# HONOR ABOVE ALL

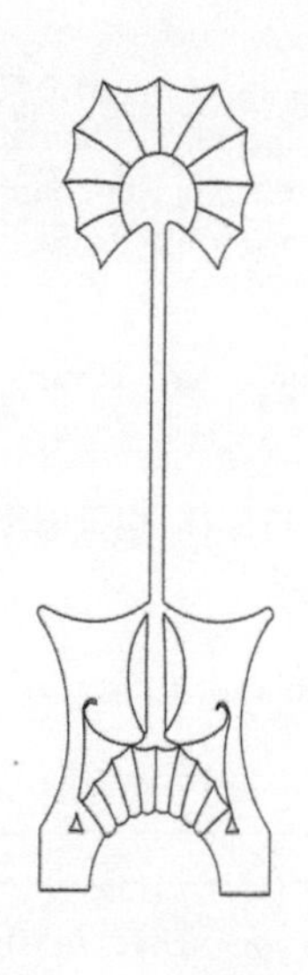

J. BARD-COLLINS

ALLIUM PRESS OF CHICAGO

Allium Press of Chicago
Forest Park, IL
www.alliumpress.com

This is a work of fiction. Descriptions and portrayals of real people, events, organizations, or establishments are intended to provide background for the story and are used fictitiously. Other characters and situations are drawn from the author's imagination and are not intended to be real.



Book/cover design and map by E. C. Victorson

Front cover image: "State Street Looking South from Monroe"
from *Picturesque Chicago* (Chicago Engraving Company, 1882)

Title page image: detail from façade of Louis Sullivan's Jeweler's Builiding, Chicago, 1882

ISBN: 978-0-9890535-7-0

Library of Congress Cataloging-in-Publication Data

Bard-Collins, J.
Honor above all / J. Bard-Collins.
pages cm
Summary: "Pinkerton agent Garrett Lyons arrives in Chicago in 1882 to solve the murder of his partner. He enlists the help of his friend, architect Louis Sullivan, and becomes involved in the race to build one of the first skyscrapers"-- Provided by publisher.
ISBN 978-0-9890535-7-0 (pbk.)
1. Sullivan, Louis H., 1856-1924--Fiction. 2. Pinkerton's National Detective Agency--Fiction. 3. Architecture--Illinois--Chicago--History--19th century--Fiction. 4. Murder--Investigation--Fiction. 5. Chicago (Ill.)--Fiction. 6. Mystery fiction. I. Title.
PS3602.A7524H66 2014
813'.6--dc23

2014027246

*To Jim, who has always been my rock*

*Mine honor keeps the weather of my fate:*
*Life every man holds dear;*
*but the dear man holds honor*
*far more precious dear than life.*

William Shakespeare
*Troilus and Cressida*

(Italicized locations are fictional)

1. Hooley's Theater
2. Borden Block
3. Tremont House
4. C. D. Peacock
5. *Eastwood Building*
6. Board of Trade
7. Portland Block
8. *Meierhoff's*
9. The Store (Mike McDonald)
10. Montauk Block
11. Chapin & Gore's
12. Inter-State Exposition Building
13. Union Station
14. *Quinn's saloon*
15. Pinkerton Agency
16. Haverly's Theater
17. Palmer House
18. City Hall
19. Grand Pacific Hotel
20. Post Office & Custom House
21. Union League Club
22. Van Buren Street Station
23. *Charlotte's house*
24. *Connell's laundry I*

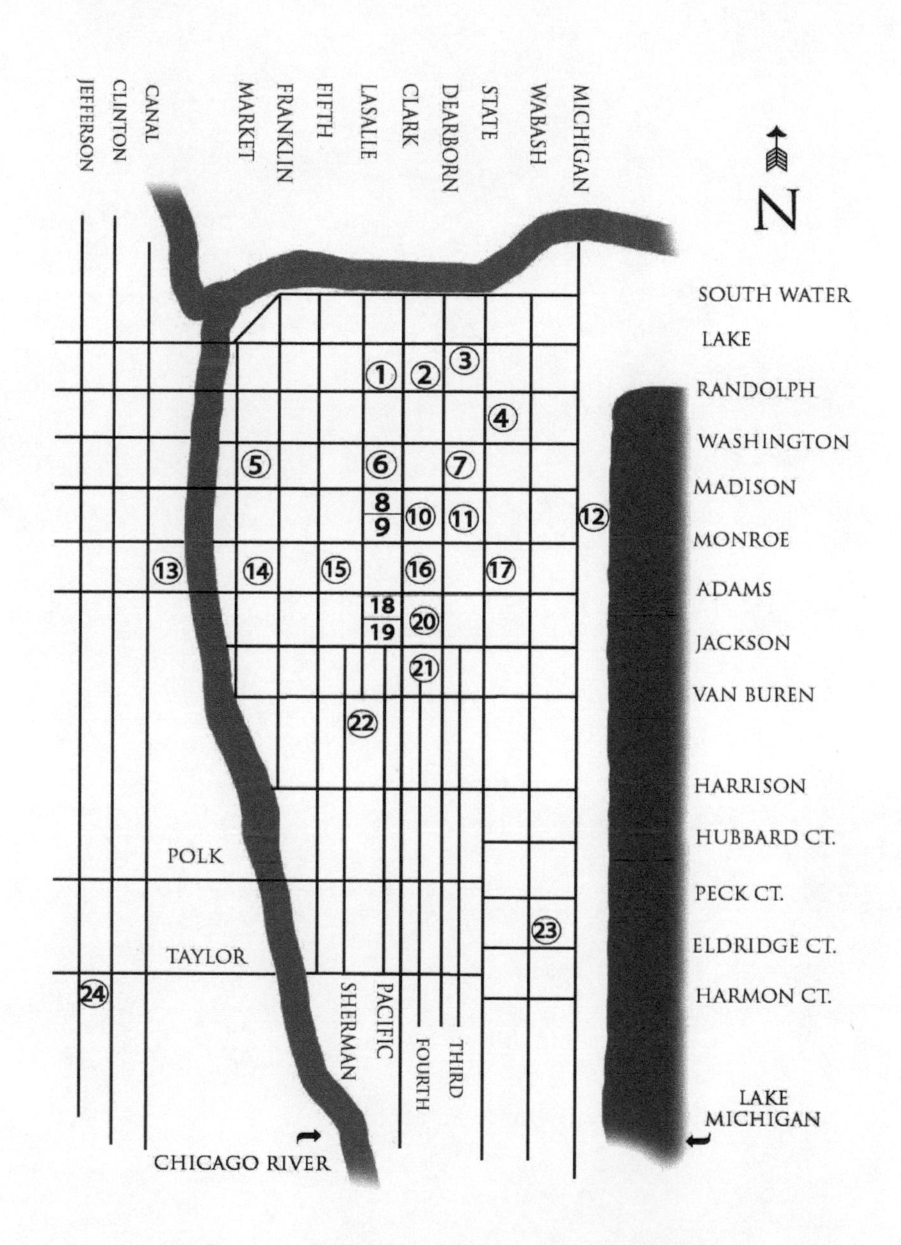


Northside Detail Map on Following Page

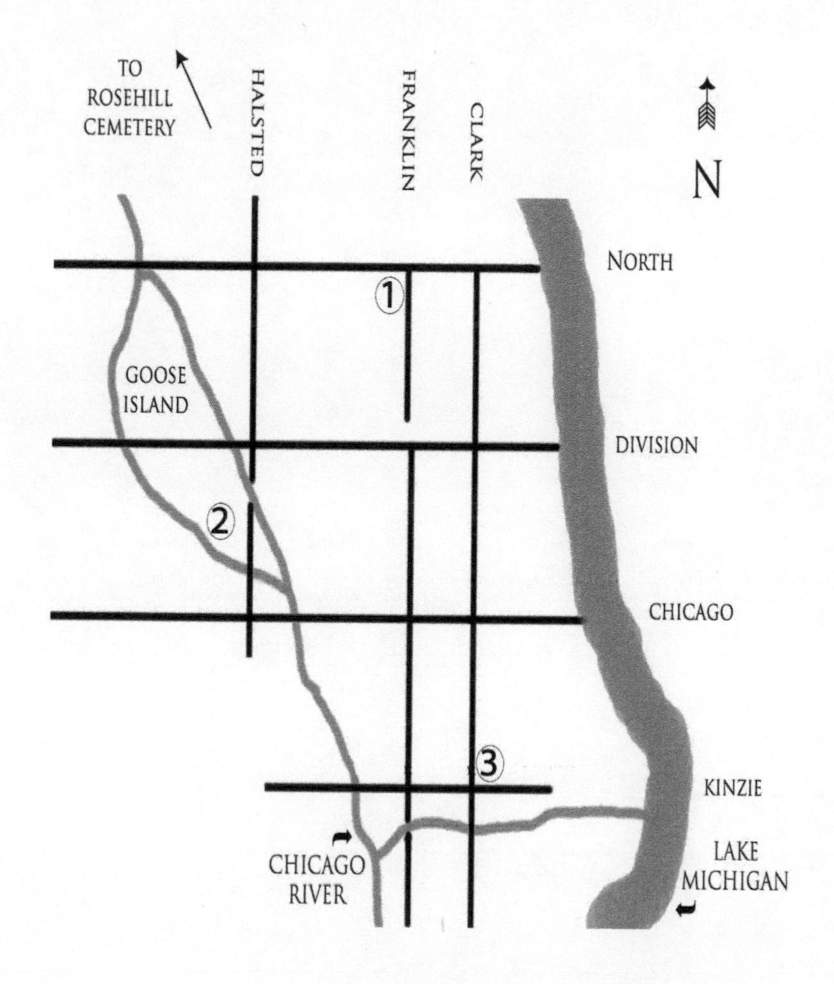


Northside Detail

1. Alexian Brothers Hospital
2. *Connell's laundry II*
3. Revere House

# HONOR ABOVE ALL

# ONE

*A decade after the Great Fire, Chicago's central business district, a mile square in size, was choked by converging networks of steel. Each day nearly one hundred trains entered the city, depositing freight and passengers at six depots. Wind-driven clouds of gray smoke covered citizenry, animals, and buildings. The Union Passenger Station served as the western vestibule to Chicago. Within a year of its construction, the brick and limestone walls of this imposing 'temple to steam' had already acquired a layer of grime. Behind the depot, a barrel-vaulted train shed, with a high-arched steel and glass roof, covered eight rail lines. No other city in America was growing faster or with such enthusiasm.*

The porter tore open the door of the Pullman car and shouted, "Chi-caw-go! Union Staaa-shun!" He stepped back as a stream of passengers spilled down the narrow steps onto the platform and hurried toward the station.

Garrett Lyons, valise in hand, walked in the opposite direction. He moved with a steady, purposeful stride, letting the crowd surge and eddy around him. As he neared the rear baggage car his steps became a brisk trot.

"Watch it! Careful boys!" His words were sharp, and spoken with authority.

The two men unloading freight stopped. Their heads snapped toward him. "Yes, sir. No offense meant."

"Well then, put him down easy."

The men carefully lowered the long oblong pine box onto a nearby trolley. They moved forward but Garrett held up a hand.

"No thanks, fellas. I'll take him now."

Lyons placed his valise on the coffin and began pushing the trolley toward the station, ignoring stragglers who gave him a quick glance before hurrying on. Midway he stopped, took a cigar from his vest pocket, lit it, and watched the flame from the match burn down to within a quarter inch of his thumb. He was shaking it out when he heard a sharp voice.

"I'm looking for Sam Wilkerson."

Lyons saw a tidy little man with gold-framed eyeglasses walking toward him. He pointed his cigar in the general direction of the trolley. "There he is."

"You must be his partner, Lyons. The Pinkerton Agency sent me to handle the funeral arrangements."

"Figured as much."

"Bill Pinkerton is not taking this too kindly. He expects your full report soon. But he did authorize payment of Wilkerson's funeral expenses."

Lyons looked down at him as though expecting to be further enlightened.

"Bill Pinkerton? I report to Allan."

"Allan Pinkerton had another heart seizure a month ago and hasn't fully recovered. His eldest son Bill's been in charge of the Chicago office the past three months. So that's who we're all answering to."

Lyons continued pushing the trolley along the platform.

The man tried to keep pace and speak at the same time. "What happened in St. Louis? I worked with Sam Wilkerson nigh on six years. Never saw anyone get the drop on him. Then I hear he was shot in the chest. Don't seem right."

The two men reached the end of the platform. Lyons took his valise off the trolley. His words were brusque. "Look, Sam's dead. He was a damned good agent, experienced, trustworthy...and my partner.

I figure he made a dumb decision, one of his few, and then it was all over for him. Sooner or later it happens in this business. You tell Bill Pinkerton that, as far as St. Louis is concerned, what's done is done. None of us can change anything."

"I'll be sure to pass your thoughts on." The man's eyes met Lyons's for a moment before shying toward the ground. "Wilkerson's mother is here for his body. Have anything else to say?"

Garrett laid his palm carefully on top of the box and paused before answering. When he spoke his voice was sharp. "Tell Mrs. Wilkerson I know who killed her son. I'll bring him in. When I do, I'll put the noose around his neck myself."

The man was about to reply when he saw something in Garrett Lyons's eyes that silenced any further remarks.

♠

Outside Union Station Garrett walked past uniformed drivers from the Parmelee Transfer Company, who were busy loading luggage onto waiting hansoms and two-horse hacks. Instead, he flagged a passing omnibus and found a seat amidst the zoo of mid-morning passengers crammed inside. He made himself comfortable as the vehicle plodded eastward along Adams Street. A weak sun shone fitfully through drifting clouds, cloaking nearby buildings in a soft haze. Only three months had passed since his last visit to Chicago, yet nothing looked familiar.

Early in his army career, a half-breed army scout told him, "You have the gift, *mon ami*." True. Lyons had an innate sense of place—not something he remembered ever learning. The ability to look at a map, a town, a street only once, close his eyes, and let the landscape etch itself onto his memory. Chicago was one city that tested this ability. Out of habit he glanced upward. A futile look. He saw canyons of gray buildings that seemed to change form with his every visit.

As always, Chicago's streets were a tangled mass of pedestrians, animals, and vehicles—wagons, carriages, hansoms, all with metal wheels and pulled by iron-shod horses. The resulting rumbling and clattering was unrelenting and, at times, overwhelming. With the amount of traffic and the number of horses in use, manure got beaten into powder and washed away when it rained. However, for the past two weeks Chicago had suffered a dry spell. Now, this powder hung suspended in the air, clinging to anything that passed through it. By the time Lyons got off the omnibus and walked a half block to the post office, a thin film covered his coat and he pulled in dust with every breath.

The clerk at the postal window handed Garrett a meager pile of envelopes. "Wait, there's something else." He turned and disappeared into a warren of shelves and cubicles.

Garrett sifted through his mail. One item caught his immediate interest, an invitation. *Open House–Poker Evening, Hosted by the Lotus Club, Tremont House.* Scrawled across the bottom in familiar script were the words, "dinner first…six o'clock, Billy's Chop House—Louis S." Garrett glanced at the date. That evening. He was half smiling when the clerk returned with a small package.

"Seems kind of strange that Mr. Wilkerson mails this to himself *and* you. There are two names on it." A long moment passed while the clerk looked at the writing on the packet, then at Garrett. Fortunately, another customer appeared behind him and further explanation was avoided. Garrett nodded his thanks, took the packet, and left the post office by the Jackson Street door.

Outside he stopped and shifted the parcel from one coat pocket to another, while casually glancing over his shoulder, then to the side. It was one of the many precautions Sam taught him that had saved Lyons more than once during the past three years. Feeling more at ease, he walked south along Third Avenue. This time of day the narrow street was crowded with pushcarts from which Chicagoans could purchase an assortment of merchandise, as well as food. Today he saw fewer carts but the usual number of customers. Enticing aromas reminded Garrett that he hadn't eaten. He bought a bag of roasted chestnuts, then shouldered his way through the crowd until he reached a cart midway along the street.

"Not many familiar faces, Jacob. Where is your second in command?" Garrett asked.

"Well, now, Lieutenant Lyons, the man went and got hisself smashed by one o' them beer wagons. Happened last month. Damn thing came barrelin' down Jackson, hell for leather, and him standin' in the wrong place." Like most veterans of the war, Jacob always addressed Lyons by his former rank. "Least it was quick. Not like this." He nodded toward his own limp arm.

The men who pushed the carts along Third Avenue were a strange lot. Many were veterans who'd managed to live though the Civil War but couldn't seem to get away from it. Jacob Masterson caught some shrapnel in his shoulder at the Battle of Stones River in Tennessee. The wound had continued seeping since then, hence his useless arm. He'd traveled to Chicago every year to reapply for his disability pension and eventually stayed on.

"How are you boys making out?" Garrett asked.

"It's a gamble. Always more traffic crowding us into smaller spaces. Ain't nothin' we can do, though. Been reading about that mess o' yours in St. Louis." Jacob reached under his cart and took out a small flyer. "The Pinkertons been passing these around. Offerin' a nice reward." Jacob's face was weathered, grim, beyond any hope of surprise. "You know what I think o' the Pinkertons. Besides, figured you'd be comin' to town and stop by."

Garrett looked at the sketch. "That's Theo Brock all right. Hear anything?"

Jacob shrugged his good shoulder. "One fella in particular told me he had information. He'll talk only to you, though. Interested?"

"Tell him. . .meet me outside the Tremont this evening at ten. No later."

♠

Lyons had discovered the Revere House on a previous visit to Chicago. Situated north of the river, the small hotel offered reasonable rates and a measure of anonymity. In addition, the Revere provided its guests with a private bathing room on each floor. Even in Laredo or Wichita, a man would find that amenity out back of the building.

After an uncomfortable train ride, followed by the dirt and noise of the city, Garrett felt the need for a good long soak. As the hot water sloshed over him, his body began to relax. He lathered more soap on his arms. Before sliding deeper into the soothing water he ran a fingertip along a scar on his forehead, a narrow miss. The "kiss of the bullet" the scout, Otwah, once told him. He looked at the round indentation that marked the center of his palm. Throughout his army career the thought of his death had been an alien one—until eight years ago at Powder River. Two of his fingers were still numb at the tips. Whenever the weather turned cold or wet his shoulder ached and the muscles in his hand tightened.

It had been a routine patrol, one of many he'd ridden during his career. But at Powder River everything went wrong. He changed orders in the field, leading his men into a Cheyenne ambush that ended his military career. The past eight years, no matter how far he ran, how much he drank, Garrett could bury the dead but never the guilt. He closed his eyes, slid farther into the warm water and tallied this trip's mental balance sheet.

Deliver Wilkerson's body to his family—done.

Report to Bill Pinkerton? Well, in due time he would, after he found Brock.

His room at the Revere contained all the essentials—bed, wardrobe, bureau, mirror, and a window facing Clark Street. Garrett dressed, then took another look at his mail. A booklet from the Remington Company advertising a new line of firearms held little interest. An invitation from a Kansas City casino to an annual high-stakes poker game was put aside. Another letter bore the return address of the U.S. War Department. Garrett turned it over in his hand but couldn't bring himself to open it, afraid of what he'd find. Once it made a decision, the U.S. Army seldom reversed itself. He put the envelope down and picked up Sam's parcel. Probably crammed full of French postcards, or the like, he thought. Sam Wilkerson, a confirmed bachelor, had lived with his widowed mother, a stern Lutheran. So his partner was in the habit of sending items of a more personal nature to their post office box. Only now Sam was dead. Nothing would change that fact. Garrett decided the package and army letter could wait.

He opened his valise and tossed the two items inside, then removed a pearl-handled derringer. It was custom made to hold two bullets instead of one and fit comfortably in his palm. A gambler's gun, but one he used with deadly accuracy. He slipped it into his pocket and reread the invitation. Though he recognized the Lotus Club and Tremont House, and was familiar with the club's regular Monday poker games, Garrett had no idea what an "Open House—Poker Evening" was. He checked his watch. Louis Sullivan was not a man to be kept waiting.

Garrett studied his reflection in the mirror and straightened his tie. As he was about to leave the room he stopped a moment, went back to the valise, and took out his Navy Colt revolver. He held the weapon in his hand, weighing it by feel. It was an older model he'd won in a poker game early in his army career. A few years back he'd had it modified to take modern cartridges. He tucked the Colt into his belt and buttoned his coat. After all, this was Chicago.

# TWO

*The original Tremont House was built in 1833. Tremont House II appeared in 1840 and was replaced in 1850 by an all-brick Tremont III, designed by John Van Osdel, Chicago's first professional architect. By 1882, the Tremont House was in her fourth incarnation. Standing six stories high, with an elaborate stone front capped with ornate pavilions, she straddled the southeast corner of Lake and Dearborn Streets like an aging courtesan. Her foundation needed support and some walls could be straighter. No one noticed. She was an old friend, one who shared the city's past. The Tremont House, like Chicago, was a survivor.*

Charlotte Reid paced the second floor hall of the hotel and, with each deliberate stride, reassured herself, *The main salon was my best choice.* After all, it was the Tremont House's largest room, extending the entire length of the building, along the Dearborn Street side—the only room that could accommodate the extra poker and roulette tables needed for this evening's entertainment.

At the end of the hall she paused in front of a gilt-framed mirror, stood perfectly straight and stared at her reflection. Her gown of plum-colored crushed silk was cut fashionably low to complement her smooth throat and shoulders. Leaning close to the mirror, she adjusted an auburn curl and murmured, "You look mighty fetching, if I do say so."

Outside, distant flashes of lightning made web-like patterns in the night sky. All day a storm had hovered over the city, promising rain, teasing with occasional claps of thunder and sporadic breezes that merely stirred up dust on the street below. The sound of voices rose and fell as the door to the main salon opened, then closed with a gentle click. Charlotte did not turn around but asked her assistant, "Well, Bernard, how is the crowd this evening?"

"Sizeable. The main salon will be more than adequate, Mrs. Reid." Bernard always addressed Charlotte as Mrs. Reid.

"I am looking forward to a profitable, as well as enjoyable, evening." Charlotte's voice was soft, low, with just a hint of coastal Georgian. When Bernard did not respond, she turned to him and, with her lips pressed tight, said, "Unless, of course, there are problems?"

He arched an eyebrow and sighed. "Just one."

"Can you handle it?"

Bernard, who barely reached her shoulder, looked up and spread his hands in a Gallic show of befuddlement. With large owl eyes and thinning brown hair, he sported a handlebar mustache that twitched as he spoke. "Alas, no. For you, it would be only a little problem." He emphasized how little by holding up his thumb and forefinger.

Monday evening was a regular poker night for the Lotus Club. Originally this group of prominent Chicago gentlemen had engaged in athletic endeavors—rowing, Greco-Roman wrestling, and boxing. Two years ago they'd added another pursuit—cards, namely poker. Thanks to an illustrious gaming reputation acquired out West, Charlotte had been engaged to manage this activity. For a moderate stipend, plus a percentage of the house, she provided Lotus Club members with a stimulating evening of poker. However, this Monday the club had decided to host an open house, which tripled the crowd, hence the added expense and worry.

Bernard held the carved oak door open, allowing Charlotte to precede him into the salon. The long, rectangular room was adorned with crystal chandeliers, green petit-point carpeting, and gold damask curtains. However, these embellishments were barely noticeable, since the room was filled to capacity. Tonight the dominant color was black—black broadcloth suits, black leather boots, and flowing black capes—all interspersed among snowy white shirts adorned with layers of ruffles that disappeared beneath black velvet vests.

Charlotte appeared at the doorway. The briefest of smiles crossed her face, then vanished.

To provide a soothing counterpoint to the slip-slip of cards and dry rattle of dice, she had engaged a string quartet. Now, barely an hour into the festivities, she found the musicians replaced by a young man standing next to the piano singing "Lorena." True, he possessed a beautiful tenor voice—clear and vibrant with just a trace of whiskey in its high tones. However, he was singing, "It matters little now, Lorena… The past is in the past…" with such a plaintive plea that the room had become as solemn as a church.

"Where are the musicians?" Charlotte whispered.

Bernard opened his mouth to speak, but lost the opportunity.

"Get them back…now. Then find Jennie and Nell. I want those girls in here, singing something, anything happy."

With a twitch of his mustache, Bernard obeyed.

Charlotte took a deep breath and exhaled slowly. Feeling calmer, she began a leisurely stroll through the salon, much like a duchess inspecting her estate. Indeed, this room was her fiefdom, the workers her vassals, its business her business. Pausing at each felt-covered table, she exchanged pleasantries with the players, while checking receipts with her dealers. These dealers, attractive young women, were attired in low cut silk blouses and black taffeta skirts. Lotus Club members felt that Charlotte's ladies provided a touch of elegance to their weekly games.

Behind a spacious mahogany bar at the opposite end of the salon four bartenders worked frantically to keep pace with the thirsty crowd. Behind the bar, a long banner that read "Welcome Back Johnny" was stretched across the mirror.

State Senator John Edward Lawlor, a robust man with a flushed red face, white hair, and sparkling blue eyes that invited trust, smiled at the crowd. A founding member of the Lotus Club, he also held the dubious distinction of being the first Illinois state legislator to be jailed on double charges while still in office. His initial offense was the theft of public funds. His second was bribing the judge to avoid prosecution. With one elbow on the bar and a drink in his other hand, he greeted Charlotte in his best political baritone. "This is a wonderful party, a marvelous welcome home."

"You've been gone a while, Senator, but your friends did not forget you."

Charlotte smiled, then leaned forward and let him kiss her on the cheek. The gaze in her green eyes sharpened when he whispered in her ear.

"Senator, my only expertise is cards. But I hear you are a serious player. I insist you join me and a few select players at my private table."

Lawlor smiled with a little twist of regret. "My dear, you are one woman with the ability to put my world in its proper perspective. I would be delighted." He raised a hand, caught the bartender's attention, and made a circular motion with his finger around the inside of his glass.

Charlotte edged away. She did a quick sidestep as a group of waiters, tall men with long aprons, walked briskly past, balancing trays high above the heads of the guests. The private tables, for club regulars and special guests, had been set up around the perimeter of the salon. The dealers at these tables were men, all attired in white linen shirts, red armbands, and green eyeshades.

Bernard appeared at Charlotte's side. She spoke softly in his ear. "I invited the senator to join me. I suggest you escort him." Charlotte glanced toward the far end of the room. "Who is at my table?"

Bernard cleared his throat, to speak over the music provided by the newly returned quartet. "Mr. Sullivan and his guest. It's Mr. Lyons."

A soft smile crossed Charlotte's lips. "Well, then, I believe it's time I joined them."

♠

Garrett Lyons shifted uncomfortably in his chair. He picked up a poker chip and attempted to somersault it back and forth across his knuckles, ignoring the conversation that came in fits and starts around him.

Louis Sullivan sat across from him, a furrow of anxiety between his brows. Not a vestige of humor resided in his tight-lipped mouth. He stopped playing with the edges of his cards, and tossed them aside in disgust. "This is not like you, not like you at all." Although his voice was a lyrical baritone, he gave each word a hard edge. "You're leaving the game early. It's simply not done."

Lyons snapped the chip off his thumb, then watched it roll over in the air and onto the floor next to him. "Why such a fuss? You're winning."

"All the more reason! I'm just getting into my game and you up and leave!" Sullivan reached into his suit pocket, extracted a cigar and stuck it in the corner of his mouth. Garrett started to say something but Sullivan raised his hand, cutting him off without a sound. He brought out a match, lit the cigar, all the time staring at his friend. "You're my luck. You know that."

"You mean you don't lose as much when I'm around." Garrett wanted to smile, but forced his mouth into a more sober expression and stared at the room's ornate ceiling.

The two men had become acquainted on one of Garrett's earlier visits to Chicago. Louis Henri Sullivan was not a hard man to classify. Always impeccably dressed, he was an articulate, intelligent gentleman blessed with all the inherent social skills that Garrett lacked. Moreover, Garrett immediately recognized that underneath Sullivan's urbane expression there lurked an insatiable lust for the pasteboards. Both men considered poker one of the essential elements of life, along with aged bourbon and beautiful women. This mutual passion became the mortar of their friendship.

During the past year Garrett's social skills had undergone considerable refinement. Sullivan, his enthusiastic mentor, introduced the former army lieutenant to literature, fine dining, and the theater. Garrett reciprocated by instructing his friend in the detailed mathematics of the poker hand. Sullivan had a naturally trained eye and, under Garrett's tutelage, quickly learned to take in every detail of the game. Although his skills kept improving, Sullivan found it difficult to cultivate a gambler's controlled detachment at the table. Despite Garrett's constant assurances, Sullivan was convinced he won only when Garrett played at his side.

"You're casting me adrift then." Sullivan's abrasive words cut across Garrett's thoughts.

"It's business. I'll be back." The last statement was an outright lie and Garrett told it in a loud, clear voice. Because Sullivan seemed to be having difficulty keeping his volatile temper in check, Garrett felt it best to tell his friend what he wanted to hear.

At that moment the man sitting between Garrett and Sullivan spoke in a soft but firm voice. "I assure you, sir, I pay my debts. This note is legal tender. You have my word as a gentleman."

Garrett and Sullivan turned to stare at him, irritated at the unsolicited intrusion. They saw a portly gentleman with a massive handlebar mustache that swept back from his nose and up to the corners of his jaw, giving him the appearance of a walrus. He looked directly at Garrett.

"Sir, my name is Shelby Oates and my IOUs have always been accepted at the Lotus Club. You can redeem this one tomorrow at my place of business, Central Casualty Insurance."

Garrett spoke sharply. "I don't take markers."

Sullivan watched the two men, stretching out the pause that followed with a long draw on his cigar and a disgusted wag of his head. "Lyons, haven't you told me repeatedly that one does not leave the game until all proprieties are observed? Either take the gentleman's marker or stay and give him an opportunity to win it back."

Louis remembered his friend's distrust of anything military. So, when he added, "Incidentally, Colonel Oates is a decorated veteran of General Meade's brigade and a Lotus Club member of long standing," he stressed the word colonel, just to see Garrett's jaw clench and his lips tighten.

Oates looked nervously around the room. Suddenly, his face paled and his eyes narrowed almost to slits. He turned to Garrett and whispered, "Sir, I regret I do not have time to play another hand."

"I'm not planning on dealing another one." Garrett nodded at Sullivan. "Be it for a military man, Lotus Club member. . .anyone."

"I sincerely hope you gentlemen are enjoying yourselves?" a soft voice interrupted.

Charlotte took a moment to delicately flip out the folds of her skirt as Sullivan stood and pulled up an extra chair for her.

Glancing first at Garrett, then at Louis, Charlotte said, "You know, I do not allow any arguments here, unless of course, they are over me." She placed her hand on Garrett's shoulder, gave it a gentle squeeze, leaned over and whispered, "His marker is good, take it."

Oates stood up, stretching to his full height of five foot three. "I trust this will suffice. I look forward to meeting with you tomorrow." He produced a business card, placed it on the table, then disappeared into the crowd.

Garrett checked the level of whiskey in his glass, sloshing it gently, while looking at the card out of the corner of his eye. He drained the whiskey in slow even gulps, then stuffed the card into his vest pocket.

Sullivan watched as Charlotte took the seat between them. He smiled, then looked at his friend. If anyone ever questioned him about Garrett's occupation—what he did while he was in Chicago—Sullivan could not answer. They were poker buddies with little interest in one another's past or present lives. After more than a year's acquaintance, Sullivan still considered his friend an interesting puzzle.

Charlotte picked up a fresh deck and began shuffling the cards as she spoke. "Gentlemen, Senator Lawlor will be joining us. And Bernard assured me that he has found two flush players. So this promises to be a profitable evening for me and, of course, my friends."

Under Charlotte's management, the Lotus Club's gaming nights had prospered. The members knew she operated a "square game." Which meant none of her dealers, including herself, would hold out an ace or keep marked cards up their sleeves. However, it was understood that Charlotte could cheat in acceptable ways. After all, if a player or dealer was able to stack a deck while shuffling, or smoothly reverse a cut, in Chicago these skills were considered both proper and necessary.

Sullivan leaned toward Garrett and whispered in a loud voice, "Since you're leaving, shall I extend your apologies to our hostess?"

Charlotte looked at Garrett and raised an eyebrow. He responded with a lopsided grin.

"He's abandoning us. Tells me it's business. And I have such good news to share." Sullivan spoke in a petulant tone.

Just then, a waiter passed their table. In a swift movement, Sullivan took a glass from his tray and drained it in one gulp. Then he announced, "I've procured invitations to John B. Drake's annual game dinner. This year it will be held at his Grand Pacific Hotel."

"A splendid affair, one I truly missed while away," came the familiar voice of Senator Lawlor. He arrived, leaning on Bernard's shoulder. With drink, his voice had taken on a husky tone. "But, this year, the game dinner will have to step aside for a more illustrious gathering."

"What would that be?" Garrett asked.

"The Grand Army annual reunion, of course!"

Sullivan sat upright, impatiently motioning with his cigar for the senator to continue.

"Next to my political resurrection, the reunion is *the* topic of conversation this evening. General Sheridan and his staff are expected. I smell an opportunity for some great poker."

The senator let Bernard help him into an empty chair. During this conversation Garrett sat rigid as a board, hands closed tightly around his empty glass. As soon as General Sheridan's name was mentioned, he stood up. Charlotte reached for his hand, squeezed it reassuringly, then turned to the senator. She spoke in a soothing voice, "I assure you the Lotus Club is prepared to host a welcoming reception and, of course, cards will be included."

At that moment two more gentlemen arrived at the table. Bernard found additional chairs while Charlotte smiled graciously. "Mr. Sullivan will explain the Lotus Club table rules."

"A pleasure," Sullivan whispered to her.

But Charlotte was looking past him to Garrett's retreating figure.

# THREE

*By 1882 Chicago was the fourth largest city in America. Half of its population consisted of an unstable mix of impoverished immigrants—packed in overcrowded neighborhoods with unregulated saloons and free-flowing beer. The city boasted one licensed saloon for every fifty-three male residents. One fourth of the aldermen owned saloons, and saloon licenses provided over twelve percent of the city's revenue. Even with limited restrictions and minimal licensing fees, illegal saloons sprouted like mushrooms. An unlicensed saloon was called a "blind pig." It might appear one evening, cater to a migrant clientele, then vanish—a saloon where the whiskey was of dubious origin, and the bartender always kept a loaded shotgun within arm's reach, and a finger's touch.*

The front door of the Tremont House, all eight feet of carved oak and quarter-inch beveled glass, slammed shut with a resounding thud. Garrett looked up and down the street to get his bearings. He saw no stars and little sky, only canyons of dark gray buildings. After the cramped stuffiness of the Tremont's main salon, stepping into the cool evening mist felt like plunging fully clothed into Lake Michigan. He flicked a thumbnail against the head of a match. When it burst into flame he held it to the tip of a cigar.

"Lieutenant Lyons, ah...that you, sir?"

Garrett heard a raspy voice, words strung out by someone careful of what he said.

"It's me, sir, McGlynn. Private Ed McGlynn."

The light from a street lamp outlined a grungy little man with a spooked look in his eyes that betrayed a lifetime of hard luck and harder living.

"You alone?" Garrett asked.

"'Course I am, sir."

If Ed McGlynn possessed an actual job skill it was unknown to Garrett. He recalled the man spending his entire army service avoiding work. These days, McGlynn spent his time hanging around saloons or the courthouse. Politics was his passion. The key to understanding McGlynn was knowing that Ed considered everything he saw, heard, or did, important. The former private thrived on having inside information, which he willingly conveyed out of the corner of his mouth.

"Got him, sir. Got your man." McGlynn took a creased paper from his back pocket and held it out. "Fits this picture Pinkerton's passin' 'round. Didn't mean much 'til Jacob told me you'd been lookin'. Then I decided to speak up."

"You mean *I'll* pay more."

McGlynn's face burst into a grin, as if feeling at ease in an old relationship.

Garrett continued. "Theo Brock's not only a forger and thief, but a murderer as well. Pinkerton's looking, but I want him first. Help me and I'll see to it you get the Pinkerton cash, too."

"Well, sir, he's holed up in a warehouse on Haddock Place near the river."

"You sure?"

"He hired a cousin's boy to do mule work. Help him pack and all."

"Pack? Let's move then. No time to lose."

Garrett stepped off the curb onto Dearborn Street, quickly jumping sideways as a carriage sped past, splattering a mixture of dirt and manure on his trousers. Swearing, he crossed as rapidly as possible. Using a street lamp as a beacon, he walked to where his memory told him a narrow alleyway, Couch Place, stretched west from Dearborn toward the Chicago River.

He set a brisk pace through dimly lit alleys smelling of rot and slops. McGlynn managed to keep up, trailing behind with the bumbling persistence of an over-affectionate dog. They turned north and, at Lake Street, the sidewalks changed from stone to wood planks and the buildings became smaller.

The heavy mist caught in Garrett's throat, forcing him to alternate his rapid trot with more careful steps. At Haddock Place he paused, giving McGlynn a chance to catch up. He could smell the river and hear the lapping of water against the docks. Warehouses in various stages of construction spread along the street with no visible signs or other markings on them.

"Which one?"

McGlynn shrugged. "Don't know. But he sends the boy for beer 'bout now."

The saloon in the corner building leaked yellow light onto the wooden walkway. Garrett strolled through the door. The building was still under construction. Fresh smells of lumber and turpentine barely held their own against the odors of beer and sweat. The room was lit with kerosene lanterns nailed to the rafters. Long banners emblazoned with the words "Workers Unite" and "Sons of Labor" were hung along partially completed walls. There were no tables, just a bar cobbled together from large planks laid across four barrels. Men in overalls leaned on it, glasses in hand. Hoarse voices from the elbow-to-elbow crowd continually called, "More beer!" and "Another round!"

Garrett left McGlynn at the door, shouldered his way to the bar, and signaled for a whiskey. A bartender splashed amber liquid into a chipped glass, then scooped up his coin without a wasted movement. The man's fingers had been all over the inside of the glass. So, when Garrett took a sip, he widened his lips and pulled in some air.

At the opposite end of the room, a speaker stood atop a barrel extolling the virtues of some political party while a boy handed out pamphlets. Garrett took one, barely giving it a glance. Then, amid the general noise, he heard a new voice—strong, vibrant—speaking with a definite Methodist tone. Garrett had spent his early youth in a

Methodist orphanage and recognized the cadence of the sound before he picked up any of the words. Curious, he craned his neck to one side until he had a better view.

He saw a young man with red hair and beard surrounding a face, unremarkable except for the intense eyes. The speaker was putting on quite a show and the crowd shouted its full-throated approval in a stew of languages. For a brief instant, though present in that crowded barroom, Garrett's spirit was back in the army, on patrol outside a Sioux camp, listening to a shaman stir up the warriors. The moment passed. He took another glance at the pamphlet in his hand and saw the image of the impassioned orator staring back at him. Evidently, this young man was an articulate spokesman for the Sons of Labor.

Garrett sensed a movement, turned, and saw the bartender fill a tin growler with beer, snap the lid on, and hand it to a thin boy. McGlynn gave him a nod. At that moment a loud hoot came from the other end of the room, followed by two gunshots into the ceiling. Garrett finished his whiskey in one gulp and quickly stepped aside as the bartender grabbed his shotgun and walked toward the disturbance. The boy left, Garrett and McGlynn following behind.

Outside, the sky was gray-black with no moon to be seen. The mist had turned to a faint drizzle. The boy held the bucket in one hand, a kerosene lantern in the other, its soft glow, like a gently swaying buoy, making it easy to trail. The two men kept a discreet distance as the boy made his way along South Water Street past a row of shuttered warehouses. Then the lad turned into an alleyway and was gone.

"Damn, lost him for sure, Lieutenant," Ed whispered.

Just then the moon moved out from behind a cloud and, for a few seconds, cast the area in a faint light. They stood in front of a row of warehouses that bordered the Chicago River. Garrett saw a horse and wagon outside one of them. The sky darkened again as he made his way along a passageway between two buildings. He walked cautiously, rounded a corner and smelled the river. Thin streaks of light crept between the wide pine boards of the warehouse door. Garrett moved his fingers deftly along the wall until he felt iron hinges. Noiselessly, he pushed the door open a crack and saw a room full of boxes and loose paper. The air was filled with the smell of oil. At the muffled sound of voices he flattened himself against the wall.

Garrett recognized the perfectly modulated Scottish burr. Could it be? He leaned forward and glimpsed a lean man with gray hair, wearing a stained coat. Yes, Theo Brock! At that moment, with two doors to cover, Garrett made a decision. This time Sam's killer would not escape. He retraced his steps along the passageway to the front of the warehouse.

"Well, Lieutenant, what now?" McGlynn whispered.

"It's Brock all right. You cover this door." Without a second thought, he took out the Colt and handed it to McGlynn.

McGlynn shook his head. "Don't know, sir. I ain't the man I used to be."

Garrett looked straight into his eyes and spoke softly in his army officer voice. "None of us are, Private! If Brock slips the noose on me again someone's going to pay. You block this door. Use a barrel, a chain, I don't care. Remember, no body, no reward."

At that moment they heard the sound of glass shattering, men shouting, then gunshots. Although the saloon was down a block and around the corner, the crowd inside had spilled out onto the street and was coming closer to the warehouse. It was time to act.

McGlynn wiped his hands on his pants then took a firm hold on the Colt. "Count on me, sir."

Over the years Garrett had developed the ability to reach a certain level of calmness within himself, just before a period of maximum stress—to step out of a situation for an instant or two. He edged his way to the back of the warehouse. He stood outside the door, took in a deep breath, emptied his mind, then exhaled slowly. Holding the derringer firmly in his hand, he kicked the door open. The wooden slats hit the inside wall with a loud crack. The sound merged with the general commotion from the street. Brock continued talking to the boy, only stopping mid-sentence when he heard Garrett's "Hands up! Step back!"

"Lyons, we meet again." Brock's voice had, if anything, a note of regret. "I thought St. Louis would end it. Why don't you just give up?"

"Only when I see you hang."

"At least let the boy go. He has no part in this."

Garrett gestured to the boy with his gun, then watched him scuttle out between two loose boards in the far wall.

Brock edged toward an inside wall. Garrett circled, keeping in front of him until they faced one another across a table littered with inkpots and paper. Overhead, a kerosene lamp swayed back and forth, its greasy light giving Brock's gray hair and long beard a grandfatherly appearance. But his eyes were cold as stone. Brock fingered a pearl stickpin on his lapel as he nodded toward two neatly wrapped parcels on the table.

"Those plates are my best work, but I've printed enough Chicago Southwestern Railroad stock. Time I moved on. The package next to the plates contains a substantial amount of cash. Take them both and I leave."

"Only if dead men walk."

"Since when did you ever turn down an easy dollar?"

"Since you killed Sam Wilkerson. He was my partner and my friend. I don't have too many of those."

"I did not kill your partner," Brock protested. "Why would I? I'm a scratcher. Damned good at forgery. But murder? That's not my style. Besides, he was shot point blank in the chest. And we both know there's no man around, including me, could ever get the drop on Sam."

The two men stared at one another while the mob from the saloon—shouting "Workers unite! Down with tyranny!"—crowded the street outside. Suddenly, they heard a loud crash, then wood splintering in the warehouse next door, followed by a loud boom. The building shook. This was all Brock needed. He flipped a can of ink at Garrett and bolted toward the front door.

"Damn radicals." Garrett sucked his upper lip between his teeth, aimed and fired.

At that moment a second explosion blew out the side wall of the warehouse, just as Brock ran past. Boards, glass, and burning oil spewed in all directions. Garrett instinctively put out his arm to steady himself.

The air filled with an acrid stench. As the smoke began to clear, he saw Brock knocked out and wedged against the wall, his leg pinned under a heavy timber.

McGlynn came stumbling through the haze. He looked down at Brock, then at Garrett. "You all right, Lieutenant?"

"I'll be a lot better when we get him out of here."

"He looks like a goner. Just leave him, that's what I say."

"No body, no money, remember? Besides, if he's not dead I want him to hang."

Frantic moments passed before Garrett was able to locate an iron bar amongst the rubble. Using it as a lever, he pried the wood up, giving McGlynn enough room to pull Brock out. Together, they managed to drag the unconscious man outside and hoist him onto the wagon they'd seen outside the warehouse as they arrived.

"Wait here," Garrett ordered.

"Lieutenant, this place'll blow any minute."

The fire, fueled by stacks of paper and kerosene, was spreading rapidly. There was no time to lose. Garrett made his way back into the warehouse and quickly pawed through the debris until he saw the two parcels. He grabbed them and left. Outside, a rapid burst of thunder was followed by the steady drizzle of rain, which thankfully slowed the spread of the fire. Charred papers and other debris floated in puddles on the street. Garrett found McGlynn sitting at the front of the wagon, Brock's pearl stickpin on his shirt, the reins in hand.

"Where to, Lieutenant? That fella won't make it down to County Hospital."

"Cross the river, then go over to Franklin Street and head north. We'll take him to the Alexian Brothers."

♠

Garrett glanced at his pocket watch as he paced the hallway, while McGlynn sat on a nearby bench, wearing a look of polite sympathy. "He's been in there awhile, Lieutenant. What if—"

"Either way, you'll get your money. Where's my Colt?"

McGlynn squinted at him. "It's in the wagon. About the horse and wagon?"

"They're yours."

"Well, then, I'd better check on 'em." He disappeared down the hallway.

Garrett's nerves were pulled tight. Hospitals always made him edgy. During his army years, they were called "vestibules to death." Yet he sensed an air of serenity about this place. An army buddy had convalesced here a while back, so he was aware of the Alexian Brothers' reputation for excellent treatment. Still, he craved a cigar and began searching his pockets for one.

The door to the infirmary opened. Garrett looked up expectantly as a brown-cassocked brother emerged, a sober expression on his face.

"The gentleman you brought us is seriously injured. In addition to the smashed leg, he has a bullet wound in his back, near the shoulder."

"Will he make it?"

"At the moment we are keeping him alive. Tomorrow the doctor will remove the bullet. After that, it is up to God. There is nothing more you can do here but pray." That said, the brother returned to the infirmary. Since he was not inclined to ask God or anyone for favors, Garrett decided there was no point in staying and made his way back towards the entrance. Another Alexian sat on his appointed perch by the admissions desk. Thick spectacles balanced precariously on his nose while fat bulged over the top of his collar, like dough rising from a bowl. He came to attention as soon as he heard Garrett's cadenced footsteps coming down the hallway.

"A moment, sir! I am Brother Andrew, the registrar. Before you leave I need information...the patient's name?"

Garrett hesitated. "The name is Smith. John Smith."

Brother Andrew dutifully wrote the name in his ledger. "His next of kin?"

"You mean who pays the bill? William Pinkerton. He'll probably be here tomorrow. I'll be visiting the patient as well."

A practiced listener, the brother merely nodded, then handed Garrett a slip of paper and smiled. "For Mr. Pinkerton then."

Garrett pocketed the paper. Outside, McGlynn and the horse and wagon were gone.

♠

It was well past midnight, in the shadowy darkness before dawn. The rain had stopped. Carriages loomed out of the darkness, then quickly disappeared again. Garrett left the hospital, walking rapidly, head down, collar up, until he found a cab.

He stared out the window at hazy swirls misting around gas-lit street lamps as the horse-drawn carriage passed from one pool of light to the next. A good night's work, he told himself. Yet he felt uneasy. Where was the surge of energy, the tingle of excitement? He'd made good his promise and found Sam's murderer. Yet, here he was, sitting in this carriage alone, with only memories for company. Somehow, tonight, this specter of loneliness frightened him. Abruptly, he leaned forward and pounded on the roof of the hansom with his open palm. The driver reined the horses and the conveyance lurched to a halt.

"Yes, sir?"

"Take me to 45 Eldridge Court."

Eldridge Court spanned two short blocks between South Michigan Avenue and State Street. Number 45 was the middle residence of a section of row houses. As the carriage reined to a stop, Garrett considered asking the driver to wait. He saw a light in the parlor, hesitated, then walked up the stairs. Before he could knock, the door opened.

The dim light from the street lamp gave Charlotte's auburn hair a golden cast. Her eyes glided inquisitively over Garrett's face. He started to speak, to tell her why he had arrived on her doorstep at this late hour. But she merely took his hand and led him inside.

# FOUR

*By 1882 urban pollution made it difficult for Chicagoans, as well as visitors, to maintain acceptable levels of cleanliness. Along with hog butchering and steel manufacturing, laundry became a growth industry. The hotels and railroads that served travelers used commercial laundries, while numerous hand laundries were scattered throughout the city. They were usually owned and operated by women and took in household laundry. A few hired out day girls to local middle-class families. An area west of the Chicago River, along DeKoven and Bunker Streets, provided a venue for many of these small hand laundries.*

The morning air smelled crisp and clean. The few puddles on the street, remnants from the previous night's storm, glistened in the morning sun. Garrett closed the carriage door and settled into the seat next to Charlotte. They waited while the boy from Evans's Livery gave the harness a final check.

"I must say, you look almost presentable," Charlotte said.

"It's the boots." Garrett stretched out one leg. "Can't report to Bill Pinkerton looking sloppy. Thanks."

"They're not a present. You purchased them in Wichita, left town suddenly, and never picked them up. Remember?"

Garrett stared out the window and smiled. He saw Bernard trotting down the walk toward them. The little man was clad in a brown wool coat that touched his ankles and a white silk scarf wrapped around his neck. The boy from the livery helped him climb up to the seat, then gave him the reins and disappeared down an alleyway.

Charlotte answered Garrett's question before he could ask. "My assistant, Bernard, accompanies me every Tuesday. I have certain business obligations today."

They felt the carriage lurch then bump against a curb as Bernard maneuvered the spirited horse along Eldridge Court and onto Michigan Avenue.

"What are your plans, besides seeing Bill Pinkerton?" Charlotte asked.

"Sam's funeral is the day after tomorrow—a ten o'clock service at Rosehill Cemetery. Sam and I started this case and I intend to finish it. I'll be back for the hanging."

"You're leaving?"

Garrett stretched out his other leg and stared at his boots. He seemed to retreat into himself. When he did speak, his words were more a personal reflection than anything else. "I always worked with Allan Pinkerton. His son is in charge of the Chicago office now. I don't know Bill Pinkerton or whether I can put any trust in him. Which means, I haven't made up my mind yet." Garrett spoke defensively and he knew it. He turned to Charlotte. "If I did decide to take on a case for Bill, I'd need a place to work from."

"There are sixty-five hotels right in the center of this city, Garrett. 45 Eldridge Court is not one of them. It is my home now." Her words slipped out before she had time to weigh them, surprising her more than him.

He raised an eyebrow, a little taken aback. "Those are strange words. Don't tell me you've decided to settle and put down roots? Never would've figured it to be Chicago. San Francisco—now that would have been my first choice...maybe Boston, New York, my second."

For a moment, Charlotte felt sorry she had spoken so bluntly. Even so, when the carriage came to a stop, she repressed the impulse to apologize. Instead, she leaned over and said, "Sullivan has tickets for Hooley's Theater this evening. Pick me up by half past seven, no later.

The curtain goes up at eight o'clock. We'll have dinner after."

Garrett nodded. That was all he could do. He opened the door and stepped out.

Charlotte watched him disappear into the crowd. A brief suggestion of a smile appeared on her lips at the memory of his visit the previous evening. There was much of the knight errant in him, the hunger to be needed, to rescue, in order to measure his strength against the dragons of wrong. Garrett Lyons had walked in and out of her life for the past ten years. They became acquainted when her husband, Colonel Reid, was stationed at Fort Fetterman. A Southern girl married to a Yankee officer, she was trying to forget the war. They met again three years later in Wichita at a high-stakes poker game. By then Charlotte was widowed. The gambling skills she'd learned from her husband enabled her to become a strong, independent woman of means. Garrett was alone, his army career destroyed, and in dire need of a friend. Looking back, these feelings were not something Charlotte had planned. Yet, without realizing it, she had opened a door and let Garrett into her life. Now, she wanted to close it and never let him leave.

♠

Charlotte adjusted the fox collar on her brown wool jacket then leaned back against the cushion as Bernard navigated the traffic on Michigan Avenue. Instinctively, she slipped her right hand inside a custom-tailored pocket in her skirt and felt the ivory-handled derringer. At the same time, her left hand tightened on the small velvet portmanteau in her lap. It held last night's gaming receipts.

She met Bernard at the first private poker game she ran in Chicago. He played well, and left the game with modest winnings. They met again, outside the hotel. Bernard came to her rescue when two disgruntled players accosted her. Although short in stature, Bernard was adept with a knife. They talked over a glass of wine and Bernard became Charlotte's assistant, organizing the Lotus Club's weekly events and private high-stakes games.

This morning, like every Tuesday morning after a Lotus Club gambling night, she had certain responsibilities. Bernard always accompanied her on her rounds. Charlotte's first obligation was at Union Trust Bank. She deposited the Lotus Club's receipts and her share of the profits into their respective accounts. Unfortunately, her share from last night had been a meager one.

Bernard was apologetic. "We had double, no triple, the usual crowd last evening, Mrs. Reid. But this crowd, they did not gamble enough. They drank. Expenses were more than we anticipated."

Her second obligation was to "King Mike." Just as Charlotte paid the Tremont House for the room, liquor, bartenders, and waiters, no gaming establishment, dealer, or croupier could operate in Chicago without paying a percentage to Mike McDonald.

Bernard turned the carriage west, skirting the other hacks and omnibuses crowding the street, then turned north. McDonald's casino-style gambling emporium, "The Store," was located a block from city hall.

Mike McDonald himself, gaudily dressed and cologne-drenched, waited at the curb. He usually handled business from his second-floor office, but made an exception for Mrs. Reid. After their initial meeting eight months before, when she'd first arrived in Chicago, he'd offered to collect his share of the club's receipts at her home. Charlotte graciously declined. So, now, he made a point of personally greeting her in front of his establishment. The usual pleasantries were observed. McDonald never opened the envelope nor checked the cash inside. Charlotte's reputation was flawless. He knew he'd receive a fair count.

Bernard flicked the reins. Before he could turn the carriage Charlotte said, "One more errand. We're going to Aileen Connell's."

Bernard's back stiffened. If he was concerned he tried not to show it. "DeKoven Street?"

"I don't think she's moved her laundry establishment."

"Whatever Mrs. Reid wishes."

The area around DeKoven and Bunker Streets was one Chicago's citizens knew existed but most chose to ignore. Life became cheaper and more sordid the farther one progressed into the district. The stench of boiled cabbage—overlaid with sewage, coal smoke, and dirt—wrapped itself around inhabitants and visitors alike. At Polk Street, Bernard turned the carriage westward and crossed the river. Connell's Laundry stood on DeKoven Street, three blocks west of the river.

The laundry! Charlotte smiled at the memory. Wherever Charlotte and Colonel Reid were stationed she soon learned an unwritten law—you stayed square with the laundress, if you didn't square up with anyone else. Posted remote from the rest of the world, those in the army became a family.

Bernard reined in the horse and stared at the row of long, sway-backed shacks that seemed on the verge of collapsing under their own weight. He wondered whether the buildings would give way first at their center, or at the walls.

"If you do not mind, I will wait outside," he said.

"You'll be out here alone."

"Madame, I am never alone." Bernard turned sideways. Inside his opened jacket she saw a Colt Peacemaker tucked firmly in his belt.

She crossed the yard, treading her way through a line of blankets flapping in the breeze, sidestepping unkempt children who raced around bubbling laundry kettles, which sat over wood fires. She knocked on the door. It opened a crack and a narrow view of a face appeared.

"I'm here to see..."

An awkward silence. Then quickly the door swung open and a woman's voice bellowed, "Well, now, Colonel Reid's wife, isn't it?" Aileen Connell stood almost as tall as the shed and as round as one of her kettles—a stylish woman, in a loud sort of way. "Whatever brings you here? Come in, come in."

Anchoring each end of the long room there stood a square cast-iron laundry stove nearly five feet in height. Their sides were hung with flatirons, sucking up heat. A kettle for hot water stood atop each stove, alongside a pan of water containing a bundle of lavender, to which a stick of cinnamon had been added. The resulting aroma failed to cover the odors of starch, soap, and sweat. Along one side of the room were the boards, long planks balanced on sawhorses, where young women pushed flatirons against linen with resounding thumps. Along the opposite wall two boys turned a linen press, while smaller children folded and piled flatwork into wicker baskets for delivery.

Charlotte found the heat and humidity oppressive.

Aileen Connell glanced sideways at her visitor, staring at her the way one recalls an old tintype or memory. "Well, now, let me look at you. Remember the long talk we had after Colonel Reid went and got hisself killed? Didn't I say you'd do all right?" She spun sideways. "You there! Don't let that tablecloth drag." She swatted a child with the back of her hand, then turned back to Charlotte and smiled. "Got time for tea?"

"I came to settle up for the girl you sent over to help Eulah." Charlotte reached into her pocket and produced an envelope.

"Sure you can't stay now? I'm just about to take my morning cup," Aileen said, as her hand folded around the envelope, a momentary flicker of gratitude in her eyes. "Eulah came by a few weeks back to see about some kitchen help. We had a nice long talk."

"Come to think of it, a cup of tea sounds refreshing."

"Well, then, follow me."

Aileen led Charlotte into the next building. She nodded toward a small mahogany table placed by one of the two windows in the room. The table was laid with a fine linen cloth and porcelain cups and saucers. "Sit yourself down. Get comfortable like." She spooned some leaves from a caddy into each delicate cup, then reached over and took a kettle from the nearby stove.

"Glad Eulah's still with you. I imagine that's a comfort." As Aileen spoke, her eyes moved from the drying room to the yard outside, then back again. Satisfied all was in order, she poured the hot water over the leaves.

"When we're done, I'll read your cup."

They sat in companionable silence, sipping tea. The smell of clean linen drifted from the airing rack winched up to the ceiling. The scent of freshly laundered cotton was one of Charlotte's favorite memories. Army life was made up of rules, regulations, and rituals. Although

Charlotte never put too much stock in any of it, she knew of more than one officer or enlisted man who'd stop at Mrs. Connell's for a reading before he went on patrol.

Charlotte finished her tea, letting the leaves settle at the bottom of the cup. After swirling the remains around three times she turned the cup upside down on the saucer, tapped the bottom another three times, then handed it to Aileen. The laundress cradled the cup in her hands and looked at the leaves that remained stuck to the bottom and sides. She moved the delicate porcelain around, tilted it up, then downward, all the while gazing at the patterns of lines, dots, and shapes.

"You do have the gift…to read one's mind," Charlotte said.

"Right now my mind is telling me you want something. I figured as much when I saw you at the door. 'Cause you could have sent Eulah or your man, the one sitting out front in the carriage, with the money."

"The girl you've been sending twice a week is working very well."

"You mean Ada?"

Charlotte nodded. "That's why I'd like her to live in. Eulah's been with my family since I was a girl but, at her age, she can use some daily help. Of course, I'll still need another girl two days a week for heavy work."

"'Course. But this is a surprise. Guess that means you decided to set down roots." The laundress abruptly turned away, began hollering orders at a group of children through the window, then turned back. "Did I tell you? Got myself a new partner. Known Ed a while. He served with my Jamie in the army out West. We've opened another laundry… near the north branch of the river, on Goose Island. So we're both settlin' in permanent, so to speak."

Charlotte rose to leave, then stopped. For some reason that she couldn't fully explain, even to herself, it was important for her to know what Aileen could decipher in those leaf patterns.

Aileen peered into the cup again. "I see money, a lot of money coming your way. You are surrounded by admirers. 'Course, you always did have them aplenty. And an old admirer has returned." She glanced up and saw Charlotte's bemused expression. A long silence followed.

When Aileen spoke again she looked fixedly at the far wall, carefully avoiding Charlotte's eyes, and with a controlled voice said, "You got two people close to you. One will bring you much happiness, the other will break your heart." She turned the cup upside down and covered it with her hands. "That's all I can say."

Charlotte was about to speak, but thought better of it. She thanked Aileen and took her leave.

Aileen Connell reeked strongly of scent, and the odors and humidity in the shed clung so, that Charlotte was almost glad to step outside and breathe in the smell of coal smoke and boiled cabbage. She walked toward her carriage, with Aileen's words occupying her mind.

Some young toughs were standing near Bernard and the carriage. She instinctively reached into her pocket for the derringer and just as quickly removed her hand. Bernard's small size proved an advantage—it made him especially unthreatening and inconspicuous. However, he was more than capable of handling tense situations. This conclusion was reaffirmed when the toughs backed away and ran.

She looked at Bernard, who smiled as he stuffed the Colt Peacemaker in his belt. "Are we finished here?" he asked.

"Actually, I think we've just begun."

# FIVE

*In 1882 the Pinkerton National Detective Agency's Chicago office was located at 191-193 Fifth Avenue. This row of identical buildings escaped damage in the 1871 fire and changed little over the intervening years. Four stories in height with long, narrow windows front and rear, these were solid, dependable structures of common brick with stone trim. The Pinkerton emblem—a large eye, under which were inscribed the words "We Never Sleep"—dominated the street.*

As Garrett walked along he remembered his first visit to Chicago, the day he'd enlisted in the U.S. Army. He immediately felt a kinship with the city. They were alike—loud, brash, and eager for a fight. The city grew over the years, sprawling across neighboring townships like a drunken sailor. Chicago may have cloaked herself with a veneer of civility but, underneath, neither one had changed. Chicago would always be a Deadwood with paved streets.

He recalled, with fondness, last night's visit with Charlotte. Old friends, they drank and talked until the early hours of the morning. She listened patiently as he dredged his memory, hauling up images of dead comrades from Powder River, then his partner's murder in St. Louis.

"Don't carry Sam's death around like you have the others. They'll bury you. I'm not saying forget, just move on," Charlotte told him.

*Not until I see Brock hang*, he thought.

After an evening spent remembering the dead, Garrett felt a

strong need to be with the living. He picked up his pace, letting his eyes search out details of city life. The babble of vendors, pedestrians, and workmen blended with the rumblings of wagons and carriages. He stopped occasionally, peering at shop windows, and scanning advertising boards touting the latest French fabrics available at Marshall Field's store. After his obligatory visit to Pinkerton, but before he left Chicago, Garrett decided he would purchase a gift for Charlotte. As a rule, he had always been uncomfortable with feminine things like shopping, ill at ease in most female company. Charlotte was different. In a sense they were a match. He felt she understood him as well as he thought he understood her.

When Garrett arrived at the Pinkerton Agency the grandfather clock standing guard in the lobby was chiming eleven. He walked briskly to the carved oak stairs and up to the second floor. At the top, a small desk guarded a long narrow hallway lined with doors, all marked *Private.* The whole floor seemed deserted, except for the clerk, a middle-aged man who long ago had learned the art of appearing busy. He did not look up, but continued shuffling papers as Garrett approached.

"I'm here to see Mr. William Pinkerton."

"Your name?" the clerk asked, curling his upper lip.

Before Garrett could reply, Bill Pinkerton walked up the stairs. He stuck his hand out, shook Garrett's, and in a booming baritone said, "Lyons, you've arrived. Let's go to my office." Pinkerton was a man in constant motion, an eldest son perpetually trying to outdistance a famous father. As tall as Garrett, he sported a lush handlebar mustache on a round face set with deep brown eyes. They passed a door marked *Allan Pinkerton.* Garrett paused.

Bill's voice softened a little. "You're working with me now. My father's mind is alert, as always. However, his body has a lot of healing to do."

Allan Pinkerton had collapsed over three months before and it was evident that he would not make a full recovery nor return to the agency. Yet Bill didn't seem inclined to remove his father's name from the door or move into his office. Garrett followed him down the hall.

Since parting company with the U.S. Army, Garrett had supplemented his gambling income with various occupations. He met Sam Wilkerson in Kansas while the detective was investigating a theft for the Merchants Union Express Company and Garrett aided him in the arrest of the culprits. In recognition of his contributions to the case, and on Sam's recommendation, Allan Pinkerton hired him. The two of them continued to work cases personally selected by Pinkerton. The "Great Detective" protected his men and they, in turn, were fiercely devoted to him. They would rather give up their tongues than discuss their work or lose a case. But now Sam was dead, Allan gravely ill, and Garrett would be dealing with Bill Pinkerton, an unknown quantity.

Bill's office was a small room at the far end of the hall. A desk, the top rolled back to expose compartments stacked with neat piles of papers, took up most of the space. Along the opposite wall were floor-to-ceiling shelves lined with books. At the far end was a window that looked out onto a brick wall.

"Sit down, Lyons. Seems you were busy last night." Bill sat down next to his desk. He leaned forward and offered Garrett a cigar from a silver container, then struck a match and lit his.

Garrett looked around. The only other seat was an uncomfortable, flimsy-looking wooden chair with a straight back and no cushion. He sat down cautiously. "Let's settle up."

"Well. . .you did leave a few loose ends. A pity about Brock."

"There was an explosion."

"I am aware of that, Lyons. Those radicals stored explosives, as well as pamphlets, next door."

"No matter. Brock was going to run. I shot him."

"The bullet's in his back. The man is still unconscious. I'm sure the Alexian Brothers are doing their best. But, if he dies, some people in this town may call that murder."

"Call it what you will. I promised Sam's mother I'd bring in his killer. I did. We closed the case." Garrett put the cigar back in his mouth and placed the two parcels he'd been carrying on Bill's desk.

"Well, now, what have we got here?"

"What Sam and I were supposed to deliver. Brock's phony plates."

"You mean these?" Bill Pinkerton opened a drawer in his desk and held up what looked like two pieces of charred metal. "They were discovered at the warehouse early this morning."

He tossed them into the drawer and faced Garrett. "The Chicago Southwestern, like all railroads, does not take kindly to someone printing and circulating phony stock. When it comes to gouging a dollar from the citizenry they want no competition. The Pinkerton Agency has done them a service and they are grateful. Case is closed."

Garrett thought of the IOU tucked in his vest pocket. "Look... they put up any reward money? It all goes to Sam's family."

Pinkerton raised an eyebrow. "Well, then, let's see what you brought me."

He opened the parcels, spread the contents on his desk and took in a deep breath. He was quiet for a long moment. "Well, now, Lyons, you've got the gambler's luck all right. Looks like you dealt yourself a winning hand."

Garrett didn't have any idea what Bill meant so he just took a draw on his cheroot and let him continue.

"This business isn't over, not by any means. Brock never worked alone. He was a middleman." Bill leaned forward and lowered his voice to a faint whisper. "Brock is a scratcher, we know that. He's good, but not this good. This isn't his work." He pointed to the packets on his desk. "Rumor has it Brock partnered with a former engraver from the U.S. Treasury. The man was dismissed over ten years ago—dropped out of sight and began printing his own money. Damn successful, too. His twenty-dollar note is near perfect."

Garrett gave his cheroot a nudge with his finger, letting the ashes fall to the floor. He thought Bill Pinkerton was a lot like his father—big on preambles. Both men had a way of changing subjects so fast that, if a person wasn't listening hard, he could get caught short. Garrett began stretching his legs, hoping Bill would get to the point before he got a cramp.

Pinkerton pointed to the contents of the smaller parcel. "These are the plates for his twenty-dollar note. I'm sure of it. The man was a master. I say was, because he died six months ago. Federals searched his home. Didn't find much. Brock must've got there first." Pinkerton grabbed a banknote from a cubbyhole in his desk, laid it next to the packet. "I was right." He handed the twenty to Garrett. "This is his. Keep it. We found a partially burned box of them in the warehouse. Hopefully that's all. I've sent flyers to banks and stores to be on the alert." Still looking at Garrett, Pinkerton reached into another cubbyhole and extracted a paper about five inches wide and charred around the edges. "My men also found this."

Garrett took the paper and held it up to the light. "Looks like a certificate."

"Lyons, this is the mother lode! That piece of paper you're holding is part of a $100 U.S. government bond, issued in 1862. It matches this plate." He held up an object that had been wrapped in the second parcel. "The same engraver designed that bond before he was dismissed and would have had little trouble copying it. I know because part of a sample printout was found in his home. They're twenty-year bearer bonds. Know what that means? Whoever presents them to a federal bank on the due date collects value plus interest."

Bill was so intent on his story that he didn't realize his cigar had gone out. Garrett struck a match on his thumbnail and held the light in front of him. Bill relit without missing a word.

"Up to now it was just rumors. Now I know it's true. The engraver made the plates, then Brock got ahold of them and came to Chicago to print the bonds."

Garrett watched the flame burn down, then shook out the match. "Not my business."

Bill stopped talking a moment, took a long pull on his cigar, then blew a cloud of smoke at the ceiling. He sat on the very edge of his chair, speaking now with the quiet intensity of a preacher at a prayer meeting. "Lyons, you're not listening. Brock is the key. The man's no help right now, got a bullet in him, thanks to you. I know Brock couldn't handle this alone. He'd need a partner to distribute the bonds, once he'd printed them. I want you to find that partner. Those bonds mature in a month's time." Bill sat back and waited.

"Not my concern. Besides, all those phony bonds were probably burnt at the warehouse."

"Don't think so. I figure there's a box out there. Brock was packed up, ready to leave town. You understand? Even one small part of that box of phony stock could do a lot of damage."

"Look, I came here to find Sam's killer. I did that. Sam was one of your best agents. He was shot, point blank, in the chest. Your father would not let that pass. I won't."

Bill sat up abruptly, dropped his cigar on the floor and stomped it out with his boot. "I am *well* aware of my obligations, Lyons. In case you may have forgotten, Sam was out alone on this case, without his partner. Where were you?" He didn't wait for Garrett's answer. "I'm not sure Brock shot Sam. So, while I wait for some hard evidence, you can help me clear up this phony bond mess."

"Let the Secret Service do their job."

"By the time they get organized, it'll be too late. Is it money you're concerned about? You always seem to be short of funds. Trust me on this. When *we* solve this case, you can be assured of a considerable monetary reward from a grateful government as well as Pinkertons."

"The answer is no. I don't need any more gratitude from *you* or the U.S. government."

"Then the Pinkerton National Detective Agency no longer needs your services."

♠

Rob Powers arrived at the Pinkerton Agency, barely awake and nursing a headache. The senator's party at the Tremont had lasted well into the early hours of the morning. Rob shifted his weight from one foot to the other as he stifled a yawn with the back of his hand.

"You're a good reporter, Powers. But remember, a *great* reporter makes his own stories," John Hosty, the editor of the Chicago *Inter Ocean*, constantly preached. "Want a desk on this paper, Powers? Go out and bring me stories with color. . .with personality." When Rob asked what that was, Hosty bellowed, "A story about a person, an individual. You know, someone our readers can recognize, or feel mighty dumb if they don't."

Rob took Hosty's advice to heart. He kept a collection of small notepads in the pockets of his jacket. These pads were crammed with information on people in the news or ones that should be. Every day he made the rounds of places where people of interest congregated. The Pinkerton office was at the top of his list. So Rob took his regular post near the main entrance door. This afforded him an occasional breeze as well as an excellent view. Along the south wall to his left was the "Black Museum," an exhibit of mementos of famous Pinkerton cases. The north wall was bare except for a full length, rather intimidating portrait of the Great Detective himself. The agency office attracted the curious as well as potential clients. But, as any savvy reporter soon learned, the real business took place upstairs, on the second floor.

After ten minutes, Rob walked up the oak stairway but was abruptly sent on his way by a clerk. He returned to his post at the main door and waited for a story to appear. The clock chimed twelve as he carelessly flipped through one of his notepads and he nearly missed a tall man wearing a black coat strolling leisurely past. He checked the notepad then quickly followed the man out the door and down Fifth Avenue, catching him as he turned the corner onto Monroe.

"Excuse me, are you Garrett Lyons? My name is Powers, Rob Powers. I'm a reporter from the *Inter Ocean*," he said, nervous as hell. "Can I have an interview? It's just a few questions."

Garrett glanced absentmindedly at him. "Depends. Let's hear them."

"Well. . ." Rob swallowed hard. "What can you tell me about the explosion and fire at the warehouse on South Water Street last evening?"

"Nothing."

"What can you tell me about the shooting? Who was injured?"

Garrett stopped and stared at the young man. In a tone that was friendly but cautious, he said, "You heard me. Nothing. Talk to Bill Pinkerton."

Powers flipped through pages in his notepad and continued. "I'm not like the rest of the reporters, filing embroidered stories based on hearsay, sketchy information. No, sir, Mr. Lyons, the *Inter Ocean* prints the facts. Rumor has it the warehouse that blew up contained a large supply of explosives and seditious pamphlets used by a workers' union, the Sons of Labor."

"You asking or telling?"

Rob walked double-time, trying to match Garrett's stride. As he kept pace, his voice rose a pitch higher. "This morning there were Pinkerton agents crawling all over the rubble. You may be a Pinkerton man, maybe not. I figure you were there, you know the real story."

Garrett continued walking.

Unaware of the stir he was causing along the street, Rob continued. "*Lieutenant* Lyons is it? Maybe lieutenant isn't the correct title. Were your army records sealed after your court-martial?"

Garrett stopped abruptly. Rob nearly bumped into him.

"Well, now, that's a question. The answer is…the U.S. Army and I parted company."

Taken somewhat aback, Rob asked, "What did you do after that?"

"I survived."

"How did you? Survive, I mean?"

"I put my years of army training to good use." Garrett's voice was a tight monotone, as if he had said this many times before and still hated it. He stared dispassionately at a display of men's pipes and tobacco in a store window.

Rob stood alongside, giving Garrett quick glances out of the corner of his eye as he flipped pages in his notebook. "I think you were a professional card player, managed a saloon, and, for a time, led hunting expeditions out West. How long did you do that?"

"'Til I got tired of smiling."

A little surprised, but somewhat encouraged, Rob continued. "I was at Senator Lawlor's party at the Tremont House. You and Mr. Sullivan are regulars at the Lotus Club gambling parties. I did a lot of listening." Rob took a deep breath and went on. "There were over forty troopers massacred at Powder River. Rumor has it that General Stannard got you off by bribing a—"

Garrett grabbed Rob by the collar of his jacket. Before the reporter could speak, he dragged the young man into the alleyway and shoved him up against a brick wall, hard. He leaned in close and said, "You miserable piece of scribbling shit."

Rob began talking fast. "Look, all I need is a story. The Grand Army reunion is this week. The *Herald*, the *Tribune*, they're all printing soldiers' memoirs. The *Tribune* ran a three-part story on General Sheridan. I'd like to write a story on General Stannard for the *Inter Ocean*. He and Sheridan were roommates at West Point, served together during the war."

"Ask the general. Don't bother me."

"General Stannard doesn't give interviews. But you were with him out West, fighting Indians. You could put in a word."

Garrett's hold tightened. Rob began gasping between words. "Look, if I can't get General Stannard's story, tell me yours. I'll promise you a fair shake. That's more than you'll get with any of the other papers. Think what I can do."

Garrett reached into his pocket, pulled out Oates's card and held it up in front of the reporter's face. "What *you* can do is tell me where I can find this company."

"Central Casualty Insurance? That's in the Borden Block. It's just a quick walk over to Randolph and Dearborn."

# SIX

*Built in 1880, the Borden Block was designed by Dankmar Adler, a German-born architect and engineer. The building stood six stories high, with a brick and cut stone exterior that did not sacrifice beauty in exchange for light. The exterior ornamentation was designed by the newest member of his firm, Louis Sullivan. The building was commissioned by William Borden to commemorate his bonanza in the Leadville silver mines and occupied the northwest corner of Dearborn and Randolph Streets. This was the site of the old Matteson House, where such noted Chicago sportsmen as Pierre Carmé and Budd Doble had gathered.*

The lobby of the Borden Block provided a quiet refuge from the hectic pace of Chicago's streets. Gas lights, spaced around the perimeter of the room, cast a rich yellow glow on the marble floors. Intricately designed bronze stair rails dispersed gently moving patterns of light and shadow on mahogany paneled walls. Garrett took his time entering, brushing dust from his sleeves, scraping his boots on a bristle board.

A uniformed porter appeared. "Central Casualty Insurance would be the third floor, sir. I'll summon an elevator. The Otis Company just installed two of their latest models."

A whirring sound signaled the elevator's descent. They looked up as the cage appeared in view. This was followed by a sharp grating noise as the cage began a precarious downward slide.

"The brakes man, use the brakes!" the porter shouted.

After what seemed an eternity, they heard an ear-shattering crunch. The cage stopped six feet above the lobby floor. Garrett could see that the cage door was partially open. Amid layers of petticoats, he saw a trim ankle encased in a black silk stocking, then a young woman's face framed in pale golden curls. She sat upright on the floor of the elevator. When she saw Garrett, her eyes widened.

Suddenly, the cage lurched downward.

"Jump!" He was about to add, "I'll catch you," when she tumbled into his arms. Taken by surprise, Garrett stiffened. He felt the curves of her body amidst the layers of material. Blonde curls brushed against his face and the scent of lavender water kindled a brief flash of memory, a fleeting image of a lithograph of a young girl with long blonde hair and porcelain skin, staring at her reflection in a pool. It had accompanied him throughout his campaigns out West. He was smiling to himself, wondering why he thought of it at all, when he heard, "Put me down *now*, or you'll discover I can be quite a handful."

Garrett found himself staring at cobalt blue eyes. "Excuse me, ma'am." He gently deposited the young woman on her feet.

"Our second elevator is available," the porter said, trying to sound reassuring.

"No thanks, I'll take the stairs," Garrett answered.

♠

Central Casualty Insurance leased a suite of offices on the third floor of the Borden Block. The company name was printed with a flourish on six of the glass-topped doors, with the seventh and center door labeled *Entrance*.

"I wish to see Mr. Oates."

"Do you have an appointment?" the young man sitting behind the desk asked.

Garrett showed him the business card he'd received the previous evening. "No appointment, but the gentleman is expecting me."

"Wait here, sir," the clerk said, then left the room.

Garrett looked around. In addition to a reception desk, the room was furnished with long wooden benches placed against the wall. An assortment of men and women were perched quietly in a row, looking ill at ease, as if they had no right to be there. Garrett did not feel like joining them, so he began pacing slowly around the perimeter of the room, returning everyone's stares with studied indifference. On his third stroll he began asking himself, *Why am I here? Because I took a damn marker, that's why.*

He had almost convinced himself to leave when the clerk returned and said, "Follow me, sir."

Garrett trailed him through a large workroom. Wooden file cases lined three walls with two rows of desks in the center. Dour-faced clerks, all wearing cuff protectors over the lower portion of their white shirtsleeves, occupied the desks. They bore identical expressions of dogged efficiency as they rustled through files or scratched pens over ledgers.

The clerk led Garrett down a hallway, stopping in front of a solid, paneled mahogany door with a carved crystal doorknob. "Unfortunately, Mr. Oates is not available. Another officer of Central Casualty Insurance has agreed to see you." He knocked on the door then, with a smile, abandoned Garrett.

The brass plate in the center of the door read: *General J. Barton Stannard, President, Central Casualty Insurance.*

♠

The office was a large corner room with one wall lined with bookshelves. The afternoon sun reflected off the leather bindings, while the grate in a corner box stove held the embers of a coal fire that attempted to take the chill from the air. At first glance, this office could have belonged to any company president. On closer inspection, Garrett saw a Fourth Cavalry flag draped over crossed sabers on one wall, opposite a painting of a lake. General Stannard was standing next to a large carved oak desk, staring out the window.

Garrett immediately felt a mask spread over his face, a kind of instinctive self-protection. He closed the door with a resounding click. It had been eight long years since the two men had seen or spoken to one another—a lifetime ago, when Garrett led his patrol out of Fort Fetterman, into the massacre at Powder River and the end of his army career.

The general rocked slowly back and forth on the balls of his feet, hands clasped behind his back. The only acknowledgment he made of another presence in the room was a slight nod of his head. Neither man moved. A wall clock chimed the half hour, cutting through the silence like a cannon shot. Finally, Stannard turned around.

Garrett stood silently, watching his former commander. The old man's face had grown hawk-like, eyes compressed to slashes. His hair was gray now, with only faint traces of the red Garrett remembered. His mouth, under an old man's mustache, was thin-lipped and grim. Without consciously doing so, Garrett found himself standing straighter, not quite to attention, but definitely with his feet together and his head up.

The first words to pass between the two men were awkward.

"It's been a long time, Lieutenant Lyons. Too long."

"Yes, sir, it has."

The general walked toward him, extending his hand in greeting. When Garrett made no move to respond, he swung his arm down in a swift motion toward the humidor on his desk. His hesitation had been slight, but sufficient for Garrett to notice.

"Have a cigar, my boy. If I remember correctly, you are fond of them."

"No thank you, sir." As soon as he spoke Garrett felt angry with himself. Here he was back in the army, routine reactions returning, as if it were yesterday.

The general took his time lighting up, inhaling slowly. "Pour yourself a whiskey. And while you're at it, pour me one too. We'll have ourselves a good long visit." He nodded toward a small table on top of which stood a silver tray holding a crystal decanter and glasses.

"Actually, sir, I came to see an associate of yours." Garrett took the IOU from his pocket, handed the card to the general, then avoided his gaze by walking over to the table and pouring their drinks.

"So...you've met my partner." General Stannard turned the card over, studying both sides. "He's not here. I haven't seen the man for two days."

"He was playing poker at the Tremont House last night."

The general raised an eyebrow. "Well now, how did he seem to you?"

"Like a loser. He left the game early and in a hurry." Garrett handed a glass to the general and continued with a decided edge to his voice. "Before his hasty departure, Oates assured me that my money would be available. Here. Today."

"Of course it is. Relax. Drink your whiskey." The general sipped his drink. As he continued speaking he seemed to drift off, plunging into reminiscences, filling the air with mindless words about the past.

Garrett watched him out of the corner of his eye. He reminded himself that the old man was at his most dangerous when he performed that maneuver. More than once Garrett had only half-listened to one of his long-winded stories, and then found he had volunteered for some wearisome job.

The general continued, "Only a few mementos here—the corps flag, my sabers—something to look at when I'm in the office. The rest are in storage. A man needs objects with a past, to see and touch, to keep him on course." He pointed to the painting of a lake and chuckled. "Remember Fort Verde? That barren hellhole in New Mexico? If the heat didn't kill you, the Apaches would. We all had pictures of lakes, rivers, some sort of water, hanging on the walls of our quarters. Still have yours?"

Garrett took in a deep breath. "Not any more, sir." He settled in a chair, sitting forward, elbows on his knees, staring at the whiskey in his glass. As the general continued talking, Garrett's mind was giving him no rest, jumping from one memory to another.

The blonde-haired girl in the elevator faded into a soldier in his patrol—firing, reloading, falling—then next an Indian camp...smoke, gunfire. Finally, he drained his glass in one long gulp. *General*, he thought, *you talk too much. But then you always did.*

"Enough reminiscing." The general put his hands down at his sides, then, as if deciding that gesture was not right, folded his arms across his chest. "I find it hard to believe my partner is such a bad poker player. Maybe he's unlucky. You still pulling cards from the bottom of the deck?"

"As I recall, sir, upon occasion you used to deal that way yourself."

"Of course...but you're good at it."

They laughed together at the remark and the general carried his laugh right into the subject he wished to discuss. "Why don't we have dinner this evening? We'll smoke cigars, drink a bottle of wine, trade stories. Like old times, heh?"

"No, sir. I've made plans."

"Finished that job for Pinkerton?" The general made a quarter turn, watched Garrett a moment, then smiled without separating his lips. "The army may have put me out to pasture, but I still keep my ear to the ground. You've been working for Pinkerton the past three years."

As he spoke, the general walked around his desk to the bookshelves. He pulled out a section, revealing a small safe, then reached inside without even looking and extracted neatly wrapped packets of money. He closed the safe, walked back, and placed two of the packets on the desk.

"This should cover my partner's debt."

Garrett stared at his former mentor. The old man's face looked sweaty even though the room was not very warm. Garrett reached for one packet.

The general grabbed his hand in a surprisingly firm grip. "Why not consider working here, with me, at Central Casualty?"

"Not interested. Sir."

The general released his hand, then put another packet on the desk. "Don't be so hasty. This is double...no, triple what Oates probably owes you."

Garrett shook his head.

"It's a small matter for Central Casualty Insurance."

"I am no longer in the army. And I no longer work for the Pinkertons. Now the only orders I take are my own."

The edge dropped from the general's voice, which became smoother. "You would be doing me a service, my boy. It won't take more than a few weeks of your time."

"I don't know anything about insurance."

"Neither do I. That hasn't stopped me from making a damn good living at it." He spread his hands and, in an almost relaxed voice, said, "Actually the job I have in mind for you has nothing to do with insurance. It's a small matter, a property investment the company made…a building under construction. They're having problems at the site. Consider my offer. You're always in need of ready cash. Think of it, my boy. Together again, like old times."

Garrett did not move. He stood quietly, trying to analyze the sound of the general's words while they still hung in the air. Finally, he let his breath out, like a man who has come up from a plunge in deep water. "I can't, sir. You know I can't." There was an awkward silence, then he continued. "Hell, I was fifteen when I joined up. You, the army, were my family. For twelve years I followed orders, mostly yours. After that mess at Powder River, what did you and the U.S. Army do? Toss me." Garrett spoke softly. "I still have a bullet lodged in my shoulder and continue to sleep with too many ghosts. It's taken eight years to bury those memories. I'm not about to dig them up again."

The silence lingered, like an unspoken chasm of distrust. General Stannard was the first to speak. "Blame Lieutenant Elliott Caultrain, the 'hero' of Powder River, not me."

The mere sound of Caultrain's name felt like a cold breath against the back of Garrett's neck.

The general took up his glass and finished his whiskey in one gulp. "Caultrain was a back-stabbing son-of-a-bitch. He'd stomp on his own mother to get ahead. At Powder River you put yourself in a no-win position, impossible to defend. You ended up in the wrong place, whatever the reason. No matter how heroic you were, when it was over there was no one to back your story, Lyons. You were alone. Caultrain had a witness. His aide's report was convincing. It sealed his case. You didn't stand a chance. Caultrain took the glory, you took the blame. By the way, it's Colonel Caultrain now. Got a promotion to General Phil Sheridan's staff and should feel right at home there with the other toadies."

"You're right, General. I didn't stand a chance at that court-martial. I was alone, wasn't I? After twelve years of service, no one came forward to speak for me."

The general leaned over, putting his face in front of Garrett's, looking directly into his eyes. "You seem to have forgotten that during your army career you had trouble following my orders, or any orders for that matter, thus you managed to dig yourself into quite a few pissholes. That was one I couldn't pull you out of. Besides, General Sheridan made damn sure I was cashiered out soon after your Powder River mess." The old man paused, looked at his former aide and let out a soft sigh. "Life is made up of many things, and fairness is not one of them. Best we both leave the past buried."

"I just want what I'm owed." Garrett took a packet of money and shoved it into his pocket.

The general poured himself another whiskey. His voice was tired but firm. "You're a gambler, Lyons, always have been, always will be." He nodded toward the packets remaining on the desk. "I'm betting these odds are too good for you to pass up. Just think about my offer, that's all I'm asking. Then come by and we'll talk. I have rooms at the Grand Pacific."

# SEVEN

*Elijah Peacock opened Chicago's first retail jewelry establishment in 1837. The small frame building on Lake Street marked the city's evolution from a trading post to a town of civilization and refinement. The founder, a third generation watch and jewelry repairman, introduced Chicagoans to silver tea services, trays, and candlesticks, enabling his upscale clientele to purchase old-world elegance. After several successive moves, the firm—by then named for Elijah's son, C. D. Peacock—settled for some time at State and Washington Streets. The three-story building was designed as a showplace for the finest in jewelry, watches, and gifts.*

Throughout his army career, whenever the pressures of the military routine began to crowd him, Garrett would volunteer for patrol. It was an opportunity to simply get on a horse and ride out a problem. In Chicago, all he could do was walk. Garrett left the Borden Block, crossing through the afternoon traffic, dodging horses' hooves and hissing carriage wheels. He reached the other side of the street and quickened his pace, angling his body through streets crowded with businessmen, shoppers, and street peddlers.

Familiar, yet troubling images flickered through his head, like an exhibit of Mr. Brady's photographs. The blood surged through his ears with such pressure that his head pounded and his vision blurred. He was back again at Fort Fetterman, the only member of his patrol to return. And he was alone, facing the cold accusing panel of officers, knowing he had already been judged and found guilty.

"Do not go back, *mon ami,*" Otwah had warned him. "Been scouting for the U.S. Cavalry too many years. The army will think better of you dead."

But General Stannard would explain, he thought—the way the old man had always defended his actions. But the general was absent from the fort. And Otwah's words rang true.

Garrett slowed his pace, finally coming to a dead stop. People continued walking around him, brushing past like a fast-moving stream around a rock. Nothing had changed. He found no escape. No matter how long, how far, how quickly he walked, he knew he would never outrun the ghosts of his long-dead comrades. The wind shifted, bringing with it a late afternoon chill from the lake. He looked around to get his bearings, searching for a landmark, a familiar structure. He saw the afternoon sun glistening on a row of buildings and realized he was near Jackson Street.

For a brief moment he felt disoriented. Smythe Tavern should be nearby. It was gone! Indeed, a whole city block had been leveled. On his last visit, the building was standing. Now, all he could see was a large hole surrounded by a fence. Sullivan was right. Chicago was a city constantly reinventing itself.

Garrett joined a group of spectators leaning against a wooden barricade that separated the construction site from the street. He stared halfheartedly at the scene unfolding before him. Mule-drawn wagons moved debris out of a large trench along two sides of the block, while workmen put the finishing touches on wood reinforcements. A group of boys—scrawny, thin creatures no more than twelve years old—had descended on the site and were busy sweeping up scraps and fetching water. Garrett remembered that was the age he'd been when he joined the Tenth Illinois Cavalry at the onset of the Civil War.

Mental pictures of his uniform, and the first camp somewhere in Kentucky, were still clear. He'd been standing around with the rest of the Chicago recruits, looking for a tent to share, when a sergeant shouted, "You there. Get up on the hill. Our new colonel needs tending." Words that were to change his life.

The camp was filled with rumors and colorful stories about a Colonel J. Barton Stannard. Garrett remembered opening the tent flap and staring at a thin man of medium height with patrician features and a flowing red beard.

"Well, enter or leave! Don't just stand there," his baritone voice boomed.

As it turned out, fate had indeed tapped his shoulder—this new colonel needed an aide. Garrett's first duty was to stand on a box holding a mirror. He watched and listened as the colonel braided his beard into two plaits.

"Won't blow into my face," he explained. "When I ride, I ride hard and fast."

Garrett soon learned that the colonel was a man of many rituals. As his star rose—until he finally reached the rank of general—these rituals became more pronounced and part of his mystique. He always wore the same uniform jacket in every campaign, one with faded insignia that had been patched over and over. Out West he added a pair of brown corduroy breeches, singed at the bottom to prevent raveling, acquiring a new pair for every winter campaign against the Indians.

Garrett's fondest memories were of the early evenings—after the marching, drilling, and endless staff meetings—when the colonel would retire to his tent. Garrett would look through the man's books and listen to him talk. The only subjects the colonel felt comfortable discussing were commanders and campaigns. Garrett didn't care, because, during those evenings, he'd learned to read and write. For the next twelve years, if anyone asked, Garrett would always state that he wanted nothing more than to live and die with J. Barton Stannard—first with the Tenth Illinois during the Civil War, and then with the Fourth Cavalry during the Indian Wars.

The mixture of men's voices, along with the sounds of digging and the movement of wagons, provided a soft background to these memories. Garrett leaned against the barricade, searching his mind for a forgotten detail, an overlooked moment of his recent meeting with the general. Something that would give him a clue, a thought, about what his former commander was really up to.

The afternoon sunlight began to take on an amber, hazy quality. It was getting late. The wind shifted, bringing with it the smell of manure and swill from the ditches. Garrett retrieved his watch from his vest pocket, checked the time, and remembered Charlotte's present. The shops would be closing soon. He saw an omnibus coming down Jackson Street and set off at a fast trot, leaping onto its rear steps.

♠

"State Street is the *only* place to shop in Chicago," Louis Sullivan had informed him.

He was right. Fancy stores of every size crammed both sides of the avenue. Garrett's decision to purchase something for Charlotte was rapidly becoming a formidable task. Out West, even in towns the size of Kansas City, shopping was easy. A man would simply stroll into the main emporium and point to a fancy trinket. Then, before he finished lighting his cigar, it would be wrapped and purchased.

Where to begin? He was eyeing a colorful display of lace shawls in a window when he noticed an attractive young woman walk by. Her blue silk dress and blonde curls were vaguely familiar. Of course...she was the young lady he'd rescued earlier that afternoon. She was carrying packages and walking in a deliberate manner. Maybe she was shopping. Although State Street was crowded, Garrett had little trouble keeping her in view. His mood brightened. Then he recognized the two neatly dressed men walking toward them. They were dips. Garrett knew their con, so he quickened his pace.

One man bumped the lady and she dropped one of her parcels. As he helped her retrieve it, his partner came up behind her. With a swift motion, he cut the strap of her purse and stuffed it into the pocket of his jacket. The incident was so smooth, so swift, the young lady did not notice. As the dip walked past him, Garrett reached out and grabbed his arm.

"Wha'?" the man gasped, then relaxed with a sigh. "Oh, Lyons. Heard about Sam. You still lookin' fer that Brock fella?"

"Caught him last night." Garrett spoke softly, keeping his voice low, as he deftly switched the lady's purse from the man's pocket into his own. "A friendly warning. Just spied a police wagon at the corner. I think they're scouting this block. Best you both keep moving."

And they did.

♠

C. D. Peacock, Jeweler was one of those stylish shops with thick petit-point carpets and marble columns, amid rows of glass cases perched on gilt legs. Garrett figured their customers probably never pointed to the merchandise, a polite whisper would suffice. He caught a glimpse of the young woman's blonde curls and blue dress. She was standing next to a glass case displaying timepieces and whispering discreetly to a black-frocked clerk.

Garrett gently tapped her shoulder. "Excuse me, ma'am. I believe you dropped this?"

She turned and looked annoyed at the interruption. When she saw her purse in his hand, her eyes widened, her bosom rose and fell in a kind of sigh. "My gracious, I hadn't realized it was missing. Why, sir, I truly thank you." A shy smile appeared on her face. "You look familiar. Have we met?"

"Yes, we have."

"Oh! That terrible elevator. I never did properly thank you. Your name, sir?"

"Lyons, Garrett Lyons."

"I am Iris…Iris Reynolds." She extended her hand toward Garrett. "Well, now, it seems I am indebted to you twice in one day."

She posed herself exquisitely against a glass display case next to a pink marble pillar. Garrett looked at her fair cloud of golden hair, long delicate face, and iridescent eyes. In his mind she became the girl in the lithograph. Only, now, she was staring at *him* and not her reflection in the pond. Garrett held on to her hand, trying to think of a suitable reply. Here she was, waiting for him to speak, and all he could muster was a silly grin.

"Thank you again," she whispered and withdrew her hand.

There was an awkward silence. Garrett could smell her perfume and almost feel the heat of her body. He began to explain. "Actually, I'm here just visiting and, well…I thought to purchase a gift." The words tumbled out. He stopped mid-sentence when he realized Iris was not listening.

The clerk returned with a velvet case. "The necklace was restrung and this clasp should not break again."

Iris inspected the pearls carefully. "This will do. Wrap it." She turned to Garrett. "So, you are here to select a present? Then I shall help. Is this a gift for your wife, perhaps?"

Garrett shook his head.

"Then your sister?"

He shook his head again.

"A friend?"

His smile brought a fainter smile to her face.

There was a brief silence, their eyes met and, suddenly, they both burst into laughter.

"She is a fortunate lady indeed." Iris led him toward another display case. "These brooches are quite lovely."

A clerk removed a tray of cameos. Garrett held one pin after another to the light. They all looked the same to him. He noticed Iris's eyes widen a little when he picked up one of black onyx surrounded with seed pearls. "What do you think?"

"An elegant piece. Any lady would be thrilled to receive such a lovely gift."

"Well, then, I'll take it."

Another clerk returned with Iris's package and she turned to leave. Suddenly, she stopped and, with a smile that dazzled, said, "Hopefully I shall arrive home unscathed after such a hectic day. Thank you again."

Garrett watched her cross to the bronze and beveled-glass entrance door, the deep blue material of her dress clinging to her body. *She has a lovely back*, he thought. And, with a smile, he wondered how she looked without the dress.

The clerk behind the counter cleared his throat. "Have you made a selection?"

"I'll take this one."

"I'll have the item wrapped, sir."

It was not that late, at least not according to the clock on the wall above the door. Garrett figured he had time to get back to the Revere Hotel and freshen up before the outing with Sullivan and Charlotte. The clerk informed him of the price of the cameo and Garrett raised an eyebrow. Sighing, he reached into his pants pocket for cash and pulled out a twenty. He immediately realized it was the phony note Bill Pinkerton had given him. So he removed the general's packet of money from his pocket instead. As soon as he placed a couple of bills on the counter he realized something wasn't right.

*Damn, that's another of the phony twenties,* he thought.

Garrett leaned over the counter and looked closely at the paper. The general's twenty-dollar notes were exactly the same as the phony note Pinkerton had given him. General Stannard had paid his partner's IOU alright, but with the same counterfeit notes. He stared at the money then quickly gathered the notes and returned them to his pocket. He reached inside his jacket, pulled out his wallet and counted out the twenties. Luckily he had enough, although his wallet was now mighty thin.

# EIGHT

*In Chicago, entertainment was continuous, diverse, and accommodated every taste. Built in 1872, Hooley's Theater was four floors high, with exterior walls of cut stone. The building fronted only twenty feet on Randolph Street but was 180 feet deep. The theater could seat 1,300 patrons without crowding. Hooley's always booked first-class attractions from New York. Located a few blocks south, Mike McDonald's establishment, The Store, was within sight of city hall. A saloon occupied the first floor, the largest gambling parlor in town the second, while the third and fourth floors contained private rooms. The Store was a favorite meeting place for Democratic politicians and the high rollers of Chicago's commercial world, both legal and illegal.*

Garrett watched Charlotte adjust her cloak and tried to gauge if her temper had improved since their meeting earlier in the day. They sat in silence, as the driver from Evans's Livery maneuvered the brougham along Eldridge Court and onto Michigan Avenue. The avenue was crowded with people, seeing and being seen, on their way to parties, dinner, or the theater. The brougham reached Monroe Street. Garrett spied a flower girl standing at the corner and signaled the driver to stop. He reached out the window and purchased her last bouquet of violets.

As he presented Charlotte with the flowers, Garrett's hand closed on hers. He watched with satisfaction as her expression changed from bemusement to a warm smile, when she looked down and discovered the black cameo brooch framed in pearls.

Sullivan joined them outside of Hooley's Theater, and the trio went in to take their seats. Garrett found the Lloyds Light Opera Company revue surprisingly entertaining and their conversation between acts was innocuous and trivial. Yet, throughout all this camaraderie, he felt troubled by something or someone. He settled a little lower in his seat and, when he contributed to the conversation, there was a slight edge to his voice. As the evening progressed his disposition failed to improve.

When the performance ended and the audience applauded, Charlotte whispered in his ear, "Who put you in such a state?"

"Bill Pinkerton's not his father. No surprise…I figured that going in. So you might say we had a parting of the ways."

She looked at him for a moment. "Does that mean you are no longer employed by the Pinkerton Agency?"

He shrugged. "It's probably for the best. Do you remember the marker I took last evening? At *your* insistence, I might add."

Charlotte merely raised an eyebrow and let him continue.

"I went to Central Casualty Insurance to collect. The gentleman wasn't there." Garrett paused a moment to be sure of Charlotte's attention. "I met his partner, General Stannard. The general hasn't seen the man for two days."

"He's the general's partner? That gentleman may be a member of the Lotus Club, but he's not one of our regular poker players. I know *all* the high rollers. Wonder why he was there at all?"

"Evidently to lose money, give me a phony IOU, and then disappear. Seems I may be stuck in Chicago awhile," Garrett replied, with a decided edge to his voice.

Charlotte unconsciously touched his brooch, which was now pinned to her dress.

He leaned over. "Don't worry. I won't be on your doorstep, hat in hand. The general offered me a job. He's having a problem with a building that's under construction."

"A man like General Stannard would not ask for help unless he needed it. You were his aide for over twelve years. You may not admit it, but he's like. . .well, like your family."

"Family? Families look out for one another. Now he's just a lonely old man who wants an audience to listen to him recite his past glories."

"You still don't understand. Family is everything." Charlotte shook her head. "Besides, did you ever consider that, if you stay and work with the general, something interesting may turn up?" She leaned over and whispered in his ear. "The Grand Army reunion festivities begin next week. I've arranged a few high stakes games. The right player—sharp, skillful, with no allegiance toward the military—could walk away with a good-sized bankroll. It's up to you."

"Would I be obligated?"

"Yes. I will not let you forget it." Charlotte squeezed his arm affectionately.

The lobby was jammed with theatergoers all determined to continue their festivities into the night. A steady babble of voices mingled with the rustling of cloaks, along with silk and taffeta swishing against one another.

"Where's Sullivan?" Charlotte asked.

"He went backstage to fetch the twirling red umbrella."

She looked puzzled.

"Second act chorus line. The third blonde from the left will be joining us for supper."

"They usually are. . .blonde, I mean." Then she added, "I'll wait in front."

The line of carriages, broughams, and hansoms stretched down Randolph Street and over to Michigan Avenue. A rumble of distant thunder was immediately followed by a sharp wind that gusted down the street, lifting women's capes and toppling men's beaver hats. Charlotte was wearing her best dark blue velvet cloak, lined with white silk. As she pulled it around her shoulders, her fingers touched the brooch pinned to her dress. Another sharp wind came in a sudden gust down the street, shaking raindrops loose from the canopy. A drop hit Charlotte on the neck, sending a shiver down her back. She stepped back inside the lobby doorway and waited.

♠

After Garrett left Charlotte at the theater entrance he made his way back through the crowded lobby. Since the debacle at Powder River, where he'd been trapped under the dead bodies of his men, Garrett did not like being confined. At times, his need for space was so urgent that it ignited a rising panic in him. Even now his face felt damp and his breathing shallow, as he angled his way through groups of revelers towards the stage door. When he felt a hand grab his shoulder he tensed. For a split second old reflexes seized him, before a stronger instinct took over. He turned around slowly and found himself staring at an army officer who wore a vaguely familiar face from his past.

"Lyons? Right? Wasn't sure at first, it's been awhile. Eight years, if I count right." The officer stepped in front of Garrett, blocking his path.

*It has been that long since Powder River,* Garrett thought, as he eyed the man up and down. *He cuts quite a figure in that custom-tailored uniform. I think I remember the face, like I'd remember an annoying burr stuck inside my boot, but can't recall the name.* "See you're still in the army and still a lieutenant."

"Not much else I can do. Don't have any talent but soldiering. Fortunately I was sick and missed your last patrol. Powder River, wasn't it?"

*Whatever I say, this isn't going to end well,* Garrett thought. He turned to leave but the officer blocked his way, then stepped closer. Garrett could see the weathered creases that edged his mouth, smell his whiskey breath.

"You know, I lost a cousin at Powder River. He served with Lieutenant Caultrain. You should have stayed out West, Lyons. What're you doing in Chicago?"

Garrett took in a deep breath. His hands felt hot and sticky. He kept clenching and unclenching them as he spoke in what he hoped was a calm voice. "If I asked you that same question, what answer would I get?"

"A straight one. We arrived earlier this week from St. Louis to finalize arrangements, see that everything runs smoothly for Colonel Caultrain."

"Colonel, is it?"

"Not for long." The officer's voice took on a self-satisfied tone. "The colonel's promotion to brigadier will be announced by General Sheridan himself at the Grand Army reunion. The opening ceremonies will be at the Exposition Building."

"A captain, then a colonel, and now a brigadier? Just remember, no matter how many skins a snake sheds he's still a snake." Garrett watched the muscles in the man's face tense and tried to hold back a smile. "I find it hard to believe you're still a lieutenant. I ask myself, why? You're probably smart, reasonably talented. I figure the new brigadier would want at least a major running and fetching for him. I'm surprised Caultrain didn't use his considerable influence and get you a promotion, too."

"General Sheridan and his staff are coming from Washington for this reunion. Civil War veterans from Michigan, Wisconsin, Indiana, and Ohio will be in attendance." The officer's voice was sharp. "General Sheridan has big plans. Since *you* are no longer on the U.S. Army's invitation list, you can read about it in the newspaper."

"Don't be too sure," was all the answer Garrett could muster. He was stuck, unable to move forward or backward.

At that moment a silver-tipped walking stick appeared between Garrett and the officers, parting the waters so to speak. It was followed by a short dapper gentleman, dressed to the nines, escorting an attractive blonde lady. "Excuse me, my good man. Let's make room." Sullivan ceremoniously pushed his way between them. "Lyons, we've been looking all over for you." He stared at the officer. "Friend of yours?"

The man nodded and stepped back into the crowd.

"Well, now, Chicago's a big town. Let's hope we all run into one another again," Sullivan called after him.

"I am definitely glad to see you," Garret said.

"And I you. We will be joining you for dinner." Sullivan turned to the lady. "And what was your name again, my dear?"

♠

It was one of those nameless hours in the underbelly of the night when even Chicago's downtown streets were almost deserted. The sky had become an ominous blue-black with occasional flashes of lightning on the horizon. A clear sign another storm was approaching. Nevertheless, The Store, Mike McDonald's gambling emporium, was going flat out.

After the Great Fire, where others saw rubble, Michael Cassius McDonald recognized opportunity. He set up Chicago's first crime syndicate, an almost exclusively Irish operation. Six years later, he took control of the Cook County Democratic Party and solidified his power. The backbone of McDonald's empire was protection and insurance. No gambling establishment of any kind was free to operate in the city without paying King Mike a fee.

McDonald first met Charlotte when she arrived in Chicago to manage the Lotus Club's gambling nights and was immediately smitten. He dispatched his most talented dealers to her games and strictly enforced a "no scamming" rule on them. Mike looked forward to Tuesday mornings when Charlotte would deliver his share of the Lotus Club's gaming receipts. Maybe there was a dash of the romantic in him, but he always chose his attire carefully for the occasion.

Even at this late hour, McDonald was in his third floor office, pacing back and forth, eyeing bolts of fabric, all of them black, displayed against a wall. Finally, he pointed to one that had a faint pinstripe. "That's the one. What do you say, Goldberg?"

"A fine decision, sir."

"It's settled. I want the suit, here, in my office, by the end of the week."

"That's in less than four days!"

"Stop lollygaggin' then! Get to it!"

The haberdasher sighed. This Tuesday evening ritual was a routine he usually endured with a weary familiarity. He was about to voice a strong protest, when the door opened. A lad with muscular arms, a broad chest, and no visible neck, stepped in. He pointed over his shoulder to the hallway. McDonald glanced at him, then turned to Goldberg.

"I want pearl buttons on the jacket, and put in that red silk lining."

Ed McGlynn was standing in the hallway, his lips shifting back and forth between a smile and a grimace, as if he couldn't decide if he should be tough or friendly.

"You'd better have a damn good reason for bothering me," McDonald said.

"Not askin' for a handout. Came to do business. Here to settle up, pay what I owe." McGlynn took a wad of bills from his pocket with a flourish, like a magician producing someone's watch after a particularly impressive conjuring trick.

McDonald fingered the money. He wasn't smiling, though he appeared to be, because of the tendency of his exuberant handlebar mustache to curl upwards at the ends. "All twenties, I see. Look a little singed around the edges. What you been up to? How did you come up with this much cash?" McDonald turned his eyes towards the ceiling, as though making an appeal to a higher authority.

"Well, last night, I was helping a fellow officer do some packin'. I got well paid for my work. Unfortunately, there was a fire. It spread fast. Had to run for my life."

Mike peered at McGlynn and could see that his clothes were singed and that he had bruises on his hands and face. He let out a snort of contempt. "What happened?"

McGlynn haltingly described the explosion and the fire, ending his story with a look of regret on his face.

"A warehouse, was it? Could it be that one on South Water Street near the river?"

McGlynn was staring straight down at the floor with the bug-eyed look of a man who had no explanation handy but needed one badly. Mike grabbed him by the collar and shoved him against the wall. He kept his voice and his eyes level. "I was just asking 'cause Pinkerton's men were all over that warehouse today, along with a group of federals. Word is they found explosives, some rabble-rousing Sons of Labor pamphlets, and guns in all that rubble. 'Til now the Pinkertons and feds have kept to their turf and me to mine. I don't want to give them an excuse to poke their noses here. So, I'm asking again...you in trouble?"

"Me? No, Mike. You know I don't want trouble."

"None of us do. But trouble follows you like shit follows a lame horse."

"Honest to god. I was next door...packin'...when the place blew... barely got out. I was hopin' you'd give me a place to stay for a while, kind of private like, to rest up. You'd be doin' an act of Christian kindness."

"Kindness my ass, what makes you think I'd do that and for you as well?"

"I'm your sainted mother's godson," McGlynn blurted out.

There was a silence. Finally, Mike whispered to his lad, "Take him to the fourth floor." He turned and looked at McGlynn. There was a long silence. "How long?" He sighed. "You heard me. How long you need the room?"

McGlynn shrugged.

"You can have it for two days. But board's extra. That's all you get. I'm taking the chance here." McDonald waited a beat to let his words sink in. "I know all you McGlynns inside and out. A McGlynn and the truth have never had more than a nodding acquaintance. So this will be your trouble, not mine. Just remember, you light the candle at both ends, you're sure to get burnt. Make sure it's just you."

McGlynn reluctantly reached in his pocket and handed McDonald the second wad of bills.

# NINE

*After the Fire of 1871 housing was a priority. Chicago hung its future on an easily assembled, inexpensive construction—the balloon frame—a method that provided cheap housing for the working man. Blocks of two-story, barn-like dwellings appeared north of the river to house the immigrants who rebuilt Chicago. The main structural components of these "balloons" were vertical studs that ran from the ground to the roofline. Since Chicago was part of the swamp that surrounded Lake Michigan, the frames were set on cedar. Setting a one- or two-story house on cedar stilts, held together by cut nails, was considered risky. Chicagoans have always been gamblers. And the good citizens rolled the dice. These homes, with simple pitched roofs, were unpretentious.*

"The peach satin, it is perfection, *oui*?" Charlotte stood in front of a large mahogany-framed mirror and, although Madame's words were reassuring, the expression on her face was skeptical. This Wednesday morning appointment at the Durand salon was an integral part of Charlotte's business schedule.

"Your creations are always exquisite, Marie. But, don't you think this may be a little too...how do you say...décolleté?"

The dressmaker took two steps backward, surveying the gown with her expert eye. She was a tall, thin woman, her features cast with an eye toward anonymity. Yet, when Madame smiled, as she was doing now, her dark eyes sparkled. "Wear this peach satin, Mrs. Reid...the men. . .they look only at you. However, if you insist, some lace perhaps?"

"Maybe just a little." Charlotte stepped behind the Japanese screen that dominated one end of the room.

Madame Durand issued orders to an assistant in rapid French, then whispered, "I shall find something exquisite. A shipment just arrived from Paris. The other dresses, you approve?"

"Can you deliver this one tomorrow?" Charlotte pointed to a dress of deep Prussian blue, a shade that suited her auburn hair and warm complexion. The collar was edged with ecru lace and the front of the skirt featured an embroidered panel.

Madame Durand picked up the dress. "Tomorrow? Of course. The ball gown and other dresses, I will personally see they are ready in time."

Chicago's fall social season was underway. With the constant round of balls and cotillions the salon bustled with activity. The private showroom, reserved for client consultations, was off the main hallway and one entered through sliding oak doors. At that moment, a muffled mixture of voices, at first soft and then louder, could be heard outside. Suddenly, the doors opened with a flourish and Iris Reynolds entered. She strode confidently across the oriental carpet, past Madame Durand, and seated herself on one of the gilded French-style chairs, as if she were conferring a favor.

"Is Mrs. Reid here?" Her words were more a command than a question.

Marie Durand nodded toward the Japanese screen and said in a gracious, but flat, monotone, "Mrs. Reid is just completing her toilette."

"I wish to speak to her privately." Iris barely acknowledged the woman's presence. She instinctively opened her purse, drew out a pocket mirror, and pretended to check the state of her hair. And, as always, was reassured by what she saw.

"Shall I send in tea and pastries?" Madame asked.

"Thank you, Marie. A pot of tea sounds delightful," Charlotte replied. Through a gap in the screen, she could not only hear but also see Iris clearly. She stopped dressing to gaze at the young woman. And when she did, it was with warmth, a definite affection, as well as a certain pride.

"These gowns, they can't *all* be yours?"

"When did you ever consider three day dresses and one ball gown extravagant?"

Charlotte stepped out from behind the screen. An assistant gathered up the ball gown and began maneuvering across the room, trying to keep the satin from dragging on the floor. As the girl passed, Iris took hold of the hem.

"Are you are wearing *this* to the Grand Army banquet?"

"Yes. It's an elegant affair and General Sheridan will be in attendance."

"I forgot. Reid was a colonel, wasn't he? But…peach satin? It is such a wishy-washy color, especially for women of a certain age. Peach has never been fashionable in any season. But, I suppose, if you are fond of bland colors…"

"Madame Durand may not be Worth of Paris, but I have confidence in her designs. What would you suggest?" Charlotte's tone was more irritated than angry. Anger would probably come later when she learned exactly why her cousin was making the effort to see her. Visits from Iris were usually generated by a need for money or a favor of some kind.

"I'm sorry. I apologize. You look lovely in everything you wear." The words were spoken carelessly, without any thought. However, when Iris stood up and made an appealing gesture with both hands, Charlotte stepped forward and the two women embraced.

Iris was five years old when her parents died and she was sent to live with the Bryants, one of the wealthiest banking families in Georgia. The child immediately became the center of attention. The widowed Arthur Bryant and his daughter, Charlotte, doted on her. When the end of the war came, the family's wealth was gone and Bryant was dead. But Charlotte vowed that Iris would still have every advantage due a southern lady. Over the years, both during her marriage to Colonel Reid and subsequent widowhood, Charlotte had kept this promise.

"Now, tell me, have you overspent your allowance again? I can send Bernard over with money. Or give me a list and let me take care of the bills. We won't tell Augustus."

Iris was not listening. She walked to the window, parted the edge of the heavy lace curtains and looked outside. "I gave the driver strict orders to return in half an hour. I don't want him idling about. He reports everything I do, everywhere I go, to Augustus."

"How is your husband? I trust he's in good health?"

"Yes, unfortunately." A note of hardness crept into Iris's voice. "It's not easy being married to that man. You don't know how lucky you are. A widow, like yourself, has the freedom to go where you want and do as you please. You have your own money...meet interesting, younger men...you have fun."

Charlotte did not respond immediately. She reminded herself that Iris's marriage might not be ideal, but then, no marriage was perfect. After the war, Charlotte sent Iris east to live with a spinster aunt in Baltimore. Although Charlotte's gambling profits were their sole support, neither of them thought it best to disclose the relationship. As Iris grew older she went to private school, made her debut and eventually married. By then this reticence had become second nature.

"You know I read the social columns. Neither you nor Augustus has been mentioned these past two weeks. So I assumed you were traveling."

"If you consider trips to St. Louis and Springfield traveling. They are such provincial towns." Iris swept the fingers of one hand to the side in a dismissive gesture.

"Today's *Tribune* had an article about John Drake's game dinner. Evidently, this year, ladies are to be included. In the past, the dinner was for gentlemen only." Charlotte tried to keep her voice cheerful. "I do know you love parties. Certainly Augustus won't miss an opportunity to show you off. Tell me, what will you be wearing?"

Over the years Charlotte had witnessed far too many of Iris's plain and fancy crying fits, so she instinctively looked for the preliminary signs—the rapid blinking of eyes, the clenching and unclenching of hands. She was somewhat surprised when Iris simply ran her tongue over her lips. However, when her cousin spoke her voice was almost inaudible.

"We did receive an invitation. However, Augustus has decided that he'll attend the game dinner alone, without me."

"Did he give you a reason?" Charlotte knew it was not necessary for Augustus, or any other husband in society, to explain his actions to anyone, least of all to his wife.

Iris was about to reply when the door opened and a maid appeared carrying a tea tray. Almost imperceptibly the two women moved toward the fireplace. They studied, with feigned interest, a display of lace fans on a side table while the maid carefully set the tray down.

Charlotte spoke quickly to the girl. "That will be all, thank you. We can serve ourselves."

The two women visited infrequently and, when they did, Iris always claimed center stage. She sat on the brocade settee and went through the ritual of pouring tea. Charlotte accepted a cup, then tactfully waited for Iris to continue the conversation. Whatever Iris's problem, she was willing to wait. They sat, sipping their tea in awkward silence. As the silence lengthened, Charlotte's initial concern became a genuine worry. Finally, she placed her empty cup on the table, then spoke, providing conversation in the hope that Iris would eventually disclose the reason for this visit.

"I understand Augustus hired Adler & Sullivan to design your new town home. It seems that many of the best people are choosing to build north of the river instead of south, near Prairie Avenue. I'm sure Louis will design the perfect venue for you. It will be impressive."

The last remark caught Iris's attention. She bit her lip and looked soulfully at Charlotte. "Last night Augustus informed me that he intends to cancel the contract. There is to be no grand house, no travel to Saratoga for the season. And any trips to Washington or New York are out of the question. We will continue living in that shabby suite at the Palmer House...forever."

From the onset Charlotte had been skeptical of Iris's marriage. She had not attended the wedding and assumed the couple would settle in Washington. However, several years later Iris had written to Charlotte to say that she and Augustus had moved to Chicago. When an opportunity for Charlotte to move her own operations from Wichita to Chicago arose, she decided that it might be wise to be where she could keep a closer eye on Iris.

Augustus Reynolds had supposedly acquired his wealth in mining ventures out West. It was not unusual for men with that background to marry late in life, acquiring a wife the way they would a painting, a house, or other property. Such notable Chicagoans as Potter Palmer and Philip Armour were married to younger women. Those unions were quite successful. Charlotte knew that Reynolds had entered this marriage as he did any business venture, with a cool head and keen eye for maximum profit. Iris was a perfect hostess. Gentlemen in Augustus's circle considered their social calendar an adjunct to their business one. However, the unforeseeable happened. Reynolds became completely besotted with his wife. And, when a man of Augustus's age falls in love, it can prove a dangerous game indeed. He pampered and spoiled Iris to excess, showing her off at gala dinners, parties, and the theater.

This worried Charlotte. She shifted uneasily in her chair, remembering a chance remark Sullivan had made at a Lotus Club gathering—"Augustus Reynolds takes a perverse pleasure in observing admirers gather around his wife, like bees around honey. As soon as they begin to swarm Reynolds steps in and swats them flat."

Charlotte spoke, in what she hoped was a soothing voice. "I'm surprised. The new town house was Augustus's idea. He's normally a very tolerant man. Perhaps you inadvertently did something to anger him."

Iris merely crinkled her nose and selected another teacake.

Charlotte knew it was pointless to reopen old arguments with Iris. So she chose her words carefully. "I know you are easily bored. Minor flirtations are allowable in your social circle and Augustus is pleased that men are attracted to you. But I trust you have *not* been indiscreet."

For a fraction of a second, Iris looked startled. Charlotte noted the expression and immediately got a sinking feeling in the bottom of her stomach.

"Iris. Why *are* you here? Tell me. Now!"

There was another silence. When Iris finally spoke, she did so in a soft, subdued manner as if she had been quietly rehearsing the words. "Just a few harmless outings, that's all."

"As long as you observe the proprieties...which I am sure you do." Charlotte eyed her cousin. "Anyone in particular?"

"Just rides and theater the last few weeks. Augustus says that I'm being too obvious and that people are talking. He says that if I don't stop he'll cut off my allowance."

Charlotte listened intently to Iris's story. She did know gentlemen were allowed brief flirtations, even lengthy affairs with women of their social circle, or even those of another class. Women did not have these privileges. Also, Charlotte knew her cousin well enough to realize that Iris had come to her because she had nowhere else to turn.

At that moment, Madame Durand entered carrying an armful of lace. "Ah, Mrs. Reid, these are exquisite, *oui*?" She walked midway into the room and stopped. She looked at Iris, then at Charlotte. "I shall leave the lace. After your tea, you will have time to make the selection." Then she backed gracefully out the door.

♠

Iris watched Madame Durand leave the room. She did not relish these meetings, when she was forced to listen to Charlotte's inevitable lectures. But she knew her cousin could always be counted on for help. By now, Iris had envisioned herself as an elegant widow with a sizeable fortune, able to travel and generally do whatever she wished. After all, that was why she'd married Augustus Reynolds in the first place. By all that was right and holy, that man should be dead by now, or close to it.

"Why shouldn't I have some fun? Augustus is getting so old and crabby. I just want to spend a little time with strong, intelligent, amusing men. Men that are my age." As soon as she spoke, Iris realized her words sounded superficial. She immediately put on a soulful expression and looked at Charlotte. "I'm certain Augustus is having me followed."

"Answer my question. Why are you here?"

"Augustus claims times are lean. He's already cut my allowance in half. If he cuts it off entirely I'll have no money."

"Be thankful that's all he threatens."

"What do you mean?"

"What I mean is he could divorce you."

"Divorce." Iris laughed. "Don't be silly. Augustus will never divorce me."

"This is Chicago, young lady, not Baltimore or New York. Here social status is based on money. Background and family are of little concern. This is a town where a man can make his own place, his own future. Augustus has done that. He may be old, but he's no fool. And, mark my words, he will not be made to look like one."

Iris heaved an audible sigh. Her cousin had never mentioned divorce before. Besides, by his own admission, Augustus was in financial straits. He couldn't afford a divorce. She half listened as Charlotte continued.

"Look, Iris, I know Augustus adores you completely. That's evident. I also know he will *not* tolerate this. You may think a few carriage rides with other men are trivial. But I am fully aware of what Augustus could do. So listen carefully, young lady. All it takes is a word, whispered about, and suddenly you are invisible. Invitations to all the ladies' teas, parties, and balls you enjoy stop arriving. Dressmakers are too busy to see you. Milliners have nothing to suit you. You call on people and are told that no one is home, even though the lights are on and carriages are lined up outside."

For a brief moment, Iris looked perplexed. Charlotte's last remarks gave her cause for alarm. This was something she had not considered. To calm herself she concentrated on pouring another cup of tea, even as her cousin's voice grew stronger.

"Stop that and listen for once. Augustus is a prideful man. Mark my words, he may dote on you, Iris, but he loves his business, his good name, and his social position even more."

Iris glanced at the ornate clock on the mantel. "Gracious, I hadn't realized it was so late." She put her cup down, stood up abruptly and allowed Charlotte to give her a long embrace.

Her cousin spoke soothingly. "Don't worry, I'll send Bernard over this afternoon with money. Give him any outstanding bills you may have. Just promise me you'll stay out of trouble."

Iris placed her forehead on Charlotte's shoulder, more for effect than from genuine emotion. She stepped back and was about to leave when she noticed a black cameo edged in pearls pinned to her cousin's dress. She recognized the piece immediately. "What a lovely brooch. It's expensive. You know I have an eye for these things."

She watched Charlotte finger the cameo then blush slightly. "Yes, it *is* beautiful. Mr. Lyons is an old and very dear friend. Unfortunately, he may be leaving Chicago shortly."

"Mr. Lyons is it?"

Iris remembered the gentleman who'd purchased the brooch as the same gentleman who'd come to her assistance in the elevator. She smiled at Charlotte and said in a sweet voice, "If your gentleman friend, Mr. Lyons, is able to purchase such a lovely gift from Peacock's, he should be persuaded to stay. There is so much to see and do in Chicago." She picked up her shawl and walked toward the door, then turned and smiled. "I feel much better now that we've had a little talk. I shall be in all afternoon. Augustus will be at his club. It would be a good time to send Bernard over."

Charlotte stood at the window and watched Iris walk to her carriage. For a brief minute, the sun shone through the clouds onto Iris's halo of blonde hair and her elegant gray velvet suit. Indeed Charlotte conceded that her cousin was a vision to turn any man's head. At the same time, the young lady was a constant worry. Iris simply chose to ignore any conversation she did not wish to hear. Charlotte knew from experience that Iris listened to her the same way she listened to an opera, a sermon, or a lecture—motionless, sometimes smiling, sometimes frowning, but never quite at the places Charlotte expected her to.

For Charlotte, family was all-important. Her parents, brothers, aunts…all gone now. Iris was the sister she'd always wanted, or maybe the daughter she would never have. So her happiness was Charlotte's happiness. Over the years Iris's escapades had not worried her, until now. Iris was a grown woman and did not seem to care about the consequences of her actions. Charlotte fingered the brooch. How did Iris know it was purchased at Peacocks? Perhaps she had purchased items there before. Iris had been reckless in the past, but only minor escapades. As she continued staring out the window, the expression on Charlotte's face shifted from skeptical to somber.

# TEN

*William W. Boyington designed the Grand Pacific Hotel in the Parisian style, with a mélange of ornate pavilions, interior courtyards, and mansard roofs. Six stories high, plus basement, the hotel sat on the spread foundations of the original building destroyed in the Great Fire of 1871. Bounded by Jackson, Clark, LaSalle, and Quincy Streets, it covered nearly an acre of land in the heart of Chicago's business district. Located near the Van Buren Street Station, the Grand Pacific was* the *place to meet and settle business. The lobby was a public club, always crowded with businessmen who filled the air with cigar smoke and trade talk.*

Garrett woke slowly the morning after their outing to the theater. The thumping in his head persisted until it dragged him to the surface of consciousness. He sat up, for a brief moment felt disoriented, then remembered—he was in his room at the Revere Hotel.

A quick sip of brandy steadied him enough to wash and shave. He studied his image in the mirror and, for the first time since Sam's death, searched his own reflection. Over the years, he'd deliberately cultivated a prolonged, piercing stare that had reduced more than one opponent at the card table to a quivering mass. Yet this morning, as he looked in the mirror, Garrett felt a stranger staring back at him. Methodically working lather in his shaving mug with brush and soap, he let his mind slip back to the events of the last two days.

*Never take a marker. When I do, look what happens.*

Garrett tilted his head to the side and began lathering his jawline. He steadied his hand, then took long, slow swipes with his razor, peeling off the foam and flipping it into the basin.

*I need you. It'll be like old times.* Those were the old man's very words.

Reconnecting with the general had been unsettling. Old loyalties were beginning to surface. He wasn't surprised when General Stannard covered Oates's IOU. Garrett remembered Stannard doing the same for him whenever he'd been short before a pay period. But why pay up with phony money? Was the general involved with Brock and his bonds? If so, it was payback. And he wanted to be the one to do the paying.

Garrett splashed cold water on his face, clearing his head as he wiped away the remains of the shaving lather. One thing he did know, his wallet was thin. He needed cash and he needed it now. He also knew that the general would be up at this hour. Like himself, the old man's personal routine was honed by years of military life. Early morning was the time to have him make good on his partner's IOU—this time with real money.

♠

Louis Sullivan woke up, grunted, flung his right arm out across the bed and faced his first problem of the day. The blonde was gone. He opened one eye, closed it again, then flung out his other arm. His groping hand came in contact with his trousers, neatly folded across a chair. He pawed at them until he found his wallet, opened the single eye again and trained it on the money inside. His next grunt was one of sour satisfaction. He'd figured her to be honest. He was right. She took only what she felt was due. And, if the Lloyds Light Opera Company was booked into Hooley's Theater next season, he resolved to look her up.

Sullivan stifled a yawn and went about the business of returning to life. There was a dry roughness in his throat. He poured a shot from the bottle on the dresser then drank the whiskey in one gulp. The potency of the drink brought tears to his eyes. He took in a deep breath, let it out slowly, and faced his second problem of the day. . .where was he?

He looked slowly around the room. Nothing was familiar. Sullivan considered himself a man of instinctive habits, one of which was discretion. At least he hadn't brought the lady back to Mrs. Greig's boarding house. He could hear carriages rattling along the street below, and looked out a half-opened window. A shopkeeper was taking his morning delivery. He eyed a sign on a storefront. Smelled the aroma of rice and pork. Ah! South Clark Street near Van Buren. . .Chinatown. Maybe there would be time for a leisurely breakfast.

These thoughts were interrupted by the sounds of doors slamming, voices shouting, hurried footsteps in the hall outside the door. In the street below two police wagons came wheeling around the corner and reined to a halt in front of the building. When he saw policemen piling out, clubs in hand, Sullivan could feel his heart pounding, the blood running through his veins, heartbeat by heartbeat.

His partner, Dankmar Adler, usually ignored Sullivan's private life as long as it didn't interfere with their business. But Adler was a conservative man and would not abide a scandal of any kind. Sullivan stuck his head out in the hallway. He heard men coming up the front stairs, so he grabbed the rest of his clothes and began scouting the hallway for another exit.

♠

The Grand Pacific Hotel had one dining room open at eight in the morning. After a few false starts, Garrett eventually found it in a far corner of the building, next to the Quincy Street entrance. The room contained a dozen linen-covered tables. Along an inside wall, potted palms partially concealed a harp and piano, a hint that later the space would re-emerge as a ladies' tearoom. A row of tall art glass windows extended along the outside wall. Even at this hour Quincy Street was teeming with carriages and pedestrians, but the art glass was so well fitted that he could not hear the rattle and bustle outside.

Garrett saw the general at a table in a far corner of the room. The old man was sitting ramrod straight, his newspaper in front of him. Garrett began walking, as quietly as possible, across the marble floor. He was within five feet of the general's table when he heard, "Well, you *are* up early. Good to see you haven't lost any old habits."

"I see you haven't lost any of yours."

"'Course not. Sit down, my boy, have some coffee," Stannard said as he lowered the paper.

"Nothing for me, sir." Garrett took the packet of counterfeit bills from his pocket. Taking a step forward, he placed it in front of the general. "Have you spoken to your partner?"

"I have neither spoken to nor seen him these last three days." The general glanced at the packet. "As I recall, you were never one to return money, particularly when it's yours."

"That money is bogus…counterfeit."

"Looks genuine to me."

"It isn't." Garrett spoke in a quiet but ominous tone that the general ignored, if he heard it at all. "How do I know? Because the money you paid me matches this," he said, as he pulled out the counterfeit bank note Pinkerton had given him. Stannard studied it reluctantly.

Garrett pulled up a chair and sat down next to him. "That was a present from Bill Pinkerton. I'm sure you'd agree he's knowledgeable in these matters." He waited and, when the old man did not respond, continued, "Seems this bogus paper is the creation of a former engraver at the U.S. Treasury. They fired him, so he began printing his own money…twenties. Same ones you paid me with. The man was a real artist."

General Stannard took in a deep breath. "Well, I have no reason to doubt your story. What do you suggest I do?"

"Replace it with real money. Write a draft on your bank—to me—payable in gold."

The general turned and looked directly at him. "That's not possible. You see, my boy, I paid you with my personal funds." He pointed to the packet of bills on the table. "Now you're telling me that money, and probably the rest of my available cash, may be counterfeit?"

"Are you saying Central Casualty Insurance is strapped?"

"Let's just say my partner made some business decisions without my knowledge. As a consequence, an officer at Union Trust Bank informed me that certain restrictions have been placed on our company's assets." The general hesitated, then spoke slowly. "At this time Central Casualty is unable to draw on its funds. You understand, of course, these restrictions are temporary."

"How temporary?"

"That depends. Consider my job offer and it can be shorter. You'll be helping me and yourself at the same time."

The general looked at the other diners, then leaned forward. "Oates invested a large portion of Central Casualty's money in shares of the Lake View Vault Company. The company is financing a building presently under construction—they're calling it the Eastwood." He moved closer. "Didn't know anything about this until Major Shoup came calling." The general looked up to see if Garrett was listening then continued. "Shoup served under General Sheridan, was on his staff until he was wounded. Phil Sheridan probably used his influence to get him a position at Union Trust. Now, Shoup has informed me the building must be 'framed up'—meaning the whole exterior finished—soon, or Lake View Vault will forfeit a good portion of its assets and that, in turn, means that Central Casualty may be forced into bankruptcy."

Garrett shook his head and tried to sound sympathetic. "I don't know anything about construction."

"Doesn't matter. What I do know is, once you start something, you follow through." Stannard leaned back, steepled his hands in front of him, and waited for an answer. When none was forthcoming, he said, "Look, I know you are fond of…no…you *love* poker. You need the game the way a drunkard needs his whiskey. That's why you're in town. With the Grand Army reunion and other notable events on the calendar, Chicago will host a lot of big games."

"Can't play without money. Those people *don't* take markers."

A hint of a smile appeared on the general's face. "Suppose I persuade the bank to appoint you their agent at the construction site? Union

Trust Bank pays you directly. With you in charge the building will be up and running in no time."

"So you still say this will be no more than four, five weeks' work?"

"As soon as the bank releases our funds, Central Casualty will make full restitution on my partner's note. You have my word." A waiter appeared with a pot of coffee. The general removed a cigar from his pocket and watched the man pour out two cups. As soon as the waiter departed he put the cigar in his mouth, struck a match, and calmly lit it. "Between the bank, Central Casualty, and your nightly poker games you'll leave Chicago a wealthy man. What do you say?"

Garrett cradled the cup of coffee in his hands. He remembered Pinkerton telling him about the treasury bonds. Had Brock printed any? If so, were they destroyed in the warehouse fire? Was the general involved? He recalled the old man had never concerned himself with money. The military had paid him an adequate salary and his marriage provided more. Only now, the general's career was a memory and his business was sinking, a good reason for the old man to add some cash to his pockets.

"That is a mighty tempting offer, sir. Just get this building site up and running?"

"Correct."

Garrett looked at his former mentor. "The building does not have to be finished?"

"Find the right people for the job, then supervise. Just like the old days."

"Those days are long gone, sir. You know it, I know it."

The general nodded, then spoke softly. "I need you."

In the back of his mind Garrett knew what his answer would be. Hell, he'd known as soon as he'd walked through the door at Central Casualty Insurance and seen the old man again.

"All right, I'm in. But..." He held up his hand. His former admiration for the general was momentarily put aside and words seemed to tumble out. "I need assurances. You're resourceful, always have been. So, I want some cash up front—enough to get me started, keep me in poker money, and give you time to deal with the bank. Don't care how or where you get it. Just make sure it's legal currency. When this is over, I want that marker paid, plus an extra percentage for my efforts. We'll settle on the amount later." He waited for the general's reaction and was surprised when he heard, "Agreed."

"Fine. Now let's clear up a few things. All I do is fix the current mess? That is, get the building up, 'under roof' so to speak?"

The general nodded.

The old man seemed too agreeable. Choosing his words carefully, Garrett said, "Sir, we've known one another a long time. I'm sure you won't be offended when I say that somehow this whole proposition of yours feels like a bad bet—like putting up a hundred dollars just to win fifty. And you're not a man to make a bad bet. Unless of course we're talking about stakes that aren't on the table."

Garrett looked at the general, waiting until he'd made eye contact, and then asked, "Are you involved in anything else?"

The old man put his hand on Garrett's shoulder and gave it a gentle squeeze. "Of course not! Would I lie to you?"

The two men stood and walked out of the dining room and down the hallway toward the elevators. Garrett half listened as the old man kept up a steady stream of conversation, speaking rapidly as if he were anxious to get the words out.

"Oates is an odd sort of fellow. My partner and I never did have much to say to one another. That is until I learned he'd invested a majority of the company funds in Lake View Vault. He tells me not to worry, that Central Casualty will own the tallest office building in Chicago. But I hear rumors, and now he's disappeared."

The general handed Garrett a slip of paper before stepping into the elevator. "Glad you joined up. I don't like riding blind. Here's the address."

The elevator door closed. It took a moment before Garrett realized he was standing ramrod straight, still wearing his "yes, sir" army smile. The smile itself meant nothing. It was something he could put on in the morning and remove at night. What bothered him was the realization that, when old habits did resurface, he stepped back into them so easily, like donning a well-worn pair of boots. He looked at the slip of paper and saw the address for the Eastwood Building, near Franklin and Madison Streets.

♠

General Stannard was in a somber mood as he rode the elevator to the fifth floor of the Grand Pacific Hotel. His mood did not change as he walked the length of the hallway toward his room. Sure, he'd persuaded Lyons to take charge of his immediate problem—the Eastwood Building—only to have his former aide present him with another more pressing one.

The general grimaced as he sat down on the edge of his bed. The flint arrow tip in his right leg, a painful souvenir from an Indian campaign in '57, was giving him trouble again. The room was silent as he sat and stroked his beard, staring first at the floor, then at the cameo of his late wife that he always kept at hand. The marriage of Mary Louise Oates and J. Barton Stannard had lasted over a quarter century. And, although Mary had died over a year ago, the general still deeply mourned her.

"Well, Mary, I sure made a mess of things. First, your cousin invests company funds in a new building that may be nothing more than a hole in the ground. Then he sticks me with counterfeit money. Your father was right—I should have stayed in the army. But the U.S. Army didn't want me anymore, did they?"

He gently kissed the image of his wife and placed the cameo in his vest pocket. Suddenly he stiffened and turned around slowly. "Oh, it's you. Heard my mutterings then? Of course, you have ears like a fox." He raised his arm. "Come in."

♠

Edward "Otwah" Le Beau shut the door with a gentle click. Dressed in a dark wool suit and white linen shirt, with his long gray hair tied in a knot at the back of his neck, the former army scout could pass for any business traveler in Chicago. The only clues to his past were a Union belt plate on his waistband, which had been a present from General Stannard, and his hand-tooled Mexican boots.

"You look tired, *mon ami*. We take a week and do some fishing." Otwah's voice still retained a raspy, guttural sound.

"Can't." The general shook his head then began talking—about his partner, Central Casualty Insurance, and the added burden of the Eastwood Building.

Otwah listened patiently, waiting for an opportune moment to speak. Lately, since his wife's death, the general had developed a worrisome habit of talking in circles. Otwah was concerned. The Grand Army reunion was fast approaching. These affairs provided an occasion for veterans to drink, parade, and dredge up memories. The purpose of Otwah's visit was to persuade the general to leave the city and thus avoid another disastrous meeting with Phil Sheridan and his former army cronies. At the very least General Stannard should not remain at the Grand Pacific. The lobby was already awash with uniforms. He half-listened as the general continued rambling.

"That building is a festering wound." The general paused a moment, as if waiting to see what Otwah's reaction would be. Since the former scout was not sure where all this was leading, he simply nodded. His ears perked up when he heard the general say, "Thank heavens Lyons is back."

"You saw Lyons?"

"He played poker with my partner Monday. Took his IOU. I paid it with my own funds. Then Lyons comes by this morning and tells me the money was counterfeit." The general sighed. "Well, I can't make good on it, and neither can Central Casualty."

Otwah placed his hand on the old man's shoulder. "Is your new house ready?"

"It was always Mary's house. Only she never lived to see it."

"Today we pack and move you there."

"But I have good news." The general smiled. "I persuaded Lyons to join me. He'll handle the Eastwood problems."

"It is like old times. Lyons will watch your back. And as usual, I will watch his."

# ELEVEN

*By 1882 the city's emergence as a railroad, commercial, and industrial center also coincided with its transformation in dining. A vast majority of Chicagoans found lunchtime a hurried, fretful venture. There were nickel-and-dime lunch spots, where uncomfortable stools, and utensils chained to the counter, guaranteed a fast turnover. Street peddlers provided quick, light meals. They remained in fixed locations on sidewalks, rented from storeowners, or pushed their carts through the streets following a regular route. However, Chicago's businessmen turned this lunch hour to their advantage. They frequented gentlemen's restaurants, which were often attached to saloons. The main attractions were liquor, good food, and a continuing business conversation.*

The Eastwood construction site covered one half block of Calhoun Place between Franklin and Market Streets. A four-foot-high wooden fence provided a makeshift buffer between the workmen and the citizenry. Besides the dirt—which was everywhere—and the noise from men and machinery, Garrett found the stench, both human and animal, the most overwhelming. He could only manage short, shallow breaths as he walked along the fence line.

The building's first floor was sheathed in gray Roman brick. Hand-cut limestone blocks outlined the windows. The second floor was in the process of being walled with brick. The third and fourth were steel skeletons silhouetted against a gloomy October sky.

Garrett joined the line of spectators spread out along the fence. They seemed fascinated by the intricate system of wooden scaffolding bracing an outer wall. Next to the scaffold were two steam-driven pulleys, grinding and belching smoke. Workmen, balanced precariously on the edge of a wooden platform, were attempting to use one of the pulleys to hoist a pallet stacked high with bricks. Garrett noticed that the crews worked in a haphazard manner, not paying attention to one another.

Above it all, he heard the hoots and hollers from the crowd. "Won't make it...Bet you a fiver they will...Sucker money."

A third try was successful, with only a few bricks falling to the ground below. Their effort was greeted by rousing cheers from the spectators, along with the exchange of cash.

In a corner of the yard more workmen mixed concrete in a large trough. A man tossed shovelfuls of the mixture into a two-foot metal cone. Then, with a quick motion, another man, wearing a red bandanna around his neck, flipped the cone over and watched the concrete mass settle into a clump. Evidently not satisfied, he kept shouting orders and gesturing. Garrett figured that he was a foreman, since the men began mixing more concrete.

At that moment Garrett felt the ground tremble beneath his feet and heard a deep voice explode in his ear. "Watch out! Bloody fool!" He looked up and saw two wagons, each drawn by a team of four draft horses, racing full gallop down Franklin Street. They'd made a sharp, wide turn and were headed directly towards him. The teamsters were cracking whips, while at the same time belching a string of abusive remarks to every animal or person in their path. Before Garrett could react, he felt two strong hands grab his shoulders and pull him out of the way. The wagons passed so close that he could see the horses' gleaming flesh, their braided manes, and smell their sweat.

"You fixin' to get yourself killed?" The deep voice belonged to a man shorter than Garrett, but solidly built with plenty of hard muscle and no spare fat.

"Caught me by surprise. Thanks." Garrett brushed some mud from his sleeve.

The wagons came to a full stop in the middle of the yard and were quickly surrounded by workmen. The lead wagon contained what looked like iron beams, while the other was piled with wood planks. Amid shouts and gestures in a medley of languages, the men unloaded the wagons. The teamsters kept a firm grip on their horses, calming them with handfuls of oats or a carrot.

Garrett looked around. "Where's the foreman, the man wearing the red bandanna?"

"Foreman? Each trade has its own—carpenters, masons, ironmongers, you name it." The man's wide mouth relaxed into a broad grin.

"Well, then, who's in charge?"

"That would be anyone's guess," the man said as he walked away.

The wind shifted, bringing cool, damp lake air. A raindrop, thick and wet, fell on Garrett's forehead. The sky was rapidly turning dark and sullen. Garrett had learned as much here as he was going to, which was little. He flipped up the collar of his coat and started to leave. After a few steps he turned and looked at the site again. His knowledge of construction was limited to building horse corrals and barracks. The longer he stared at the unfinished building the more he realized that, despite General Stannard's buttery assurances, he needed help.

A crowd surged by and someone bumped him. Garrett instinctively patted his pocket for his wallet then checked his vest for his watch. It was noon. He needed food and answers to important questions. He knew where to find both.

♠

Located at the entrance to Arcade Court, Meierhoff's Restaurant occupied the first floor of a narrow four-story building. Like many buildings constructed after the fire, it was a simple design of common brick walls with three windows per floor, front and rear. Arcade Court was a few feet wider than an alley and served as a link between LaSalle and Clark Streets. Its close proximity to city hall made Meierhoff's a popular eating establishment. Garrett chose it for two reasons: first, the food was good and he was hungry; second, Louis Sullivan lunched there.

He shook rainwater from his coat, then pushed open the glass and oak doors. Once inside, he walked through the saloon and went directly into the grill. Paneled walls were crammed with the Meierhoff brothers' hunting trophies—elk, moose, deer, and buffalo heads. On the far side of the long, narrow room a row of booths provided a semblance of privacy, while tables took up the remaining floor space. Waiters passed nimbly between them, balancing trays on their shoulders, setting dishes and tankards down with flair.

Sullivan was ensconced at his regular table. Located next to the entrance off Arcade Court, it afforded him the best possible view of his fellow patrons. He was eating a large plate of stew and, at the same time, nodding to every judge, banker, and bureaucrat who entered the grill and passed near him. A copy of the *Inter Ocean* lay next to his plate, opened to an article titled, "Police Raid Chink Town." He looked up. "This is a surprise. Thought you were leaving."

"I'm staying." Garrett pulled up a chair and sat down. "I've decided to take General Stannard's offer and work with him at Central Casualty."

Sullivan wasn't listening. His attention was centered on the gentleman wearing a beaver coat and carrying an ivory-tipped cane who had just walked into the restaurant. "Mr. Reynolds, how are you, sir?"

The man in question nodded absentmindedly in Sullivan's direction, continued across the room, then stopped and returned to the table. Augustus Reynolds was a tall man of over fifty years who carried himself like a man ten years younger. When he spoke it was with the confidence of someone used to being listened to and obeyed.

"I have a meeting with Mr. Adler tomorrow."

Before Sullivan could reply, another gentleman appeared and Reynolds turned to greet him. They walked toward a booth at the back of the restaurant.

Sullivan edged his chair closer to Garrett. "Know who's with Reynolds? Ferdinand Peck, that's who. Just a nod of his head and a new building, or warehouse, or factory goes up. A snap of his finger decides which architect gets the commission. Damn! Peck and his cronies pay more attention to that stuffed moose head on the wall than to me. Know what that feels like?"

"No, but I'm willing to listen." Garrett signaled a waiter and pointed to his friend's plate.

"Look! Peck and Reynolds are lunching with Burnham. Christ! He's such a glad-hander. No wonder he and Root grab the big commissions." Sullivan turned abruptly and stared at his friend. "So you're staying then? I suppose you'll be selling insurance now?"

Garrett shook his head. "I'll be in charge of the Eastwood building site."

"What do you know about building construction?"

"More than I do about insurance…but not enough. The general says it doesn't matter since the job will probably take no more than a month of my time." Garrett carefully unfolded a napkin and placed it in his lap.

"You believe him?"

"As much as I believe anyone. Remember your guest at the Lotus Club? The gentleman that gave me that IOU?"

"He was *not* my guest. Since we were at Charlotte's table maybe she invited him."

"In any case, he's the general's partner. I figured maybe you knew that already. Well, that gentleman has taken a powder."

A waiter approached, balancing a tray of glassware. In a quick, fluid motion he set down two steins of beer, scooped up the one that Sullivan had already emptied, then continued on without missing a step. Garrett waited a moment to see if Sullivan was listening.

"The general tells me Central Casualty Insurance—meaning Oates and himself—are unable to make good on my marker until the damned Eastwood building is up and running. Evidently that was Oates's job. The old man would like my help to get things moving. I'm to hire someone to run the site."

"I assume that's why you joined me for lunch." Sullivan's voice grew a trifle sharp.

"Well, that and your stimulating conversation." Garrett tilted his chair back and drained his stein. A group of businessmen entered the restaurant. As they passed the table one of them, a short man with bushy sideburns, patted Garrett on the shoulder. "Good to see you again."

Garrett smiled and nodded after him.

"You know that gentleman?" Sullivan whispered, leaning forward and, at the same time, stretching his neck to one side to get a better view.

"Played poker with him a few months back, at one of Charlotte's private games."

"That's Sam Ryerson. Family's in the steel business. Mr. Mayer and Mr. Schlesinger are with him. They're all hand-in-glove with Peck's business ventures. Look! They're at Burnham's table. Damn! Something's brewing, I'm sure of it."

A waiter arrived with a plate of stew for Garrett and a pot of fresh coffee.

"It's fortuitous for both of us that you plan to stay in Chicago." Sullivan kept an eye on Burnham and Peck as he spoke.

"This is quite tasty," Garrett said, trying to change the subject.

Sullivan was having none of it. He leaned over and whispered in a conspiratorial tone, "I recently joined the Iroquois Club. Many of the city's most influential people are members. The club's monthly soiree usually includes a few tables of poker—good players, high stakes. Since I see you're acquainted with one of the members, who knows? The next time Peck and his cronies have a new project in mind, the firm of Adler and Sullivan could be their choice. I know I'll definitely make a favorable impression, particularly if you play at my table."

"You're sure?"

"I'm a man of few faults—being wrong is not one of them." Sullivan spoke in a toneless voice that made it difficult for Garrett to tell whether he was serious or merely sarcastic. "I know Burnham and Root will be there."

"How's that?"

"They're members. Burnham is nothing but a salesman and Root is a designer...of sorts." Sullivan sat back in his chair looking well fed and delighted with himself. There was a flicker of humor in the depths of his eyes. "This is no free lunch, my friend. You need help. And, for a price, I'm willing to accommodate you. Is it a deal?"

Garrett put down his fork, wiped the side of his mouth with his napkin, and nodded.

"Then I suggest you visit Quinn's Saloon. It's a grand establishment. You'll like Padraic Quinn. He runs a few monte and poker tables in the back and, depending on the odds, will bet either side of an issue. Quinn can fix you up with the right people."

"Where is this grand establishment?"

"Three blocks west of the post office at Adams and Franklin, careful you don't miss it. Just mention my name." Sullivan drained his coffee cup in one gulp, then tore his napkin loose from his collar and tossed it on the table.

Garrett took a long, slow drink of his coffee. "When is this get-together of yours?"

"Thursday evening...tomorrow. Why? Are you doing anything important?"

"Yes. Tomorrow morning I'll be saying goodbye to a friend."

# TWELVE

*Rosehill Cemetery, the largest nonsectarian cemetery in the Chicago area, was established in 1859. Its three hundred and fifty acres were nestled between Lake Michigan and the upper branch of the Chicago River, just north of the city in the town of Lake View. The name Rosehill was the result of a mapmaker's error—the area was originally called "Roe's Hill" for a nearby tavern owner, Hiram Roe. The cemetery's most prominent feature was its ornate limestone entrance gate, designed by William W. Boyington. The serene setting of Rosehill became the final resting place of many Chicago and Illinois Civil War veterans, from privates to generals.*

It rained the morning of Sam Wilkerson's funeral, a sudden downpour that left the ground sodden and the sun hidden behind slow-moving, dirty gray clouds. Garrett figured that said a lot for Sam's life. After all, funerals were miserable things. The dead were dead and why prolong grief for the living?

Funerals attract a variety of mourners. There are the usual relatives, maybe a few friends, and then the curious. Outside of Sam's mother's fellow churchgoers, the crowd was sparse. Garrett figured Sam would have wanted it that way. Like himself, Sam never could abide a lot of personal clutter in his life.

Garrett had been working hard to keep his face motionless, with a token expression of passive interest in the words he heard. They were empty words. All spoken by people who hadn't known Sam, or people who were clearly too shocked by the circumstances of his death to pretend to mean anything they said.

Mrs. Wilkerson was standing across from Garrett, her shoulders slumped, her back bowed forward, and her face pulled by the gravity of grief, as if every muscle was attached to a weight. Garrett remembered her words earlier that day.

"Children are all a woman has, Mr. Lyons. We bring them into the world, love them, listen to them. Then, after a time, they leave us. I'm sorry my Samuel is dead. But I will not weep for him. He would not want that."

Garrett watched the people clustered around her, fellow members of the Swedish Lutheran Church. He noted a common feature among them—thin, tight mouths in unsmiling faces. As if life was a burden they must somehow endure. He saw Bill Pinkerton standing off to one side and nodded towards him. Pinkerton nodded back. It was as much acknowledgement of the other's presence as either was willing to give.

The sound of the chapel bell traveled across the cemetery lawn. The minister intoned a final prayer to the eternal. The undertaker, his face wearing a look of professional sorrow, merely nodded. Garrett stepped forward, along with five men from the church. Each picked up a rope end and together they lowered Sam's coffin to its final rest.

Once it was all over Garrett began walking toward the cemetery entrance and was midway along the path when Bill Pinkerton caught up with him.

"I thought the reverend gave a nice service. Wanted you to know I presented Mrs. Wilkerson with a check from the Chicago Southwestern Railroad. She was most grateful. That was a nice gesture, giving the reward money to Wilkerson's family."

"Just my share. After all, Sam certainly earned his."

Pinkerton removed a cigar from his vest pocket. "Guess you'll be leaving."

"Maybe I'll stay in Chicago awhile."

"That would not surprise me. With such a heavy military presence in town for the army reunion I imagine your hands are itching to turn a few cards." Pinkerton stopped to strike a match on a nearby headstone, lit his cigar, and watched the smoke he exhaled fade into the air.

"Actually, I'll be working with my old commander, General J. Barton Stannard. Heard of him?" Garrett did his best to pin Bill with a steady gaze. Pinkerton gave no reaction, so Garrett continued. "Then I'm sure you're familiar with Central Casualty Insurance. I'll be here at least a month. Figure Brock will be out of the hospital then, so I won't miss the hanging."

"Look here, Lyons, this isn't Wichita or Laredo. Chicago courts won't go hanging a man on your say-so, not without surefire proof."

Garrett let out a snort. "Brock killed Sam. Shot him right in the chest. Didn't even give my partner a chance to draw. Sam was one of yours, a Pinkerton agent. Thought you'd want to see his killer hanged."

"You seem to have forgotten Brock is a scratcher, always has been. He deals in forged paper. I don't know one that even carries a weapon. Theo Brock may break the law, but not the rules. Besides, he claims to have an alibi. I had an associate in St. Louis check it out." He waited, letting Garrett grasp the full implication of his words.

"What are you saying, Bill?"

"I'm saying...I made a deal." Pinkerton took a quick step back, giving Garrett some room to accept the news. "Brock turns over the government bonds, any other plates he has, whatever he's printed, plus the names of his partners, then he walks. The U.S. government is quite willing to pay handsomely for their return."

Garrett felt as though the wind had been knocked out of him. For a moment, all he could do was stare at Pinkerton. When he did speak, his words came out soft, slow, and under control. "I'm not surprised. You get a feather in your cap, and line your pocket at the same time. Just remember I have questions for him."

"Brock isn't fit for talking. The doc plans to operate today—take out the bullet you put in him."

Pinkerton hesitated, then looked at Garrett. "The man has more questions to answer, about his enterprise, Sam's death. Only, maybe you shouldn't be the one asking them."

"Sam was my partner. Who else but me?"

Bill Pinkerton's otherwise pleasant voice grew a trifle sharper. "My father always considered the Pinkerton agency his family. Sam Wilkerson was with him from the beginning."

"Your father hired me," Garrett answered in a hard, even tone.

"Three years ago, in Kansas, the Merchants Union Express theft went down and the agency needed an extra gun. My father kept you on 'cause Sam took you under his wing. I call the shots now. Since you are no longer an employee, I'm saying the Pinkerton Agency will do the investigating. We'll find Sam's killer. It wouldn't do any of us any good to hang the wrong man now, would it?"

The sun emerged tentatively from behind a cloud, as if it might consider shedding some warmth on the city. Bill Pinkerton strode purposefully toward the cemetery entrance, while Garrett walked in the opposite direction, with no particular destination in mind.

*Brock has an alibi.* Even as Garrett mouthed the words he had trouble believing them. If not Brock, then who killed Sam? His partner had left a note on the dresser in their hotel room. Said he had a lead and wanted to play it. But why go out alone? Sam had always been the cautious partner, never taking any unnecessary risks.

Garrett turned a corner, found himself staring at neat rows of simple headstones, and realized he was in the military section of Rosehill Cemetery—an area reserved for Illinois veterans of the Civil War, and a final resting place for many comrades from the Tenth Illinois. He walked slowly down a row of stone markers, stopping now and then to read a name that looked familiar. Suddenly, a wave of sadness engulfed him, as a barrage of frightening images flashed through his mind. He sank down until he was kneeling on the grass.

♠

Winter never died easy on the plains. A routine patrol became a nightmare—sleet, rainstorms, injured men, marauding Indians. It was near dawn. Garrett and his men were three days overdue, ten miles from

Fort Fetterman when Otwah found him. Garrett was staring through his scope at a party of Cheyenne camped next to the rain-swollen Powder River. The remnants of his patrol were hidden on a ridge behind him. Otwah knew of another river crossing downstream. They started out, and had almost cleared the camp when a bugle sounded. Out of a stand of cottonwood, Lieutenant Caultrain and his patrol attacked the Cheyenne, looking for some quick glory. Only this was not war in the grand style—only shafts of early morning light, and Indians you could not see. Screams of wounded horses and men wound their way through the sound of popping pistols, thudding hooves. Lieutenant Caultrain panicked, ran, and left his men. Against orders, Garrett led his patrol back. And when dawn broke through the overcast, Garrett was alone—his men and Caultrain's men all dead or dying. From that day on, the faint sound of distant thunder, and the whistle of the wind turning the grasses, continued to haunt his dreams.

♠

Garrett kept staring at the neat row of headstones, reading the names, until they became a blur. Every soldier knows that wounds and death are the currency of battle, but the thought of his own death had always been an alien one. You figure you'll be the one to make it. And when you do, all you feel is the cold chill of your own mortality. Those thoughts were miserable company. For the past eight years, no matter how fast he ran, how much whiskey he consumed, Garrett could not erase the guilt that continued to bleed him like an invisible wound.

*Shit, Sam, you're gone. Now I have another ghost to live with. Never thought we would end like this. No, I figured to be standing at the foot of the bed in a high-class club when you made your departure to the other side. All this accompanied by the girls chanting a hymn, while you had your fading eye on the madam's ass. Damn it, Sam! It's not my fault. It's yours. Why the hell did you go out without me? I was your partner. We were a team. You the old-timer, the professional. Don't trust anyone, you'd say, watch your step, you'd say. Why give advice you don't follow? It's not over though, is it? Not until I catch the bastard. And I will, just like you taught me. God damn you, Sam Wilkerson, I miss you like hell.*

Funerals are not final. Garrett felt as though Sam had died all over again. Throughout his army career—during the war, even out West—whenever a friend was killed, everything else that day made you angry. You forgot the big picture and concentrated on little things. Only now, too many thoughts were competing for attention in his head. Garrett had fixed his vision on droplets of moisture sparkling on the grass and saw a small flag next to a headstone. He reached over to straighten it. As he did, he sensed a presence next to him. For a moment Garrett didn't recognize her. Charlotte seemed to have materialized from nowhere. He swallowed hard and, when he spoke, his voice sounded remote.

"You were at Sam's funeral? I didn't see you."

"I arrived just after the service began."

Garrett stood up slowly and stretched his legs. The lines of strain were deep in his face. His voice was barely audible. "It was nice of you to come. I didn't think you knew Sam."

"We met once, in Wichita. Actually, I came here for you."

There was an awkward silence, as if neither one knew what to say next. When Garrett's military career had disintegrated, Charlotte was the one person he could talk to, the person who would listen. He looked at her and smiled his thanks. Memories seemed to be everywhere. If he stood still any longer they would engulf him.

"Walk with me?"

"Sure."

Charlotte handed him a basket containing an assortment of ribbons and small flags. "When I moved to Chicago I joined the Ladies of the Grand Army of the Republic."

"The Grand Army? A southern girl like yourself?" The edge had dropped from his voice and a faint smile appeared on his face.

"It's the ladies' auxiliary. Weather permitting, we come to Rosehill once each month and tend the graves. Of course, with the Grand Army reunion nearly upon us, there will be more visitors and ceremonies." She held up a small banner.

"That should duly impress General Sheridan and the Washington brass."

They spent the next twenty minutes walking up and down the rows of headstones. Charlotte would read the names and Garrett would rummage through the basket to select an appropriate flag, banner, or ribbon. He watched her movements, always calm and self-assured—each natural gesture linked to the next. After a while he found a certain comfort in the routine.

"Surely you haven't forgotten—the blue chevron is infantry. The yellow?" she asked.

"Cavalry."

At the end of the last row they found themselves next to the memorial statue of General Sweet. Charlotte sat down on one of the limestone steps surrounding the monument. "After the service I saw you speaking to someone. I have always made a point of never interrupting an angry conversation between two gentlemen."

"That was Bill Pinkerton. A man who'd sell the flowers from his own mother's grave."

Garrett leaned back against the stone base, stretched his legs and began to talk. The words flowed smoothly. He told her about his conversation with Pinkerton, the deal with Brock.

Charlotte's eyes had a way of opening a little wider when he talked, then closing a little, like they were capturing what he was saying and holding onto it. She could do that. Pull it all out of him. The way Otwah's poultices had drawn the pus from his bullet wounds at Powder River. She watched his face as he spoke and noticed a grimness she'd not seen before.

"The general offered me a job and I accepted. But I still intend to find Sam's killer." He glanced at her. "First thing, I should move out of the Revere." Garrett took in a long, deep breath. The Revere Hotel was becoming a little too comfortable. He made a point of never staying in the same hotel more than three times. "If and when I find a place, I'll be sure to let you know."

Charlotte ignored the remark. "General Stannard's wife is buried here. He visits her grave regularly. Some days we sit and talk. He's planning to live north of the river."

"I thought he had rooms at the Grand Pacific."

"The new manager at the Grand Pacific has little tolerance for the general's social habits. So many visitors at all hours—veterans from his campaigns, even his Indian scouts, you know he always considered them family. So the general is moving to a house of his own."

Charlotte checked the watch pinned to her lapel. "When I left this morning, Eulah was baking apple pie. She'd be disappointed if you didn't come for lunch. Besides, you can't do much on an empty stomach. We can work out a plan to find Sam's killer."

"We?"

"Remember, you're on your own now. The Pinkerton Agency will give you no help. Do you know any scratchers here in Chicago? Do you know anybody who distributes phony paper?"

Garrett didn't answer.

"I didn't think so. Admit it, you need help. Consider me your new partner."

She looked over at him. They both smiled.

# THIRTEEN

*For most of Chicago's workers, life was a constant struggle to find housing, food, and a job. There were agencies and hiring halls, all located downtown, many of which were shady. Another option was to frequent one of the saloons, where you could both buy a drink and find an employer. In Chicago, the neighborhood saloon became an institution as important as family or church. It served as the workingman's chief source of information about housing, jobs, and politics. The barkeep was landlord, employment agent, and occasional banker. In other words, the neighborhood saloon met all the workingman's social needs.*

As usual, the Chicago streets were choked with traffic. Garrett crossed Franklin Street and turned south, walking quickly to keep pace with the late afternoon crowd. After his lunch with Charlotte, Garrett had decided to work on clearing his obligation to the general. That done, he would be able to focus on hunting down Sam's killer. He needed to see Brock, talk to the man. But first he must deal with the Eastwood site and that meant a visit to Quinn's.

The afternoon sun drenched the buildings along Franklin Street in a warm glistening light, leaving the doorways in shadow. If he hadn't glanced down, Garrett would have missed the faded No. 3 sign tacked to an iron grille. P. J. Quinn's Saloon and Eatery occupied the basement of a five-story office building at Adams and Franklin Streets and was reached by a half flight of stone steps. In the daytime Quinn's served as a meeting and clearing house for the construction trades—a place where most building contractors in Chicago kept a table.

Garrett pushed open the battered oak door and stepped inside. The saloon was dark, the way all good saloons were dark, with only the barest light filtering down from kerosene lamps hung from the low ceiling. The long, rectangular room was furnished with plank tables and simple straight-backed chairs of the sort that were easily broken in fights and just as easily replaced afterwards. The walls were brown with smoke and the layer of sawdust on the floor had already been kicked into a carpet of whorls and ridges. Low, rumbling voices, alternating with short bursts of laughter, filled the room.

Garrett's body tensed. He crossed the room, walking on the balls of his feet with hands hanging loosely at his sides, ready. But he received no more than a casual glance from the other patrons. The brass-railed, ornately carved bar was a sight to behold, stretching the entire length of an inside wall. Closer examination revealed that it was a work in progress—the far end still bare wood, with cases of hand tools and lumber stacked in the corner against the wall. A short, stocky man, with sand-colored hair and wire-rimmed glasses balanced precariously on the tip of his nose, stood behind the bar wiping a glass with the edge of his apron.

*Quinn's the man to see. Got his fingers in a lot of pies.* Those had been Louis Sullivan's very words.

Garrett tapped a coin on the counter and signaled for a whiskey.

In a quick, fluid movement the man poured a shot, scooped up the money, picked up another glass and continued his methodical wiping.

"I'm looking for a Padraic Quinn," Garrett said.

"Who's askin'?"

"The name's Lyons." Garrett drained the glass in one swallow. He took in a deep breath as he ran his tongue around the inside of his mouth in an attempt to remove the taste of raw liquor. "My friend, Louis Sullivan, told me Quinn was the man who could give me the answer to any building problem."

"Well, now, it's himself you're talking to. Whether I can help, or even care to, depends." Quinn's face wore a carefully composed expression of boredom that told Garrett the man had already heard most of life's problems and would not waste time on his.

"My associate has a building under construction. I'm to handle the day to day—"

Quinn held up his hand, stopping him midsentence. "Well, now, Mr. Lyons is it? You've come to the right place, but the wrong time. Top crews are all spoken for. Even the middlin' ones are busy. See for yourself—I got bids for masons, trenchers, blasters, carpenters, metalworkers." He jerked a thumb at the framed piece of slate nailed to the wall behind the bar. Letters and numbers were scribbled on the board, folded papers stuffed around the frame. "This isn't one of Sullivan's jokes now is it?" Quinn tilted his head to one side. "That look on your face tells me that what you know about construction wouldn't fill up this glass."

"I know enough to realize I need a good man to run the job. I need someone to hire the best workers and then push them to get a building up fast."

"I'm guessin' you need this man right away?" Quinn chuckled. "Maybe this here building of yours is having problems…like the Eastwood?"

"If it's a question of money, I'll pay the going rate."

At that moment the far end of the room erupted with sounds of crashing chairs and men arguing in what sounded like guttural French. Quinn did a quick half turn. "SILENCE! Now, that'll cost ya. It's goin' right on your bill. No more idlin'. Get to it."

Quinn spoke to the offenders in the same slow, even voice he probably used with old people and small children. One man stepped forward as if he had something to say, thought better of it, and joined his comrades collecting the tools and materials stacked near the end of the bar. The response from the rest of the patrons was impromptu laughter—a short, quick nervous fit of it. A few glanced up, but soon went back to their drinking.

"Belgian…woodcarvers at that," Quinn explained, pointing toward the carved lion's head at a corner of the bar. "The boys have been plyin' their trade at hotels like the Grand Pacific, private clubs, and those mansions on Prairie Avenue. They're true artists, with big talents and an even bigger thirst. So, they're workin' off their bill."

Quinn removed his glasses, folding them carefully before slipping them in his pocket. "Now to business. You'll be needin' a person with special talents. Findin' that person won't be easy. Depends on what you're willin' to spend." He poured more whiskey into Garrett's glass. "I can work up quite a thirst lookin' for just the right man for this job."

Garrett stared at the murky liquid, then at Quinn. Quinn stared back. Garrett removed a roll of bills from his jacket, slowly counted out a few and placed them on the bar. Quinn looked around, saw that no one was watching, and slipped the money into his pocket.

"It'll take a few days, a week at most. You stop by then." He strolled to the end of the bar where the Belgians were busy chipping away at a block of wood. "How you boys comin'?" he shouted.

Odd, Garrett thought, the way one instinctively raises one's voice when talking to a foreigner, as if loudness would make the words more understandable. From the corner of his eye Garrett saw someone get up from a table near the door and begin walking his way. Although he couldn't immediately place the man, there was a familiarity about his face.

"Quinn, my man, I'm ashamed of you, treating one of your own like that." The man's deep voice rumbled down the length of the bar like an approaching storm. "Look at his face. 'Tis the map of Ireland's, like your own. So, bring out your best—I mean that bottle you keep under the bar—and set us up. The name's Froelich, Josef Froelich," he said, sticking out a hand big enough to crush a brick. "I'm the man you're looking for."

Close up, Garrett recognized him immediately. "We met yesterday at the—"

"Eastwood building site. That's right."

"You saved me from a serious injury," Garrett said, reaching out to shake the man's hand. "My name's Lyons, Garrett Lyons. I never got a chance to thank you."

"Well, now's the time."

♠

The two men sat at a corner table, in a small pocket of silence not shared by others in the room. Garrett watched as Froelich carefully poured two long drinks from Quinn's private stock. They raised their glasses in a silent toast then slowly sipped the whiskey.

"Ahhh, smooth as silk," Froelich sighed, staring at his glass. "So… am I to understand you're wanting assistance at the Eastwood? What do you know about construction?"

"Enough."

"I mean *Chicago* construction."

"I'm not familiar with Chicago buildings, how they go up or down. Don't care to learn. Figure on hiring someone to do that for me."

They both laughed, then sat in silence for a moment.

"Who you work for?"

"Does it matter?" Garrett leaned back in his chair and stared at Froelich. The man's face probably looked younger than his years. Only the decided cut of his jaw line and cold blue eyes gave Garrett a clue to the real man.

Froelich raised an eyebrow. "So you're a gambling man then? Rumor has it the Eastwood is to clear over ten stories. Am I right?"

Garrett didn't know one way or the other, so he merely shrugged.

"Hasn't been done, you know. Don't know if it can, at least here. But, my God, wouldn't it be great to see, built in Chicago, the first building to scrape the sky." Froelich leaned back in his chair and visibly sighed. He looked at Garrett. "I've been keeping my eye on that site. The Eastwood's going up mighty slow, too slow if you ask me. Wait much longer and the weather'll turn and your employer won't see a building, let alone any profit. Of course, the right man just might be able to make things happen."

"How do I know you're the right man?"

"You don't. But I've been in this business since the fire of '71. Worked for the best—Burnham, Jenney, Boyington, just ask them…if you have the time. It'll be at least a week or so before Quinn can find someone, if he can."

"If you've worked for the best, and are so knowledgeable, why are you sitting here? Chicago always seems to be tearing down and building up. Isn't there a big demand for your services?"

Froelich's eyes narrowed to little slits. His hand clutched his glass, his knuckles turning white. "At the present time, I am between jobs. Why aren't you working a case for Pinkerton? Saw your name in the paper. There was a warehouse fire."

Garrett didn't respond but instead let the silence linger. His jaw tightened as he took a small sip of the whiskey, then another, finally draining his glass. Garrett sensed he and Froelich were alike in many ways. Both men had a part of their lives they kept buried.

Froelich put a cigar to his mouth, lit it, and laughed the smoke out. "Look, you can sit here a day or a week but you won't see anyone else lining up for this job. Why? Because the Eastwood construction site is a pitiful mess, that's why. You need someone *now,* and that someone is *me.*"

Garrett pushed his lips together and listened.

"Don't understand, do you? Let me explain," Froelich continued. "Chicago is growing fast, office buildings have to be bigger and taller. At the same time, old construction methods have to change. They're too slow. Up 'til now, when a man like yourself needed a crew, he'd come to Quinn's, put in an order. Then, come back later to see who turned up to bid on the job. Each trade—masons, carpenters—had their own foreman, ordered their own materials."

Froelich drained his glass and leaned forward. "Today the word is *speed.* Speed in construction is based on two things. One is looking ahead, knowing when you need materials. The other is having them at your hand at the right time. Workmen give their best when materials come in as fast as they can handle them or, in my case, faster. Are you listening? 'Cause this is the only way you'll get the Eastwood built."

The grin on Froelich's face never faltered, just gradually widened at the corners. He poured himself another drink then laid down his rules.

"Number one, everything goes through me. I get a free hand, no interference. That means I hire the men, purchase the materials, I run the job. And that job is to put up the building shell and seal it in. That's phase one and what you hire me for…now. To do this we have to keep costs under ten cents a cubic foot or the whole project goes belly up. If the initial phase goes up fast and efficient, that'll keep Shoup and his bank happy. That done, then we can talk about the next phase. Just show up with the pay packets on Saturdays." He paused a moment and took another sip.

"How much will you be charging for this service?" Garrett asked.

Froelich assumed an air of resignation, raised his eyes heavenward and whispered, "Christ! That's the trouble with you Irish…even when you're beggars, you got to be choosers."

"Well, this isn't my money, now, is it?"

"Whatever my price—and believe me it's a fair one—you'll pay it."

It was amazing what two men, virtual strangers, could learn in a short time with the aid of a bottle of good Irish whiskey. Interesting, too, that each had weighed up the other so quickly and decided he was to be trusted. Garrett did not consider himself a betting man. Betting men eyed fast ponies or how many peanuts in a jar. No, he was a gambler, a thinker, a man who followed his hunches and premonitions. He had a good feeling about Froelich. But it would be prudent to consult with Sullivan. His friend was familiar with the world of Chicago construction. Froelich was right—the sooner he hired someone, the sooner the job would be over. Then he could get down to the business of finding Sam's killer.

"This isn't my decision entirely. I'll meet you tomorrow morning with an answer."

"'Til then." Froelich got up and started toward the door.

"Want to know where?"

"Don't worry, Lyons. I'll find you."

# FOURTEEN

*The Iroquois Club, although not the most prominent men's club in Chicago, maintained a selective member list, which included the city's leading bankers, politicians, and architects. The club's headquarters were located in the Haverly's Theater building, on Monroe Street, just west of Dearborn. The first of six stories of this building was constructed of iron, and the upper ones of white Lemont stone. The Iroquois Club considered its mansard roof and Italian Renaissance façade a beacon of refinement in a culturally barren area of the city.*

"Who dealt this mess?" Louis Sullivan clamped his teeth on an unlit cigar and grimaced good-naturedly. "Whoever it was forgot to shuffle."

The other players at the poker table chose to ignore the remark. Senator Lawlor wore his usual jovial expression. He spoke in a stern but mocking voice. "A pity we're not at my former residence. Any man who dealt this would end up in solitary."

"I wholeheartedly agree." John Wellborn Root leaned back in his chair. "Don't know about you, Sullivan, but I haven't seen a good hand all night."

"Dealer takes two." The soft voice belonged to a fourth player, J. C. Forsyth. The banker carefully placed his throwaway cards face down, then looked at the other players.

John Root's blue eyes twinkled as he reshuffled the cards in his hand.

"Move those pasteboards around all you want, Root, they ain't gonna change." Senator Lawlor looked at his hand, then tossed a handful of chips into the pot. "I'll raise."

Garrett was sitting next to Sullivan. "If your cards are that bad, Louis, why don't you just quit?" His words had a decided edge. The events of the day—Sam's funeral, his meeting Bill Pinkerton—were beginning to take their toll. "I'm out," he said.

"Listen to the man. I bet twenty," Louis said, anxious to keep the game moving along.

"Well, I fold." Forsyth spoke with a quiet firmness.

Root hesitated a moment, gave his cards a closer look, then carelessly tossed them on the table. "I'll follow your lead."

The senator took a sip from his glass while contemplating his hand. "Well, Sullivan, seems we're the only ones left. So I'll see that and raise you." He pushed a stack of chips to the center of the table.

Sullivan stared at his cards, then let his gaze travel around the table from Garrett to the senator, then back again.

Garrett ignored his stare and looked across the room. At the same time he tapped his cards once on the table then put them face down. He was tired and wanted the game over.

"I call." Sullivan picked up Garrett's signal and quickly moved two stacks of chips to the center of the table.

The senator looked at his hand and shook his head slowly. "It's yours."

Sullivan grinned as he turned over his cards.

"Damn!" John Root sighed. "I'm impressed. Your game has improved."

"It's late, gentlemen. Time we settled up." Without further hesitation, Forsyth removed a pencil from his coat pocket and began scribbling figures on slips of paper.

Senator Lawlor stood up. "Well, I don't know about the rest of you, but I'm in need of liquid sustenance. Care to join me?"

The main lounge of the Iroquois Club was a long, narrow, oak-paneled room with a wall of windows facing Monroe Street. It was decorated in typical gentlemen's club fashion, with groupings of leather armchairs scattered across thick Oriental carpets. A large fireplace anchored one end, while a circular table, laden with a late evening repast, occupied the center of the room. The aroma from Havana cigars and aged bourbon mingled with the scent of logs crackling in the fireplace and gave the room a relaxed atmosphere.

Earlier, Garrett had played a game of billiards with Sullivan, then wandered alone through the hallways, scrutinizing the club's art collection, which consisted of gilt-framed Rubenesque nudes frolicking amid pastoral settings. On the whole, he'd enjoyed the evening. The atmosphere was elegant, the company congenial, the poker players mediocre. If he'd put his mind to it, Garrett could have won himself a sizeable sum. Only he found it difficult to concentrate. He kept trying to put the events of the last two days into some order. Usually he could do this activity best alone, in his room at the Revere Hotel.

*Brock has an alibi.* Garrett remembered Pinkerton's words. Bill Pinkerton might be looking to boost his own reputation, but surely not at Sam's expense. The sooner he spoke to Brock, the better. Sullivan was engaged in conversation with two gentlemen at the buffet table. Garrett was about to let him know he was leaving, when a deep baritone voice interrupted his thoughts.

"I might have known. John Root got himself bluffed with a pair of sixes."

The voice belonged to one of the handsomest men Garrett had ever seen. Daniel Hudson Burnham had a beautifully molded head, topped by a crown of dark brown hair that curled low over his broad forehead. A thick reddish-brown mustache served as a pediment above a firm, powerful jaw. A tall man, nearly six feet in height, Burnham was standing next to Garrett and staring with deep blue eyes at his partner, John Root.

"I trust you were gambling with your personal funds and not the firm's." Burnham said.

"You know I always empty my pockets first before reaching into yours," Root answered good-naturedly. It was apparent the two men enjoyed this bantering. "You evidently heard the club just received a shipment of Cuban cigars. Always a temptation, isn't it? You may have guessed, Lyons, cigars are my partner's vice."

"Only one vice, Burnham? What a pity," Senator Lawlor said as he joined the group. He was accompanied by a short, rotund gentleman, whose neatly trimmed beard failed to hide his thick lips and gourmand's cheeks.

Burnham nodded at the gentleman. "A good cigar is all the vice I need. Although, I dare say, Major Jenney would probably vote for vintage claret."

If anyone could be considered Chicago's senior architect-engineer, it was William Le Baron Jenney. The "Major"—who served with distinction in the Civil War—opened his office after the fire of 1871 and took the lead in rebuilding Chicago. His atelier had trained many of the architects present in the Iroquois Club lounge that evening.

Jenney raised his glass. "Well, Daniel, tonight I chose port. The club has acquired a few cases of excellent vintage. At my suggestion, of course."

As Garrett half-listened to the conversation, previous thoughts of leaving disappeared from his mind. Instead, he concentrated on selecting a cigar from the humidor on a side table. Finding one he liked the look of, he struck a match against the mantle, lit the cigar, then tossed the match into the fire. He decided that now was the time to observe and gather facts. He'd sort them out later. He made himself comfortable in a high-back chair, with a fresh glass of whiskey at hand, and watched the scene unfold before him.

"Here's the news." Forsyth distributed the tally slips to the senator and Root.

"Well, John, how did you fare?" Burnham peered over his partner's shoulder and raised an eyebrow. "Better dig deep. Looks like Sullivan acquired a second vocation."

"What does that mean?" Lawlor asked.

Burnham took a long draw on his cigar, then let a turban of thick smoke unravel around his head. "It's common knowledge that our esteemed member, Mr. Sullivan, has only three years left on his contract with Mr. Adler." He looked about him, making sure no one else in the room was close enough to overhear, then continued. "Since our colleague has a tendency to put his foot in his mouth, there's speculation among us as to whether this partnership will last. I understand you are a betting man, Senator. Care to join the pool?"

Jenney let out an exasperated sigh. Although his voice was soft, he spoke with a blunt certainty. "Daniel, in every business partnership one man does the pulling and one does the prancing. You, of all people, should be well aware of that."

There was a lingering silence as Burnham examined his cigar to keep from looking at his former mentor. Jenney continued. "This evening, Daniel, I suggest we combine our vices. Join me for a glass of port?"

Burnham looked at Jenney and produced a charming grin. "A splendid idea, I'd relish not only a glass, but one of your stories...about Paris perhaps?" He wound up the sentence with a vague gesture, then looked over Jenney's shoulder. "What do you say, Sullivan?"

"Glad you're here," Senator Lawlor said. "We were just talking about you."

Sullivan looked directly at Burnham.

"I was telling my partner how your game has improved." John Root spoke in his usual soothing voice.

"Thank my friend Lyons. I'm lucky he's staying in Chicago awhile."

"Well, Lyons, what do you plan to do here, besides spending time at the poker table with Sullivan?" John Root asked.

"Work with General Stannard at Central Casualty Insurance."

"The general should consider himself fortunate to have your assistance. I feel Central Casualty is sailing into perilous waters." Forsyth's words were slow and deliberate.

"You seem well informed, even though you don't make sense." Senator Lawlor chuckled.

"Bankers know everyone's business. That's how they make money." John Root poured himself a whiskey. "What can you tell us about Central Casualty Insurance?"

Forsyth studied Garrett a moment before he answered. "I know as much as anyone and maybe more than most. Central Casualty is an old Chicago company. Dealt mainly in maritime insurance until '55 when they added life insurance. About the time Quentin Oates's daughter married a young cadet from West Point, Barton Stannard."

"Then who is General Stannard's partner?" Garrett asked.

"Quentin's nephew. Old Mr. Oates pretty much ran things while he was alive." Forsyth paused. Once he was sure of everyone's attention, he continued. "Central Casualty is a long-valued customer of the bank. However, this past month, rumors have circulated up and down LaSalle Street. And those rumors, along with certain facts—which, as a bank officer, I am privy to—have led me to conclude that this company is in serious trouble. I speak now only because I feel their predicament will soon be public knowledge."

"What kind of a cockamamie answer is that?" Burnham muttered under his breath.

Forsyth ignored him and continued. "Over the last two months Central Casualty purchased a considerable amount of shares in the Lake View Vault Corporation. So many that the general's company became the primary investor."

"Never heard of them. Willard Nixon handles all the vault transactions here in Chicago. He would have mentioned it." John Root looked at Burnham, who nodded in agreement.

"I'm certain Mr. Lyons here will help set General Stannard along the proper path." William Le Baron Jenney looked at the group and raised his now-empty glass. "Gentlemen, all this talk makes a man thirsty. I insist you all join me in a glass of port." That said, he led the group out of the lounge and into an adjoining room.

Senator Lawlor put a hand on Garrett's arm. They stopped momentarily and waited until Jenney's entourage had left. His voice, although low, was clear. "Central Casualty bought shares in the Lake View Vault Corporation, in order to build the Eastwood Building. I heard it is to be the first ten-story building in the city. I find it worrisome that no one knows Lake View. I *do* know Willard Nixon's reputation.

Lake View is one vault company that he did *not* organize. I wonder why?"

"What's a vault company?" Garrett asked.

Lawlor picked up his whiskey glass and took a sip. "A vault company is an investment group. According to Illinois state law, a corporation cannot construct or own a building unless that building is used in their business operations, but a majority of investors want to construct a building they can rent out, to make a profit. The law doesn't make sense."

Garrett shrugged. He didn't know what else to do.

"It's shortsighted. Would those idiots in Springfield listen? Of course not."

The senator had a self-satisfied, almost smug, look on his face. "Hell, there's no law I can't get around. Before my enforced sabbatical, I was instrumental in getting the state legislature to pass the Vault Act. That's a piece of legislation that allows a company to incorporate under Illinois law with the sole right of building, maintaining, and operating a safety deposit vault. The corporation doesn't have to specify where they plan to put their 'vault.' There's nothing in Illinois law that prohibits these vaults from being put into a new building, which they always are. Then the rest of the building can be rented out. This fueled our present construction boom. Look inside any of these new buildings and I dare say you'll find a vault room."

Garrett felt a hand grasp his shoulder. He stiffened, spun around, and found himself staring at Forsyth.

The banker looked tentatively around the room before he spoke. His voice was soft but firm. "I wanted to speak to you in private. I am in a quandary. General Stannard is an honest man and well thought of here. As I mentioned previously, Central Casualty acquired a great deal of Lake View Vault stock. But recently a considerable amount of that stock has been deposited in our bank by another party."

"He means someone else will soon hold a majority of the Lake View Vault stock," the senator whispered.

Forsyth nodded his head. "I suggest you advise the general to act quickly or it will be too late." That said, he silently retreated into the next room.

Garrett stared after him then turned to Lawlor. "You hear that?" The senator nodded.

"I wonder, who's been acquiring the Lake View Vault stock and why was Oates letting it go?" Garrett asked.

The senator meditated for a moment. "I could find out for you, at a price. A lot of things have been said about me, Lyons. Don't pay them heed, my real love is poker." He held the glass of whiskey in front of him. "A good game of poker is better than a barrel of this."

"I agree. And I know just the person who can arrange a private game for you."

"Well, then, it's a deal." The senator smiled as he drained his glass.

♠

Garrett felt a poke at his arm.

"Hear the music?" Sullivan whispered. He nodded toward the other end of the room.

John Root had settled himself in front of a grand piano and began to accompany himself in a rousing rendition of "Lucille."

At that moment Forsyth re-appeared at their side and discreetly handed Sullivan a roll of bank notes. "Congratulations. Here are your winnings. I certainly hope your luck continues."

Sullivan murmured his thanks, then took Garrett's arm and led him off to the side of the room. "Just listen to the man. Root sounds as good as one of those tenors we heard the other evening at Hooley's."

Garrett nodded his agreement. John Root not only had a lovely tenor voice but also what Charlotte would call "parlor room polish."

Sullivan continued. "Did I ever tell you my father owned a dance studio in Chicago? I'm well versed in the piano. Although I don't sing well, I have a large repertoire of Strauss waltzes."

Garrett took his arm. "Louis, it's time to leave. You've dazzled us enough this evening."

# FIFTEEN

*In 1869 Potter Palmer started construction on his first hotel at the corner of State and Quincy. Just two years later he began another hotel at the corner of State and Monroe. Both hotels would perish in the Fire of 1871, although their architect, John Van Osdel, was able to save the plans by burying them under the clay basement floor. As the ashes cooled, Palmer vowed to rebuild. Palmer House III—bigger and grander—was completed in 1873 on the State and Monroe site and included such amenities as a vertical steam railroad, otherwise known as an elevator. The hotel catered to travelers and provided suites of varying sizes and prices for those Chicagoans in need of long-term lodging.*

Iris Reynolds watched the raindrops tick against the window. When they were followed by loud claps of thunder she mouthed a silent "Damn." In this weather Augustus would never permit a carriage ride along the boulevard or even shopping on Wabash Avenue. Hopefully, he wouldn't refuse a visit to Charlotte.

At the present time, Iris wasn't in her cousin's good graces. Fortunately, Augustus didn't know that. She let out an audible sigh and walked over to the carved walnut settee and sat down. Even the bouquet of red roses and enormous box of candy on the table next to it did nothing to relieve the monotony of the room.

Iris picked up a copy of the *Inter Ocean* and flipped through the pages until she found the personal message column. There was nothing, the same as yesterday, and the day before. She slid a little farther back on the settee and forced herself to remain calm. Thankfully, news of the explosion and warehouse fire was relegated to a small article on page three. A Pinkerton agent, named Wilkerson, was buried yesterday. Listed among the pallbearers was a familiar name, Lyons. Mr. Garrett Lyons. Iris smiled, recalling their meeting and his connection with Charlotte. Her cousin always had luck with men and money.

Last month, before their St. Louis trip and without even telling her, Augustus had sold his house on Prairie Avenue and insisted they take up residence in this suite in the Palmer House. "More convenient, my dear," he assured her. He could make daily trips to his broker's office in the hotel lobby.

Iris did not know how her husband had acquired his wealth and, until this unexpected move, she hadn't cared, as long as there was plenty of it. Augustus's money seemed to be connected with stocks or bonds, and the bewildering operations of the Board of Trade. She half-listened when he mentioned bulls, bears, and something called the "Pit," where he would buy and sell grain or at least his broker would. Grain went up, and then down. Strange, when grain went down, they had a lot of money. Unfortunately, last week Augustus had informed her that grain went up, so the money had disappeared. Hence no new house up north of the river, or trips to New York or Washington. Augustus assured her it would be temporary. He had other investments, long term he said, that would eventually prove profitable. She had to be patient. And, he teased with a wink, she mustn't forget their new venture. A quick fix that would give them needed cash.

She heard voices in the adjoining parlor. Augustus's visitors were still there. Earlier, she had tiptoed over to the door and tried peering through the keyhole, without success. Iris recognized the voice of one of Augustus's guests and toyed with the idea of simply walking in, but decided against it. Her husband had been moody lately and easily provoked.

The voices grew louder, then stopped. When she heard the sound of a door closing Iris immediately shoved the newspaper behind a pillow and began polishing her nails. Chicago's ladies had recently discovered this popular East Coast fashion. Iris's polisher was made of India rubber with an ivory knob on one side and a surface of chamois on the other. She dipped a finger into a paste of crushed stone, oil, and rouge, then daubed the stuff on her nails. She was rubbing her nails with the chamois when Augustus entered the room.

"What are your plans for the day?" He put his hand on Iris's shoulder, bent over, and gently kissed her forehead. He looked at the flowers and chocolates. "Presents?"

Iris did not take her eyes off her task at hand. "The roses are from Tom Ryerson."

"The chocolates?" Augustus touched Iris under her left ear.

Iris bit her lower lip thoughtfully, while a faint smile lingered at the corner of her mouth. "John Peck. You know he has a sweet tooth. I find him amusing. He speaks French and gives me news of Paris. They are friends, nothing more." She made a kissing gesture and looked into Augustus's eyes. Her smile was brilliantly unconvincing. "Remember, you did ask me to be nice to them, for business reasons? You know, darling, I always do what you say."

"I'd like to think so, my dear." Augustus noticed the *Inter Ocean* tucked behind the pillow and picked it up. "What's this?"

"Nothing. I picked it up because I thought your associate would have contacted you by now. Besides, I couldn't find any St. Louis newspapers in the lobby."

"We'll hear soon. But he'll use the *Tribune*, not this rag." As he spoke, Augustus slowly caressed the back of Iris's neck with his fingers, much as one would stroke a cat. "Now I must visit my broker." He hesitated, then unexpectedly thrust his hand into his waistcoat and drew out a small package. "Here is a little something for you."

Iris eagerly opened the box. Her eyes widened when she saw a familiar large black cameo—a companion to Charlotte's—only this one was encircled in diamonds.

"Well, my dear?" Augustus watched her reaction.

Iris took the brooch from the box and held it. "It's beautiful, really beautiful."

"A clerk at C. D. Peacock's told me that you were in the store earlier this week. And you helped a gentleman select a similar brooch, one with pearls. I think diamonds suit you." He bent over and gently kissed her forehead again. "Wear it to the game dinner."

"The game dinner! You know I've been dying to go. How wonderful! But darling, I can't help thinking—"

Augustus pressed his fingers into her shoulder. Iris winced. He leaned over and whispered in her ear, "My dear, when have I ever asked you to think?" That said, Augustus Reynolds walked purposefully out of the room.

A shadow crossed Iris's face. She returned the brooch to its case and then continued polishing her nails, but soon stopped. Her hand was shaking.

♠

It was mid-morning when General Stannard arrived at his office in the Borden Block. He'd spent the previous day, with Otwah's help, moving personal belongings into his new home. Today the former scout was organizing the deployment of his remaining furniture and household goods, which had been in storage since his wife's death. Yesterday he'd persuaded Lyons to take charge of his immediate problem, the Eastwood Building, only to have his former aide present him with another, more pressing one. All this upheaval put him in a testy mood.

The general burst through the door of Central Casualty Insurance and stopped abruptly at the reception desk. Without even a "Good day," he leaned over and spat out, "Has Oates arrived yet? You don't know? Well then, find out!" He tossed his coat and walking stick on a nearby desk and bellowed, "I will tolerate no intrusions. Is that clear?" At that remark, the remaining staff took refuge behind their files.

Once inside his office the general immediately opened his safe and removed the cash resting inside. Earlier that year, when rumors of a financial panic circulated throughout the city, he withdrew all of his personal money from Union Trust Bank. Ironic name. He never did trust banks. Like most soldiers, he preferred keeping his currency at the ready. Mary's wealth, and that of her family, was allied to the fortunes of Central Casualty Insurance. But this money, well, this money was his.

He knew that each packet of currency should be secured with a strip of paper bearing the bank's seal. A closer examination revealed that a good number of packets bore no identification mark at all. Of the twenty-two on his desk, twelve bore a proper seal and were rightly his, but the others? He selected four of the questionable ones at random, broke the wrappers then fanned the currency in semicircles, like a deck of cards, on his desk.

"All twenties. Hmmm...seem genuine enough, but who am I to tell?"

Of course, this alleged counterfeit money was a concern. But what angered the general most was the fact that someone had the effrontery—without his knowledge or permission—to enter *his* office and open *his* private safe. Only one person would have had the means and the opportunity. And that person was Shelby Oates.

In reality the two men had little in common. The general was a widower, his partner a bachelor. The general had spent the majority of his life in the U.S. Army and still maintained a military-style schedule, favoring his outdoor pursuits. At every opportunity he would escape the rigors of the business community and go hunting or fishing with Otwah in the Fox River area west of Chicago. On the other hand, his partner had been raised by maiden aunts and never worked a day in his life. He spent his early years traveling throughout Europe, developing a talent for idling, a taste for good liquor, and was most comfortable at ladies' teas or art exhibitions.

Originally, the day-to-day business of Central Casualty had been handled by Quentin Oates, the company's founder and chairman. After his death, Shelby Oates had taken over that responsibility. Until three months ago Central Casualty had seemed to be running smoothly enough, or so Stannard thought. True, at times he sensed that something was amiss, but refused to think about it. Now, the general realized he would pay dearly for his lack of oversight.

He sat back in his chair and let his mind plunge into memories of the events of the past few weeks, which emerged in a series of disconnected but vivid pictures. Oates had been acting stranger than usual, coming into the office at all hours, rummaging through papers. Apparently he had visited the Tremont House on Monday, where he found time to lose at cards and give Lyons an IOU. But the man had no time for their meeting the next day?

The sound of voices, followed by a sharp knock, interrupted his thoughts. The door swung open and a clerk entered the room. The general raised his hand. Although he spoke quietly, his voice was like a gunshot.

"Well, do you know where Oates is?"

"No."

"Then bring me all the information we have on the Eastwood Building and specifically the Lake View Vault Corporation. I want to know exactly where Central Casualty stands." He removed his watch from his vest pocket. "I expect it within the hour."

The clerk stiffened, gave a slight nod, and backed out of the room.

♠

Bernard entered 45 Eldridge Court through the rear door. He walked past the laundry room, through the scullery, then into the warmth and comforting smells of the kitchen.

Eulah was at the table trimming the crust on a pie. She looked up and exclaimed, "Get out of that wet coat. You'll catch your death."

"Where is—"

"She's in the front parlor doing accounts." Eulah stepped back, wiped her hands on her apron and snapped, "Ada!"

A tall, scrawny girl with mouse-brown hair coiled in a braid on the top of her head rushed in from the pantry.

"Ladle a bowl of my chicken soup from the pot on the stove and pour a glass of cider. When you finish, tell Mrs. Reid that Bernard is here."

"Yes, ma'am." Ada barely glanced up as she gave the tasks her full attention.

Bernard had finished his soup and was drinking a second glass of cider by the time Charlotte entered the kitchen. She sat down at the table and waited as Ada poured her a glass. "Thank you, my dear. Now, I'd like you to go upstairs and find my purple shawl and bring it down." She watched Ada's figure disappear down the hallway then turned to Bernard. "Well?"

"I delivered the envelope to Mrs. Reynolds and she gave me this list. There was no message. I could see she had a guest."

Charlotte glanced at the paper then put it aside. "The other errands?"

"Everything is arranged. The hotel manager was not available. But his assistant assured me he would reserve the Lotus Club's regular room. The Tremont House is completely filled. As you know, the army reunion is this week. Many veterans have already arrived." There was a silence as Bernard dabbed a corner of his mustache with a napkin. "I am confident the crowd will be manageable. I also assume the club members will bring guests, most probably from the U.S. Army?"

"Yes. All men love to gamble, the military more than most." Charlotte hoped this Monday's poker night would be more profitable than usual for everyone.

"With that in mind, madam, I took the liberty of reserving an adjoining salon, at the assistant manager's suggestion, with your approval, of course."

"Anything else?" Charlotte expected more and waited.

Bernard adjusted his shirt cuffs, then spoke guardedly. "I went to the Alexian Brothers Hospital, as you requested. I learned that the patient, a Mr. Brock, has survived the operation and is recovering."

"Were you able to see him?"

"No."

"Then how do you know Brock is recovering?" Charlotte did not look pleased.

"Simple deduction. Mr. Pinkerton was in the hallway with two agents. However, I did speak to a Brother Andrew, who told me Mr.

Pinkerton wants Brock moved out of the hospital. The doctors were not in agreement. Pinkerton stationed an agent in the patient's room."

He raised his hand before Charlotte could interrupt and took a long drink of the cider.

"One of the brothers suggested that Sunday would be a more opportune time to visit."

# SIXTEEN

*Chicago was a city "on the move." Early architects and builders, such as John Van Osdel and William W. Boyington, began their careers as carpenters, then worked their way up through the trades. The Great Fire of 1871 destroyed much of the city and at the same time created a building boom. Chicago became a nurturing ground for high-rise construction. This, in turn, produced a new breed of architect/engineer. William Le Baron Jenney and Dankmar Adler, two of Chicago's emerging architects, had served as engineers in the U.S. Army under Generals Grant and Sherman. One characteristic these architects had in common was ingenuity—based on their conviction that whatever their clients wanted they could build.*

The Borden Block is a gem of a building! After all, I designed the façade. My office is on the top floor." Those were Sullivan's words, usually spoken over a late night whiskey.

The elevator jerked to a stop, the door wheezed open, and Garrett stepped out. He walked down the hallway, reading signs on doors, half-listening to the slow cadence of his own footsteps against the wood floor. At the end of the corridor he found a door with ornate lettering—*Dankmar Adler & Company, Architects.*

"Somewhat late in the morning. Thought you would be at the Eastwood site by now."

Louis Sullivan stood behind him, immaculately dressed in his usual attire—a custom-tailored brown wool suit.

"If God wanted us to enjoy the dawn, he would have made it later in the day," Garrett responded. "How'd you get here?"

"I took the stairs. Keeps me fit."

Sullivan reached past Garrett, opened the door, and ushered him into the reception room, a rectangular space with framed drawings of classical Greek buildings spaced along the oak-paneled walls. In the center an empty desk sat between two armchairs atop an oriental carpet. A beaver hat, ivory-tipped cane, and black coat were carelessly draped over one of the chairs.

Louis gave the objects a cursory glance then nodded toward a door on his right. "That's Adler's office. He's probably with a client. My office is just ahead, through the drafting room."

He opened a door in the paneled wall behind the reception desk. They entered a long, narrow room, well lit with windows along one side and gaslights hanging from the ceiling. Two rows of drawing tables dominated the space. These "tables"—actually sawhorses with large boards laid over them—were piled with ink drawings and rolls of blueprints. Groups of young men, wearing white starched shirts and bow ties, stood nearby, shuffling papers and whispering quietly. Next to each man was a small wooden box crammed with rulers and pencils.

An architect's office was a totally foreign place to Garrett and, for a moment, he stood off to one side, fascinated by the scene in front of him. Sullivan strolled down the aisle, pausing at a desk, glancing over sketches, making comments. As Sullivan approached, the young men tensed and clustered together, reminding Garrett of a flock of prairie hens sensing the presence of a hawk in the area. On the other hand, Sullivan was thoroughly enjoying himself.

"These are my apprentices. I do the hiring. First I examine the man's sketchbook. Then, if it's any good, I'll take him on for a trial period, a month, maybe two. Once he's employed the man can start to draw some pay." He glanced over at Garrett. "I consider that more than reasonable."

"If you say so."

They stepped to one side as two young lads rushed past carrying long rolls of paper. Garrett pointed toward an apprentice stretching a sheet of fabric over an ink drawing. "What's he doing?"

"When a draftsman finishes the rendering, a thin sheet of linen is laid over it and he traces the drawing in ink. These tracings are used to create blueprints. By the way, you should have a set for the Eastwood site."

Sullivan continued his parade and monologue. When he bellowed, "What's this? You call this drawing? It's unacceptable," at one unfortunate draftsman, Garrett retreated to the far end of the room. He spied a door labeled *L. Sullivan, Private* and opened it.

Louis Sullivan's office was a corner room with windows along two sides. The shelves underneath the windows were crammed with books. Garrett settled himself in a chair next to a large, polished oak desk that dominated the center space. Tacked on the walls, amid framed sketches of Paris, were drawings of what he concluded were some of Sullivan's current projects. The sketches were residences of one kind or another with the client's name written at the bottom. Garrett mouthed the names—Reynolds, Nicholson, Kimball, Wineman, Rothschild—in an attempt to ignore the voices emanating from the drafting room. He was lighting a cigar when his friend entered in his usual rush and sat down in the leather chair behind the desk.

Sullivan leaned back and sighed. "Didn't I tell you the Iroquois Club would be top notch? Admit it, you had a memorable time. Since you'll be staying in Chicago we must cast a wide social net."

Garrett nodded. "Look, I went to Quinn's and—"

"You haven't forgotten? Remember I told you I had tickets for Drake's game dinner?" Louis interrupted. He reached into his pocket and withdrew a paper, waving it like a trophy. "This is a social opportunity neither of us can ignore. What do you say?"

Garrett did not respond immediately. He studied the self-satisfied expression on Sullivan's face then stared at the ceiling as if in deep thought. He would probably attend, but he didn't need to tell Sullivan that yet. Let him stew awhile. In any case, an evening at the Iroquois Club was a fair trade for information on Quinn and his ability to find someone to run the Eastwood job. General Stannard's problem had to be settled, and the sooner the better. He needed time to visit Brock and check the man's alibi. What if he wasn't Sam's killer? Who else was there?

He let the silence linger and, just when Sullivan was about to speak, Garrett shook his head soulfully. "I'm sure you feel this invitation is an opportunity. It's not that I'm ungrateful."

Sullivan stared at him for a moment, then smiled. "All right, what do you want?"

"Considering my ignorance of Chicago construction, and *if* Quinn is able to find someone, how would I know whether the man is doing his job? He could 'palm an ace' on me, so to speak. I need an expert, like yourself. A man who'll visit the site, check things out. Then I can assure General Stannard the building is making progress, running smoothly."

"In other words, you want me to visit the Eastwood site in exchange for your presence at the game dinner," Sullivan commented with a sniff. "How many…visits I mean?"

Garrett shrugged. "Does it matter? How can you pass up the chance to poke your nose into someone else's construction site?"

"You have a valid argument. I'm agreeable. But is this a fair exchange?"

Before Garrett could answer, the office door opened wide, ushering in a neat-looking man with a fine gray beard and a head of gray hair. Although he spoke quietly, Garrett could see anxiety written in the way he held his body and the tightness of his shoulders.

"Do you know who was in to see me this morning, Sullivan? Mr. Balke, that's who. Evidently, he and his partner, Brunswick, came to our office yesterday. They wished to discuss the progress on their building and spoke to *you* at great length. Now it seems our clients have concerns."

There was a long silence. Sullivan took in a deep breath and sat for a moment looking down at his hands. The expression on his face was almost contrite. Garrett tried to hide a smile, because, when Sullivan did speak, he was his usual brash self.

"Look, Adler, concern is not the proper word. Mr. Balke is simply confused."

"*What* did you say to them?" Adler's voice was edgy.

"I simply told them, 'Look, I've discovered that the soil underneath your proposed building is a swamp. God Almighty did that, not me. So the foundation will cost you $25,000 more.' While they were digesting that, I informed them that the building would be faced with limestone, not common brick. Now, it's expensive—an extra of about $20,000. I also designed a terra cotta frieze around the third floor, which will cost another $15,000. However, I did tell them that they would have a building in which they could take pride. I also added that their offices will have fine views."

Louis sat back in his chair and sighed noisily, as if to tell Adler that he felt he'd answered the question satisfactorily. When he looked up and realized that his partner was glaring at him, he changed the subject. "By the way, have you met my friend?"

The gray-haired gentleman turned, noticed Garrett and announced himself. "I'm Dankmar Adler."

"Garrett Lyons."

They shook hands.

"Lyons is working with General Stannard at Central Casualty," Louis said.

"How is the general these days?" Adler asked. "He's kept to himself since his wife died. Will he attend the Grand Army reunion this Saturday?"

"I don't know his plans yet, but I'm almost certain he'll attend."

"I've been advising Lyons on building construction," Sullivan added.

"How?" Adler asked.

"He needs someone to run things. Well, I sent him to Quinn's. It might take a week or so, but Quinn'll come through."

"That's why I'm here," Garrett joined in. "I want an opinion on a Josef Froelich. I met the man yesterday at Quinn's. He seems knowledgeable and is ready to begin work at once."

"Not *the* Josef Froelich? Why—"

Adler raised his hand, halting his partner mid-sentence. "Your friend could do worse."

"I've heard the rumors," Sullivan said.

"And that's what they are…just rumors," Adler replied testily.

"Just what have you heard, Louis?" Garrett asked.

"I heard—on good authority, mind you—that Froelich is as shady as they come, that's what."

"Well, I'd rather hire a crook who knows what he's doing than an honest man who doesn't. I can manage a crook." Adler stared at his partner. "I dare say so can your friend Lyons. You can't teach a man the skill—either he has it or he doesn't. Froelich has the skill, plus the experience to bring a building in on time and *on budget*."

Adler pulled out a chair and sat down, as though preparing for a long stay. "I'm here to discuss budgets, Sullivan." He leaned back, squeezed the bridge of his nose between his thumb and forefinger, and continued, speaking softly at first. "Our agreement with Brunswick and Balke was to keep costs to under fifteen cents a cubic foot for the entire project. That includes all the exterior, as well as the interior, finishes. You've used close to ten cents per foot already. And we haven't put in floors or windows yet."

Sullivan raised an eyebrow. "I thought *I* was in charge of architectural design."

"It's a warehouse for God's sake, and a small one at that. Haven't I mentioned *again* and *again*, Brunswick is a close friend of Peck and Ryerson? This can lead to bigger commissions."

By now, Adler's voice was getting louder. Sullivan began to squirm.

"No limestone. We use common brick." Adler spoke sharply.

"And my terra cotta façade?"

Adler shrugged his shoulders and slowly shook his head.

"Never!"

Their conversation continued in a rapidly escalating tone. Garrett began edging toward the door.

He gave Sullivan a good-bye nod, then escaped into the drafting room, dodging a group of apprentices huddled outside the door pretending to look engrossed in a set of blueprints.

Earlier Garrett had wondered why Sullivan and Adler did not have adjoining offices. Now he realized Adler felt it best to keep his partner away from prospective clients—for good reason.

# SEVENTEEN

*The first steam-driven elevator in Chicago appeared in 1864 and was installed in the Charles B. Farwell store on Wabash Avenue. In 1870 the Hale Elevator Company of Chicago developed a hydraulic elevator, which was faster and smoother than steam. The first one was installed in a warehouse on Lake Street. This was one factor that fed Chicago's growth. The invention of the passenger elevator meant buildings could rise to scrape the sky. The city's audacious developers could attract tenants by offering these modern conveniences. The Borden Block boasted two such elevators and was considered one of the most modern office buildings in Chicago.*

After his strategic withdrawal from Sullivan's office, Garrett walked down to Central Casualty. The young man at the front desk was engrossed in a new issue of the *Gazette* so he was able to pass through without an unpleasant confrontation.

He found General Stannard in his office, smoking a cigar and staring out the window. The old man did not turn around, merely acknowledged his former lieutenant's presence with a nod of his head. Garrett tried to gauge the old man's present disposition. After a few moments, he began reporting on the events that had occurred since their last meeting. He described the Eastwood site, his lunch with Sullivan, and how he got roped into an evening at the Iroquois Club—omitting the rumors circulating in the financial district regarding Central Casualty. As Garrett continued speaking, his mood became less serious, more relaxed, for no particular reason other than this was a familiar scenario. He was back in the army, coming in from patrol, reporting to the general. God, he realized just how much he missed it all.

Garrett recounted his visit to Quinn's saloon, his meeting with Josef Froelich and how, thanks to Sullivan again, he would be attending John B. Drake's game dinner.

"Froelich can start immediately. Sullivan's skeptical…he would be. His partner, Adler, feels the man's capable and eventually will work out. I'll have to keep a tight rein on him."

He stopped, took a step forward, and raised his voice a little. "Have you been listening? What do you think? Should we hire Froelich? Look, I need some direction here."

The general turned around. His brow was furrowed and he was biting his lip. The old man was definitely in a somber mood, so Garrett thought it best to adopt a lighter tone. "Remember, sir, things are never as bad as I report, or as good as I hope them to be."

General Stannard pointed his cigar at the money fanned across his desk. "Look at that. You were right. Found all this in my safe. The packets with the bank seal are legit, the others most probably fake. I never checked closely, until now."

Garrett picked up one of the banknotes and turned it over in his hand. "You found this in your safe?"

"*I* didn't put it there. No reason to. The only person that has access to the safe besides myself is Shelby Oates." The faint smile on the general's face broadened into a grin. "His office is next door. Let's see what he's hiding in his own safe."

♠

The partners' offices were located across from one another at the end of the hallway. Thus the two men were able to enter Oates's office without being readily observed by any Central Casualty staff. General Stannard stood in the doorway, uncertain what to do or even where to start. The few times he'd had occasion to visit, he'd felt uncomfortable.

This office was the same size and same shape as his, yet so different.

In the half-light of drawn blinds the room looked somber. The place smelled faintly of wax, polish, and stale flowers, not the more familiar aroma of cigars and whiskey. The room's predominant color was blue. The carpet was dark blue, with a border of red and pale blue latticework. A fireplace of polished marble dominated the outside wall with a large Fantin-Latour painting of flowers and fruit positioned over the mantel. Smaller paintings hung on the oak-paneled walls, while sculptures of young women and animals were displayed on cabinets and shelves.

Garrett squeezed past the general and began a search of the room. He quickly located a safe, built into the wall behind a row of framed Audubon prints.

"Let me see. I may have a combination here somewhere." General Stannard began fumbling through his vest pockets.

"No need." Garrett pointed to the gouge marks on the safe then moved the door back and forth on its hinges. "Empty. Someone was looking for something."

The two men stood in silence for a while—one of those silences peculiar to them, during which each tried to read the other's thoughts. Finally, the general spoke.

"You may be right. Oates is a dabbler, no grit or spine to finish anything. Lately he fancied himself a poker player. Only he kept losing, digging himself in deeper and deeper. Being such a prissy southern gentleman, he never would come right out and admit it. That is until I confronted him with the facts, here, in this very office. Laid it right out, everything Shoup told me. That's when he owned up to investing in the Lake View Vault Corporation." He watched Garrett probe under the fireplace mantel. "What are you doing?"

"Scouting." Garrett began dismantling a small bookcase. "So your partner fancies himself a high roller?"

"Doesn't make sense. Oates never goes outside his circle of friends for cards."

"And these friends let him accumulate enormous gambling losses.

Did he ever consider that maybe it wasn't a straight game? Maybe he swapped phony twenties for your real ones, when he started getting over his head in debt."

"I never got a chance to ask him anything more. We were to meet here earlier this week, to square things. He never showed."

Oates's investment in the Eastwood had put the reputation of the company at risk. If the public felt the slightest twinge of doubt, well... an insurance company is built on trust. The general shifted his weight from one foot to the other and stood silent for a moment. Suddenly he spoke.

"After a while you could get pretty tired of him. We kept our distance. It does make a person feel sad, though. I think the man could have amounted to something if he'd been raised right."

"You mean spent his life in the army?"

"He could've done worse," the general snapped, then walked back to his office.

Garrett continued his methodical search, concentrating on Oates's desk, pulling out drawers, then searching through papers as various thoughts went through his mind. Something was beginning to stir in his memory. An image of Oates appeared, a soft chubby man, with a haughty air, and his sudden look of panic as he tossed his card on the table. As if Oates had seen someone or something that frightened him.

If the Eastwood building was in trouble, why didn't General Stannard have it put right? He remembered that the general was a man born with an inspectoral eye, who rarely passed up an opportunity to exercise it. He'd built a successful military career based on his ability to evaluate a difficulty, find a solution, and then implement it. Whether coordinating troop movements, supplying men in the field, or planning a winter campaign, General Stannard could smell out trouble where it started. And he certainly never let anybody else bark orders when he could. But that had been the way he was eight years ago.

Garrett recalled a few occasions over the past several days when the general had seemed vague, lost. Maybe he was getting old? No. There had to be another reason. During their years together in the army, the old man always kept his contact with civilians to a minimum. Maybe he'd forgotten how to talk to regular people.

*Damn, something's stuck*. Garrett jiggled the drawer, reached in, and retrieved a thick packet. *Well, now, what have we here?* He began unfolding the documents, then stopped.

Over the years, Garrett had developed an instinct, a warning system. It wasn't much, just a series of faint signals that would suddenly appear. He learned to rely on them. So, when he sensed a presence, he slowly unbuttoned his coat, inched his hand backward, and felt for his holster. He was about to draw his gun when he heard a low, raspy voice.

"Did I not teach you, *mon ami*? Always watch your back."

"Otwah." Garrett whispered the name as he spun around.

"It does this old warrior's heart good to know he can still stomp on a dried branch covered with dead leaves two feet from your ear and you do not hear."

The two men stared at one another, grinning, then approached with measured strides. They threw their arms around each other and slapped backs hard enough to hurt the other's shoulders. They laughed and spoke in a mixture of quick gestures and short sentences.

♠

Garrett locked Oates's office and found the general at his desk with Otwah beside him. They were staring at the documents he'd found in Oates's desk.

"Stock certificates?" Otwah asked.

"No. U.S. government bonds," Garrett answered.

The general walked to his safe, opened it, pulled out some papers, and held them up. "They're twenty-year bonds issued during the war. Mary and I purchased these ones back in '62."

"Why would Oates hide bonds, *mon ami*?" Otwah asked.

Garrett smiled. "His are as worthless as those bank notes," he said, gesturing to the bills fanned across the general's desk. "Bet both of you a tenner."

The general glared. "These bonds look the same as mine."

"Look again. I'm not saying there's anything wrong with your bonds, General. But take a closer look at the ones we found in Oates's office. I'll spot you another ten the serial numbers are the same. Your bonds will have the numbers in sequence."

"First bad money, then bad bonds. I think they come from the same place, same person." Otwah waited a moment then added, "This partner of yours, where is he?"

"The gentleman did a bunk after sticking me with a worthless IOU," Garrett said. "I suspect that someone talked him into swapping his Lake View Vault shares for these bonds. Forsyth, over at Union Trust, told me someone else had acquired a big block. After a while, Oates must have realized the bonds were phony."

General Stannard looked both uncomfortable and angry, as men do when they don't quite believe something that they instinctively feel must be true. Without another word, he gathered up his own bonds, walked over, and returned them to his safe.

"The army reunion, it is soon. That is why I am here," Otwah whispered.

Garrett nodded, then lowered his voice. "Lot of veterans in town. And that—"

The general interrupted. "That means Phil Sheridan will be here with his entourage of toadies. My invitation arrived last week. I certainly plan to attend." He put his head back and wrinkled his nostrils like an animal sniffing the wind for danger. "Remember the itch behind the ears, the kind that used to come just before an Indian raid? I've been getting that itch. When I get these feelings, I listen to them. They're all out there, just circling, ready to attack. I know it."

Garrett and Otwah exchanged glances.

"Sir, those 'itches' of yours got both of us nearly scalped by more Apache and Cheyenne than we care to remember."

The general ignored the remark. "Too many things happening lately—to me, to Oates. I suspect that Phil Sheridan has some interest in Union Trust Bank."

Garrett remembered a rumor that had circulated at Fort Fetterman. Stannard and Sheridan attended West Point together and were roommates for a time. Two different personalities—one a plodder, the other all flash and dash. Some incident happened their last year and there'd been bad blood between them ever since.

"Sir, you still haven't answered my question."

"What question?" The old man narrowed his eyes and looked at Garrett closely.

"The one I asked when I first got here. Do we hire Josef Froelich to run the Eastwood site?"

Stannard gestured with his hand, as if he didn't give much credence to the question and was trying to erase it from the air. "As I recall, I put you in charge of the Eastwood project. You give the orders. Just come to a successful conclusion."

"Lyons, where are you staying?" Otwah asked.

"The Revere. I'm paid up 'til Saturday."

"Nonsense!" the general interrupted. "No use wasting money you don't have. Plenty of room in my new place. Otwah will move your things after dinner. It'll be like old times."

Garrett found himself wanting to smile. Instead, he forced his mouth into a more appropriate expression. The old man hadn't changed. His new house was as good a place as any. Besides, that way Garrett could keep an eye on the general, maybe see what he was really up to.

As they started to leave Stannard took an envelope from his pocket and handed it to Garrett.

"What's this?"

"What you asked for—a draft on the Central Casualty account at Union Trust Bank. Don't worry, it's good, I made sure. The man in charge at Union, Major Shoup, initialed it. He's Phil Sheridan's man. That means you can trust him just as far as I can spit. I suggest you redeem the draft soon."

# EIGHTEEN

*Chicago sits atop a quagmire of sand and clay, interspersed with pockets of water—a sort of "gumbo"—which could give way when a heavy weight is placed on top. It was the custom to set a building four or five inches above the level of the sidewalk, then slant the sidewalk up from the curb. Settlement would eventually bring the building to the desired level…most of the time. If the building did* not *settle, the façade crumbled or fell. If the building settled too much, it collapsed. By 1882 engineering designs had been developed that could address these problems. A ten-story building no longer presented a formidable challenge for the builder or architect. It was simply a matter of time—which architect would design, and which company would build, the first skyscraper?*

The faint, first rays of daylight filtered through the skeleton of the Eastwood building as Josef Froelich rolled off his makeshift cot. He sat for a moment, tried to focus, then reached for his pants. He struggled with the buttons, his fingers numb from the cold. Once dressed, he went outside and took in a deep breath.

The early morning air felt crisp. Sleeping overnight at the site was a good idea. He would be here when Lyons arrived. This field office wasn't much, but a darn sight better than a cramped six-to-a-room boarding house. Time was of the essence. And he was not a man to waste it.

*Ahhh, perfect, the sand is loose, easy to work. Insulate the concrete with some hay or straw and it'll cure slowly. So far, this is passable building weather.*

From the time Josef Froelich had dug his first trench, laid his first row of brick, he considered buildings to be living, breathing things. Not at first, mind you. A building had to grow brick by brick, stone by stone. As a building grew, every man who worked on it left a part of himself, until the time came when the building began to live, to breathe on its own. Josef Froelich could sense the precise moment this occurred. Right now the Eastwood was still an inert shell. But Froelich knew he was the man who could bring it to life, whatever it took.

*I will not let anyone…anything…stop me this time.*

The night before, as he sat alone inside the shed, he'd heard strange noises, not the usual sounds of stray dogs or rats. But, now that it was morning, when he looked around nothing seemed out of place. Theft at any building site was always a problem. Construction was booming in Chicago and materials were in short supply. Late night was the perfect time for crews to go "shopping."

*It's late in the season. The weather will turn soon. This building should be farther along. Not a good sign, materials stacked around untended, half used.*

Lyons had officially hired him late the previous afternoon. No surprise there. After all, the man had little choice in the matter. The job had to get done. And Lyons realized that he, Froelich, was the man to do it. They spent what was left of the afternoon walking the Eastwood construction site, which proved to be thirsty work. Afterward, they retired to Quinn's for refreshment. While there he wrote up his work order. Quinn was familiar with the foremen and the crews he favored.

Froelich checked his pocket watch. Hopefully Quinn was successful and the men would arrive soon. He reached into the back pocket of his trousers, removed a small notebook, and flipped through the pages. He began scratching notes with the nub of a pencil that he kept licking with the tip of his tongue. He heard a rumbling sound and looked toward the entrance. A wagon crammed with workmen was coming down the street at a steady gallop. The driver slowed his team to a trot, let five men jump off, then flicked his whip and immediately took off amid a slew of curses. Froelich waved. "Here, over here." He tore sheets of paper from his notebook and handed one to each of his foremen. There were nods, a few muttered comments.

Over the next half hour, singly and in groups, the regular workmen began filing into the site. His foremen organized the crews, handed out materials. Soon he heard the sounds of men moving, of machinery being oiled and tested, the slow hum of a construction site coming alive. Froelich smiled contentedly.

♠

A construction site at midday is like nothing on earth. Garrett might as well have been in the Siege of Vicksburg for all the noise, the stink from men, animals, and machines. He was standing off to one side, near the entrance, taking it all in, when he felt a hand grasp his arm.

"You Lyons?" a foreman bellowed in his ear. Garrett nodded. They did a quick sidestep as a laborer hurried past pushing a wheelbarrow. The man pointed toward the far end of the site. "Herr Froelich...office," was all Lyons heard.

The "office" was a makeshift shed with a pitched ceiling, plank walls, and one small window. Garrett shut the door and took a moment to catch his breath. There was little space to move around. It reminded him of the general's office at Fort Fetterman. From outside he could hear the deep rumble of steam-driven engines. *Sounds like artillery,* he thought, and the ping of rivets reminded him of the high chatter of musket fire.

A small wood stove in the corner seemed to be holding up one end of the building. A plank table covered with papers took up the center, along with two straight-back chairs. Josef Froelich was sitting on one of them. Next to him stood a tall, thin man with a way of holding himself that made him look as though he was standing under a low leaking roof on a wet day.

Froelich spoke. "This is Major Shoup. Tells me he's here on behalf of the Union Trust Bank."

Garrett leaned forward to shake the man's hand but lost the opportunity.

"Evidently Stannard thinks the Lake View Vault Corporation will be the first to put up a tall building." Shoup's voice sounded dry, crackling, as if he needed to gulp down a glass of water. "But the whole thing smells of day-old fish to me. That old fool is taking a big gamble investing Central Casualty's funds in Lake View. At Union Trust we don't cotton to bad investments. I'll be here daily, if need be, or send someone." He eyed Froelich. "So. . .Lyons here hired you to get this job on schedule. Just keep expenses down. No more problems at this site."

Froelich looked sideways at Garrett. "I plan to be here twenty-four hours a day. And Lyons will be available."

"I smell any trouble, I'll close you down. Saturday is half day. I'll be finished dispensing pay packets by one."

As the door closed behind Shoup, Froelich's face grew somber. "Someone has to be here at all times. I checked the site yesterday and again this morning. Nothing's missing, but I know someone was poking around last evening. Even if they ain't stealin', they're up to no good."

Garrett looked at him. There was no gleaning anything from his face. Garrett sensed Froelich was a man who could handle most anything that came his way, yet he sounded worried. "What are you saying?"

Froelich explained. "In construction, crews work a six-day week and a ten-hour day, Saturday being a half day. When Shoup hands out those pay envelopes, decisions will be made. Some men I keep on and some I let go."

"You expect trouble?"

"This past month I've heard rumors about the Eastwood. That's not unusual. Every newspaper in town prints a daily story on the buildings going up. Sometimes it's like adding kindling to fire. Even a hint that a certain vault company is shaky, or there are too many accidents at a site, and the vultures step in to feast on the carcass. Everyone is edgy. I could use another set of eyes and ears here."

Froelich kept staring out the window. The construction noise had come to a halt. "Look at that," he bellowed, pointing to a group of men idling near a pile of bricks. "They're worse than children. Don't move, or even think, 'til you tell 'em to." He opened the door and turned to Garrett. "We can talk again later."

♠

Later that afternoon a chill settled over the city, penetrating everyone and everything, turning the sidewalks dark and slippery. The wet metal framework of the Eastwood's third and fourth floors seemed black against a darkening sky.

Garrett found Froelich in the office, sitting at the table. The flame of a single oil lamp lit his face. He did not look up when Garrett shut the door. Instead, he focused his attention on the set of blueprints spread out in front of him. "How are things out there?" he asked between short quick puffs on his pipe.

"Seems quiet." Garrett leaned over the table into the light. He adjusted the lantern, studying the blueprints that were spread out, looking at the pencil lines Froelich had made. "What's your opinion? Can you get this done on time?"

Froelich reached down next to the stove and wrapped his hand around a bottle of whiskey. With the other he clamped two small glasses between his fingers, then turned and set the glasses on the table. "Join me? Something to take away the chill." He poured the whiskey.

"There are two groups of contractors in this town. The old school—good, experienced men—they know Chicago's building problems and give you a safe, practical answer within a blink of an eye. The second group are like myself. We can look architects—like your friend Sullivan, or Burnham—right in the eye and say, 'If you draw it, I'll build it.'" He raised his glass. "So, here's to the Eastwood, may she rise a full five floors to glory."

Garrett took a sip of the whiskey, held it on the back of his tongue, then swallowed. He cleared his throat and spoke slowly. "It's my understanding that the plan was for a ten-story office building."

Froelich pointed his glass at the blueprints. "A lot's missing—all the foundation plans for one thing. I see most of what's been built so far. But I don't know what was originally planned. A lot of changes are made in the field." There was a touch of contempt in his voice as he drained his glass.

"Answer my question...can this be done?"

"If it's ten floors you want, it's ten floors you'll get."

Froelich poured another round of drinks, then laid down his rules. "You listen, because this is the only way you'll get the Eastwood built. To start, I've taken on a forty-man crew. Forty is safe enough to get a good day's work done. More than that and you won't be safe from yourself. I don't hire any bad apples, no wheezers, and none of them rabble-rousers. I pay my crews eight cents an hour. That's more than fair. By the middle of the week I'll know how many more men I'll need. My job is to get this building framed up and sealed. And we don't have much time to do this. Like I said, I'm keeping costs under ten cents a cubic foot or your whole project'll go belly up."

He paused to see if Garrett had taken it all in, then leaned back in his chair and looked down at the floor. "Isn't that right, Bailey?"

Garrett saw a mangy dog emerge from under the table. The animal had a droopy ear and a scar along one side of its face.

"You need an extra set of eyes and ears? Looks like you already have one."

Wreathed in whiskey fumes, Froelich ignored Garrett's remark. "I figured to bring in more men for evenings. Help me keep an eye on things. You square it with that Shoup fellow." Then, with a remarkably steady hand, he poured the remains of Garrett's glass into his own.

♠

A burst of cold, damp air greeted Garrett as he left the Eastwood site. He shivered involuntarily and pulled his coat tightly around him. Chicago traffic was the usual chaotic battle of pedestrians crossing haphazardly between a jumble of carriages, broughams, and omnibuses.

He checked his pocket watch—nearly seven o'clock. Even though his body ached for a hot bath, he felt an even stronger need to unburden himself, to talk to someone who knew his mind. Charlotte was the one person who would listen and help him put his thoughts in order. Quickening his step, he turned the corner onto Franklin Street, and was about to signal a passing omnibus, when he heard someone call out his name.

"Lyons. You're still in the city. I'm not surprised."

He turned and saw Bill Pinkerton standing in front of a tobacco shop. Garrett spoke in what he hoped was a casual manner. "The last time we talked you mentioned some counterfeit bonds. You sure Brock wasn't the engraver?"

Pinkerton raised a questioning eyebrow. "My father always said counterfeiting is a crime of genius. I checked with some scratchers at the state prison. Those boys recognized the work straight off. And it definitely was *not* Brock's."

At that moment Rob Powers emerged from the tobacco shop. The reporter saw Garrett, and stepped warily to one side. Bill put his arm around Rob's shoulders. And, with a smug look on his face, asked, "Tell me, Lyons, do you believe in the power of the written word?"

Without waiting for an answer, he went on. "Well, I do. The *Inter Ocean* is printing Power's story about the warehouse explosion. What a grand story it is! How you single-handedly nabbed a notorious forger. How you entered a flaming building, at great risk to yourself, and salvaged crucial evidence. How you saved a critically injured man and transported him to the hospital. And how he gasped his final words to you before falling into a coma."

"The only items I found were those two packets. I turned all that over to you. Brock was never conscious after the explosion."

"'Course you did. But Brock's partners don't know that."

Garrett didn't like the way this conversation was going. "By the way, how is Brock? I still want a chance to talk to him."

Bill Pinkerton removed a cigar from his pocket. He turned to one side, away from the street, and waited while Powers struck a match and lit it. His otherwise pleasant voice grew a trifle sharper. "The poor man went under the knife yesterday. Unfortunately he is unable to receive visitors at this time." Pinkerton tipped his hat in a mock salute and walked off.

Powers started to follow, but Garrett grabbed his arm.

"You still nosing around for news?"

"Look, my warehouse story is in the pressroom as we speak."

"What if I give you a better one?" As Garrett leaned forward, Powers instinctively pulled back. "An exclusive story, what I'm really doing here in Chicago...in exchange—"

"For what?" Rob asked.

"Information...on a regular basis. Yes, or no?"

"That depends."

"On what?"

Rob took in a deep breath and swallowed hard. "There's a building going up at Monroe Street, near Dearborn, called the Montauk. A reporter I know at the *Herald* is writing his own column with daily progress reports. And the *Herald* is selling a lot of papers." He continued with a steady stream of words, afraid to stop. "I convinced my editor, Mr. Hosty, that the *Inter Ocean* should do a series of articles about the Eastwood. I told him I'm the person to pen these stories, since I know the man in charge, namely you. It's an even trade."

Garrett released Power's arm and thought a moment. "All right. First, find out what you can about a Shelby Oates. He's—"

"A partner at Central Casualty Insurance." Powers reached inside his coat pocket and extracted a small notepad. "Where do I find you?"

Garrett hesitated. Best not give out the general's new address. "You're the reporter, you find me. Remember, keep your pencil sharp and don't write the ending to this story 'til I tell you to."

# NINETEEN

*Peter Brooks lived in Boston, where he made his fortune in shipping, but saw his future in Chicago. Since he seldom came to the city he hired local attorney Owen Aldis to be the agent for his first purchase, the Portland Block. Built in 1872 and designed by William Le Baron Jenney, this six-story building stood on the southeast corner of Washington and Dearborn Streets. Brooks approached his next project with single-mindedness and daring. He wanted to build Chicago's first "skyscraper." So he commissioned the ten-story Montauk Block. However, Brooks instructed Aldis that he wanted the most value for his money, and that a building was intended for use, not for ornament. In order to comply with these dictates Aldis hired the firm of Burnham and Root.*

Mike McDonald stood at the second-floor window of his office and stared at the scene below. Chicago's streets presented a more sober, depressing sight in daylight. Last evening's rain had dirtied everything, leaving dark traces on the façades of buildings, turning their colors ugly. Suddenly he felt tired, as if all the energy had been drained from his body.

*Long nights and early mornings will be the death of me yet*, he thought, as he sat down at his desk and took a long gulp of coffee from the mug in his hand.

After the Great Fire—when members of Chicago's gambling community moved their residences from "Gamblers Row" to fancy areas like Drexel Avenue—McDonald stayed put. While they built elegant homes King Mike consolidated his empire. Those were the years when the lines were still being drawn, when nobody held a place without pushing someone out. And, if a man fucked up, he paid the price. Mike knew, even then, that if he spent his money lavishly or trusted too many people he would never live to be an old man. The more links in a chain, the weaker it is. Until this past year he'd felt comfortable, almost content, living in the private rooms on the fourth floor of his gambling emporium.

He leaned back and closed his eyes. An image of that mansion on Drexel Avenue appeared. A gentleman's life could be within his grasp. Over the past few months these thoughts had become more frequent. The moment McDonald had met Mrs. Reid he immediately made it his business to learn as much as he could about the attractive widow.

In Mike McDonald's world knowledge could be bought. He was suitably impressed by the top-drawer gambling reputation she'd acquired out West. In Chicago Charlotte kept her business confined to the Lotus Club gambling nights and select private games. He admired that. These present arrangements were evidently profitable and enabled her to live comfortably at Eldridge Court. She was a woman of refinement and good taste, he told himself. It was no wonder that moneyed men, gentlemen of influence, wished to play cards at her table. Mike McDonald wanted to provide that table.

Busy with these thoughts, he almost failed to hear his office door close. He sat upright and found himself looking at McGlynn, who reeked of stale beer and clutched a battered felt hat.

"You wanted to see me?" he asked sheepishly.

McDonald pointed to a chair at the farthest corner of his desk. He pulled open a drawer, removed a bottle of whiskey, and poured a shot into his coffee. At the same time he placed a roll of currency on the desktop. He stared at McGlynn and waited a few moments before he spoke. When he did, his words held an unmistakable warning.

"Life is hard, Ed, but it's one hell of a lot harder when you're stupid. Tell me straight out, what have you been up to?"

"Don't know what you mean. I always play it straight, Mike, you know that." Ed looked at the roll of bills on the desk. "I paid you up front, fair and square."

"These twenty-dollar bills you've been handing around are phony. They may look near perfect, but they're bogus just the same. Knew that all the time, didn't you?"

McDonald kept his tone quiet. Less a reproach, more like a question from a friend. He kept staring at McGlynn, watching him squirm—not so much interested in what the man said, as how he said it. Scaring people was easy. What was hard? Making them fear you little by little. Letting the fear seep in that would keep them awake at night. Then fear became respect. If he had to choose, Mike McDonald felt that it was better to be respected than liked.

"Pinkerton's men passed out flyers—looking for this Brock fella. Seems he's a master forger. They promised a fat reward for anyone with information."

The blood rushed scarlet to McGlynn's face and then, after a moment of terrible silence, fled, leaving him pasty white. "Swear to God, Mike, I thought the bills were real. Don't suppose you'd let me pay it back, whenever—"

"First, tell me more about your adventure at that warehouse on Monday. *Why* were you there? *Who* was with you? *What* happened? And none of your excuses."

As Mike listened to Ed recount his meeting with Lyons, the warehouse explosion, and the subsequent transportation of Brock to the hospital, he looked out the window and, as always, kept his thoughts to himself.

McGlynn's breathing came in short gasps as he concentrated on his every word. "That's all I know, Mike. Honest. What can I do to make it right?"

McDonald stubbed out his cigar and looked at his empty mug. "You say this Lyons fellow is managing the Eastwood site? Well, now you go and get yourself a job there."

"Doing what?" McGlynn looked perplexed.

"I don't care what. But you, my lad, will be my eyes and ears. Report only to me. I want to know everything about that building and this Garrett Lyons. Understand?"

"Sure, sure, Mike. When do I start?"

"When do you think?"

♠

Charlotte watched as the elderly gentleman sitting behind the desk consulted a large maroon ledger spread out in front of him. After a few moments she politely forced a smile and said, "I don't think you heard me, Mr. Danforth. The Lotus Club is a long-standing client of the Tremont House and, as such, deserves consideration. I have merely requested *two* gaming rooms. I was told that this had been arranged with your assistant."

For this occasion Charlotte had carefully dressed in a suit of dark brown velvet decorated with frog clasps and with Garrett's cameo pinned to the lapel. She studied Danforth's face and knew she had his full attention. If truth be told, Charlotte didn't care one way or the other. That was not the purpose of this visit. What she wanted was information. Iris's recent visit and her conversations with Garrett had rekindled a long-buried curiosity regarding Augustus Reynolds. In particular, his gaming habits and their relationship to his business ventures.

"I *am* listening, Mrs. Reid." Danforth's words were rich with the sort of pious sincerity she associated with politicians and priests. "But, with the Grand Army reunion next week, our resources are stretched to the limit. And, yes, I know the Tremont has always kept its third floor available for private functions. However, these salons have already been booked. I hope you will bear with us."

"*All* of the salons? The Grand Army is only a temporary guest at this establishment. We have used your facility every Monday evening for nearly a year. Who booked them?"

Milford Danforth crossed his hands, interlacing his fingers.

"Of course I can't tell you. Client loyalty will not permit it. However, you can assure the Lotus Club that their regular room will be available for them this Monday. You have my word."

Charlotte allowed herself a brief smile, then said, "I will endeavor to make sure our members are satisfied with that. And, now, I feel the need for that glass of sherry you graciously offered earlier."

"Mrs. Reid, it will be my pleasure." Danforth's voice was an ingratiating whisper. He rose from his chair and left the room.

As soon as the door closed Charlotte walked round the desk and began leafing through the ledger. She paged back until she found the list of private third-floor gaming rooms. She began checking dates and names. There was no mistake. Reynolds held regular private card games. She rechecked again and looked at the expense list and noted one item in particular. She allowed herself a brief, bitter smile, then closed the ledger.

The wall clock chimed four, the door opened, and a waiter carrying a silver tray holding a decanter and crystal glasses walked across the threshold, followed by Danforth and Mike McDonald. For no apparent reason she could fully understand Charlotte found herself patting her purse to feel the shape of the derringer inside.

McDonald pulled up a chair, bowed slightly, and sat down next to Charlotte. If she was surprised to see him she did not show it. "Good afternoon, Mrs. Reid." He turned and looked at Danforth. "I was just informed there's been a miscommunication. Like any good businessman wishing to be ahead of the game I made arrangements to secure the hotel's facilities for the week."

His jaw tightened. He removed a cigar from his vest pocket, then lit it. Assured of her attention McDonald continued. "I was never informed by the Tremont staff that Mrs. Reid requested the use of an additional gaming room for Monday." He continued staring at Danforth to see if the man had grasped the full implication of his words. And indeed he had.

Charlotte could readily see that Milford Danforth was a man whose loyalties had just become conflicted by people and events over which he had little control. He wisely chose not to press the matter. Instead, he rose from his seat, then deftly poured sherry into the glasses. He handed one to Charlotte, another to McDonald, and finally took one himself. He raised his glass and said, "Be assured that the Tremont House is more than willing to make the necessary accommodations for both of you." Charlotte graciously raised her glass and smiled in return.

McDonald leaned over and spoke softly. "If you need any additional dealers for any other games during the reunion be sure to let me know."

His words were so unexpected that Charlotte didn't answer for a moment and her face lost its trained mask of politeness. She finished her sherry in one swallow, stood up and turned to Danforth.

"Since I have your assurance that we will have use of our regular room I am more than satisfied." She looked at McDonald. "However, I do appreciate your kind offer. Good day, gentlemen." She glanced at the clock, then left the room.

♠

Garrett walked east on Calhoun Place, barely keeping pace with the late afternoon crowd. The number of people on Chicago streets constantly amazed him, like herds of deer running nowhere. When he reached Dearborn he turned north, walked a few yards and stopped. He realized that—other than being hell bent on finding an omnibus or any means of conveyance—he didn't know where he was going.

Otwah had moved his belongings from the Revere Hotel to the general's new house, a quiet place located north of the river. Garrett didn't mind bunking there. The price was right and it was still relatively close to the business district. He could keep an eye on the general *and* be close enough to visit Brock. Over the last few days he'd spent most of his time at the Eastwood site, leaving early and returning late. He found himself looking forward to his visits. He knew that if he was in the house General Stannard would put him to work sorting the boxes from storage. This was not the time, nor was he in the mood, to unpack a lot of memories. Right now what he wanted was a double whiskey, so he looked up and down the street for an appropriate venue until he spotted one.

He pushed open the front door of the Tremont House and a wall of conversation assaulted him. The hotel lobby was filled to capacity. He eased his way through the crowd and soon found himself overwhelmed by the heavy aroma of whiskey and tobacco. In addition to the usual salesmen and business travelers he saw a large delegation of U.S. Army officers. Groups of them were huddled in corners, while others had positioned themselves in the center of the room. He noticed that most were loud-voiced young men wearing crisply tailored uniforms. These men of the new army were busy waving big cigars and proclaiming grand ideas with the mindless flourishes of those who will share no responsibility for them. Garrett stopped, half listened to one such speech, felt uncomfortable, and moved on. He did manage to make eye contact with some older officers he remembered, but received no nods of recognition.

He was about to enter the bar when something made him turn around. For one awful moment the scene in the lobby held him. His jaw tightened and he felt a sudden wave of melancholy. He looked at the uniforms, heard the voices, and realized that a part of him still missed all that camaraderie from the old days. Then he remembered the general's words, spoken at dinner the evening before. "A man can't spend too long remembering what he was, or he'd take a closer look at what he's become." He still felt the need of a whiskey, but suddenly regretted this choice of venue. He started to leave and spied a woman walking quickly though the lobby toward the front door. It was Charlotte. Garrett quickened his step, came up beside her, and put his hand on her shoulder.

Charlotte spun around. She took a deep breath and let it out very slowly.

He smiled, hoping to see her smile in return. When she did, he asked, "And what is a lovely lady like yourself doing in this mad house?"

"I've just completed the final arrangements to fleece them out of their money." She gestured toward the sea of uniforms crowding the lobby. "It's exhausting work. What are you doing here?"

"*I'm* thirsty and looking for a whiskey. Only this is not the place."

"I agree. I'm looking for a hansom."

"And you shall have one. Wait here."

Garrett turned on his heel and walked through the entrance, straight to the curb, waving to attract the next hansom that passed. When one stopped, he returned, took Charlotte's arm and escorted her out the door.

She looked up at Garrett. "I know a nice quiet place where you can secure a whiskey. We have a lot to discuss."

# TWENTY

*In 1881 and 1882 the firm of Adler and Sullivan had a number of commercial buildings under construction in Chicago, including the Jewelers Building, five stories high, at 15 South Wabash Avenue; the Rothschild Store, five stories high, with a cast-iron front, at 210 West Monroe Street; and the Revell, six stories high, at the corner of Adams Street and Wabash Avenue. These buildings exhibited a radical departure from the conventional masonry architecture. To achieve maximum interior light, Sullivan's designs narrowed the piers, thus widening the open span of the window bays. Isolated stone footings carried the weight of the piers and interior columns. Thus the offices had more interior light and space. According to Louis Sullivan, no other city had warehouses and offices designed with such architectural nobility.*

Garrett's chance meeting with Charlotte had resulted in a delicious dinner, good whiskey, and a long conversation that evening at Eldridge Court. After hearing of Bernard's experience at the Alexian Brothers Hospital, any plans Garrett had to see Brock were postponed. The next day Charlotte sent him back to the general's house with baskets of food and Ada, claiming the general needed a day girl, even a temporary one, until he settled in.

"She'll come three days a week to help with the housework until you and General Stannard get settled. I can't send Eulah, she's getting too old." He remembered her smile when she said, "Then

I'll be able to keep you informed about my progress on our case."

Garrett was skeptical about Charlotte's self-appointed role as his "partner," preferring to work alone. In any case, on Monday he was up at dawn and arrived at the Eastwood site along with the work crews. Now he was sitting in the office, next to the stove, trying to get warm. He took his pistol apart, cleaned it, and started reassembling the weapon. This gave his hands something to do while his mind reviewed the events of the past week.

As a general thing, two serious bits of trouble seldom arrived on the same train. Over the years Garrett had learned that destiny, although not the kindest of mistresses, usually gave him time to clear up one mess before shoving him into another. Still, after almost two weeks in this city, there were a couple of things that wouldn't leave him alone.

The first was finding Sam's killer. "Why waste time searching for Brock's partners? Just let them come looking for you," were Bill Pinkerton's very words. Then Bill told him that Brock *didn't* murder Sam. If he didn't, who did? Had he made a hasty decision? It was vital that he speak to the man again. Maybe Brock *hadn't* killed Sam. But he knew or saw something, Garrett was sure of that.

The second was the IOU from Oates that led to the reunion with General Stannard and, from there, to the Eastwood site. "This job will take just a few weeks of your time," were the old man's very words. How was the general involved in all this? Garrett's gut told him the two situations might be connected. Right now, though, nothing made sense. He felt that if he kept shuffling these thoughts around, sooner or later he would find the key that linked them together.

The incessant sound of hammering and pounding, and the hissing and thumping of machinery outside, formed a background to his thoughts. Garrett did not hear the door open but immediately sensed a presence. He spun around and drew his pistol.

"Whoa!" Sullivan hollered, as he held up his hands.

"What are you doing here?"

"Remember? I visit the Eastwood site and you attend Drake's game dinner. I always make good on IOUs." Louis returned Garrett's stare.

"Our client Mr. Reynolds asked for an appointment this morning. Adler felt it would be prudent for me to absent myself. So I decided to check the progress of our designs now under construction in the city. I finished and now I'm here." He snatched a set of blueprints and spread them across the table. "Let's see what we have." He adjusted the papers and stared at the maze of lines.

"What do you think?" Garrett asked.

"Anything is possible, if a client is willing to spend the money. A ten-story building, if it ever comes to be, would prove profitable. Building tall is not a problem, but building safe on Chicago soil is. A tall building, one that scrapes the sky, has never been done before. I'm skeptical to say the least."

"You were born skeptical."

"These all the plans you have? This isn't much." Sullivan stepped over to the window and began studying the construction site with his expert eye. "Heard you've had some problems. What does Froelich have to say?"

"I'll be spending more time here than I figured."

Louis sighed. "Well, as long as I'm here, suppose I take a look around." He walked out the door.

Garrett followed, trailing him through clouds of dust. Crews were unloading wagons, mixing concrete, and hauling bricks. Garrett recognized the sounds—men working with their backs. Sullivan set a brisk pace, climbing a series of wooden ladders on the scaffolding up to the fourth floor of the Eastwood, then following a boardwalk until he reached the front of the building. When Garrett finally caught up, his breathing was loud and labored. He put his hands on the railing and leaned forward, gasping for air.

"What a view." Sullivan spread his arms wide in a dramatic Moses-on-the-Mount pose.

At this height the construction noise was somewhat subdued. However, a sudden gust of wind brought the dust and the smell of men and animals upward. Garrett began to cough. Sullivan shot him a brief glance. "Join the Lotus Club rowing team. We meet every Sunday at the boathouse in Lincoln Park. You need to keep fit if you work in the construction business."

Garrett ignored the remark and looked down at the site. Everything seemed the same—the noise, the general confusion. He spotted Froelich. The man wasted no speech or motion as he kept wagons moving in one direction, brick masons and carpenters in another. His actions reminded Garrett of the general, the way the old man used to position himself at the far edge of the battle and command his troops.

Sullivan kept up a steady stream of conversation, pointing out the different trades, giving brief descriptions of the work to be done and in what order. In a far corner of the site, near the entrance, he pointed out a line of men waiting for the grinder to sharpen their tools. Closer to them, groups of boys moved at a brisk trot, carrying pails of water between the masons, carpenters, and laborers.

One redheaded man in particular looked familiar. Garrett tried to place him in his mind and kept an eye on the red hair as it moved from one group of workmen to another. Then Garrett remembered—he'd seen the man at the bar near the warehouse. He was the rabble-rousing orator, who extolled the virtues of the Sons of Labor. Garrett watched the man zigzag his way through the site then into a supply shed near the entrance, exit it, then disappear underneath the scaffolding.

For a long moment Sullivan seemed lost in thought. Then he turned and said, "Lyons, do you realize that every great building you see in this city is the image of a man who you do not see? It is the image, the idea, the soul of a man, like myself, who designed it."

"Let's talk about *this* building. What's your opinion?"

Louis gave him a disdainful look. "Froelich is knowledgeable. Adler tells me the man is obsessive, totally committed to his projects." A gust of air surged upward, carrying with it the stench of construction. Sullivan made a face. "Time for lunch. I want to leave before I lose my appetite. We'll get a good pint and a decent spread at Quinn's."

Garrett felt queasy. The only food in his stomach was Ada's breakfast porridge. It was still there, like a block of cement. "I'm ready for lunch."

Their exit, across boards and down various ladders, was slower than their ascent had been. Sullivan kept up a steady monologue on the merits of different types of brick. Midway, one of the masons tipped his cap to him. Louis stopped, shook his hand, then turned to Garrett and described the talent needed to lay a perfect row. Garrett thought, *You're as obsessive about buildings as Froelich.*

Sullivan continued his dissertation on mortar then stopped mid-sentence. His hand was on the scaffolding. "Did you feel that?"

"What?"

Sullivan put his other hand on the scaffold, waited a moment, then spoke calmly. "See that knife sharpener by the gate? Last one there buys lunch. And I'm running!"

He took off, jumping down the steps two at a time. Garrett followed close on his heels. The instant they reached the ground they heard a loud CRACK! The sound was followed by another, then another in rapid succession. The ground shook. The scaffolding quivered, then fell to the ground with a thunderous crash.

♠

The dust was thick as fog. As it cleared Garrett could see a pile of lumber and stone where the scaffolding had stood. He quickly retraced his steps, pushing through the gathering crowd of workers, following shouts of "Anyone hurt?" and "What happened?"

"Out of the way! Out of the way!"

Garrett used his voice with cold, calculated effect. He became the officer in command, authority in the flesh. The workmen stepped back, letting him pass. He saw two men stranded out on a beam at the third floor of the building. Another man hung precariously from remnants of the wood scaffolding.

"All right now…back to work…nothing to worry about." Froelich's voice boomed loud and reassuring.

Men carrying ladders and ropes came running at a fast trot from all areas of the site. They positioned the ladders against the wall and pitched the ropes upward. On the third level two shirtless men leaned over, caught a rope and attached it to a column. Then, with a final groaning heave, they began pulling their stranded co-worker to safety.

Everyone—workers, foremen—was surprisingly calm. Garrett wondered if accidents like this were a regular occurrence. Froelich pointed to a small fire at one end of the pile of brick and lumber. He shouted, "Douse that, before the horses get spooked."

Garrett circled one side of the debris, Sullivan the other, both men looking for the trapped or injured. Midway around, Garrett spied McGlynn rushing past carrying a pail of water. "Can't stay out of trouble, can you?"

Ed stopped in his tracks, recognized Garrett and flinched. He struggled for words. "I ain't got nothin' to do with this. I'm just a runner for one of the grinders."

A vivid picture flashed through Garrett's memory—the rabble-rouser at the bar last Monday evening, then the explosion at the warehouse. Was McGlynn a member of the Sons of Labor?

"The big surprise is finding you doing manual labor." Garrett brought his hand up, palm out, and hit McGlynn in the chest, knocking him back. "I want some answers."

Drops of sweat appeared on McGlynn's forehead. He wasn't a coward. But he did like to work both sides of the street. He only double-crossed a little, less for the money than for the thrill of living on the edge. "Lieutenant, you know me. Always got my ear to the ground. Let me square things."

"Lyons, over here! Someone's trapped," Sullivan shouted, pointing to a jumbled pile of lumber and bricks.

"You I'll deal with later," Garrett said to McGlynn over his shoulder as he made his way over to two burly teamsters who were levering the rubble apart with metal rods. After a long five minutes, they were able to drag the man out.

"Leg...leg," he moaned in a thick Teutonic accent. His pant leg was slick with blood.

Froelich took a kerchief from his pocket and twisted it around the man's thigh, just above the wound. The bleeding slowed. A workman ran up, carrying something that looked like the door from the coal shed. "Make a decent enough litter. Take him to the field office and send someone for Hampson," Froelich said. Then he shouted, "All right, back to work. We're behind already."

"This man you sent for…is he a doctor?" Garrett asked.

"Hampson served in the war, got captured, and learned the trade at Libby Prison. He's the closest thing to a doc you'll see this part of town."

The injured man's breath moved in and out, catching whenever a spasm of pain shot through him, but he didn't cry out. The workmen reached the office, angled the litter through the doorway, and set it down on the floor. Froelich picked up the man's hand and turned it over, palm up. "He's not a brickie."

"He sure as hell ain't with the trades I'm runnin'," a foreman answered.

At that moment a short, thin man, wearing a too-large wool coat and carrying a black leather satchel, arrived. "Doc" Hampson spoke softly. "Alright, let me take a look at him."

Garrett took Froelich's arm and pulled him aside. "If that man isn't part of your crews, what's he doing here?"

"Causing trouble. Happens too often, at this site and others around town." Froelich lowered his voice to a whisper. "Look, a site…like the Eastwood…gets targeted. First materials go missing, not a lot, but enough to slow down the job, then come the accidents. In construction there are always accidents, only now it's a regular occurrence. A building gets a reputation. Crews quit. Work slows. Then someone waltzes in and buys up everything for pennies."

"Who's behind this?" Garrett asked.

"Wish I knew."

Meanwhile, the injured man was shouting what sounded like curses, his voice rising to a shriek whenever the pain grew worse. Froelich, Sullivan, and Garrett moved next to the door, giving the man as much distance as they could in such a tight space.

Doc Hampson stood up. He'd cut away the man's trousers and put a temporary bandage over the gaping hole in his thigh. A clean white rag was knotted loosely above the wound, the ends left out for quick tightening. "It's broke alright. And it's bad."

"What're you saying?" Froelich asked.

Hampson's face darkened. "I'm saying I can't piece those slivers back together here. That leg should come off. Gangrene travels fast. It'll start mortifying by tomorrow. Take it off now or he'll need a shovel, not a doctor."

"You ain't cutting here. Go over to St. Stephen's. Let the nuns tend him," Froelich growled. "You can move him when the shift ends."

"How soon is that?" Hampson asked.

"Hour or so."

"Then get the laudanum and the whiskey in my bag."

"Is that a good idea, Doc? Mixing drink with laudanum can kill a man," Garrett said.

"There are worse ways to die. Besides, the whiskey's for me."

Suddenly, the injured man lifted his head and began moaning words. Sullivan spoke for him. "He wants to know if Doc's going to cut. He loses a leg, he won't find work."

"Let the Sons of Labor whittle him a new one...if he lives," Froelich responded.

The injured man wasn't listening. His back was arched and his mouth worked, moving air in and out in shallow breaths.

"I've seen surgeons cut off arms and legs close to a hundred times during the war," Garrett said. "Maybe thirty of those men lived. It wasn't the gangrene, the loss of blood, or even the fever. They all got that. Thing is, they just gave up."

"Then why bother?" Froelich muttered.

Garrett glared at him. When he spoke his voice was quiet but firm. "I asked the surgeons the same question. Why bother? They told me that it wasn't their job to stand by and watch a man die if they could help. Now if it wasn't theirs, then it sure as hell isn't ours."

A lamp hissed on the table. Froelich looked down at the injured man, then at Garrett. "I'll get the teamsters to bring a wagon around."

Sullivan tapped Garrett on the shoulder and whispered, "There's nothing more we can do here. Let's get some lunch."

# TWENTY-ONE

*Following instructions from Peter Brooks, Owen Aldis purchased a lot on the north side of Monroe Street, between Dearborn and Clark. Thus construction began on the Montauk Block. Brooks preferred a plain structure of at least eight stories, hopefully ten, with a basement and a flat roof. Still, Brooks was no pinchpenny builder. The money he saved by eliminating what he called "gimcrackery" allowed many new engineering designs to be incorporated into the Montauk—cast iron for interior columns and wrought iron floor beams, all set on a unique spread foundation.*

The line at Quinn's bar was three deep. A loud undercurrent of conversation ebbed and flowed around shouts of "Whiskey here," or "Fill 'er again," from the lunch crowd. Regular customers were engaged in their daily polemics about the lack of jobs and skilled labor. Young boys scurried in and out, carrying pails filled with beer back to construction sites. All this noise and movement reminded Garrett of an election party that had lasted two days too long.

Sullivan greeted Quinn with a cursory nod and edged his way toward a group of tables set up in an alcove at the rear of the room. Along the way he stopped and spoke to, or shook hands with, a variety of tradesmen. Garrett realized that one of the remarkable things about Sullivan was his ability to function at all levels of Chicago society. Louis was fluent in French, German, and Italian but also in some universal tongue, derived from half a dozen root words. This talent enabled him to converse in a multitude of dialects.

Quinn walked to their table holding two steins of beer in one hand and a pitcher of the brew in the other. Garrett took his stein and drained the contents. Sullivan did the same. He wiped his mouth with a clean white handkerchief retrieved from his suit pocket, then leaned forward near Garrett and spoke in an undertone, letting the activities of the saloon continue around them.

"During the general confusion after the accident, I did some investigating." He reached into a vest pocket and removed a piece of metal, which he placed on the table.

Garrett turned it over in his hand. "Where did you find this?"

"Underneath the poor bastard we pulled from the rubble."

At that moment, Quinn arrived at the table carrying plates heaped with beef, boiled potatoes, and gravy. He deposited the food with a grand gesture.

Sullivan raised his fork in salute. "As usual, Quinn, the beef looks cooked to perfection."

Quinn wiped his hands on the towel wrapped around his waist, then picked up the piece of metal. "This from the Eastwood? So, you had a blasting accident then?"

"Why do you ask?"

"Because that's an Irishman's job. Only kind a Mick can get nowadays. It keeps food on his table if he works hard and stays lucky." He stared at Garrett. "This morning one of your foremen came running in to fetch Hampson. The doc ain't back yet." Quinn looked over his shoulder at the bar. "So…a blasting accident. Well, now that puts a different light on things."

"What's he talking about?" Garrett asked.

"The pool!" Sullivan's words were sandwiched between mouthfuls of beef. "See that framed slate back of the bar? It gives the weekly betting odds on all the buildings under construction in the city, including the Eastwood."

Quinn explained. "The letters on the left stand for the buildings under construction. Now the letters EC, that's your site. The numbers are today's odds. First column is thefts, the second for accidents, and the last is a total collapse, which is not too rare these days."

Garrett counted ten buildings on the board. The Eastwood was at the top. The odds did not look favorable.

"Saturday I pay the winners. Then we start a new round. 'Course the house always bets against anything happening." At that moment a noisy argument ensued at the far end of the bar. "Damn, it's too early for this." Quinn left to quell the disturbance.

Sullivan emptied his stein then raised his voice a little in order to make himself heard above the noise. "That injured man was Belgian."

"Belgians, Swedes, Krauts, does it make a difference?" Garrett asked.

"Yes, it does. Belgians specialize in carpentry and plaster work. They're not comfortable with blasting materials, which was painfully evident."

"What did the *Belgian* have to say?"

Sullivan nodded toward the entrance of the saloon. "Why don't you ask Froelich? He understood every word the man said, even though he didn't let on."

Froelich was standing in the doorway. He spied Sullivan and began walking toward their table. On the way he exchanged a meaningful look with Quinn, who raised an eyebrow, then erased the numbers next to the Eastwood. Froelich sat down and signaled for another pitcher. He spoke as he poured. "Before you ask, that poor soul is with the nuns at St. Stephen's. Hampson says his odds are fifty-fifty."

"How did he get onto the Eastwood site?" Garrett asked.

"Probably came in with the day labor."

"Can you find out who sent him?"

Froelich shook his head. "Don't think he'll last the night."

"Are there any more of his ilk at the site?" Sullivan asked.

"Can't take the chance. I'm hiring some extra muscle. Lyons here can see we're paid. Just tell that bank fella, Shoup. It'll be worth the cost."

They finished their meal and drank their beer in silence, each man following his own train of thought. Occasionally Garrett or Sullivan would stare at a person or object in the bar as if seeking support or an answer to a silent question. Froelich sat uncomfortably, staring straight ahead. He was not a companionable man and whatever his thoughts were he was disinclined to share them. He finished first and stood up.

"Best get back." He looked at Garrett. "I figure this evening should be quiet. But if you stop by, get there before dark."

Garrett and Sullivan left Quinn's mid-afternoon, after the consumption of another pitcher of beer to aid their digestion. This had become a day of quickly traveling clouds, sunlight switching on and off, and cool currents of air blowing in from Lake Michigan, breathing hints of winter only weeks away. Even so, Louis insisted they detour past Monroe Street, since he wished to monitor the progress of a building under construction.

"I'd like to see what Burnham is up to these days." After they walked around the Montauk site he promptly dismissed the building as being "dull as dishwater and downright ugly as well." However, he suggested that Garrett compare that building's progress to the Eastwood. "See if Froelich can deliver. Helps to know where you stand." They continued walking toward the Borden Block with little or no conversation. When they reached the entrance of the building, Louis broke the silence. "An extra gun wouldn't hurt."

"What do you mean?"

"What I'm saying is…I'm willing to lend assistance. Admit it, Lyons. You could use some help."

"You mean *you* don't want to miss out on any excitement. Tell me, how many shooting lessons have you had? Two? Three? Remember the first thing I taught you?"

"Yes. 'Never draw your gun unless you are prepared to use it,'" Sullivan intoned. "And I've been practicing."

"Have any of those practice targets been moving or capable of returning fire?" Garrett put a hand on his shoulder and, as an afterthought, said, "Look, there is something you *can* do. Find out what lots around the Eastwood site have been sold this past year and who's been buying them."

Sullivan cast him a disdainful look. "That's all?"

"It will help. It doesn't look like we'll learn anything from that Belgian." Garrett took the piece of metal from his pocket. "I agree with Froelich, he was there to make trouble."

"Well, then ask yourself—trouble for who?"

Garrett fingered the metal. "This wouldn't bring down the Eastwood. A man would need more charges, more time and planning. Even I can figure that out."

"Correct. I would say this is a spur of the moment type accident. Agreed? He was not aiming at the building, but the scaffolding. And who was on the scaffolding?"

"Beside you and me? Just a few workmen."

Sullivan smiled. "Well, *I* haven't an enemy in the world."

"Mine wouldn't go to that much trouble. They'd just as soon put a bullet in my back." Garrett shook his head. "Froelich was right. This could be just the beginning. Someone wants this property and won't stop 'til he gets it."

♠

It was ten minutes to five when Garrett walked through the door of Central Casualty Insurance. The clerks were making half-hearted efforts to look busy, keeping one eye on their ledgers and the other on the clock. Garrett found General Stannard sitting at his desk. He closed the door with a gentle click and noticed the general hurriedly return the cameo he was fingering to his vest pocket.

"Well, Lyons, report. How is the construction business?"

"In Chicago, I'd say good. At the Eastwood, not so good."

Garrett settled himself in a chair and reviewed the events that had occurred since that morning at breakfast. The general listened without comment. If he had an opinion he gave no indication, beyond the smoothing of his finger over the palm of his hand.

"Could *you* have been the target of this accident?"

Garrett shook his head. "Froelich tells me this has happened at other sites. Evidently someone doesn't want that building to get finished.

When it goes belly up they can buy it cheap. We're both certain whoever it is will probably try again."

"What do you think of that Mr. Froelich? Can he get the job done for us?"

"Remember Fort Mesa? I bought a mustang from that half-breed Apache?"

The old man nodded.

"Froelich's a lot like that horse. Don't trust the man, but I need him to get where I'm going. All the while, I figure he'll throw me first chance he gets."

The general chuckled, then his face assumed a more solemn air. He closed his eyes and seemed to retreat into himself. After a moment he looked up and focused again on Garrett. "I had a visitor today. I believe he's an acquaintance of yours—William Pinkerton."

"What did he want?"

"A number of things. First he informed me that a gentleman's body was discovered last evening at a burned-out warehouse near the river. He wanted confirmation the body was that of my missing partner, Mr. Shelby Oates."

Garrett didn't respond, but listened intently. Stannard continued, his voice a mere whisper. "Pinkerton did point out that the body was placed there *after* the fire. He evidently wanted to assure me that, had it been there earlier, his agents would have found it when they searched the warehouse after the blaze you probably started."

The general took a cloth bag from his lap, slowly untied it and let the contents fall into a neat pile on top of his desk. "These items were found on the body. Most of them belonged to Oates. This was found in his vest pocket." The general handed Garrett a folded sheet of paper. Then he cleared his throat and sat back again, not looking at his former lieutenant. "What do you make of it?"

Garrett read the words aloud, "Nine o'clock, Lotus Club, Tremont House. Garrett Lyons." He handed the note to the general. "Look, sir, I never met your partner before that poker game."

"Figured as much." The general straightened up and spoke slowly, deliberately. "I told Mr. Pinkerton this paper had *no* significance. I reminded him that Shelby was a long-standing member of the Lotus Club and most probably frequented their Monday night parties. Since you evidently have acquired a reputation as a poker player, he was simply looking for a game."

"Thanks." Garrett looked at the items on the desk, then picked one up and placed it in his pocket.

"Secondly, Pinkerton showed me another item. It was a Navy Colt, an older model that had been retooled. Asked me if it was familiar. I told him I have seen a lot of Navy Colt revolvers in my army career. One looks much like the other. He kept the Colt, then asked if I knew where you were staying in Chicago. I chose to be vague on that topic. I distracted him by telling him that I had not seen Oates for nearly a week. A situation at first I considered only irritating, but now...well." The general continued staring out the window. "You and Oates meeting at the Tremont, was it just bad timing or bad luck?"

"Look, I didn't murder him. What reason would I have?" Garrett's voice was tense.

"And *I'm* still not sure it was Oates who put those phony banknotes in my safe or why he had those phony bonds. Tell me everything that occurred last Monday evening. Start with your poker game at the Tremont."

Garrett sat down and made himself comfortable. He began with his arrival in Chicago with Sam's body. "The game at the Tremont was not the Lotus Club's regular Monday game. You know me, I never take a marker when I play poker, but Oates insisted and Charlotte backed him up. Oates wasn't one of the regular players but your partner told me straight out he would make good on it."

Garrett described his meeting with McGlynn and the incident at the warehouse. "Sam and I'd been on Brock's trail nearly three months. When he tried to run, I shot him. It all happened at the same time as the explosion. Then I took him to the Alexian Brothers Hospital." He explained his visit with Pinkerton, the government bonds, and how everything fell apart at Sam's funeral. "Pinkerton informed me he'd cut a deal. Brock walks—in exchange for the bonds he's printed and the names of his partners."

The general had been listening quietly. "Then talk to Brock."

"Can't. Pinkerton won't let anyone near him. Charlotte sent Bernard with no success. Went there herself, she told me. Neither of them could get past the front desk."

"I was thinking—the Eastwood Building, the warehouse explosion and fire, those bonds, Oates's death—everything is laid out right there in front of us, only we don't see the connections. Maybe we're looking at this all wrong." There was a wistful tone in the general's voice.

*We?* Garrett thought. The old man was using "we" like he had finally decided to step up and be a part of this. He was about to reply when the general held up his hand. "By the way, Oates's office is now your office. Just like old times." He said the words with what passed for a smile.

"No thanks. Don't need one." Garrett looked at him, then tried to sound more reassuring. "You know I'm better 'out on patrol.' Never have been a desk man. You hired me to finish the Eastwood and that's where I should be."

For a second the general looked irritated, then he nodded. "You're right. Well, then, what are your plans this evening?" There was a weariness set deep in the old man's eyes. His face wore the look of a man to whom time and space had come to mean very little.

Garrett looked at him. "I'll go find us a hack and we can go home."

# TWENTY-TWO

*John B. Drake's annual game dinner was an event unique to Chicago. Invitations were always kept in exact ratio to the city's population, one guest per thousand inhabitants. The first game dinner was held in 1855 at the old Tremont House. Seventy-five guests were in attendance. The twenty-seventh game dinner would be held in the great dining-hall of Drake's Grand Pacific Hotel. At last count the invitations numbered six hundred and fifty. By tradition, Drake assembled a tableau of animals in the center of the dining room. This year his pièce de résistance was a prairie scene of roasted deer, complete with hide and horns, surrounded by a grouping of stuffed and baked sandhill cranes, raccoons, and prairie chickens.*

Garrett stepped out of the tub, wrapped a towel around his body, and proceeded to walk down the hall. Midway, he stopped. The door to his room was ajar. He distinctly remembered closing it. He stood outside, listened for a moment, then slowly pushed the door open.

"Miz Reid sent this here fancy suit over. I laid it out on your bed," Ada explained, staring at the towel-draped figure in the doorway. "You have a visitor, sir, in the kitchen. A reporter, he tells me." She edged her way past him and went out into the hall.

Having any woman in the house, even a cook or housekeeper, would take some getting used to. Garrett wondered how the general was dealing with it. He finished dressing, pulled out his valise, unlocked it, and found his derringer. Fancy dinner or no, he never went out in Chicago, or any city, unarmed. He was about to close the bag when he saw Sam's package. He took it out, broke the string and tore off the paper. Inside were packets of French postcards, which was no real surprise. Then he felt something else between the packets.

The handkerchief was definitely a woman's. It was bordered in hand-knotted lace, with an embroidered emblem in one corner. He rubbed it between his fingers. There was a faint scent of perfume, flowery, a hint of lavender mixed with heavier spices. Garrett unfolded the papers that were wrapped in it. One was familiar, a flyer on Theo Brock. But the other...he held it under the lamp for a closer look. This was a U.S. government bond, one of the counterfeit ones to be exact.

Garrett sat on the bed and looked at the wrapping. *Sam mailed this on our last day in St. Louis, probably when he left the hotel. Why didn't he show it to me? He could have waited. We were partners. Maybe he was playing a hunch. He went out alone.* Garrett took a deep breath to collect himself. *No time to sort it out now.* He returned the items to the valise, locked it, and went downstairs.

Rob Powers sat at the kitchen table devouring a piece of apple pie. The reporter stopped chewing momentarily, looked at Garrett, and smiled. "I have the information you wanted. You still interested? Considering this Oates is dead and all."

"How'd you find me?"

Powers ignored the question and posed one of his own. "So you're attending the game dinner? I *am* impressed. For a once-in-a-while visitor to Chicago, you keep illustrious company." He retrieved a notepad from his pocket. "Want to know who'll be there besides yourself?"

"No. What have you found out?"

Rob fingered one of Garrett's sleeves. "Good quality. Well, getting down to business, Mr. Shelby Oates, the nephew of—"

"Don't waste my time."

"Ah...the late Mr. Oates was expelled from two colleges back East. Drinking, gambling mostly...he ran up a lot of debts. His family sent him to Europe for an extended visit. Upon his return he spent time out West." Powers recited the information dryly, as if the man were as boring as the details.

"He was a remittance man. I met a lot of them in Wichita and Dodge. Their families paid them to stay away."

Garrett let Ada pour him a cup of coffee.

"Oates returned to Chicago when his uncle died and took over Central Casualty Insurance, along with General Stannard. Only Oates still had his gambling habit. He usually played with a select group of friends. From what I gather they were small, gentlemanly games and he always covered any debts." Rob began flipping pages in his notepad. "That was until two months ago. My source hinted that a femme fatale entered Oates's life. Women will do it every time." Powers looked up, figured he had Garrett's attention. "I heard this lady introduced him to some big stakes players. At first he won, then he began to lose. Oates dug himself into a hole. Word is he owed big money. Still interested?"

They'd already figured out that Oates paid off his gambling debts with his own funds, which were quickly depleted, then apparently traded Lake View Vault shares for government bonds. Probably seemed like a sure thing.

Garrett nodded at Powers to continue. "Who did he play with? I need names."

"Well, Oates moved in a somewhat refined social circle. Not Potter Palmer or Philip Armour you understand, but close. The man was friendly with a lot of people—Peck, Smythe, Fields, Reynolds, Blair, to name a few."

"They don't need his money," Garrett said. "They wouldn't kill, at least not for a mere gambling debt. I understand he paid the debt off. So, he was killed for another reason."

Not dismayed, Rob continued. "Well, I did learn that Oates was shot in the chest. Must have been someone he knew. 'Course you'll not be reading that in the *Inter Ocean* or any other papers. Pinkerton is keeping the information to himself. Also, Oates's body was placed in the warehouse *after* the fire."

"I know all that. The poker game at the Tremont and the warehouse fire occurred Monday evening. Oates left the game in a hurry. Either he was meeting someone or running away from someone."

"Is any of this important?" Rob asked.

"What's important is—who paid for the bullet?"

♠

"I hardly recognize you, Lyons. Why, you're dressed to the nines." Senator Lawlor grinned from ear to ear as he pushed open the door of the shiny black brougham.

"I'd better sit carefully. Promised Charlotte not to crease the jacket or lose my cuffs up my sleeves." Garrett's last remark produced chuckles all round.

It was dark inside. He found a seat and, when his eyes grew accustomed to the faint light filtering in, began to inspect the interior. The carriage was impressive, with gray broadcloth upholstery, a cut-glass vase for flowers, and cream-colored silk shades on the square windows. The mingled odors of expensive tobacco and Florida Water emanated from the senator, who lounged contentedly in a far corner of the carriage.

"Do you know who'll be there?" Sullivan was busy adjusting the starched cuffs of his dress shirt. Without waiting for a reply, he removed a newspaper clipping from his vest pocket and began a recitation of the important personages attending the dinner. "I'm sure Lyons is acquainted with one or more of these gentlemen, on a friendly card-playing basis, of course."

"Hope you boys enjoy the evening," the senator said as he relit his cigar.

"All I need is an opportunity to meet these gentlemen in a social atmosphere. When they have another big project, trust me, the firm of Adler & Sullivan will top their list of architects." Sullivan tapped his cane impatiently against the carriage roof. "Get a move on."

Their driver chirruped to the horses, a pair of fine bays with long bushy tails, as he slowly maneuvered them through Chicago's streets.

At Jackson he joined an assembly of carriages, four-in-hands, and broughams. Each one was exquisitely turned out—leather polished, brasses gleaming, horses groomed to perfection, servants in full livery—all moving west to the Grand Pacific Hotel entrance on LaSalle Street.

From the glass-domed carriage rotunda, through the carved oak doors, and into the main lobby, the Grand Pacific provided its guests with a dazzling array of sights and sounds. Across from the entrance was an ornate marble staircase carpeted in a red and blue Oriental pattern.

As Louis straightened his tie one more time, Garrett took a moment to survey the scene before him. Jewels sparkled around ladies' throats, as well as on their hands and wrists. Scattered among the colorful gowns and black suits he spied dress blue uniforms of the U.S. Army. A few faces were familiar. Men he remembered as lieutenants back in '74 were now dressed in the braid and ribbons marking them as majors and colonels.

Suddenly the voices of the crowd rose and hit a crescendo of oohs and aahs, as a group of dress blues emerged from the elevator. General Phil Sheridan was making a grand entrance, surrounded by his entourage. Garrett hesitated, but just for a moment. If General Sheridan was here, then most likely so was Caultrain. He felt uneasy, meeting face to face the man who'd ruined his army career. But there was no turning back now. He quickly joined Louis and the senator as they walked through the lobby and up the main staircase.

At the top of the stairs, outside the door to the main dining room, a circular marble table rested on a gilded base. In the center of the table sat a Sèvres porcelain statue of Bacchus holding a platter of roasted partridge and quail in full plumage. An immaculately dressed man with a tall, slender build stood next to the table. He was their host, John B. Drake. No other man was better suited to this task. Suave, dapper, and always tactful, Drake attended to every detail of his annual dinner, while maintaining an air of serenity.

"Senator Lawlor." Drake walked over and extended his hand. "It's been some time since you've attended one of our game dinners. And, I might add, we have sorely missed your presence."

This was Drake's way of saying that, whatever the senator had done in the past, as far as he was concerned the slate was wiped clean. He handed Lawlor a card and continued talking, while steering the trio toward the dining salon.

The Grand Pacific's main salon was located on the second floor and extended the entire length of the hotel, along the LaSalle Street side. It was the largest private hotel dining room in Chicago. Four imported crystal chandeliers hung from the ornate plastered ceiling. Round tables, each seating groups of ten, were draped in white linen and set with gleaming silver, china, and crystal. The focal point at each table was a centerpiece of stuffed, roasted game birds. Placed strategically on the floor around each table were gleaming brass spittoons.

Louis nodded a greeting to anyone with whom he had even a slight acquaintance. He was somewhat surprised when Daniel Burnham walked over. "Sullivan, I saw you and your friend, Lyons, at the Montauk site yesterday. Well, what do you make of it? Of course, you know that Root and I redesigned the building to increase the number of floors. Now it will be ten stories."

With a deft wave of his hand, Louis just laughed. "I lay odds it will sink, sooner rather than later. Ten, twelve, why not construct a twenty-story building?"

Burnham leaned closer and gave Sullivan a pitying look. His blue eyes looked amused. "Capital idea, Sullivan. One should never make small plans."

Before Sullivan could reply, Burnham's wife appeared and took his arm. Louis was staring after them when the senator held up the card John Drake had given him. "I believe our table is near the window, if that centerpiece on it is a pintail duck. What do you say?"

Garrett followed them, edging himself between groups of guests. Suddenly, he stopped. On a platform in the center of the dining room was a tableau of whole roasted deer and smaller animals, all placed in a forest-like setting. This was indeed a sight. He was so engrossed with the display that he failed to notice a woman walk in front of him. He took a step forward and they bumped into one another.

Iris Reynolds gave a little start, turned sharply, and smiled. "Sir, I do believe your foot is on my dress."

She wore a gown of pale sea-blue satin, décolleté in front and embroidered with tiny crystals. The deeply plunging neckline accentuated a perfectly corseted waist, her ample bosom, and creamy white shoulders. Pinned in the center of the ecru lace bodice was a large black cameo encircled with diamonds.

Garrett bowed slightly. "My apologies."

After a moment's surprise, then recognition, she said, "Why, Mr. Lyons, isn't it?" Then, not waiting for a reply, she continued. "Tell me, sir, do you believe in fate? I say this because we seem destined to meet again and again." Iris glanced over her shoulder, then looked up quickly and met his eyes. She spoke so softly Garrett had to lean over to catch her words. "I hope our next meeting is soon. I never had the opportunity to thank you properly."

Garrett flinched as he felt a jab at his elbow. It was one of the waiters edging by. When he turned back around Iris was gone, so he found his table and sat down. Louis and the senator introduced themselves to their fellow diners. He heard the name Wentworth, glanced up, and nodded a greeting to the gentleman. Sullivan's face immediately acquired a solicitous look. Sensing he was about to be pestered for an introduction, Garrett whispered, "The man plays a good poker hand and has a mind that can track every card in the deck. Regular players seldom push him on a hand, 'cause he rarely bluffs. That's all I'm telling you."

He studied his menu with curiosity before finally slipping it under his plate.

# TWENTY-THREE

MENU
TWENTY-SEVENTH ANNUAL GAME DINNER
GRAND PACIFIC HOTEL

Blue Point Oysters in Shell
Game Soup ~ Venison Broth

*Roast Dishes*
Prairie Chicken ~ English Hare ~ Partridge ~ Wild Turkey
Spotted Grouse ~ Black Bear ~ Opossum ~ Leg of Elk
Loin of Buffalo ~ Red Head Duck ~ Black Tail Deer ~ Coon

*Broiled Dishes*
Blue-Winged Teal ~ Jack Snipe ~ Blackbirds ~ Reedbirds
Pheasant ~ Quail ~ Butterball Ducks ~ Marsh Birds ~ Plover

*Entrées*
Antelope Steak with Mushroom Sauce
Ragout of Bear, Hunter Style
Filet of Grouse with Truffles ~ Braised Rabbit à la Colbert
Venison Cutlet

*Ornamental Dishes*
Boned Quail in Plumage ~ Red-Winged Starling on Tree
Pyramid of Game en Bellevue ~ Partridges in Nest

John Drake walked to the center of the dining room, hopped up on the platform and stood next to the stuffed roast deer. The general murmur of voices, the rustling of silk and taffeta, and the clatter of china ceased. In a booming baritone he welcomed everyone. His remarks, including a recitation of the history of his annual game dinner, were humorous and mercifully short. Then, with his usual showmanship, he tossed a red silk handkerchief in the air and shouted, "Let the Twenty-seventh Annual Game Dinner begin."

The doors at the far end of the room swung open, disgorging a line of waiters, smartly dressed in dark blue Grand Pacific Hotel uniforms, led by the maître d'hôtel, his uniform adorned with copious amounts of gold braid. The waiters marched in step while balancing trays laden with ornate silver tureens. Two servers were assigned to each table and they were kept busy holding trays, removing plates, and keeping everyone's glass filled with champagne.

"Game soup, venison broth, or blue points?" each guest was asked in turn.

"Ah, the game soup, of course." Senator Lawlor closed his eyes, inhaled a long deep breath, then leaned back. "This is truly a feast for the gods."

"We'll have the venison broth." Sullivan looked sideways at Garrett and whispered, "The napkin goes on the lap."

"That man is tucking his under his chin." Garrett nodded toward an adjoining table.

Sullivan replied, "The gentleman in question trades wheat and corn and is worth over three million dollars, which allows him to put his napkin anywhere he wants."

Once they'd gotten that point of etiquette out of the way, they found that the conversation at their table had turned to real estate.

"Now, I grant you, Prairie Avenue is fine enough, but dirty," Marcus Harper was saying. "The North Side, that's the coming part of town."

Leander McCormick took a spoonful of soup and glared. "Well, I don't live there."

"Don't be an ass. If we've learned anything, it's that nothing stays the same for very long in Chicago. That's why we came here. Chicago allows every man to spread himself."

Garrett concentrated on his soup, trying not to slurp or spill, and failed to notice John Drake walk up to their table. He seated a latecomer—a uniformed officer—then continued on. When the soup bowls were removed and the table cleared, Garrett took the opportunity to take a closer look at the late arrival. With the flickering candlelight and the constant movement of the waiters, he couldn't readily identify the man. Then he heard a soft eastern-accented voice say, "It is indeed an honor to be invited to this unique gathering. I'm looking forward to an enjoyable evening."

It was Caultrain. They had not spoken to, nor seen one another, since the debacle at Powder River. Caultrain had made himself a hero, while Garrett lost his army career. Ever since Stannard had told him that Caultrain was now on Sheridan's staff and would no doubt be at the reunion, he'd anticipated that they'd meet—only not here at the Grand Pacific but in some dark alley, just the two of them.

The colonel looked resplendent in his dress uniform, his mustache and goatee carefully groomed. He was effortlessly charming to everyone and Garrett remembered that had always been his manner, cool but pleasant. His face wore its usual discreet half smile. The kind you achieve by practicing in front of a mirror. He was nodding circumspectly to the gentlemen and smiling discreetly at the ladies around their table. If he saw or even recognized Garrett he did not let on.

Garrett motioned a server to refill his wine glass and drank it down in one gulp. *The man has aged well*, he thought, although he noticed lines running in deep trenches on either side of his mouth that were almost hidden by his carefully groomed mustache.

The next course was announced with a flourish. Conversation at the table immediately centered on the platters containing varieties of roasted game. Garrett signaled to a waiter and pointed to his glass for another refill. He quickly drank half, then forced himself to stop and eat a piece of wild turkey. He chewed slowly, trying not to stare at Caultrain, instead concentrating on the bits and pieces of conversation drifting around the table.

The topic had turned from real estate to the Grand Army reunion. The ladies were bombarding the colonel with questions. "You are with the War Department? Washington must be ever so exciting." General Phil Sheridan's name was bandied around a few times, followed by queries about the Grand Army parade on Michigan Avenue, as well as the famous veterans who would be in attendance. Meanwhile, the servers removed the plates with quiet efficiency.

"Delicious, simply delicious. Good food, good companions, right Lyons? This promises to be a memorable evening." The senator held his glass up, as if admiring the crystal facets and also discreetly pointing its emptiness out to a nearby waiter.

"I certainly agree." Louis looked at Garrett. "You've been mighty quiet."

Garrett did not realize it but he'd been sitting as rigid as a board, with his hands clenched. He glanced rapidly around the table. When he'd first seen Caultrain, he immediately felt a flood of heat spreading up the back of his neck. All of his anger and his memories of Powder River—buried for the past eight years—boiled to the surface. He hadn't been able to relax, even after several glasses of wine. He clenched his jaw and spoke with barely tempered ferocity. "It's getting stuffy in here. Some people at this table are blowing too much hot air. Maybe I should ask a server to open a few windows and let it out."

More entrées arrived with the usual fanfare. Garrett pointed to his glass and a server immediately filled it. Louis raised an eyebrow. He reached over for Garrett's wine glass, but saw the expression on his friend's face and pulled his hand away. "This is not your usual beverage, which is whiskey. I suggest you watch yourself. Best to keep eating," he whispered from the side of his mouth.

"Fine, I'll have that." Garrett nodded halfheartedly toward a platter of venison cutlets.

"What's this? Rabbit 'à la' what?" Marcus Harper asked the waiter in a loud voice.

"'À la Colbert' is a cheese sauce. You've eaten it at my restaurant," Herbert Kinsley said.

The server placed the dish on the table. Marcus Harper swiped a finger through the sauce and tasted it. "Why didn't Drake say so in the first place, instead of giving it a fancy name?"

The senator eyed his antelope steak from different angles before stabbing it with his fork. "I imagine you'd call this real army food, right Lyons?"

Garrett didn't respond, but drained his glass. Amid the clatter of silverware and the clink of china he could hear the ladies' conversation with Colonel Caultrain.

"You served out West? How exciting! I've read about your exploits at Powder River in the *Herald.* Oh, ladies, we have a real hero with us this evening."

Caultrain merely smiled, in the manner of one hearing exactly what he expects to hear.

Kinsley asked the servers to fill everyone's glasses. Then he stood. "Gentlemen, ladies, I wish to propose a toast. To our guest from Washington, welcome to Chicago."

"Hear, hear!" Glasses clinked. Silverware scraped against china.

Caultrain stood up and, once he was certain all eyes were on him, raised his glass. No one else would dominate the conversation and no one else would be the center of attention. He graciously bowed, then nodded in the direction of Kinsley and the ladies. "I also wish to propose a toast. To my generous hosts, on behalf of myself, and of course my fellow officers present here this evening, let this humble soldier extend his appreciation for your hospitality."

Garrett sat uncomfortably, shifting his position, crossing and uncrossing his legs, studying Caultrain's performance. What he saw was the prim satisfaction of a man who felt the need to shed light on his own importance. When the clapping and the smiles subsided, Garrett stood up, a movement so sudden he caught his fingertips on the table. Steadying himself, he said, "I wish to propose another toast." He turned to the servers. "Fill 'em up—to the brim."

The rest of the diners stopped talking and looked at him. Louis gave Garrett a warning glance, which he ignored. At that point Sullivan looked anxiously at the senator who had abandoned his steak and was trying to spear a lone carrot on his plate with a fork. Deciding there was nothing further he could do, Sullivan stared up at the ceiling.

"Who should we toast? Colonel Elliot Caultrain—the man of the hour? No! Ladies and gentlemen, let us lift our glasses and salute the *real* heroes of Powder River." Garrett was surprised at the depth of his anger and his own eloquence. It had led him farther than he meant to go. Not a man to turn back, he continued to speak in a quiet but firm voice. "I propose we toast the *brave* men this *brave* colonel abandoned to die at Powder River."

Garrett raised his glass and, when no one joined in, drained it. He tossed his napkin on the table and sat down. There was an awkward silence. Louis saw the stunned and uncomfortable expressions of his fellow diners and inwardly moaned. The senator looked at Garrett, raised an eyebrow and asked in a loud whisper, "Am I to understand that gentleman is an army acquaintance of yours?"

"We served together...at Powder River," Garrett said, keeping his voice deliberately level as though the matter were of no more than casual importance.

Caultrain turned slowly towards them, staring directly at Garrett with intense, bright eyes. He shook his head ever so slightly, looked at his dinner companions, and shrugged in an effort to appear unconcerned. However, his jaw tightened and his features grew harder. He looked as though he was about to say something but, instead of words, what appeared on his lips was only the briefest suggestion of a smile. And his smile was as sharp as the blade of a knife.

Louis looked at Caultrain and thought, *It would be unwise to have any unsettled business with a man capable of a smile like that.*

The servers appeared and the maître d'hôtel announced the final entrée of the evening—platters of grilled quail and red-winged starlings on rice. Everyone at the table looked relieved. There was a nervous burst of compliments from the guests on the food and wine, as the servers hastened to refill glasses.

Garrett noticed that Caultrain was no longer wearing his smug, self-confident look. The color in his cheeks had faded and he paid scant attention to the attempts at polite conversation that the others at the table directed toward him. *Yes, you bastard, I did not bury myself*, Garrett thought. There was a contented smile on his face as he savored a moment of triumph, however brief.

In the distance they heard Johnny Hand's orchestra strike up a waltz. As if on cue, the guests gravitated toward the double doors at the far end of the room until only Senator Lawlor, Louis, and Garrett remained at their table.

"I'm not much for dancing. Think I'll find someplace to sit and visit." The senator stood up, lit a cigar, then strolled toward an adjacent clubroom. Soon he was ensconced in an armchair, holding court, surrounded by a group of admirers.

Garrett looked over at Louis. "What do we do now?"

"We get you some fresh air," Louis replied. He began skillfully maneuvering his friend out of the dining room toward a bank of windows that overlooked Jackson Boulevard. It was a slow process, since Louis could not miss an opportunity to greet any notable personage within earshot. All the while he whispered an incessant torrent of complaints in Garrett's ear.

"I have never seen you like this. Frankly, I don't know what to make of it. Did you forget why I came to this dinner?"

They reached a row of potted plants and Garrett suddenly stopped. He was not really in the mood for Sullivan's social maneuverings. Sullivan walked a few steps past him then came back.

"Well, for God's sake, stay here then. But pull yourself together and...keep out of trouble." With that, he turned on his heel and left.

Garrett smiled indulgently as he stared after the retreating figure. Sullivan be damned. He felt a trifle uncomfortable and stretched his arms as if his cuffs were riding up. What to do? Sit? Stand? Light up a cheroot? While he decided what to do next he inspected a painting of a woodland scene, complete with a regal buck. He heard a woman's voice, at first soft, lilting, then sharp, ending on a pleading note. Curious, he decided to investigate.

Iris Reynolds sat in a corner chair, half-shaded by one of the huge palms, its exotic leaves throwing a dark pattern over her creamy shoulders. The pale billows of her gown shimmered in the soft glow of the candlelight. For a moment she looked startled as she turned to face him. Then she smiled.

Garrett noticed a retreating figure and thought he recognized the uniform, the profile, of Caultrain walking down the hallway.

"Mr. Lyons, we meet again."

Garrett noticed that Iris's skin was pale and that there was a light color to her cheeks. At that moment she seemed especially vulnerable. When she spoke in a hushed voice her eyes did not lose their troubled look. "I so hoped to see you again, alone. Please sit." She motioned to the chair next to her.

"I'm at your service, ma'am." Garrett smiled as he sat down. His smile brought a fainter smile to her face and for a few seconds they stared at each other. Laughter sounded yards away, although it was merely around a corner, and, in the distance, the orchestra struck up another waltz.

"Mr. Lyons, I could use a friend."

"Friend? I would think a beautiful woman, such as yourself, has many friends. Friends who take you on carriage rides, friends you visit for tea."

Iris smiled rather shyly at him, an expression Garrett found strangely exciting.

"It's the quality of friendship that matters, not its length," she said. "One can have an acquaintance with people all one's life and never share a moment's total understanding. Then you meet a stranger and feel kinship." Iris leaned forward, her lips at his ear. "What I mean is—do you have a true friend? I mean a person to whom you could entrust your life? That is the kind of friend I need, the kind of friend I'm looking for."

"Well, Mrs. Reynolds, if that's the case and you are in need of assistance, I'll do what I can to help you."

Iris gave him a long look, as if trying to judge the sincerity of his words. Then she laughed.

Garrett followed suit. When her lace handkerchief slipped from her hand onto the floor he picked it up and returned it to her. Their faces were only inches apart. He gazed into those luminous eyes, down her bare throat to the delicate suggestion of a collarbone beneath the skin, then finally to the voluptuous pulse of smooth skin that formed a soft triangle next to the black cameo between her breasts. When she spoke again it was in such a low voice that Garrett had to lean even closer to hear her words.

"I am alone, with no friends. So...I seldom go riding, and I never take tea."

Iris was breathing hard. He could almost feel the delicate scent of her lavender water on his skin. He swallowed with slight difficulty, as if his mouth were dry. At that moment he felt an overwhelming desire to hold her in his arms, to touch her hair, releasing its neat curls from their pins, and thread his fingers through the softness.

He stood up quickly, deciding the best maneuver would be a strategic withdrawal.

"Mr. Lyons, are you quite alright?" She rose and moved close to him.

A waiter strode by, holding aloft a tray of brandy snifters that clinked as they touched one another. Garrett stepped back, nearly tripping over a small table. Before he could steady himself Iris stepped forward and purposely put her hand to his chest. Suddenly she froze and stared over his shoulder. Garrett turned slightly and saw an angry looking, gray-haired gentleman standing several paces behind him.

"Mr. Lyons, that is my husband, Augustus Reynolds." Iris's voice was an intimate whisper as she gave his arm a gentle squeeze.

"Shit." Lyons had dealt with irate husbands before and this time he hadn't really done anything.

Augustus Reynolds simply stared at the two of them. Then a smile crossed his face, as shadowy as a ripple of cold wind over water.

# TWENTY-FOUR

*Chicago was a city of unending demolition and construction. While commercial buildings rose higher and higher, homes sprouted like weeds north of the river. The designs and styles of these residences, a reflection of each neighborhood's citizenry, ranged from brick row houses, to three-story limestone dwellings, to simple frame structures dressed up with ornate trim. Developers promoted these new homes as the best of urban living as they were within a short streetcar ride of the business district. However, on a daily walk in Lincoln Park residents of this area could still see raccoons, squirrels, and even an occasional deer.*

Ada sat at the kitchen table and chewed on her lower lip, a thoughtful expression on her face. She wore a gray dress and plain white apron. Her thick hair was tied back in a knot, a white cap balanced precariously on top of her head. The daily chores were done—the wooden table scrubbed, gleaming pans hung on racks by the stove, the china set out on the dresser. Now she stared at the blackened stove, at the live embers behind the bars. It was more than just the fire. Ada thought it had something to do with the smell of the room, the echo of voices, the feeling of a home. This could be the place she dreamed of...her place.

She was five when her mother left and Mrs. Connell took her in. For the past twelve years this dream had hovered about her like a cloud. She couldn't stand on it, cling to it, or even hold it tight during the dark hours of the night. But the dream never left. Ada forced the thought to the back of her mind. One thing she did know was that the house chores here would not be a problem. After all, Mrs. Connell had sent her out for day work for the past year. Her big worry was the cooking.

At Miz Charlotte's house Eulah never let her near the stove except to clean it. When she was told that she was to stay in this house, "'til everyone was settled in," Ada had been a little fearful. She soon realized the old general was a nice man, but sad. Mr. Garrett was usually out. And that Indian, Otwah, showed her how to clean and bake the pheasant and ducks he brought, helped her set up the pantry. Now she felt a certain comfort here.

Ada was so wrapped up in these thoughts she almost missed a muffled sound at the rear of the house—a door closing, then footsteps. She found herself clutching a piece of linen and hastily placed it back on the pile when Otwah appeared in the doorway.

"Lentils, flour, sugar—for the pantry." He placed the parcels on the table then looked around. "You have things in order, good."

"Yes, sir," Ada said, trying to keep her voice casual.

Garrett had followed Otwah into the kitchen. "Where's the general?" he asked.

"Ah...in the library. You want me to fix something?" Ada asked.

Otwah gave Garrett a sideways glance. "Just slice meat and bread. We make sandwich."

♠

The library was at the front of the house, to the right of the entry and across from the parlor. Garrett found Stannard stretched out on a burgundy velvet chaise next to the fireplace. His eyes were closed, his face pale. Garrett had been bunking there for only a few days, yet he sensed a change in the man. Occasionally he saw brief flashes of the old warhorse. But something had happened to dilute the general's spirit. Was it his wife's long illness and her subsequent death? There was also the end of his army career...perhaps it had all been too much for him.

Garrett sat in an overstuffed wing chair next to the chaise and instinctively glanced at the clock on the fireplace mantel. Then he stretched his legs out, leaned back to a comfortable position, and took a closer look at the room. A fire was blazing, reflecting scarlet in the leather bindings of the books on the shelves along the wall. A large oak desk—littered with an inkstand, pens, paper, and a miniature field cannon—stood guard at one end of the room. In between was an assortment of tables, chairs, and unopened boxes. Nothing in the room looked new. Everything bore a gentle patina of age and quality. It reminded him of their quarters at Fort Fetterman, enveloping him in a familiarity, a feeling of comfort, as if he had come home.

The old man was still resting. Garrett closed his eyes, listened to the hiss and crackle of the fire, and let his thoughts wander. The general could no longer claim his problems at the Eastwood site were minor annoyances, something Garrett could clear up in just a few weeks. There was no doubt someone wanted to shut the site down. If the project fell behind schedule Union Trust would take over the property, as well as the management of Central Casualty—because of their heavy investment in Lake View Vault. What would the old man do then? Garrett was contemplating various scenarios when he heard a mumbled "Mary, Mary."

Suddenly, the general sat upright. He looked at Garrett, peering at him with eyes slightly narrowed, as if he needed spectacles. He glanced around the room, waving a hand at the ivory and silver picture frames arranged on the tables and mantle. He spoke almost apologetically.

"Sometimes, when I doze off, I think of Mary. I've put her things about, can't get rid of them. There'd be nothing left of her. The army was the only life that was ever real to me. Mary liked glitter, parties, the 'Washington Whirl' she called it. I like to think we were happy. I hope I wasn't a disappointment to her." He was silent for a moment. His thoughts seemed to drift with the memory.

"I'm sure you weren't, sir." Garrett spoke quietly.

There was an awkward silence. Neither man quite knew what to say next. Thankfully, Otwah appeared at the doorway holding a plate of sandwiches and a jar of pickles. The general cleared his throat. "I'll need a whiskey with that." He pointed impatiently toward a tray holding a decanter and glasses. "Pour us some, Lyons."

Garrett filled three glasses, passed them around, then raised his glass. "Here's to your continued good health, sir, and a quick, successful completion of the Eastwood."

The general acknowledged the toast with a nod before taking a drink. "Well, report. How is this man you hired working out? Any more problems?"

"None I've heard of yet. That doesn't mean we won't have any. Froelich doesn't think the scaffold collapse did any real damage. But I plan to have Sullivan look at it. If he can't he'll send someone from his office. Not all of the building plans are available." Garrett picked up his sandwich, took a few bites, then looked over at the general who evidently expected more of an answer. "How long have you had problems at the Eastwood?"

The general shook his head. "I knew nothing until Shoup paid me a visit. Gave me a month to get the place in order, something built or...I'm not sure what."

"Froelich tells me other building sites are having trouble. The same story—missing materials, accidents, then work stops, the bank gets nervous. That's when someone steps in and buys cheap."

"This all began with Oates and his cards?" Otwah said.

"I think it's been going on for a while. Didn't you tell me he was not usually a reckless card player?" Garrett added.

"My partner wanted to be a gambler. He just didn't have the spine for it. Usually played to his limit, then stopped. Always came into my office to strut a little when he won. It was not like him at all to dig himself in so deep."

The general selected a fresh cigar from the humidor and lit it. He looked grave, his mouth pinched at the corners. Otwah found a chair near the window, sat, and stretched his legs. The three communed quietly for a while. Evidently, the general was in one of his meditative moods. Garrett recalled that, at Fort Fetterman, the two of them would sit on either side of the desk in his office and sometimes not a word would pass between them for close to twenty minutes.

Finally, the old man spoke. "For all his faults, Oates was a decent man. I'm sure he convinced himself that he was doing no harm by trading Lake View Vault stock for government bonds." Evidently, the general did not wish to speak ill of the dead.

Garrett said, "Oates probably thought the bonds were legitimate when he made the original trade. But then he discovered they were counterfeit and he panicked. Maybe that's the real reason he wanted to talk with me."

"What do bonds have to do with this?" Otwah asked.

"That's what I intend to find out." Garrett stretched to ease the tension he felt in the muscles of his back. "Those bearer bonds are the biggest scam Brock ever planned, bigger than his usual bogus railroad stock."

"Brock is the man you shot?" Otwah asked.

Garrett nodded. "I was certain he killed my partner, Sam. Now, I don't know. Evidently he's recovered enough to strike a deal with Pinkerton."

"When Pinkerton paid me a visit he took great pains to mention that a Navy Colt was discovered near Oates's body, an early model that was retooled. I simply listened. He did not ask my opinion."

Garrett explained that it was McGlynn who'd led him to Brock. "He was my rear guard. In all the commotion I loaned him the Colt. Damn, I'll probably never see it again."

"This McGlynn, he was in your patrol at Powder River?" Otwah asked.

Garrett nodded. "Yeah. He's carrying it around like the rest of us."

The room became silent. The general and Garrett stared at one another. The mere mention of Powder River brought back memories. Both men were thinking about their past—a time when they'd trusted and relied on one other, when there was an unwritten, unspoken bond between them that went beyond duty or orders, almost a psychic link between thought and action. Powder River and the events afterward had shattered that bond. Over the past eight years Garrett had not even thought, nor wanted, to mend it…until now.

The general reached for his whiskey, held the glass in his hand, and looked intently at Garrett as he spoke. His voice was soft, yet filled with tension. "Damn them all. I was a good soldier, we both were. I did my duty. Nearly got myself court martialed! Hell of a way for a man to end his career. It nearly killed Mary." His voice cracked. He was losing control, trembling. "What can a man do, when he's a victim of men sealed away in their Washington offices, men who make decisions based solely on the preservation of their jobs?"

"You did the only thing possible that was honorable. Never doubt it. We were all given jobs, sir. What it comes down to is—you did what the army ordered you to do."

Garrett exchanged a worried glance with Otwah. The old man was rambling again. The general had lost the two things that were most dear to him, his army career and his wife, and now he felt as though he'd betrayed them both.

"*Mon ami*, the army reunion?" Otwah's words to Garrett were a bare whisper. "I tell general, we go camping on the Fox River. He does not listen."

Garrett lowered his voice. "The town is teeming with uniforms." Remembering the incident in the bar at Hooley's, and the confrontation with Caultrain at the game dinner, he said, "You know, General, a camping trip sounds like a good idea for both of us."

"The Grand Army reunion?" the general's voice interrupted. "My invitation is on the desk. Don't know about you boys but I look forward to watching Phil Sheridan prance around in his gold braid and medals." He looked at his former lieutenant. "Learned a long time ago, a man can't run forever. Besides I've never known you to back down from any brawl. Therefore, I've decided we'll all attend the reunion."

"Aren't you forgetting a few things?" Garrett asked. "What about Oates, his death? Your first priority should be the Eastwood Building. Mine is finding Sam's killer."

"No! I haven't forgotten." The general dismissed his remark with a quick wave of his hand. "We may learn something. You're not the only person who's been busy. I've been doing a little scouting on my own. I paid a visit to the Alexian Brothers Hospital." He picked up a sandwich and took a halfhearted nibble.

"Told the brothers I was visiting an old comrade…a good tactical approach. Then I wandered the halls and discovered where Pinkerton is keeping that Brock fellow. The sign on the ward door says 'Quarantine.' Don't pay it any mind. He keeps an agent there all the time. But one of the brothers mentioned there's a good half hour between when one man leaves and the replacement arrives. Not good planning. Never leave a post unattended."

The general stood up, walked to his desk and began moving papers and books around. Garrett wondered what the old man was doing. It was impossible to tell.

Finally, the general opened a drawer and pulled out a wooden box, then came over and set it in front of Garrett. Inside the velvet-lined case was a presentation set of ivory-handled revolvers. "Mary had the Colt factory make them special for me. They were to be a surprise. They're yours now. Try not to lose them."

Garrett thought he detected a wistful tone in the old man's voice. He picked one of the revolvers up and held it near the light of the fireplace. He weighed it by feel, first holding it on its side in the palm of his hand, then turning it on end. "This is a beautiful piece, sir."

"Remember, Chicago may not be Apache country, but it is dangerous nonetheless. Can't have you carrying a piss-ass derringer around. That's a lady's gun. You can always count on a Colt." The general wrinkled his nostrils like an animal sniffing the wind for danger, then smiled. "Well, we can sit here and toss ideas on the table, shuffle them around, or we can bring all of this mess to a head. What do you boys say?"

For a brief moment Garrett thought he saw a sparkle in the general's eye, like the old man was back in the game again. "Yes, sir."

Otwah's grunt could have been anything. Garrett chose to interpret it as a yes.

# TWENTY-FIVE

*In 1853 Chicago's first mayor, William B. Ogden, formed the Chicago Land Company, which purchased 160 acres along the north branch of the Chicago River. The company dug clay for bricks, which they sold to builders. By 1857 their excavations had formed a canal and unintentionally created the only island in the Chicago River. The property was inhabited by a succession of squatters, beginning with the Irish who named it Kilgubbin, then finally Goose Island. The island's daily life hovered precariously between rural and urban. Surrounded by a river that provided a ready supply of water, as well as limitless industrial sewerage and dock sites, the population found employment in shipbuilding, charcoal baking, and other less savory industries. There were over one hundred two-story frame houses crammed into a three-block area, along with numerous taverns. Goose Island residents raised cows, pigs, chickens, geese, and children…all of whom wandered the island at will.*

The lobby of the Palmer House Hotel, fitted with an abundance of plush furniture and broadleaf plants in large pots, was in its usual flurry of midday activity when Iris Reynolds stepped out of the elevator. She was dressed in a soft blue-gray dress. Although the neckline plunged deeply, she had filled in the cleavage with lace, so that it would be appropriate for a Grand Army ladies' luncheon. Hopefully this would not be a waste of a perfectly good afternoon.

Iris had realized it was time to take matters into her own hands. She knew that Charlotte—as an army officer's widow—would receive an invitation to the luncheon, so she simply asked her cousin to include her. Charlotte's note had arrived that morning and was very clear, "Eleven thirty—Monroe Street entrance." Naturally, Iris arrived early. She could not miss an opportunity for a leisurely stroll through the lobby, basking in the gentlemen's admiring glances.

From early childhood Iris Reynolds knew precisely what she wanted in life. Never moved by passion, only practicality, her instinct for survival was honed to perfection. She could fabricate a falsehood without blinking an eye. And she could appear trivial on occasion, all of which was socially acceptable.

Today Iris found herself standing at the Monroe Street entrance talking polite nonsense with Abigail Ryerson. It was nonsense because neither woman particularly cared about the subjects they discussed—the weather (always of interest in Chicago) and current fashions (Iris felt Abigail had money but no style). Indeed their whole conversation was simply a social device to pass time. A lady could not simply wait for her cousin's carriage to arrive without exchanging some words, however meaningless. Both women nodded a polite greeting to Bertha Palmer and Alicia Peck as they walked past. It was at times like these that Iris wished Augustus had not sold their brougham. Today, Charlotte's hired carriage would have to do.

When Iris spied Charlotte walking down the street, her stomach churned. She immediately murmured a few polite words to Abigail. "It's so close in here. Please excuse me." Iris edged her way toward the door, stepped outside and managed to meet Charlotte before she reached the hotel entrance. "I see you're on time," she said. The arc of her eyebrow rose no more than a millimeter, but conveyed her thoughts.

"I thought it was hardly worth seeking a hansom. Bernard needed the carriage for business errands. It's such a short walk to the Union League Club. I understand their dining room is quite elegant. Really, Iris, it isn't far." Charlotte continued the conversation as they walked along.

Iris noticed that Charlotte was wearing the cameo she'd received from Lyons. She thought wistfully of their encounter at the game dinner. Garrett Lyons was a man, hard and real. She longed to have a man like that in her life. Until yesterday she thought she might be able to, and perhaps today she would be able to remedy the situation.

The air was brisk and Dearborn Street clattered with the noise of broughams, landaus, and carriages. Iris glanced over her shoulder, hoping no one of her acquaintance would see her walking, and only pretended to listen. Let Charlotte talk, she had more important matters on her mind. Iris knew she had beauty, wit, and style, those indefinable qualities that marked winners from losers. Above all, she wanted to be a winner. And she finally realized that, if it was going to happen, now was the time to act. She had come too far to turn back now. Of course there was a danger in it but, as Augustus always preached, danger and risk were the very essence of fortune.

Iris suddenly realized Charlotte had stopped. She looked back and saw her cousin talking to a drab-looking girl in a patched, brown dress. When she saw Charlotte press some coins into the girl's hand, she murmured, "Oh, good God, what *is* she doing?" She walked faster, in order to distance herself from them.

Charlotte caught up with her at the corner. "That was Sally Dunn. Only last year she was one of my dealers at the Lotus Club's Monday gatherings. The girl has fallen on hard times. I couldn't ignore her."

Iris forced a smile. It was a slight gesture.

"It only takes one bad turn and suddenly a person's life goes upside down. Do you appreciate that you and I are more fortunate than many other people?" Charlotte asked.

Iris's face relaxed slightly, as if the thought had just occurred to her. "Actually, I don't think I've ever met or even known anyone *really* poor. Although, every Sunday, the vicar assures us in his sermons they do exist. Now I suggest we hurry. One should never be the last to arrive at a social function. It's simply not done."

They reached the corner of Adams and Dearborn. A landau sped past, pulled by matched bay horses, flanks gleaming, manes braided, closely followed by a hansom. Iris started to cross the street just as a brewer's wagon rounded the corner at breakneck speed. Charlotte grabbed her arm and pulled her back onto the curb. "Iris! Be careful. You could have been killed!"

♠

Goose Island made no attempt to disguise what it was, no effort to control the stench or noise. It presented itself to the world like a moving machine with all of its parts exposed. Garrett went there with one purpose in mind, to find Ed McGlynn. He had questions that needed answers.

*McGlynn led me to the warehouse, I loaned him my Navy Colt, he helped me take Brock to the hospital, then he disappeared. A week later, he shows up at the Eastwood site. What was he doing there? McGlynn and any type of manual labor have always been mortal enemies. He definitely knows more than he's telling about Oates's body being deposited in the burned-out warehouse.*

Garrett knew the key to finding him was Aileen Connell. He had a vague memory of the laundress from his stint at Fort Fetterman. Charlotte had mentioned her recent visit to Aileen's laundry, and that she and McGlynn had opened another one on the island. Garrett figured that was where McGlynn would go to ground. Garrett also knew the populace of Goose Island would sense an outsider. Behind the half smiles and blank stares, they were as careful as misers and as suspicious as dogs in strange territory. He could spend the whole day searching the island's warren of alleys and streets, or take a different course.

At the third tavern Garrett finally saw a familiar face. The place was small, dark, cramped and his eyes took a while to adjust. He heard the slap of playing cards before he could see them, while the pungent odor of beer, whores, and workers moved like a storm cloud through the passages of his nose. The few men drinking there had probably lived and worked the same central mile of Chicago ever since they could push a barrel or wield a hammer.

Garrett signaled for a beer then sat down. "How are things?"

Jacob Masterson's one good hand was clenched around his beer mug. It shook slightly, rippling the liquid. "Same as last time we talked, Lieutenant. Ever find your man?"

"Yes." Garrett looked at Jacob. He could see the lines of weariness in his face, the tightness around his mouth. "You live here on the island?"

He nodded. "Never thought I'd be stayin', but the past two months, with just me out every day, it's getting harder to move that cart. 'Sides, with winter comin', I'm lookin' for inside work."

The sounds of the tavern's daily life were all around them—the clink of glasses, the shuffle of feet, the splash of beer. Jacob took another drink. The liquid trickled down his chin. He set down his mug and wiped it away with the back of his hand. Neither man spoke, as there seemed nothing sensible to say. Finally, Jacob drained his mug. "So, Lieutenant, why're you here?"

Garrett searched for an answer that would not invite too many questions. "I'm looking for an Aileen Connell. I understand she recently opened a laundry on the island."

Jacob nodded. "Place is over between Haines and Bliss Streets, if she's there. Outside, go straight ahead, then make a hard turn. It's just 'fore you get to the dock."

"Thanks." Garrett slid some coins across the table, stood up to leave, then sat back down.

"Looking for winter work are you?" He told Jacob where he was bunking, gave him the general's address. "Could use an extra hand... get the old man settled in. Just sign on at least through the cold spell. As I recall you make a great pot o' coffee."

"Indeed I do, Lieutenant." Jacob's hand closed over the coins.

♠

Outside, the mist in the air had thickened and now the sky was a uniformly pale gray. Garrett joined the animal and pedestrian traffic, made that hard turn just before the dock and found Bliss Street. He took a moment to get his bearings. Nothing was moving. Usually

Chicago streets teemed with life, but here it seemed as though the city was holding its breath. He counted at least ten buildings crammed onto a street just a few feet wider than an alley and not as long. The laundry was at the end. The one-story building leaned downhill at a subtle angle that made Garrett look twice to see if the roof was tilted or if he was.

Ed McGlynn was sitting outside. Goose Island was not his usual haunt, but times dictated what a man had to do. When Aileen hired him to manage the place he reluctantly agreed, telling her it would be just temporary, a refuge. When he'd used up his allotted days at Mike McDonald's, the timing worked out. He saw Garrett Lyons walking toward him but made no effort to move. He just pointed to the sign next to the door. It read, "*Collars Washed, 25¢ per doz. Cuffs, 50¢ per doz.*"

He smiled. "Afternoon, Lieutenant. Pickin' up your wash?"

Garrett grabbed the front of his shirt and yanked him up. "Not here for my laundry, Ed. I'm here for answers. After that explosion, we took Brock to the hospital and—"

"Hey, hang on, you said, 'Take the horse and wagon,' remember? I couldn't let it sit outside."

He gave Ed another jerk so his feet were dangling. "My Navy Colt...where is it, Ed?"

"Don't know. Why you askin'? Looks like you got a fine enough firearm now." McGlynn's eyes dropped to the ivory hilt of the pistol stuffed in Garrett's belt.

"I was partial to that Colt. But not to this." Garrett set McGlynn down, then pulled a pearl stickpin from his pocket. "I saw you take it off Brock when we loaded him on the cart."

"You didn't say nothin'. I figured it was like payment."

Lyons leaned over and spoke slowly, right in McGlynn's ear. "Well, then, suppose you tell me how my Colt and this pearl stickpin ended up at that same warehouse, near Shelby Oates's dead body, a day *after* the explosion?"

McGlynn squinted at him, a bewildered expression on his face. "I went back the next evenin', give the place another look. You know me,

Lieutenant, always got my ear to the ground. Keep my eye out, see what I can find. I heard people arguin'. Crawled closer to get a better look."

"Recognize anyone?"

"Couldn't really see 'em clearly. Just heard 'em. None of their voices sounded familiar. I saw 'em dump a body. That's when I—" McGlynn started coughing. After a moment he caught his breath and continued. "I stumbled, must 'ave dropped 'em. That's the truth. I swear."

"You and the truth have never had more than a nodding acquaintance."

A tall, heavyset woman appeared in the doorway. She stood, hands on hips, and stared at Garrett, eyebrows arched. "Listen to the man, 'fore you string him up."

"It's all right, Aileen. This here is Lieutenant Lyons. We served together."

"Lyons, is it? Well, now, Fort Fetterman, am I right?" She laughed, a rich gurgle deep in her throat. "In that case, you take it easy on him."

Garrett liked the woman straight out. He recognized her as one of life's survivors, like himself.

"Let the man catch his breath. He's got somethin' to say," Aileen said.

McGlynn took a deep breath and began. "Well, sir, after they left, I saw that body, not a pretty sight, and decided right on not to stay. Any commotion were sure to bring someone. Don't need any mix-ups with a Pinkerton. But I did a quick look 'round. Found somethin' a couple of feet from the body." He groped in his pocket and handed Garrett a small packet. There was a prolonged silence as Garrett unfolded it. Inside was part of a metal belt buckle.

"Is it important?" McGlynn asked.

"Could be. Appreciate if you didn't tell anyone about this."

"Don't worry. My Ed's a good man. Well, he's as good as the world allows him to be," Aileen said with a smile and a wink. "But, remember, he'll stick his neck out only on my say so."

♠

The dining hall of the Union League Club glowed with light. The air was clouded with the scent of lavender water and tobacco. The room hummed with women's chatter, now and then rising in excitement, signaling the arrival of yet another officer in full dress uniform. Amid the rustle of taffeta and swish of silk, ladies gracefully moved toward the linen-draped circular tables spaced around the room.

"I believe our table is over there, to the right." Charlotte looked at Iris.

"You go ahead. I'll follow." Her cousin smiled ever so slightly, letting her eyes wander from one uniform to another, her face only mildly interested.

Iris reminded Charlotte of a general surveying his troops. She watched admiringly as Iris took a circuitous route around the room, gravitating toward the head table. *Well,* she thought, *I don't know why you're here, but this is your hand, my dear. Let's see you play it out.* Charlotte had little belief in coincidence. Iris was here for a reason.

A chime sounded. There was a crush as the ladies moved toward their respective tables. Charlotte could see Iris in flirtatious conversation with some junior members on General Sheridan's staff. The general was standing next to the head table, his arm on one officer's shoulder, as he looked at him with the smile of a father proud of his remarkable son. Charlotte turned to the woman standing next to her. "The officer next to General Sheridan, who is he?"

"Colonel Elliott Caultrain, the general's new protégé. He bears a striking resemblance to the old one. You remember...Custer."

Once seated, Charlotte spoke with old friends from Washington, in town for the reunion. She learned which officers had been promoted or had retired, and whose careers had been cut short by unfortunate circumstances. Any other time she would have considered this an enjoyable addendum to the Grand Army celebrations, but she could not dismiss an uneasy feeling about Iris.

Waiters glided smoothly from table to table. They served thinly sliced cucumber sandwiches on brown bread with cream cheese; and white bread sandwiches with smoked ham, mayonnaise, mustard, and finely grated cheese. All accompanied by numerous bottles of wine.

Iris finally returned to their table. She found a seat next to Charlotte but focused all her attention on the officer who served as their host. Between sips of wine, and bites of sandwich, Charlotte listened to snippets of their conversation, which ranged from her husband, to his business, travel, and, of course, herself. Sometimes Iris spoke of Augustus in the past tense, as if he were already dead and out of this world, then in the present tense, as if he would come through the door and join them at any moment. As the last course was served—French pastries and thin slices of fruit—Iris took a breath and smoothed her skirts thoughtfully.

"It was so kind of Mrs. Reid to invite me." Iris smiled at their host.

*Invite you!* Charlotte thought, refraining from commenting that her cousin had invited herself. There was movement at the head table, signaling General Sheridan and his entourage's imminent departure. The remaining guests were beginning to leave. Charlotte put a hand on her cousin's shoulder and whispered, "I'll have the waiter get us a carriage."

"No need, I'm sure I can find my way back to the Palmer House," Iris answered in a patronizing whisper.

"But Iris! We really haven't had time to visit properly." Charlotte squeezed Iris's arm, which kept her attention. "You came as my guest and you will leave as my guest."

At that moment a group of ladies passed by and an old friend stopped to speak to Charlotte. When she turned back around Iris was gone. Her reactions were mixed, first anger, then alarm. The crowd was thinning. She scanned the room and finally found Iris's blue-gray dress in startling proximity to an officer's uniform. Her cousin appeared to be in an intimate, yet heated, conversation with the general's protégé. Charlotte quickly made her way across the room to intervene, before anything more unseemly transpired.

Iris's eyebrows rose a millimeter when she saw Charlotte approach. "I was just congratulating the colonel on his recent engagement. I believe the young lady's father is in the Senate.

I wanted to wish the couple all future happiness." Her eyes glistened and she spoke in a voice that could have chipped stone. "Is our carriage here?"

♠

Charlotte sat across from Iris and waited. The carriage ride from the Union League Club had been one prolonged silence. When the driver made a sharp turn on Monroe, heading toward Michigan Avenue, she finally spoke.

"Ignore me all you want, my dear. I have all the time in the world. I'll keep this carriage driving up and down these streets until you give me an explanation."

Iris's face lost its trained mask of politeness. "For what? Can't we simply spend a pleasant afternoon together?"

"You have no interest in the Grand Army ladies' auxiliary, never had, never will. But you were dead set on going to that luncheon. So what was your purpose? To see Colonel Caultrain?"

"You heard. I merely wished to congratulate him on his recent engagement." The carriage slowed to a near stop due to traffic. Iris grasped the door handle. "I don't intend to sit here and listen to one of your lectures."

Before she could open the door, Charlotte grabbed her arm and flung her across the coach and against the seat...hard. When she spoke, her voice sounded like someone else's. "No lectures, my dear, just answers. That's what I want. How involved are you with this Colonel Caultrain? And don't lie to me!"

Iris studied her for a moment, then lowered her voice as if giving more weight to her words. "I don't need to hide anything. I have done nothing wrong."

"I don't believe it. What have you been up to?"

"The colonel is an *important* acquaintance. He will soon have a lot of influence in Washington. Augustus has always encouraged me to be gracious to his business associates."

"I'm sure you have been...all too gracious."

Iris hesitated. "This was business, you understand. Only things moved too quickly."

"How much does Augustus know? Is that why he cut your allowance and stopped construction on your new house?"

"It doesn't matter anymore. Elliott wasn't supposed to get engaged. We had plans...at least I thought we did."

*You foolish girl*, Charlotte thought. "Tell me, did these business meetings with Augustus and his associates include private card games at the Tremont?" She did not give Iris time to reply. "You were there. Don't deny it! The ledger at the hotel lists the dates and expenses per client. And, in all the poker games I've hosted at the Tremont, players do not order champagne."

Iris gulped a few breaths then told her cousin about Augustus's business venture, ending with, "Augustus is bankrupt. He tells me he *will* recoup his fortune, but how long do I have to wait? I'll be old, like you. I want a life *now.* I first met Elliot in Washington, then he came here to meet with Augustus and I felt he was my chance."

An ice-cold knot had formed in the pit of Charlotte's stomach. "One thing I have learned—everyone pays a price in this life, Iris. And sometimes it is too late when you realize what you've paid." She took in a deep breath and sighed. "You can get out here."

"Here?" Iris stared at the crowded street.

"It's a short walk to the Palmer House. The air will do you some good, I hope."

# TWENTY-SIX

*The Inter-State Exposition Building, designed by William W. Boyington in 1872, was located in Lake Park. It was initially constructed to house commercial exhibitions touting Chicago's recovery from the Great Fire. The building hosted political conventions, art exhibits, and cultural events, such as orchestral concerts and opera festivals. It featured a 140-foot-wide auditorium, a stage with a proscenium arch, and an assembly area with eleven dressing rooms. Two thousand people could view the stage without obstruction. However, the echo was noticeable. It was difficult to hear speakers, unless you sat close to the stage. The Inter-State Exposition Building was the perfect venue for a Grand Army reunion.*

Although the Chicago skyline made a dramatic frieze against the setting sun, Garrett was in no mood to appreciate it. He was late. Ahead, he could see banners proclaiming the Grand Army reunion fluttering from the rooftop and blazing torches lining the entrance to the Exposition Building.

Just before he reached the front entrance he spied Sullivan lurking in the shadows. Louis's face bore the decidedly weary expression of a reluctant guest. He'd told Lyons that he could see no advantage in attending any type of military celebration. But yesterday Lyons had insisted, reminding him that Dankmar Adler would be there. A decorated army veteran, Sullivan's business partner had served with

General Sheridan. Therefore it would be prudent for Louis to make an appearance.

"I played poker with Senator Lawlor last night," Sullivan said. "Remember you asked about the buildings listed on Quinn's tote board?"

"Find out who owns them?"

"No. But I know how to locate the information."

As soon as they crossed the threshold of the Exposition Building Garrett, too, regretted his own decision to attend the reunion. He should have worked harder to convince the general to go on that camping trip. He saw veterans clustered about their respective banners and guidons. They were laughing, joking, patting one another on the back. All this camaraderie from the old days made him uncomfortable.

"Right now we need to locate General Stannard." Garrett began edging his way through the crowd, letting Sullivan trail behind him.

"The general is probably in the assembly area, which is to our left." Sullivan raised his voice over the hubbub.

"How do you know?"

"Buildings are my business. Besides, Adler has a set of blueprints. I checked them before I left the office."

The Exposition Building's main hall was fitted out in style. The ladies' auxiliary of the Grand Army had draped the space with as many headquarter and regimental banners as they could find. Chairs were arranged in orderly rows, with sections separated by corps' flags. Next to the stage a regimental band in full uniform, their brass instruments gleaming, played a march.

At the back of the hall, a raised platform stretched the entire width of the room. Displayed on it was an idyllic representation of what the ladies imagined to be a typical army bivouac. In the center sat a row of spotless tents, while in front were piles of drums and bugles, next to tripods of neatly stacked muskets, as well as a faux campfire with cooking kettles hung over it. As a final touch, two brass Napoleon cannons, polished and shining until their own gun crews would hardly know them, flanked the tableau. Evidently, it was the intention of the ladies to bring back only the *good* memories of army life.

The semicircular assembly area was situated behind the stage. It was crowded with soldiers milling about, buttoning their uniforms, lining up, waiting for orders. The odor of damp wool and cigar smoke was turning the air musty.

"This looks like utter chaos," Sullivan said.

"This is the army, Louis, get used to it."

They began a systematic search of the assembly rooms, until they saw Otwah standing at the end of the corridor. The former scout acknowledged their presence with a raised eyebrow.

"You finally arrived, *mon ami*. The general, he was worried."

Voices filtered out through an open doorway. They saw General Stannard pacing slowly, back and forth, talking to a group of officers.

"Well, now, Barton, you left a mighty big footprint," one was saying.

"He sure did. You were the most consistent man in the brigade—always in a rage."

"Damn right!" the general said. "I was in the army too long just to be pushed aside. Still remember the years it took to work my way up the chain of command. Years of serving under old men who only wore their uniforms so they could impress the ladies at parties."

The men laughed quietly and nodded agreement.

Garrett stood at the door and listened. Most of these officers were strangers to him. They were faceless names that, during his years serving with the general, had filtered down through the hierarchy of command in dispatches from the Division of the Missouri or from Washington.

"Field experience is the sure way...hell, the *only* way for promotion," one veteran said, then squirted a yellow-brown stream of tobacco at a brass cuspidor six feet away, hitting it square.

General Stannard saw Garrett and Sullivan, nodded a greeting in their direction, and continued, "Well, fellas, we all had our chances."

"You're right. Generals who say it can't be done do *not* get promotions."

"When we saw a problem...Barton Stannard saw opportunity," another added, amid quiet murmurs of agreement.

Garrett heard a voice whisper in his ear. "You and I both know, Lieutenant Lyons, that a general who wins battles and lives to tell about it will never lack for enemies in Washington."

He turned around. Standing next to him was a short, thin man sporting a sardonic smile along with his neatly trimmed goatee. He looked vaguely familiar.

"Saw you walk in and figured you'd be with General Stannard. I know the general was ignored in past reunions. This year I made sure he received an invitation." The man leaned closer and smiled. "Glad we met up. You know I never carry tales, but I have it on good authority that General Phil Sheridan is planning something big."

Seeing a face from his past was not unexpected. Even so, Garrett was cautious but friendly. On hearing that last sentence, his body stiffened, then relaxed. "Al Bloche?"

"You remember." Bloche smiled.

Garrett signaled to Louis. "I want you to meet the best news-walker in the Tenth Illinois." There was an awkward moment, as they all eyed each other. "What are you up to these days?"

"I live west of Chicago, in Oak Ridge. Own the local paper, the *Vindicator*. Well, time to pay my respects. We'll talk later." Bloche limped over to greet General Stannard.

"An Indian who speaks French, then a man you introduce as a news-walker. This evening is full of surprises." Sullivan looked somewhat impressed. "By the way, what is a news-walker?"

"After every battle a few selected men would slip away and wander up and down the lines visiting other campfires. They exchanged news, judged how the battle was going, what the prospects were for the morrow," Garrett explained. "You *never* gave them false information. And no announcement from headquarters was believed unless it jibed with what a news-walker had picked up. Often we had a better line on the situation in the field than most of the generals. Also had a pretty fair notion of what had happened and what was apt to come."

Sullivan shook his head. Garrett could not tell whether it was disbelief, feigned amazement, or utter boredom, so he added, "Always kept a close eye on them. News-walkers were notoriously light fingered."

Louis looked at him for a moment, then checked his pockets.

In the distance, they could hear the regimental band strike up another march. As if on cue, there was a lot of shuffling and a general ruckus in the hallway. A few of the officers began to take their leave, filling the air with various good-natured sentiments. *Look at them*, Garrett thought. Old soldiers in a land that had once honored them, but now just tolerated them and would more than likely forget them. But this evening was theirs, a last hurrah.

Bloche returned. Sullivan pointed to his leg. "A war wound?" he asked.

The former news-walker tapped his leg with his cane, producing a hollow, wooden sound. "It was a buggy accident. Too bad though, a war wound is always better copy." He turned to Garrett and spoke softly in a conspiratorial manner. "I hear General Sheridan brought his *full* staff with him from Washington."

"Sheridan always travels with an entourage. I know Caultrain is with him."

"Do they realize that you and General Stannard are here this evening?"

"They'll know soon enough."

"Did you ask yourself why General Sheridan's in town?"

Garrett looked at him. "For the Grand Army reunion…or is it something more?"

"You know me, Lieutenant, wouldn't speak if I wasn't certain." Bloche leaned closer. "I've heard Sheridan's laying the groundwork for a member of his staff to run for public office."

"Here in Chicago?"

Bloche raised an eyebrow. "Not sure. I'm guessing maybe on a state level."

Garrett was not convinced. "I recall Sheridan never shared a stage… if he could help it."

Bloche let this information settle in, then continued. "Want my opinion? Sheridan's building himself a power base, similar to the one he has on the east coast. The man has expectations."

General Stannard made his way over to them. "No surprise there. Phil Sheridan was cut out to be a politician, the way the righteous are chosen for the church. That was clear even when we were classmates at the U.S. Military Academy."

"Well, sir, this must be quite an evening, seeing old comrades again," Sullivan said.

"I intend to write this up in the *Vindicator*," Bloche added. "The general participated in many notable battles during the war and out West. He didn't know fear."

"You're all wrong," General Stannard replied. "Every man who isn't a maniac knows fear. All of us have been in hazardous campaigns. Just ask any of my colleagues here. We never started on them without wishing they were finished. 'Course, once you were in the battle, it got easier. By the time it was over, we were sorry to leave. But at the start your feet were icy."

Everyone was so busy nodding in agreement, adding comments, that they failed to notice the young officer, in a spanking new uniform, enter the room. He walked over to the general.

"I have a message for a General Stanrodd...or is it Standard...and his fellow veterans attending today's event." The officer smiled with a smug confidence. When he was sure of everyone's attention, he spoke with the arrogance of a man with a big message and no responsibility for it.

"General Sheridan sends his regrets. He does not have time to personally greet you. Unfortunately, his staff has informed him that, due to constraints in space, there will not be room for you on stage." He looked at General Stannard. "With respect, sir, if you wish to remain, perhaps the sergeant at arms can find a vacant seat for you in the gallery."

While the officer had indicated that his words were said "with respect," there was not a shred of it in his voice. A heavy silence filled the room. Garrett felt the tension. Things could get nasty. He looked over and tried to gauge General Stannard's mood, at the same time ignoring the stern gaze of the other officers. Finally, he took a step forward, stood next to the old man and whispered, "Give the word, sir, and we'll all leave."

Instead, the general turned to the young officer and leaned hard into his face. The skin on the back of his neck turned a dark red, the past eight years of simmering anger nearly boiling into an explosion. His jaw was clenched and he spoke with barely tempered ferocity. "Listen, son. You go back and tell…" Then he paused and turned away. When he turned back again there was a sly smile on his face and his voice was dangerously calm. "Young man, I don't know what you heard, but my name is *Stannard*, General J. Barton Stannard. Can you remember that?"

As he spoke, the general leaned forward and straightened the officer's collar, looking all the while like a kindly father getting his son ready for school. "Tell me, am I correct in assuming the army is your chosen career?"

The officer nodded.

"Then you're a drinking man?"

"No, sir." The young man swallowed with difficulty, as if his mouth were dry.

"I am wary of men who claim to be champions of sobriety. How about a good swear word now and then? I imagine that is not in your repertoire either?"

"No, sir. I can't say that I have mastered the use of profanity." The officer glanced self-consciously around the room, his confidence rapidly fading.

"Swearing, my boy, is an art, a convenient skill. I advise you to learn how to use it properly." The general paused, then said, "Most of the young men in today's army do not understand this. Why, a well-placed curse can effectively punctuate, even enforce a point. I strongly suggest that you try it sometime. I am certain any of my officers, particularly Lieutenant Lyons here, would be a good instructor."

*He's rambling*, Garrett thought. *It's as if there's something the old man wants to say, but he's looking for anything else to say instead.*

General Stannard smiled and patted the young man's shoulder. "Now, I want you to go back and tell Phil Sheridan that I understand his situation. I know there's always intrigue when so many peacocks get together. And since we're in such close quarters here, there's not enough room for Phil to strut."

By now the smile had gone from General Stannard's face. Garrett saw something bitter, angry, a cold, hard stare, replacing it. However, the old man continued speaking in the same even tone of voice.

"You tell General Sheridan that I'll be glad, even honored, to take a seat. But not in the gallery. I'll be somewhere in the auditorium. You see, I've always felt an officer should stand with his men. He knows that."

The young officer's face had changed during Stannard's speech—the initial arrogance turning to red-faced embarrassment then to bewilderment. At the end he snapped to attention, saluted, and left as rapidly as possible.

The room became quiet. Everyone glanced self-consciously toward each other, shuffling from foot to foot, as a long moment passed. Finally, one old brigadier took a step forward and broke the silence.

"We all agree on one thing, don't we, men? Barton Stannard was a good soldier. He was a commander who never shamed his men. There's no call for Phil Sheridan to shame you."

There were nods of agreement all around.

"You should be sitting up there on that podium, not pushed aside like an old shoe."

"I say we all leave now," one officer commented.

"What are your orders, sir?" another asked. "Do we leave or stay?"

The general rapidly scanned the room. His voice was soft, yet still filled with tension. "Remember campaigning, fellas? We took our luck when it came and never worried about what might have been. I was invited to this party. I am staying."

"That settles it. We're staying too," one man said. The rest of the officers loudly agreed.

"You boys go along now. I'll see you in the auditorium." The general stood quietly and watched the officers leave the assembly room. No one spoke.

Finally, Garrett broke the silence. "You really plan on going out there? Is that the best strategy?"

The general turned to Garrett, cocked an eyebrow, and said, "I have always been a soldier. I keep my word and don't back down. Regardless of the outcome, the important thing is that I'll be able to look myself in the mirror from now on."

Garrett stared at the old man's face and saw a grimness, a determination, that he hadn't seen since Fort Fetterman. If Garrett had any doubts about why he was in Chicago standing here next to the general, they were put to rest. He realized that this was where he was meant to be. He was home. "Well then, sir, I'll be standing with you."

Otwah let out an audible sigh. "*Mon general*, Lyons, what you both have in courage you lack in horse sense. But I will be with you."

Al Bloche took a paper from his pocket and stepped forward. He began drawing a rough sketch of the stage, the main aisle, and the rows of seating on either side. "The way I see it, General, this here is the layout of the hall." Then he made a few quick notations indicating where each regiment was seated. "Seems most of the Tenth Illinois are deployed here in the back, next to that fake army camp. And right next to it…" he marked an X on a spot to one side of the paper, "is the only door currently leading into and out of the auditorium."

"How's that?" Sullivan asked.

"Because I saw those cadets closing and bolting the others," Bloche replied.

"*Mon ami*, first he directs all the veteran officers to the visitors' gallery. Then he gives you no way to get there."

"Looks like Phil Sheridan has us outmaneuvered," Garrett stated quietly.

"Not necessarily," Sullivan interrupted. He reached for the paper Bloche held in his hand, looked at it a few moments for dramatic effect, then in his best baritone announced, "I know another door the general can use."

# TWENTY-SEVEN

*The U.S. Army Military Division of the Missouri—which stretched from Canada to Mexico, between the Mississippi River and the Rocky Mountains—was commanded by General Philip Sheridan. Sheridan was a politician-soldier and he considered the only good Indians dead Indians. In 1882 the division headquarters were located in the Honoré Block. Designed by architect C. M. Palmer, it stood six stories high, with frontage on Adams and Dearborn Streets. The outer walls were probably the most ornate in Chicago, with the exception of the Palmer House. The Honoré Block contained two passenger elevators, twelve stores on the ground level, and three hundred rooms or offices on the upper floors—ample space to comfortably house General Sheridan and his staff.*

Colonel Elliott Caultrain acknowledged the audience's applause with a slight bow of his head, along with a sardonic smile, then cleared his throat and began to speak. He had been assigned the task of delivering the first of three speeches introducing General Philip Sheridan, written for him by the general himself. He finished and returned to his chair on the stage with the satisfaction of a soldier who has followed orders and, at the same time, been able to shine some meager light on his own importance.

Most generals were content to leave mundane matters, such as speeches, in the hands of junior officers. Not Phil Sheridan. Throughout his career he'd insisted on directing every aspect of an operation, owing no doubt to an exaggerated dread of complications.

Colonel Caultrain sat onstage, along with the rest of the general's staff, listening intently to the remaining speeches. Then, on the last word of the last speech, as if on cue, they all stood and snapped to attention. Sheridan made his entrance, accompanied by a trumpet fanfare from the band. Dressed in full dress uniform, medals gleaming, he walked confidently to center stage holding his arms above his head acknowledging the accolades. He stepped onto a platform hidden behind baskets of flowers. This move enabled Sheridan to expand his height of five feet and five inches to a more impressive six feet. After a few minutes, even though the veterans were still applauding (if somewhat halfheartedly), he began to speak.

It was immediately apparent to everyone present that Phil Sheridan thoroughly enjoyed the sound of his own voice. He enunciated each syllable, thereby implying that everything he said was important. As he welcomed individual brigades, calling them out by name, the men stood and cheered. Although the veterans seated in the center and in the back of the hall had difficulty hearing his words they were caught up in the excitement.

No one took any notice when Louis Sullivan entered the hall at the same time that General Sheridan made his appearance. He edged past the band seated in front of the stage and found a narrow service door, barely noticeable, located along the outside wall of the exhibition hall. He waited patiently for just the right moment. When General Sheridan began a lengthy description of his exploits at the Battle of Chattanooga, Sullivan opened the door and General Stannard entered the exhibition hall. He walked forward until he reached the center aisle.

In the crowded hall General Sheridan did not see them. Otwah and Garrett followed, positioning themselves the usual two steps behind the general, with Sullivan as rear guard. The panorama in the exhibition hall—colorful battle flags interspersed between veterans and officers—was indeed a sight to behold. Garrett turned to Otwah and was about to say, "This will give the old man a new lease on life," when he saw the general hesitate.

Sullivan whispered to Garrett, "It's been a long time. Will the men recognize him?"

Garrett realized that he might be right and had almost convinced himself to step up to take the old man's arm. Suddenly, General Stannard thrust his shoulders back and began to march down the main aisle, toward the back of the hall. The general walked slowly, ramrod straight, eyes ahead. Meanwhile, Phil Sheridan continued his oration, unaware of anything but his own words.

The general paused every few steps and kept looking at the faces in the audience as though noticing them for the first time. Most of the veterans were still looking toward the stage. Finally, after what seemed like endless minutes, the crowd began to murmur, softly at first, then gradually louder.

"It's him. Yes, sir. He's back."

Then the cheers came and, as more veterans picked up the call, the sound began to echo through the rows. Some of the men reached out to touch the general.

"Quiet down now!" a veteran hissed. "General Stannard wants soldiers, not yawpers."

When Stannard reached the area of the hall where the Tenth Illinois had congregated, he stood motionless, facing them. The men snapped to attention, dipped their colors, and gave him a formal salute. He began a slow, military walk, bowing his head ever so slightly at the unit as he reviewed his former troops.

Phil Sheridan paused mid-sentence and peered out over the auditorium. He seemed to have finally become aware of the commotion in the back of the auditorium and that the audience's attention had been diverted. He turned toward his staff, seated behind him, and with a quick motion of his head signaled Caultrain to handle this minor irritation. Then, with fists clenched, he turned to the audience and continued his speech. Sheridan was not a man to back down or let his former classmate steal his thunder.

As Garrett followed General Stannard down the main aisle of the exposition hall he told himself that, no matter what happened, he was glad he was there. And, although Otwah's facial expression seldom varied, Garrett sensed that the former scout took the same pleasure he did in this display of respect shown their general. He turned around and looked at Phil Sheridan. *Of course*, he thought, *this is why he and the others don't like Stannard. This outpouring of affection is not for them.*

General Stannard stood next to the tableau set up at the back of the hall, hands clasped behind his back. His face wore a broad smile as he reminisced with a former sergeant. More officers crowded around, waiting their turn to shake his hand. Garrett stood a few feet away, at the edge of the crowd. *The old man looks almost happy*, he thought. This moment in time, no matter how brief, was something they both needed.

His eyes half closed, Garrett listened to the clamor of voices. He was back in camp with the Tenth Illinois, standing near the general, listening to the old man lay out his campaign. This mood was broken by Sullivan's loud whisper, "What's your plan? You have one, don't you?"

Otwah touched his arm. "Watch your back, *mon ami*."

Garrett caught a quick glimpse of an angry Colonel Caultrain walking rapidly in their direction. This was no surprise.

Stannard stood only a few feet away, calmly talking to Bloche and other officers when Caultrain appeared in front of them, red faced and clearly enraged. Stannard glanced from Garrett to Caultrain, then back again to Garrett.

The colonel offered a half-hearted salute, which the general ignored, then dropped his hand with a sarcastic flourish. "Sir, you are to leave this hall immediately—General Sheridan's order. You are creating a disturbance." He turned to Garrett. "Leave *now* or I will have you arrested. And...take that Indian with you."

Garrett leaned forward and looked him straight in the eye. "Colonel, let me remind you, we are all invited guests. Surely you remember Otwah. He was General Stannard's scout at Fort Fetterman."

Otwah grunted his displeasure at Caultrain. "He not look familiar, *mon ami*. Ah! Maybe it is because, like the Cheyenne and Sioux, I only remember the shape of his back, not the color of his eyes."

At that moment, a group of soldiers entered through the side door, rifles in hand. They advanced toward the Tenth Illinois, who blocked the advance. There was a lot of pushing and shoving on both sides.

*This could get nasty. We don't need a riot,* Garrett thought. He turned to Sullivan. "Go back to the band. Tell them to play 'Gary Owen.'"

General Stannard stepped between Caultrain and Garrett, ostensibly to take charge and calm things down. Suddenly, he stumbled forward. As he tried to straighten up, he grabbed hold of his left arm, his face contorted in pain. Before the old man crumpled, Otwah grabbed a stool from the bivouac display and Garrett eased him onto it. To the rest of the regiment, it looked as if it were all one natural movement, not a collapse, just a tired man taking a seat. Garrett leaned over and spoke with a gentle tone. "Sir, maybe we should consider—" Then he noticed the blood.

The general looked up and said lamely, "Lyons, I've been hit."

"It's his arm," Otwah said in an undertone that was barely audible. "Only a flesh wound. It could be worse." The scout pointed to the general's chest. "But all this…not good for heart."

"See who did it?" Garrett asked.

Otwah shrugged. "Big crowd, things happen fast."

"And you have the eyes of a hawk."

"The knife was meant for you. *Mon general* was in the wrong place."

Garrett felt something brush against him hard. He looked down and saw Caultrain's hand slipping what looked like a dagger into his pocket. He did not give the colonel a chance to speak. "I doubt if you've ever taken a stupid breath in your life. So, I advise you not to start now." Garrett smiled. "I can still out draw you. But I won't touch my gun. Why? 'Cause, if I drew, I'd shoot. I wouldn't miss and I'd make sure you took a long time to die."

Caultrain looked at Garrett, then over at his aides, as if to reassure himself that he was in control and would get out of this.

In the distance they heard the opening bars of "Gary Owen." Most of the men in the hall did not realize what had happened and began clapping along with the music. General Sheridan pranced back and forth across the stage, leading them in song, apparently finished with his speech. One of the younger officers walked over, stood next to Caultrain, and asked sarcastically, "Shall I escort them out, sir?"

"I will leave—with General Stannard—in good time." Garrett swallowed hard, but did not take his eyes off Caultrain. "Like the general, I do not leave wounded men in the field."

Garrett and Otwah positioned themselves on either side of Stannard and escorted him toward the rear entrance of the hall. The old man took his time, walking slowly, taking one last look at his troops. The men of the Tenth Illinois lined the aisle to the back door and drew aside to let them pass. There was something trusting, friendly, in the way all the men looked at him, not so much out of curiosity, but as if they wanted to remember that here was a true soldier. When the trio reached the door, General Stannard held Garrett's arm and turned for one last look. The men snapped to attention and gave him a farewell salute.

♠

The evening traffic along Michigan Avenue was moderate. A glittering web of stars covered the indigo-blue sky as the wind gusted along the street. Garrett heard a rumble of distant thunder as he and Otwah escorted the general down the front steps of the Exposition Building. Sullivan had preceded them. He flagged a passing hansom and held the reins. The driver was buried in blankets. His horse stomped the ground, snorting, and shifting uncomfortably in the cold night air.

Otwah helped the general inside and the others followed. Sullivan closed the door of the cab and said, "I guess we're hightailing it out of here?"

"In the army this is referred to as a disengagement," Garrett said.

The driver flicked his whip and, as the carriage began to move, General Stannard looked out the window. His face was pale in the faint glow of the streetlight, yet when he spoke his voice was firm. "Just a flesh wound…in the arm…could have been worse."

"Yes, sir," Garrett said. *But you were standing in my place*, he thought. They watched as the driver edged the hansom out into the evening traffic, then proceeded north. He turned to Sullivan. "Well, the night is still young. Let's drop by Chapin's for a drink and a meal."

"It has to be a quick one. I'll be knocking at your door early tomorrow morning."

"Why? Tomorrow's Sunday."

Sullivan laughed. "Remember, you asked me to find out about the properties listed on Quinn's tote board? And, earlier, I told you that I knew how to find that information?"

Garrett nodded. "What are you getting at, Louis?"

"Well, tomorrow morning, bright and early, you and I are going to pay a visit to city hall."

# TWENTY-EIGHT

*After Chicago's courthouse and city hall were destroyed in the Fire of 1871, a new city hall was constructed at Adams and LaSalle Streets. It contained all of the city offices, a law library, the county recorder, and some of the courts. The building was constructed around the brick substructure for an iron water tank. The tank was used to house the newly founded public library. Work on a new city and county building was begun in 1878, but in 1882 it was still far from complete.*

The taste of fear—naked, utter fear—is a horrible thing. Garrett did not believe there could be so much noise in the world. His eardrums throbbed, his stomach tied in knots. He was crouched in a trench, unable to move, listening to the whistle of bullets overhead, certain that at any moment he would die. He tried reason, then threats, but nothing would get rid of that lump in his stomach. When he could no longer stand it he began running like hell, over ground battered by artillery, finally stumbling into a ditch and landing on a fallen comrade. When the man's eyes suddenly opened, and he began to speak, Garrett woke and sat upright.

The sound of his own breathing, and his heart beating, seemed unusually loud in the pre-dawn stillness. He leaned back, afraid to close his eyes, lest that melancholy face returned. He grabbed a blanket and wrapped it around his body. Still, the noise would not stop! As his head began to clear he realized someone was pounding on the door.

"Sir, it's me, Ada."

He opened the door a crack.

"A Mr. Sullivan is here. Another man came last night. Said you sent him."

"That would be Jacob."

Ada nodded. "Well, he made your coffee. Said to tell you he fixed himself a place on the top floor."

"What about the general?"

"Sleeping. Your Mr. Jacob said he'd draw his bath." She turned and stomped down the hallway, muttering something unintelligible under her breath.

Garrett spun away from the door and took in a couple of deep breaths to clear his head. Through the partially opened window he heard the noise of horses' hooves, carriages passing in the street, and people calling to one another. He felt a sort of sanity return, a reassurance in the pedestrian, ordinary sounds of a day beginning. As he dressed he put his thoughts in order.

First, it was evident that someone wanted to shut down the Eastwood site, which could damage the Lake View Vault Corporation, and thus Central Casualty Insurance. Should that happen, the Eastwood site would be sold. Who wanted that property and why? How much of a stake did Major Shoup and the Union Trust Bank have in all of it? Whatever the answers, the general stood to lose everything. Well, everything except his meager army pension.

Sure, the old man had made enemies in Washington, but he'd been gone from the army for nearly eight years. In any case, Colonel Caultrain was involved in some way. Why? Garrett had a gut feeling and that had never steered him wrong before. Caultrain had shown up in town early and was mighty cozy with General Sheridan at the game dinner. Not surprising, as he only attached himself to people who could advance his career. Rumor had it General Sheridan was grooming Caultrain for bigger things.

Whatever happened, he could not forget Sam. He had to talk to Brock soon. That phony government bond was connected in some way to all of this. The engraver was dead and Brock was hanging on. And what did the handkerchief he'd found in Sam's package have to do with it? Maybe a visit to city hall would shed some light on things.

♠

The early morning air was cold. Dark clouds moved slowly across a sky the color of frosted glass. The temperature had dropped during the night and everything seemed touched by it. Garrett waited, his coat pulled tightly around him, as Sullivan paid the driver. "Where is the senator meeting us?"

"City hall, on Adams."

Sullivan was smiling as he set off down LaSalle Street. Garrett followed, keeping his head down, and his hands pushed hard into his pockets. He moved with careful steps, his boots sliding on the small patches of ice that had formed. They turned the corner and, after a few false starts, found the entrance.

"Didn't I say it would be easy?" Louis smiled.

Garrett did not look impressed. "We aren't in yet, Louis. So stop grinning like this is a card game and you have an ace up your sleeve."

"Maybe I do." He reached into a small slotted opening in the stonework, extracted a key, unlocked the door, then returned the key to its place. The door opened onto a central hallway with a staircase at the side. The building was cold, semi-dark, and as quiet as a church. Louis shivered. "In any case, I just hope we aren't caught."

A deep, rich baritone said, "Then I shall be most disappointed and deny all knowledge of you both."

Senator Lawlor emerged from an adjoining cloakroom. He was fastidiously groomed in a fur-trimmed coat, with a silk scarf draped around his neck. He held a cane, which he used to push the door closed. He seemed right at home in these high-ceilinged corridors and offices.

"You boys know full well this is a dirty world. One cannot prosper without dipping one's hands into the muck from time to time."

Garrett guessed the senator knew the location of not only every closet in the place, but any skeletons to be found inside and, when an occasion demanded, was not above turning a key or two. "Tell me again, why are we here?" he asked.

"Because this is where you'll find the information you need," the senator responded. "Sorry I can't stay. The mayor's hosting a meeting of party faithful upstairs. However, I found someone to assist you." His whisper echoed along the hallway. "Driscoll's a decorated army veteran and has worked for the county these past ten years. I asked him to render some assistance." The senator leaned forward, balancing on his mahogany cane in the gravity-defying posture that is second nature to the semi-inebriated. "I'll leave you here. Driscoll will be out any moment." He glanced at the ornate clock above the door, then turned on his heels and began a slow, steady ascent up the stairs to the second floor.

A prolonged silence enveloped the hallway. After a few moments they heard a door close. A short, stocky man with a round cherubic face emerged from a nearby office. He walked with a decided limp.

"War wound?" Sullivan mouthed silently to Garrett.

Driscoll spoke in a soft, lilting voice with just a hint of a brogue. "You must be the senator's friends. I understand you're looking for records of some kind."

"Property records to be exact, Jack," Garrett said.

"Ah, now, those are..." He took another step towards them and peered closely at Garrett. "Lieutenant Lyons? Is that you?" A flicker of distress crossed his face.

Sullivan looked at Driscoll, then at Garrett. "You two know each other?"

"Tell him, Jack." Garrett smiled, but without a hint of humor.

"Well, now..." Driscoll was seeking a delicate way of framing the information. He glanced furtively at Garrett. "During the war we... ah...served together."

"That's right. Private Driscoll spent his entire enlistment with one foot in camp and the other in Chicago's First Ward. So tell me, Jack, what will you do for us?"

"It's property records you want? That department is on this floor, just down the hall."

"I'm looking for permits. You understand?" Sullivan spoke slowly. "Records listing who owns a structure or site, as well as who's going to build on it."

"You mean tax rolls?" He raised an eyebrow. "Don't think I can help you."

"But you'll try, right, Jack?" Garrett's voice was quiet but insistent.

Driscoll leaned forward and spoke out of the side of his mouth. "You understand, I could get into a heap of trouble for this, Lieutenant."

"You'll be doing me a service. And it wouldn't hurt to curry favor with the senator."

"Well, then, Lieutenant, don't be too long. There are a lot of people about, too many for a Sunday morning."

The county Department of Records was in actuality a suite comprised of three separate, but connected, offices. Driscoll extracted a ring of keys from a pocket and after a few halfhearted attempts succeeded in opening the center door. "How long you planning to be here?"

"Can't say," Garrett answered. "We can let ourselves out."

"No, I'd better check back after I make rounds. It'll be about half an hour. That gives you more than enough time." He returned the keys to his pocket, then limped down the hall.

Garrett pushed the door open with one hand and grabbed Louis's arm with the other. "The first principle of covert entry is always take a moment to memorize the scene."

What they saw was a medium-sized room, one wall of which was lined with wooden shelves holding leather-bound ledgers stacked in rows. Three desks took up most of the center space, and a door and tables were on the opposite wall. Garrett gave Sullivan a nod. "The second principle is—"

Louis shot him a dubious look. "Work fast. Don't worry, I will."

He removed a paper from his pocket and began methodically checking it against the labels on the ledgers, finally stopping in the middle of the row. He pulled one off the shelf and began rifling through it. Not satisfied, he continued the same routine, working his way along the row and ending near the door.

"If you take something out, return it to the same place. No one should know we've been here," Garrett reminded him.

"I tried matching the buildings listed at Quinn's with construction permits. Nothing!"

"How many buildings on his list are near the Eastwood?"

Louis showed Garrett a street map. "I drew this before we came. Those red dots are buildings on Quinn's list. The blue dot is the Eastwood. Only these two buildings are close."

"Who owns them?"

"A company called Liberty Development."

"What about all these buildings?" Garrett made a circle with his finger around the blue dot. "This is near the center of the business district. Have any buildings in this area been sold this past year?"

"I would need to see property transfer records."

Garrett looked at the door labeled, *County Clerk, J. Riordan, Private*. It was locked. He reached into his pocket and extracted a shiny object that resembled a teaspoon, with the exception that half of its bowl was cut away and the remaining edge was notched.

"You are a man of many talents." Sullivan peered over Garrett's shoulder and watched as he inserted the metal object into the keyhole, then jiggled and rotated the tool. With a flick of his wrist Garrett tried the doorknob. It turned easily in his hand.

The adjoining room was larger, with a small window at one end, a door leading to the hallway opposite, and a desk in the center. Shelving that contained bound property transfer ledgers lined the three remaining walls. Each ledger was carefully labeled with the month and the year, as well as a particular area of Chicago.

"This looks like the place." Sullivan began reading the labels on each ledger, now and then pulling one off the shelf and placing it on the desk. "Ah, finally…success." He retrieved the list from his pocket, then began opening the books and running his finger up and down the columns. "Tell me about this Driscoll fellow. I sense you feel he's untrustworthy."

"Let's just say Driscoll wouldn't give someone the steam from his breath without a payoff." Garrett leaned against a cabinet and spoke in a casual manner. "It was just before Grant's Wilderness Campaign. The Tenth Illinois was in reserve, what you call a rear guard. Our job was to keep supplies moving up to the front and catch any stragglers coming away from the fight. We called them runners."

He watched Sullivan progress. His friend moved from one ledger to another, all the while making notes. "Driscoll's a veteran. But decorated? No. His war wound? It's in a rather uncomfortable place."

"How do you know?" Louis asked.

"I shot him."

There was a pause. Sullivan digested the information, then grinned and pointed to a list. "Found something. It looks like over half of the properties near the Eastwood have been sold within this past year and—"

Garrett raised his finger to his lips and nodded toward the hallway.

They heard the click of footsteps on marble, followed by muffled voices, a pause, then the faint sound of a key being carefully turned in the lock. Garrett pointed toward the door to the adjoining office. "I've just started," Louis mouthed as he closed the ledgers. Garrett pushed him into the next room, making certain the door was locked behind them. They stood, bodies pressed against the wall, and waited. There was absolute silence. After what seemed an interminable time, they heard steady, low voices in the next room, then the doorknob rattled.

Garrett pointed to the desks in the center of the room and immediately hid behind one. Louis followed suit, hiding behind another. They heard the sound of a key being inserted into a lock. The door opened.

"No one's here. See for yourself, nothing's been disturbed." It was Driscoll's voice. "Don't worry. They probably got discouraged and left."

The door closed on the rest of his conversation. Garrett and Sullivan concentrated on trying to relax, conscious of their breathing, careful about making unnecessary sounds. They heard the thump of ledgers being returned to the shelves, a door slamming shut and voices drifting down the hallway. Finally, Sullivan could contain himself no longer and whispered, "Who is—"

Garrett raised his hand. After waiting a full two minutes, he reached for his pistol. Then, he silently turned the knob and pulled the door open while raising his weapon.

The room was empty.

"Whew! That was close," Louis whispered. "Let me show you what I found." He went to the shelf and began searching through ledgers. Suddenly, he turned to Garrett. "It's missing! The ledger, the transfer records I found, every last one of them…gone."

Garrett stood by the door and watched Sullivan make a compulsive search through the ledgers. "What are you doing?"

"I thought whoever was here might have just moved that ledger to another shelf."

"Louis, make sense. Driscoll took it. He probably figures if *we're* looking for the information, other people will want it too. That man wouldn't pass up a chance to turn a dime."

*'Course he could be working for whoever is behind this,* Garrett thought.

He pushed the door to the hallway open a fraction and peered first in one direction, then the other. It looked deserted. "By the way, did I mention the third principle of covert entry?"

"An exit plan?"

"I hope so." Garrett took two steps forward and was about to signal Louis to follow when he heard voices. He quickly backed inside and silently pulled the door closed.

"Who is it?" Louis asked.

"Don't know. But it sounds like they're heading this way."

Sullivan hurried toward the only window in the room and, after a brief struggle, managed to get it open. He knew that, like most civic buildings, this one had been constructed with a one flight walk-up to the first floor. Underneath was a high-windowed basement. He looked out onto a ledge approximately a foot wide that went underneath the windows and around the building. "Follow me. We'll take this to the corner of the building then jump down," he whispered, then climbed out onto the ledge.

Garrett followed, letting the window close behind him. "That's one hell of a drop."

"No it isn't. We're just up one floor, no more than ten feet and there's that mound of sand to catch us." Sullivan hugged the wall and began edging his way toward the corner of the building. He waited for Garrett to catch up, then jumped out, rolling onto the sand and coming to rest near a pile of bricks. "We're lucky they're still under construction."

He was methodically brushing sand from his coat when Garrett followed behind, landing with a thump. "I suggest we retire to Chapin & Gore's," he said. "It's not only close by, but the only restaurant open at this hour."

# TWENTY-NINE

*Gardner Spring Chapin and James Jefferson Gore met out West and became partners in Chicago, where, in 1865, they opened a grocery store at State and Madison Streets. Gore convinced Chapin to add liquor to their inventory. Soon that was their major enterprise and they became Chicago's leading whiskey wholesalers. After the Fire of 1871 they reopened, adding a bar to let customers sample their merchandise. Naturally, they soon included food. Chapin & Gore's restaurant, located at 75 Monroe Street, proudly boasted that it never closed. During the racing season the eatery was headquarters for Chicago's bookmakers. If you couldn't find a bookman at C & G's, he was in either the hospital or the morgue. Diners like Peck, Armour, and even Pinkerton (when he wasn't tracking one of the restaurant's patrons) enjoyed the finest steaks in Chicago, cooked on open ranges. This was a male-only eatery, no women were admitted.*

A rumble of thunder, followed by a sharp gust of wind, ushered Garrett and Louis along Monroe Street and into Chapin & Gore's. Even at this hour the restaurant contained a sizeable crowd of early risers mixed with last night's leftovers. Garrett found an empty table in the corner. He always gave Sullivan the needed time to extend his customary handshake greeting to anyone of importance in the room.

Although the racing season was over Garrett spied a few bookmakers in the room. Since all of their business transactions were done in cash, these gentlemen frequently found themselves with more money than it was wise to carry down a Chicago street. Chapin & Gore's provided individual tin boxes, properly labeled with each man's name, to house any extra funds, which were then stored in the restaurant's vault. Garrett had heard rumors that, at times, the vault held close to half a million dollars. But, in one of those uniquely inviolate agreements of the law-breaking fraternity, Chapin & Gore's had never been robbed.

Louis returned from his rounds and sat down. "You are indeed a creature of habit."

"What do you mean?"

"I mean you *always* pick a table near a wall, or sit facing the door. And I've noticed that, on every one of your trips to Chicago, you never stay in the same hotel more than twice."

"Not true. This was my third visit to the Revere." Garrett nodded at the waiter standing next to them. "The man is waiting for your order."

"The steaks are mighty fine this morning, gentlemen. Our manager, Mr. Peace, sent a hack over to the Yards to pick up some fresh cuts." As if on cue, a column of smoke erupted near the lunch counter, followed by the sound and smell of grilling meat. The waiter leaned over and whispered just loud enough for them to hear. "Mike McDonald is one customer who insists his meat be absolutely fresh."

"Guess I'll have coffee, eggs, and one of your steaks," Garrett said.

Sullivan nodded in agreement, adding two dozen oysters to the order. He stretched his neck to look around the room. "Well, now, so it *is* King Mike himself sitting in that far corner, next to the mural. His manners are appalling, but having money covers a multitude of sins. He'll give you a run for your money at the poker table."

Garrett changed the subject. "Let's see your notes before our food comes."

Louis pulled some papers from his pocket and spread them in a neat row on the table. "Here's my map of the buildings on Quinn's list that were near the Eastwood." He took a pencil from his pocket and began comparing lists, making notations. "I wondered which had been sold recently. I made a good start before being interrupted."

Garrett noticed Louis's map was drawn on his personal stationery. The paper bore an intricately styled border and was engraved with *Louis Sullivan, Architect* above the name of the firm. He thought it interesting that the words "Adler & Sullivan" were in smaller type. "Find anything?" he asked.

"That hunch of yours was a good one. Over the past year more than half the parcels around the Eastwood site were sold. Interesting to note—all the transactions were handled by Liberty Development. The name is familiar. But right now I can't place it, at least not on an empty stomach."

At just that moment the waiter appeared, balancing a tray carrying the first part of their meal. The two men concentrated on their food, letting the ebb and flow of the customers arriving and leaving C & G's swirl around them. Sullivan was about to ingest the last oyster when he stopped and nodded toward a gentleman who had just walked through the door. "Now I remember! There's the man himself—Liberty Development."

Garrett glanced up and saw the imposing figure of Augustus Reynolds walking towards them. Reynolds returned Sullivan's greeting with a quick nod of his head, then stopped and glared at Garrett. The tension between the two men was palpable. The waiter hastily removed the dish of oyster shells, as he gestured Reynolds on to his own table.

"What do you know about him?" Garrett asked, watching Reynolds's retreating figure.

"Very little," Louis whispered between mouthfuls of coffee. "Man made his fortune out West in silver. Doubt if he actually mined the stuff. He was probably selling, trading, or stealing claims. Moved to Chicago three years ago, formed Liberty Development, and evidently amassed enough money to hire our firm to design his new home... although it seems he came to talk with Adler the other day and put that plan on hold."

"That all?"

"There have been rumors around the Iroquois Club. The man has his fingers in a lot of pies. Not all of his ventures are on the up and up.

However, you could say that about most of the businessmen who live on Prairie Avenue and lunch at the Commercial Club."

Their steaks arrived, along with more coffee, and the waiter removed their empty plates. As they continued eating, Garrett and Louis reviewed their morning activity—poking at this, recalling that, speculating about other just remembered bits and pieces, most of them inconsequential. They stopped when it became apparent they were getting nowhere. A silence descended and did not lift until nearly five minutes later with Senator Lawlor's arrival.

He stood at their table and the faint smile on his face broadened into a grin. "Did you boys have a pleasant morning? The mayor himself mentioned to me that he'd never heard so much commotion in the building on a Sunday." He did not wait for their answer but leaned forward and spoke in a voice barely loud enough for them to hear clearly. "My morning was profitable. Next election I shall be on the ballot." He raised his palm just as Louis was about to speak. "It is alderman, which we all agree can be a bountiful office. So...until I am in a position to dispense my political loaves and fishes, I suggest you gentlemen confine your escapades to evening poker and any more visits to city hall to regular business hours." He gave them a wink and walked on.

They continued eating in relative silence, broken only by occasional comments pertaining to the quality of the food. Garrett eyed Augustus Reynolds, who was ensconced at a corner table. Between bites of steak and sips of coffee, he continued to watch the crowd. *Like shuffling cards*, he thought. *Never know which card will land where, ergo who'll visit Reynolds's table.* He saw Mike McDonald. No surprise there, it just confirmed what he had already surmised. The parade continued. Evidently, Reynolds had many business contacts, some were army—a few faces and uniforms looked vaguely familiar, some former army, such as Shoup. Various scenarios went through his mind. His gut told him there was an important deduction to be made here. "I don't know," he muttered.

Louis whispered, "You're talking to yourself and chewing at the same time."

"If I am it's not helping."

"Well then, are we finished here?" Sullivan asked.

"Yes, I've lost my appetite," Garrett replied as he tossed his napkin on the table.

Sullivan signaled a waiter, then pulled some banknotes from his wallet. "Well, I'm on my way to Lincoln Park to meet some of my fellow Lotus Club members. We spend Sunday afternoons rowing on the lagoon. Care to join us?" When Garrett did not respond, he added, "The Lotus Club is more than Monday evening poker, you know."

"I'm sure, but you can take me as far as General Stannard's."

"How's he feeling?"

"As well as anyone, I guess. Just a minor flesh wound but, with his heart, I hope he'll take it easy for a while."

Smoke from grilled meat and diners' cigars made the air in the restaurant a bit hazy. Garrett stood up and began a rather circuitous route toward the exit. Sullivan paid their bill and started to follow, but stopped midway to talk to someone. When Garrett reached the door he gave the room a final glance. McDonald was gone. Reynolds was in earnest conversation with some army officers. He could only see the backs of their heads. Still, he sensed it was possible that one of them could be Colonel Caultrain.

Once outside, Garrett was surprised at the number of people on the street on such a cold Sunday morning. He paused a moment and stepped back a few steps, feeling the need for some space. It had been nearly two weeks since he'd arrived in Chicago to bury Sam. Now he was even more convinced than ever that Oates's IOU, his murder, the phony government bonds, and the Eastwood building were all connected in some way. Seeing Reynolds in full conversation with his business contacts set him thinking. Liberty Development was buying blocks of property. According to Louis's map, the Eastwood site would be needed to form a large enough parcel to interest an important client.

Then he recalled an earlier remark made by Rob Powers. The reporter's very words—Oates continued gambling even though he was out of his league.

*Why keep on if you're losing? The general said that Oates got suckered into high-stakes poker games, then lost and paid off his debts by trading Lake View Vault shares for government bonds. Who did those come from? Was it Brock's partners?*

Garrett looked at his watch. Where was Sullivan? The general would be up by now and finished with breakfast. Thank goodness for Ada and Jacob. The old man had someone to order around. They could help him sort through those boxes stacked around the house, a good enough job for a Sunday. He returned the watch to his pocket and retrieved a cheroot. He smoked pensively as he waited for Sullivan to reappear.

He had never been a person encumbered by family. His mother's early death had been followed by dismal years at a Methodist orphanage. By now, her long dark hair and soft lilting voice had become nothing more than a fading memory. He'd enlisted in the army as soon as he was old enough and, for the next twelve years, the army had become his family. In the end *that* family had cut him adrift, too.

What he really wanted was to see Charlotte, to go over the past events with her. Garrett realized something that he'd probably known for a long time. She was the only woman who understood and respected the lone hand he played. It was a strange contradiction, but Charlotte's understanding of his need to stand alone served to make him feel closer to her. She was not a woman to place any strings on him. Charlotte not only listened to his ramblings, but usually managed to put his ideas in their proper order. He was fumbling for his watch again when he heard a familiar voice.

"Mr. Sullivan will be joining you shortly." Rob Powers struck a match and lit a cheroot. "Your esteemed colleague is just about to complete his grand promenade around Chapin & Gore's."

Garrett could not help but smile. "Still looking for a story? I'll take you back with me to General Stannard's. You can hear his report on the Grand Army reunion."

"That's old news." Powers shook his head impatiently.

"Not 'til I say it is."

"What about the Eastwood site? Been mighty quiet lately. Pinkerton office isn't. I was there yesterday and could sense something brewing.

There were a lot of people from Washington in and out. Heard a rumor Bill Pinkerton was about to close a big case." Powers spoke quickly, as if afraid he might forget something if he stopped.

At that moment a group exited the restaurant, laughing and talking, among them Sullivan. Garrett turned to Rob. "Why don't you see if you can flag a hansom."

Sullivan appeared at his side. "Who is that fellow?"

"He's a reporter for the *Inter Ocean*."

Louis raised an eyebrow. "Since when have you ever wanted to see, or even speak to, any reporters?"

"Since the general is sitting home recovering. Powers can write a story about him for the *Inter Ocean*."

"Stannard dislikes reporters even more than you. Remember last summer, after our first poker game at the Tremont? Your regaled all of us with that story about the general having a patrol run a reporter out of Fort Fetterman."

Garrett thought a moment and nodded. "The old man may just surprise you. He has lots to tell about his Civil War battles and fighting the Apache."

"The general may have been a great soldier but the man is as dull as dishwater."

"You mean he's not Phil Sheridan?"

Sullivan nodded. "That reporter is interested in scandal, murder. That's what sells newspapers. Take my advice, let the old man be. He's caught up in a world he doesn't belong to anymore, and living by rules from a life that's gone."

"Thank you, Louis. You know I always welcome your advice."

"Like hell."

# THIRTY

*In 1843 a hospital for the treatment of contagious diseases was built at the northern edge of the city, on land originally purchased for a cemetery. In 1850 the Illinois General Hospital of the Lakes opened a twelve-bed ward in the old Lake House Hotel at Rush and Water Streets, charging three dollars per week, per patient. In 1852 it was renamed Mercy Hospital and in 1863 relocated to Twenty-Sixth and Calumet. By 1882, as Chicago's immigrant population increased dramatically, the number of public and private hospitals in the city continued to grow. The Alexian Brothers Hospital, a three-story brick and stone edifice at North Avenue and Franklin Street, contained all the necessary spaces for the pursuit of modern medicine—offices, patient wards, and a dispensary. Within these rooms were found the modern tools needed to perform surgeries and autopsies, including knives, saws, and chisels.*

General Stannard shut the library door and told Rob Powers to sit, nodding toward a vacant chair near his desk. He walked around the young man once, then twice. The general looked unimpressed. One newspaper was the same as the other as far as he was concerned. "Lyons tells me you're a reporter. For what paper?"

"The *Inter Ocean*. It's the fastest growing daily in the city." If Rob Powers felt ill at ease he didn't show it. He removed a notebook and pencil from his pocket, indicating to everyone that he was, as always, ready for a story.

On the ride from Chapin & Gore's Garrett had delivered a persuasive argument to him on the value of an interview with General Stannard. He reminded the reporter of the man's war experience, his exploits hunting the Apache and fighting the Cheyenne, and concluded with a subtle hint at Rob's future dime novel greatness if he published the general's story. "Just ask the right questions, that's all," he directed.

Now General Stannard was looking at Rob and shaking his head vigorously. "What do you mean? For the people who fought, it happened yesterday. That's what wars are like. Just talk to any old soldier; it'll be the first thing you notice. It lives with them, day in, day out, often for the rest of their lives. Usually it's the most important event that ever happened to them."

Rob appeared to be asking the right questions. Garrett was surprised at the knowledge Powers already had about the war and General J. Barton Stannard. Evidently all those notebooks the reporter crammed into his pockets contained more than random scribbles.

Hands clenched behind his back, the general paced the room in full military mode. He looked pensive, mulling over Rob's last question. "Of course I liked the army, always wanted to be a soldier. Got to be damned good at it, if I do say so myself. Most people like doing what they're good at. I guess I was as surprised as anyone when I made it through the war. Those memories still march though all our dreams, don't they?"

Garrett nodded. He himself had gone from being terrified he'd die, to not caring either way. And then, the final stage, wishing it would happen. Since then Garrett had convinced himself that, except for his guns, material possessions were unimportant. Now, as he sat in the general's library, the smell of candle wax, cigars, and wood polish mingled with burning logs in the fireplace and evoked a pleasant feeling. There was a buffalo head mounted on the wall—a souvenir of a hunting trip near the Powder River—and next to it hung a war shield from an early, brutal campaign against the Cheyenne. He used to think about those days all the time, even when he didn't want to. Then, as the years went by, it got easier to forget. Now, he found a certain comfort here, in this room.

The general's voice was getting shaky. "Sure I fought the Apache. That glory? It's all moonshine. Only those who never fired a shot, or heard the shrieks of the wounded and dying, think it's all medals and accolades. You learn soon enough, men—in the right time, the right place—are capable of most anything. There is no hell like war."

Garrett sat up. The old man was working himself into quite a state. His face looked pale. Although it was only a knife wound in the arm, the general was clearly still feeling the effects of the attack at the army reunion. Thankfully, at that moment the door opened. Otwah made his entrance carrying a tray that held a pot of coffee and cups. He was followed by Jacob, who brought in a plate of sandwiches. Otwah gave Garrett's foot a nudge with his boot as he set the tray down on a side table. "*Mon ami.* Time you go."

Rob flipped through the pages of one of his notepads, then tossed out another question. "I hear General Sheridan was your bunk mate at West Point? What can you tell me about him?"

The room went quiet. General Stannard turned around and stared at Rob. Garrett noticed the old man had a little spark in his eyes. "You mean *the* Philip Sheridan? Well, the best I can say is that Phil always thought everyone should love him as much as he loved himself." His remark brought laughs all around.

Rob's attention turned to Otwah. Garrett made an introduction and gave the reporter a brief history of their relationship, ending with, "Otwah is half French, half Potawatomi. He may be retired from the army, but he can still trail a fox through a henhouse and neither the fox nor the hen will know it." Powers began bombarding the former scout with questions. Otwah, in his typical fashion, answered with as few words as possible.

Garrett caught the general's eye and nodded. The old man walked over to where Garrett stood near a window. He handed the general a piece of metal. "McGlynn claims he found this at the warehouse. He went back after the fire. Oates may have grabbed it as he fell."

The general motioned Garrett to move away from the window, then held the metal up to the light. "This is part of a belt buckle,

U.S. Army issue. Both pieces of an army belt buckle are numbered, the plate and the hasp. This is the hasp."

"It may be important." In actuality Garrett wasn't convinced it *was* important. He had given it to the general hoping to distract him, much as one would give a toy to a child to keep it entertained.

"Could be. That Pinkerton fella did mention Oates's body was dragged to the site. Whoever did it might've used a belt placed around his chest." The general cocked an eyebrow. "They may have retired me, but I still have a few friends in the War Department. Let me find out who was issued this buckle."

♠

"This the right door, Jacob?"

"Only here once, Lieutenant. It was night and black as pitch. Was helping my partner, God rest his soul. He delivered merchandise to one of the Alexians every week."

Garrett closed the door as quietly as possible, then began walking. Jacob followed, matching him pace for pace, stretching his legs to keep up. The two men had entered the hospital through a service area, which, in turn, led into the dispensary. Garrett glanced at the chaotic wealth of jars, holding all manner of substances. One of the Alexians was standing behind a huge marble-topped table, an intense expression on his face, bottles and vials all around him. The brother had a beetle-like brow below a halo of curly brown hair. Before he could question their presence, Jacob spoke up. "Dignan sent us. We're to pick up a body for burial." The brother nodded and went back to his mixing and stirring.

The two men stepped out into a hallway bustling with visitors and staff. After all, this was Sunday afternoon, a time many Chicagoans set aside to visit the sick and elderly.

"General Stannard scouted the place earlier this week. Told me Brock was in a special ward. Where would that be?" Garrett asked Jacob.

"Let's see. The brothers reside on the top floor. This here is all the offices and such. I'd guess the east wing, second floor. The docs operate there. If they took a bullet out of Brock he'd be kept close. You need me anymore?"

"No, I should be fine from here."

When Jacob disappeared into the crowd Garrett took the stairs up to the second floor. To his left was a set of double doors, which probably led into the operating theater. In the other wing he saw a ward with approximately twenty beds, but only half were occupied. Scattered groups of men and women hovered near patients, most likely friends and relatives. Garrett walked over to the double doors, opened one a crack and saw a stoop-shouldered man with a mournful face leaning against a wall. He was squinting at his pocket watch. A Pinkerton, no doubt about it. Garrett recognized the world-weary stance. When the detective glanced up and stared at him Garrett immediately turned and walked into the other wing. A group of men were standing next to a bed near the door. They all carried themselves with a definite military air. In any case, Garrett took a chance and walked over.

"You in town for the reunion?"

A thin gray-haired gentleman replied, "Hell, yes, wouldn't miss this one."

Garrett nodded towards the man's shaky hands. "The war?"

"McClellan's Peninsula Campaign, picked up a fever, never could shake it."

"I'm looking for an old comrade. Don't see him here, must be in one of the other wards." As he spoke, Garrett kept an eye on the hall. That Pinkerton seemed edgy. He remembered the general saying the men guarding Brock worked in shifts. This one looked as though he was ready for a break.

"If your friend isn't here, try the Marine Hospital up in Lake View," another man added.

"There's a ward across the hall, only four beds. But it looks empty."

Garrett caught a movement out of the corner of his eye and saw the Pinkerton walking down the stairs. He smiled and nodded at the group, then eased his way out the door and across the hall.

Brock was the only patient in the ward. Overlaying the medicinal smells he'd come to associate with the hospital, Garrett detected a faint and unexpected hint of lavender. There was an eerie stillness about the room—nothing moved, not even the air. Garrett remembered the same unnerving silence at Shiloh, just before the Rebs sent over an artillery barrage from hell. He forced that thought to the back of his mind, walked over and touched Brock's hand. It felt cold, clammy. Brock stared at him and tried to focus. His face was pale and there was a weariness set deep in his eyes.

Garrett leaned over. "Yep, it's me, Theo. You don't look so good. Thought the doc took that bullet out, put you on the mend. In any case, we're going to talk."

When his voice came out, Brock's throat sounded like it was clotted with cotton. "Lyons…want you to know…didn't kill Sam." He grabbed Garrett's hand and held it in a vise-like grip.

"I figured that out. But you were there or close by. In St. Louis, am I right?"

"I was in…a warehouse, right off that alley. Sam came to meet her… stumbled onto our setup. Put it together. Everything happened…so fast."

Garrett noticed a medicine bottle on the table next to the bed. He picked it up, smelled it, then held it in front of Brock. "Where'd this come from?"

"Lady…had me drink…made it special." His words were short, stifled gasps. Then he made a choking sound and his body arched. Garrett watched, horrified, as the man's body convulsed. Finally, Brock fell back onto the bed and lay still.

"Damn it, Theo. First Sam, now *you* go and die on me!" Garrett felt a sense of panic, of being late again. Helplessness was the one emotion he never could abide. It got under his skin, like an itch he couldn't scratch. He took a deep breath and stepped back from the bed. If Theo Brock, lying on his deathbed, claimed he didn't kill Sam, Garrett believed him. But who had killed Sam? According to Pinkerton, the original engraver had died in St. Louis of influenza *before* Sam was shot. So it stood to reason that Brock had been working with someone here in Chicago. And, now, that someone had gotten Brock out of the way. Maybe they'd been the one who killed Sam.

Garrett heard a rumble of voices in the hallway outside. He reached into the pocket of his coat and felt for his gun, then thought better of it, too much noise. Instead, he looked around and saw a pitcher and basin on a table near one of the beds. A bar of soap and towel were next to it. He grabbed the soap, placed it squarely in the center of the towel. Holding the towel at the ends, he spun it around, securely embedding the bar, then went into a crouch near the door.

The Pinkerton detective walked in and stood for a moment, staring at Brock. Sensing a presence, he spun around, saw Garrett, and immediately lunged toward him. With the ends of the towel in his right hand, Garrett swung it and lashed his homemade weapon into the man's midsection. The towel-wrapped bar of soap delivered a surprisingly wicked blow, for which the man was unprepared. He gasped and staggered backward, knocking over a pitcher of water. He slipped, then fell, hitting his head with a resounding thump. He was out, but not for long.

Garrett made a rapid exit down the stairs then slowed his pace to blend with the crowd.

He reached the hospital entrance and found Brother Andrew roosting on his usual perch. "Mr. Lyons, isn't it? Here to visit your friend?"

"I understand the docs operated on him?"

"Ah, it is indeed a miracle. The gentleman was near death when he arrived. But, with good medicine and prayer, he's on the road to recovery."

"I don't believe in miracles. The man was damn lucky I brought him here."

Brother Andrew had one of those curiously round faces in which almost everything pointed up—his nose, the corners of his mouth and the ends of the gray thickets that were his eyebrows. Whatever the situation, Brother Andrew would always meet it with a stubborn good humor.

"It *was* a miracle, Mr. Lyons. The thing about miracles is, if you are a man of faith, you don't need them. But, if you are one of the doubters of this world, well then, no miracle is ever enough, is it?"

Garrett pressed his lips together and reminded himself not to let his mouth get him into trouble. There wasn't much time before the Pinkerton man would raise an alarm. He kept his voice under control. "Has the gentleman had any visitors today?"

"None are allowed, Mr. Pinkerton's order. That's precisely what I told the lady earlier. She inquired about the patient. Then, of all things, she offered to pay his bill. I checked my ledger and told her the exact amount."

Garrett thought of the lady's handkerchief he'd found in Sam's packet of cards. That's what the lavender scent in Brock's room had reminded him of! He leaned forward and raised an eyebrow expectantly.

Brother Andrew looked at him and continued. "The lady opened her purse and laid out a bundle of crisp right here on my desk. She counted out the money without batting an eye. Then she smiled... such a lovely smile. Asked me if I knew who she was. I told her that if I'd seen her face, I wouldn't know where. She put another note in my hand. Said it would help me to forget. At that point a group of people arrived. So I assume she left."

"What did this lady look like?"

"I forget." Brother Andrew's eyes met Garrett's, then returned to the ledger on his desk. The conversation was over. There was a commotion upstairs, a mixture of voices, first soft, then louder. Garrett immediately took his leave.

Outside he was greeted by a chill, damp wind that slapped his face and reddened his skin. He stopped abruptly and stood for a moment, deciding which way to go. That first evening in the warehouse, Brock had steadfastly claimed that *he* did not kill Sam. Garrett hadn't believed him, until today. Now the man was dead. The Pinkerton man had found Garrett in Brock's room. Bill Pinkerton would assume that *he'd* killed the man. After all, he not only had the motive but had vowed to bring in Sam's killer and see him hanged.

Garrett walked fast, his pulse racing. There was little time left. He heard the hospital door burst open, then men shouting, shouting at him. He began running, bumping into people as he passed, his feet clattering on the pavement, his breath coming in short gasps. Just as he thought that he wouldn't be able to escape he saw a familiar carriage coming towards him. He dashed into the street and waved it down. As soon as it slowed he jumped up, grabbed the door, and shouted at the driver. "Get going, now, and make it fast!"

# THIRTY-ONE

*In 1882 Chicago was not only a leading industrial center but also the most radical city in America. It was home to the Socialist Labor Party, the International Working People's Association, as well as the more moderate Knights of Labor. These groups wanted a decent wage and forty-hour workweek for their members and were quite vocal about it. In response, Chicago enlarged its police force and local businessmen called for a stronger state militia. Workers reacted by organizing quasi-military, self-defense units such as the Irish Labor Guards, the Bohemian Sharpshooters, and the German Lehr-und Wehr-Verein.*

Garrett scrambled into the carriage, just catching the door. He steadied himself against the doorframe, then looked out the window. No one was following. "You can slow down now," he yelled.

Bernard ignored his request, concentrating all of his energy on avoiding potholes and scattering pedestrians. He deftly turned the carriage around and, amid the clatter of hooves and rattle of wheels, headed south at a hell-for-leather pace.

Garrett sat down and turned to Charlotte. "What are you doing here?" As soon as he'd seen her, the thought that she might have been Brock's lady visitor flashed through his mind. He immediately dismissed that as preposterous. Surely she had any number of reasons to be in the area.

She looked him in the eye. "Why were *you* running?"

"I think Brock's dead. He was dying when I got to his room." The words tumbled from his mouth. He started to add, "Someone poisoned him," but thought better of it.

"Did he say anything?" she asked.

"Only that he didn't kill Sam. I'm inclined to believe him." Garrett took a deep breath. Calmer now, he told her about his altercation with the Pinkerton detective. "I heard Brock was on the mend. But when I got there, he was practically on his last gasp. I didn't kill him, but Bill Pinkerton won't believe that. He wants to be a hero, solve a big case, and prove he's his father's son. And he's not above putting my head in a noose to do it."

"I've seen you in worse spots. You can't go back to the general's. It's the first place any Pinkerton agent will check." Then she added, "Do you have any other friends in Chicago?"

"I don't know where Sullivan's bunking now." He looked at her expectantly.

Charlotte shook her head. "Not my place. Well, not *this* evening. I'm expecting guests. Some old friends from Washington are here for the reunion. Besides, my house is the second place Pinkerton's men will check."

As Bernard turned the carriage from Michigan Avenue onto Eldridge Court, Charlotte relented. "You can stay just long enough to catch your breath."

When Garrett walked into the front parlor the porcelain clock on the mantel chimed the hour. It was late afternoon and relatively dark, except for the flickering glow from the fireplace. Whether in Chicago, Wichita, or Kansas City, Charlotte's home was always an elegant and comfortable refuge, a place where Garrett could relax.

"I'll have Eulah fix something for you. Go pour yourself a whiskey." Charlotte looked at him and smiled. Garrett found himself smiling back. Instinctively he reached over and caressed her cheek, tracing her jaw with his fingertip.

"I have to dress. We should talk, maybe tomorrow. We can review this Brock situation. Louis made reservations at Kinsley's. I'd invite you to join us, but I think it would be wise for you to lay low. Just make sure you're gone by the time I come down. Whatever you decide to do, remember, be careful." She walked out to the hallway and up the stairs.

Garrett lit a cheroot and flicked the match into the fireplace. He noticed an album on the table, casually picked it up, and began leafing through the pages. There were tintypes of Charlotte as a young girl, family pictures—her mother, father, and brothers. He turned a page, then stopped. His smile turned somber. He tossed the cheroot into the fire, picked up the album, and walked to the back of the house.

Eulah was standing at the kitchen table assembling sandwiches. As long as Garrett had known Charlotte, Eulah had been with her. She'd arrived at Fort Fetterman with Charlotte and her husband, Colonel Reid. He'd assumed Eulah was a former house servant. Freed since the war, she opted to stay with Charlotte, and was now a trusted friend and member of the household. That meant Eulah was privy to all the history, gossip, and intimate things one could know about a family.

Garrett put the album down in front of her and pointed to a page. He was careful to watch her face as he asked his question. "What can you tell me about these pictures?"

Eulah paused for a moment, considering. Finally, she answered. "I been with Miz Charlotte near twenty years, first in Georgia, then out West, and now here in Chicago. I do know that she's almighty fond of you. The Lord only knows why. And, in your own way, I know you feel the same. So you wouldn't be askin' if this weren't important." She poured a little coffee into his cup. Her tone was polite, respectful, but there was a reproachful look in her eyes. She peered at the album.

"That is Miz Charlotte and Colonel Reid taken out West." Eulah looked at the photo again. "I think that was Fort Fetterman. In the small picture she's with Miss Iris in Baltimore, when Miss Iris was in school, and the other is at Miss Iris's big debut party."

He pulled the lace handkerchief from Sam's package out of his coat pocket and held it out to her. "And this?"

Eulah paused and poured him another scant spoonful. It was evident to Garrett that Eulah intended to dole out information in the same manner that she poured coffee. Her voice was stiff and her words carefully measured.

"That hanky is one I made for Miss Iris myself. Hers I embroidered with blue flowers, and Miz Charlotte's I did with red flowers."

Which explained why the handkerchief had looked familiar to Lyons.

"Miz Charlotte thinks the sun rises and sets on Miss Iris. Always has, ever since that child's parents died and she came to live with the family. Now she's the only kin left." She moved closer and whispered, "They's cousins. That's why, when Miss Iris and Mr. Reynolds moved to Chicago, Miz Charlotte moved here to be near her."

Garrett took a moment to digest the information. He had never asked Charlotte about her past. And she'd never questioned him about his. Out West everyone started with a clean slate.

Eulah poured him another half cup. She looked over her shoulder at the doorway. Certain no one was within earshot, she folded her hands on the table. "Don't think I'm speakin' out of turn. But mind you, just 'cause something's tied up in a pretty package don't mean there's anything pretty inside. Knew from the get-go that child was evil. Miss Charlotte can't see it. Or, don't want to." She paused a moment, then shook her head slightly. "Mark my words, Miss Iris would take the pennies off a dead man's eyes."

Garrett put down his coffee and pushed the plate of sandwiches away. He no longer felt hungry. His stomach was tied in a knot.

♠

When Garrett stepped outside 45 Eldridge Court he was greeted by scattered raindrops that quickly became a steady downpour. By the time he reached Quinn's, a chill had settled over the city, penetrating everything, turning sidewalks dark and slippery. The saloon was filled with fellow refugees from the storm. There was a fire burning in the stove on the far side of the room and the smell of wet wool, mingled with wood smoke, had settled over the place like a cloud. He saw Froelich sitting in a corner staring morosely into his glass of whiskey.

"Is that all you have to do on a Sunday?" Garrett signaled to Quinn, who promptly sent a lad over to his table with a bottle and glasses.

"Watch yourself before you sit. Those Belgians Quinn has working here are a mite careless with their chisels. Just got me a bad stab." Froelich drained his glass. No sooner did he put it down than Garrett refilled it, then poured one for himself.

"You remember the accident at the site? The poor sod died." Froelich took another drink, his face looked bleak. "The nuns at St. Stephen's learned the man's name and residence 'fore he passed. So the task of delivering the news of his demise fell to me. He had no family or relatives, least not in Chicago. So we take care of the funeral."

"You're saying Central Casualty Insurance gets the bill?"

He nodded. "I searched his room. Found army discharge papers. He was a sapper, served with a New York regiment. The man knew explosives all right. I also found this." He reached into his pocket and handed Garrett a newspaper. "It's the *Svornost*, that's Czech. I read the *Staats-Zeitung*, when I bother. In any case, it's all drivel about an eight-hour day, better working conditions. With more men looking than there are jobs, things aren't gonna change."

Froelich kept turning his glass around with his fingers as he spoke. "After the strike in '77, Chicago doubled its police force. Workers got angry, started printing these broadsheets, organizing militia groups. Right now they march and hold shootin' contests. Mind you, tomorrow someone or other will decide a bomb is the answer." There was an edge to his voice.

Garrett saw lines of strain etched into Froelich's face. "You think the deceased was a member of one of these groups?"

"No. . .they take care of their own. Men would've been sent to pick up the body, pay for the funeral. There was no one but me and his landlady." Froelich took a deep draft of his whiskey. "It's happening again. They'll disrupt *my* work site. Put everything I do at risk." His words were quiet, firm. This was obviously something he felt deeply.

Garrett felt a sudden wave of sympathy for the man. "Well, someone hired him. Nice to find out who."

"Doesn't matter. They'll find another to take his place. Like taking a bucket of water out of the lake, can't see where it's been." Froelich stood up, unconsciously wiping his hands on the legs of his trousers. "That's the least of our worries."

"What do you mean?"

"That fella from the bank?"

"You mean Major Shoup?"

"This is bound to get back to him, if it hasn't already. He'll make it his business to find something...anything...to shut us down. This is the excuse he needs to send people around looking at every brick and board. Well, best I get back."

Garrett watched him disappear into the crowd. He took a sip of whiskey, held it on the back of his tongue before swallowing. Regular saloon sounds were all around—talking, laughter, the clink of glasses. As he stared into his drink a thousand thoughts raced through his head. He tried to put them in order.

It all started with Oates. He was lured into high-stakes poker games by Augustus Reynolds. Or was it Iris? Or both? Powers had mentioned that Oates kept playing because of a woman. Garrett slid a little farther back in the chair and sipped at his whiskey. Reynolds, Brock, and those phony bonds were all connected. Only now Oates and Brock were dead, which left Augustus and Iris Reynolds. The knowledge that Charlotte and Iris were cousins brought out mixed feelings in him, like walking on the edge. Perhaps Charlotte had been Brock's lady visitor after all. Garrett continued staring at the liquid in his glass. Then, from deep inside, he felt something swell up inside—a new and dreadful feeling, a fear like no other.

♠

Padraic Quinn knew his patch. He'd walked these streets as a youngster just off the boat, as a runner for Mike McDonald and, finally, as his own man, with his own saloon. His neighborhood was all about rhythms. When you knew the rhythms, you knew when the music didn't sound right. For the past week he had sensed a dissonant current in the air.

Quinn's main occupation was dispensing liquor. His secondary one was listening to the usual complaints about the lack of jobs or, conversely, not enough skilled labor from the clientele who frequented his establishment. Lately he'd sensed an undertone of violence in their daily discourse, a rage boiling under the surface. This evening, at this particular moment in time, the laughter arising from the crowded tables in his saloon was good humored. But he knew full well it could turn on a dime.

Earlier in the evening he'd kept busy, darting back and forth, threading his way between tables, dispensing beer and whiskey. It felt like a party where everybody had come, not to take part, but to look on. Now he stood at his regular spot behind the bar, a pistol stashed in his waistband and a shotgun within arm's reach. When he spied a tidy little man with gold-framed eyeglasses walking through the door, he was immediately alert. Quinn's face tightened as he eyed the man's progress through the crowd. When he saw him stop and sit at Lyons's table, Quinn moved the shotgun to within a finger's touch.

Garrett slid a little farther back in his chair and stared at the man. "Do I know you?"

The man sat down, poured himself a large whiskey, and drank half the glass.

"Remember the last time we spoke? It was at Union Station. I was there to pick up Sam Wilkerson."

"What do you want from me?"

"Those of us who've been with the agency awhile had a lot of respect for Sam. We all heard what happened at the hospital. I don't care if you killed this Brock or not. Sometimes things happen for the best anyway. Only Pinkerton's not in agreement with us. Right now I would say Bill Pinkerton is not pleased at all."

The man took a handkerchief from his vest pocket, removed his glasses, wiped them, and returned both items to their proper places. "I'm in this neighborhood on other matters. And, if anyone at the agency asks me, I haven't seen you." He finished his drink and poured another. "One ray of hope though, you're off Bill Pinkerton's shit list and you're on a whole new list he's just created. I believe he calls it the 'shoot-first-then-disembowel' list. You're at the top."

"Anyone else on it?"

He gave a little grunt that was almost a laugh. "No…just you."

Garrett observed that, for a small man, he had an authoritarian way with a large drink. The man had already downed two whiskeys with no apparent effect. At that moment Quinn walked over. He was followed by a boy who began clearing their table. Garrett placed his hand around the bottle. "There's almost half left and we're thirsty."

"Not my concern. I'm closing early, a private social function." Quinn nodded toward the bar where two more lads were draping Sons of Labor banners around the mirror.

"We've time enough to finish the bottle." The Pinkerton man filled his glass and held it up in a silent toast to Quinn. His face bore the look of a man who asks questions for a living and expects nothing in return but lies and evasions.

"Seems there's been a lot of these 'accidents' on building sites lately, too many. You know anything about that?" he asked Quinn.

Quinn paused a moment before answering. "Men doing a little extra scavenging. A wagon breaks an axle, material being loaded falls off. Someone gets hurt. Accidents happen. A push turns into a shove and before you know it there's a melee."

Garrett just sat back, taking it all in, listening to the conversation.

"Unfortunately, Mr. Quinn, we both know there's what you'd call 'volatility' in some areas of the city. There are always people ready to foment dissatisfaction. These people usually exploit the ignorant working man. If there were more order there'd be less likelihood of trouble."

Quinn stared at the man with eyes both level and sober. "You're giving an opinion on things you know nothing about." Then he shrugged—a gesture implying that, in Chicago, "order" was a relative term. "Time to settle up. Whoever's payin' get your money on the table, and be damn quick about it. The lad here will take your coin." He leaned over and pointed to a spot at the far end of the bar. "And by the time I reach that lion's head I want your sorry asses outta here."

Garrett noticed that in addition to the bar the windows were festooned with banners. Over the general murmur of conversation he picked out the sound of a fiddle. The music, happy and melancholy at the same time, rose and fell in gusts of sound. It fit the place and formed an appropriate background. Quinn's was a typical Chicago saloon where, during the day, every patron was welcome. However, in the evening the establishment became a neighborhood social club. In effect, when he said, "We're closing," Quinn was telling Garrett, and anyone else within earshot, "This is now an Irish saloon. And anyone who isn't Irish, or a member of the Sons of Labor, will be sent packing."

The Pinkerton man drained his glass then looked at Garrett. "Time it is then."

# THIRTY-TWO

*H. M. Kinsley's first restaurant, located in Crosby's Opera House, was destroyed in the Great Fire. In 1874 he purchased a restaurant called Brown's but it soon closed. Kinsley auctioned off the furnishings and fixtures but leased enough space in the building to continue his successful catering business. Undaunted, he opened his namesake restaurant, Kinsley's, in 1880, finally meeting with success. At once it became Chicago society's first choice for fine dinners and parties. Chicago hostesses eagerly read his monthly catalogues, which outlined proper etiquette in such matters as* Afternoon Receptions, The Art of Formal Dressing, *and* Ballroom Etiquette.

Garrett left Quinn's with the smell of whiskey in his nostrils and the beat of "The Minstrel Boy" ringing in his ears. He stood on the pavement and took in deep breaths to clear his head. There was a chill in the air. A sudden gust of wind sent a newspaper rattling along the gutter.

"Don't tell me where you're heading. Best I don't know." The Pinkerton man walked off without looking back, and disappeared into the crowd.

The street was full of people taking the evening air. Garrett decided to take a circuitous route to the Eastwood site. As he walked along, his mind worked its way through a multitude of thoughts. *Oates discovered that the government bonds he'd been given were phony, just like the twenties he'd gotten earlier. That was probably what got him killed. Sam had one of the same bonds in his package. Why? Maybe safekeeping. Reynolds and Caultrain were involved in those shady card games with Oates. No surprise. Caultrain had a pile of gambling IOU's at Fort Fetterman. He hasn't changed. It has to be the bonds. Is Caultrain partnering with Brock and Reynolds to distribute them—most likely without Phil Sheridan's knowledge? His career is on the rise. Would he be that foolish? Who could organize private card games? Charlotte?*

But his gut told him she wouldn't. And his gut was seldom wrong. And, last of all, Iris and Charlotte were related. There must be a thread, however slender, that united it all. Something that would later turn out to be obvious and he would curse himself for not seeing it sooner.

He turned the corner, spied an oil lamp that illuminated the entrance to the construction site and quickened his pace. Even at this short distance from Dearborn Street, the traffic noise had dwindled to near silence. Froelich was standing at the gate. A group of carpenters carrying their toolboxes were leaving and Garrett edged his way past them.

"You've got crews working evenings and Sundays?" he asked.

Froelich glared. "Time is money, for both of us. They're willing to work extra hours for short wages. No one's the wiser. You want the building up, on time, on budget? Well, this is the best chance to do it. That a problem?"

"If it's going to affect me or Central Casualty Insurance it's my business."

"Not if you look the other way." Froelich secured the padlock on the gate. "Ready for a nightcap?"

"Where're the sinks?"

Froelich pointed over his shoulder. "Dug a new one this morning, the other side of the field office."

The 'sinks' was a shallow trench dug across the rear portion of the site. Garrett used the moonlight and a meager lamp near a pile of bricks as a guide. He'd finished relieving himself and was buttoning his trousers when he sensed a movement off in the shadows. He took a step back, stumbled over some boards, and fell hard against a brick pile. When he looked up he found himself staring at Froelich's mangy, lop-eared dog, who was crouched no more than two feet away. Garrett slowly inched his hand toward the derringer in his pocket. Just as his fingers closed on the weapon, he heard a sharp whistle. The dog jumped down and ran off.

Garrett took in a deep breath. His mouth felt dry. He definitely felt the need of a nightcap. This had certainly been a day. First, an early morning romp through city hall with Louis, followed by a deathbed visit with Brock. Meeting Charlotte had only added to his dilemma. He found Froelich sitting in the office, staring into his glass, the dog stretched out on the floor next to him. Neither gave him a glance.

Garrett sat down and poured himself a whiskey. The dog nudged at his trouser leg. He reached down and ruffled its head with affection.

"Seems Bailey's taken to you. Don't take to everyone. Know it 'cause he didn't make no sound when you came through the door or tear at your leg."

Garrett took a sip and tilted his chair back a little. He rocked his chair slightly, keeping the balls of his feet on the floor. "How soon can you get this building up and closed in?"

Froelich pointed his glass at the blueprints tacked on the wall. "There's a lot missing—foundation plans to be exact. I can see what's built so far, not *how* it was built. That's important. We're making progress. Not fast enough for that bank fella though. He was here again today. I'm putting more crews on tomorrow." Froelich put his glass down and with an unsteady hand reached for the bottle, hesitated, then poured the remains of Garrett's glass into his. He leaned forward making certain his words, wreathed in whiskey fumes, went home. "Tell me, what do you get out of this?"

"Like you, I was hired to do a job. General Stannard and I go way back. I don't want his Central Casualty to go under. And it just might if Union Trust closes us down. "

"Then, here's to success." Froelich raised his glass in mock salute, took another drink and muttered a low, obscene curse.

Garrett realized the man was more than a little drunk. "Need an extra hand tonight?"

Froelich took out his watch and tried to focus his eyes as he checked the time. "Wake me in an hour. Meantime things should be quiet."

"What happens in an hour?"

"I hired members of the Lehr-und Wehr-Verein. They patrol, I get my rest." Froelich stretched out on a makeshift cot near the stove and was soon snoring.

Leftover whiskey fumes churned in Garrett's stomach. He opened the window. The wet metal framework of the building's third and fourth floors seemed blacker against the night sky. He was listening to the distant peals of thunder and watching the lightning flashes crackling across the dark sky when he saw it. A faint light was moving along the first floor of the Eastwood. He immediately extinguished the lamp, shrouding the office in darkness, and went back to the window. There it was again, a faint light, then another one. Only hand-held lanterns, but in this gloom they shone as conspicuously as beacons.

♠

"Mr. Sullivan is it? I'm afraid I don't see your reservation." H. M. Kinsley's voice was a low baritone, very meticulous, his diction perfect.

Louis smiled at Charlotte, and their companions, a Major Dexter and his wife. Then he turned on his heel, took a step forward, and stared at Kinsley. He spoke in a clipped whisper. "I suggest you look again, a party of four. My clerk delivered the request yesterday."

"Of course, Mr. Sullivan." H. M. Kinsley was a man whose courtesy never failed. He slowly scanned his book one more time, then signaled Louis and guests to follow him. A thin man with graying hair, Kinsley moved with the same precise grace as his diction.

When they were seated, Sullivan whispered to Charlotte. "I have always felt that if Kinsley were to stab someone in the back he would do so politely, so as not to soil his glove or leave a stain on the carpet." They laughed together as the waiter arrived with menus. "Well, now, what shall we order?" Louis looked round the table, then answered his own question. "I think we'll start with champagne and oysters."

Kinsley's main dining salon was all burgundy velvet, gold-rimmed and monogrammed china, and servers who stood near your table to refill your wine glass after every sip. The room glowed with soft candlelight from wall sconces and crystal chandeliers. This evening a string quartet added to the ambiance. They listened to the buzz of conversation and clink of goblets that rose from surrounding diners—it seemed as though everyone in the room was determined to have a pleasant evening.

Louis indulged in his usual trivial conversation, pointing out anyone notable who passed near their table, then following with bits of gossip. A waiter and two servers appeared, carrying trays of oysters and an ice bucket holding a bottle of champagne. Louis was about to propose a toast when there was a burst of activity at the main entrance. They saw Kinsley effusively greet a group of new arrivals. Diners at surrounding tables stood and clapped when General Phil Sheridan appeared in the doorway.

"There he is—the hero of the hour." Sullivan raised his glass in mock salute.

"As usual, Sheridan is studded with medals like a porcupine with quills," Major Dexter added. "All he has to do is turn up and the man is cheered 'til people are hoarse."

Sheridan walked toward his table, stopping frequently to shake hands, exchange greetings, and generally allow the diners to bask in the reflected glory of his presence. Following at a discreet distance were members of his staff in full uniform. Among them were his present aide, Colonel Caultrain, and former aide, Major Shoup.

After a short while, a waiter arrived at their table carrying a platter of roasted guinea hen, accompanied by boiled potatoes and carrots. Louis took the opportunity to change the conversation to a favorite subject…himself. After an eloquent description of his latest design, Louis offered to give his guests a personal tour of Adler and Sullivan's buildings. Charlotte merely smiled as they concentrated on their meal.

"What an attractive woman," Major Dexter remarked, nodding toward the doorway.

Iris Reynolds, radiant in a gown of pale lilac embellished with lace and pearls at the bosom, was making her usual dramatic entrance. Her husband would normally have stood beaming at her side, proud of his possession. However, he appeared to be in an angry mood that evening. He exchanged words with Kinsley and then, without warning, walked resolutely toward General Sheridan's table, with Kinsley trailing behind. Iris was left standing in the entrance, abandoned and alone, without an escort.

If she felt even momentarily perplexed by Augustus's behavior, Iris showed no sign of it, only giving the room a cursory glance. Charlotte's presence was acknowledged with a slight nod of her head. She eyed Sullivan with the wariness one would give a nameless insect, something best avoided. It was only a moment or two, though it seemed longer, before Augustus Reynolds finally stopped midway across the room, made a remark to Kinsley, and walked back to Iris. He made no apology and she apparently expected none. She put her hand on his arm, resting her fingers lightly. If he brushed her off she would be able to pretend not to have noticed.

Charlotte sipped her wine as she monitored the couple's progress across the room. Augustus's face looked strained. He took a chair next to Colonel Caultrain, leaving Iris to fend for herself. Iris's face tensed, only slightly. She glided past Colonel Caultrain without a glance toward Major Shoup, as he stood and offered her his seat. Iris gently squeezed his arm as she settled herself at the table. He replied with an overly warm smile. All subtle gestures, but duly noted by Charlotte. Something was amiss. "Tell me, Louis, do you have any family?" she asked.

"At this time only aging parents who totally adore me, and an older brother who, on rare occasions, will listen to my opinions." Louis spoke with a blunt certainty that Charlotte found soothing.

While General Sheridan garnered the interest of Mrs. Dexter, and Iris Reynolds, the admiration of Major Dexter, no one noticed William Pinkerton's arrival at their table. He nodded a polite greeting to Charlotte and glared at Sullivan.

"I know you are both acquainted with Garrett Lyons. Where is he? Have you seen him?"

Sullivan grimaced. "Do you mean have I seen him *recently*?"

Pinkerton went straight to the point. "I mean since your visit to city hall early this morning."

"I can honestly say I haven't seen him since about midday." Louis wiped the corner of his mouth with his napkin then signaled the waiter to serve the crepes he'd selected for their dessert.

"Won't do you any good to hide him." Pinkerton's voice was on edge.

"Neither of us knows where Mr. Lyons is at the present time." Charlotte spoke quietly. It was a simple matter of fact. She did not care if he believed her or not.

"Well, your friend Lyons is in serious trouble. I mean to find him, one way or another."

They watched Pinkerton walk toward General Sheridan's table.

"Well, now, what do you make of that?" Louis asked.

"Nothing to worry about," Charlotte said. "Garrett Lyons is one man who can take care of himself."

♠

Someone was out there, Garrett was certain of it. He held his pistol in one hand, touched the cartridge box in his coat pocket with the other, then moved in a silent glide toward the office door. Froelich was snoring away. No help there. Bailey barely raised his head.

Garrett stepped outside and began edging along the wall of the shed. The darkness gave him an advantage. While it canceled much of the light, it magnified sounds. He moved carefully from one stack of building material to another...closer and closer, finally reaching a pile of brick and lumber near the entrance of the Eastwood. He peered around the corner and saw a brief spurt of flame, someone lighting a cigar. An undercurrent of sounds curled through the open areas of the building. He heard a muffled mixture of voices, mingled with the dull rhythmic thud of what sounded like a shovel or spade hitting dirt.

It happened quickly. Garrett sensed a movement in the shadows behind him. He caught a flash on the periphery of his vision and instinctively went into a crouch. The gunshot sounded like a stout stick being snapped in two. The wood next to him splintered, small pieces spraying in his face. His ear immediately classified the weapon as a Colt .45 and the shooter to be about ten yards away. His heart pounded cold in his chest. He forced himself to think. Who was shooting? How many were there? At the same time, he felt a slight tingle of excitement go down the back of his neck. He was out West again, on patrol, having to live constantly with his senses on high alert. Things had been different then. He was younger and they had all looked out for one another. Now he was alone. He peered over the edge of the lumber pile, raised his gun, and fired two rounds. They were answered by more shots. He heard a dull smack of lead on brick and felt a sharp pain along his forehead. A trickle of blood wandered like a thin stream down the side of his face.

*Damn it. Now I'm mad.*

He flattened his back against the brick pile and checked the load in his pistol. His first impulse was to take a quick look around the side, then fire a couple more rounds to gain some idea of what he faced. Instead, he decided to hold the weapon close and wait. All he heard was the faint howl of wind sweeping through the steel skeleton of the building and the natural sounds of the night. He began a reconnaissance, saw abandoned shovels and a series of holes dug along the perimeter of the foundation. He considered expanding his search, but was beginning to feel light-headed.

No time to roust Froelich. Bailey was next to useless.

He took a step back, stumbled over a broken board, and steadied himself. He should have looked up. Someone landed heavily behind him, dropping from the brick pile. Then one, two more came from the side. Garrett shoved the Colt into his pocket. As they closed in, he stood loose, then veered and rammed into them. The men cursed and screamed. He punched and kicked. He could feel the satisfying crunch of his fist on a skull. In a way Garrett felt set free. For the past week he had held everything inside. Now he was out West again, in the army, like the old days.

Someone jumped on top of him, rolling so that his shoulder slammed into Garrett's chest, pinning him to the ground. Garrett felt the air burst from his lungs. He dug his boot into the brick pile and tried twisting away. Warm blood dripped from his head onto his shoulder, as thick fingers gripped his neck. His heart quickened. He was sputtering for air and blinded by his own blood. He managed to pry off the fingers and struggled against the onslaught until something metal hit his head.

He could feel his body being dragged along the ground. His fingers clawed at the brick, the wood, anything to hang onto, until suddenly the world became smaller. Pinpoints of light spangled a blanket of fog. The lights faded and the fog closed in. He fell into blackness.

# THIRTY-THREE

*The* Inter Ocean *began publication in 1872 and by 1882 was firmly ensconced at 85 Madison Street. Ideally located, this four-story building was also well adapted to the purposes of publication. The first floor, at ground level, contained business offices along the Madison Street side and the pressroom in the rear. The mailing rooms were on the second floor, while the third contained editorial rooms surrounding a well-lit vestibule. It was on the fourth floor that the paper was prepared for publication—in the composing and stereotype rooms, the former of which was directly connected to the pressroom via one of W. E. Hale Co.'s water-balanced elevators. Also found on the top floor were rooms for proofreaders, and the night and telegraph editors.*

Garrett opened his eyes and found himself staring into a murky haze. When he blinked, his eyes stung and what he could see was out of focus. He concentrated on trying to relax, conscious of his breathing. When he inhaled, his lungs filled with the damp smell of his own sweat and his chest pushed painfully against the pile of lumber and brick above him. He heard a faint hum of voices, the clink of shovels, the ping of hammers nearby, and immediately concluded that he was probably still at the Eastwood site. But where?

He took small, tight breaths, blinked hard and fought past the odor. The sinks! He was at the far end of the site. His fingers found a jagged piece of brick and grabbed ahold of it. As he pulled himself toward a slim crevice of light he was suddenly aware of a sharp pain in his shoulder. His hand gave way. Momentarily drained, he lay back. The mist and damp wrapped around him like a muffling blanket. He was so close to putting this puzzle together. This mental dialogue would offer him little comfort unless he found a way out of his present predicament.

The pain in his shoulder was a steady ache now. Garrett felt something scrabbling up his leg, then along his side. His first thought was of rats and he tried edging away, with no success. Whatever it was followed along. Then he remembered his derringer and was groping blindly in his coat pocket when he felt a hot breath on his neck. He looked over and found himself staring at a familiar lop-eared dog who immediately licked his chin. Garrett smiled. If Bailey had found his way in here, then Bailey could show him the way out.

A firm hand grabbed his arm as he crawled out from beneath the slag pile. Garrett took in a long gulp of fresh air. He stood up and focused his watery eyes on the figure silhouetted against the tall skeleton of the Eastwood Building.

"You smell worse than day old fish." The slight hint of a smile crossed Sullivan's face.

"How'd you find me?" Garrett's voice sounded hoarse. His throat felt as if someone had rubbed grit into it.

"I went looking for Bailey, and this fella next to me was looking for *you*," Froelich said. "If you need a whiskey, there's a bottle in the office. I'm going to take a look around."

Louis took Garrett's arm. As they walked toward the field office the ground trembled. They staggered, then BOOM! It took a few seconds before Garrett realized what had happened. A bomb! Bits of lumber and brick rained down on the site. Figures drifted through the smoke and dust from the rubble like souls in purgatory, while voices shouted, "Get water! Quick!"

Members of the Lehr-und Wehr-Verein scattered throughout the site. Some took buckets of water and doused the fire. Others went from floor to floor, through the skeleton of the Eastwood. The initial commotion had died down when Froelich finally returned with Bailey at his side.

"How many more do you figure are still out there?" Garrett stared at the blasting cap and wire in Froelich's hand.

"Don't know. Looks like someone set charges around the outside of the building. The patrol found most of them. They're checking now. With this weather, if the charges get wet, can't be certain they'll even go off," Froelich said, as if he were trying to believe it himself.

"Anyone hurt?" Garrett asked.

Froelich shook his head. "They weren't sappers…did a sloppy job… probably wanted to put a scare in everyone." He took a closer look at Garrett and crinkled his nose.

"While you were getting forty winks, someone was at the site. I took a closer look. We traded shots. I emptied my pistol at 'em, got jumped, ended up buried near the sinks." Garrett stared at Froelich. "When did this patrol you hired, the Lehr-und Wehr-Verein, show up?"

"Not more than thirty minutes ago, at the most. Why?"

"And you didn't hear a thing?"

"Not 'til one of them woke me up."

"I suggest you take a closer look at the Eastwood, particularly along the foundation and first floor," Sullivan said, looking grim. "That structure may look sound, but I'll send over an engineer from our office."

"Could've been worse, no one was hurt. Most of our supplies are ruined. It was that pile of slag near the sinks that blew up. Don't worry I'll take it from here." With that, Froelich and Bailey walked off again.

Garrett's shoulder ached and he needed a long soak and a change of clothes. A glance up at the sky told him the weather was beginning to turn. The heavy mist that made every surface of the Eastwood slick would soon be a thin drizzle. He turned to Sullivan. "Why'd you come here?"

"Pinkerton and his men are searching for you. They were at the general's."

"I imagine the old man didn't take too kindly to that."

"Pinkerton searched your room, came across a valise. According to Jacob, the man seemed mighty pleased with himself."

Garrett remembered the packet Sam had mailed to him. The general could end up in the middle of this, through no fault of his own.

"You definitely need a bath. And I must return to my office." Louis handed him a key.

"What's this?"

"A room at the Hotel Clifton. And, if anyone asks, you are Mr. Henri List. The general sent Jacob to my office with the news and a change of clothes for you."

"Who the hell is Henri List?"

Louis smiled. "He was my maternal grandfather."

♠

It was late afternoon the following day when Garrett next saw Sullivan. His friend was walking briskly down Madison Street. He took a last pull on his cheroot, let it drop, then stomped it out with the heel of his boot.

"You look rested. Did you find your room comfortable? It wasn't easy finding a decent hotel room on short notice, especially for a man on the run." Sullivan put extra relish into the last words as they walked toward the Inter Ocean Building.

"The Clifton is comfortable enough. Why're you asking?"

"Mrs. Greig, my usually gracious landlady, was quite upset when Pinkerton's men searched her entire establishment. She suggested I find other lodgings…immediately."

"Then take my room. I'm a man on the run, remember? Best I keep moving."

Sullivan opened the door and preceded him into the business office of the *Inter Ocean*. He stood for a moment and surveyed the surroundings. "A pleasant, well-designed space. Quite unexpected. Don't you agree?"

What they saw was a long narrow room, paneled on three sides in maple trimmed with cherry and ebony. While Sullivan admired the ornamental glass panels near the Madison Street windows, Garrett made a polite effort to get the attention of one of the clerks. Everyone seemed intent on their tasks. "Powers. I'm looking for Rob Powers."

Garrett said the name in a loud voice, so that the nearest clerk, a thin fellow with curly hair, would take heed.

The clerk finally looked up. "Who'd you say?"

"Powers. He's a reporter at this paper." Louis spoke slowly, emphasizing the words.

Another gentleman pointed toward the far corner of the room. "Just start walkin' up. The stairs are over there. You'll find him sooner or later."

The next floor, the 'mailing room', was relatively deserted. They continued to the third floor, a rabbit warren of rooms surrounding the vestibule, each containing an identical scene—desks piled with paper, copyboys grabbing sheets, then rushing upstairs to the typesetter. All this noise and activity proclaimed to the world that Chicago's newsmen were alive, well, and earning their pay. Garrett and Louis peered into room after room, asking for Powers and receiving only shrugs or silence. They began moving on to the next floor and nearly passed Rob by—he was sitting at his desk in a narrow, ill-lit hallway near the elevator.

"You told me you had an office at this newspaper," Garrett said.

"No. I told you Mr. Hosty would give me a desk. My editor is a man of his word. This is the only place I could find to put it."

"Thought you were working on a story about the warehouse fire."

Rob seemed a bit irritable. "No. The regular reporters scooped me again."

Sullivan noticed a stack of foreign-language newspapers on the desk and held one up. "Ah, the *Staats-Zeitung*. Evidently, young Powers is planning a story decrying the plight of the working man. You're *not* promoting an eight-hour day, I hope? We'll never get anything built."

Rob waved another foreign-language paper in Louis's face. "Read this. I recently learned that certain construction sites are pulling night shifts, Sundays too. The Sons of Labor consider this a dangerous and exploitative use of manpower and are mighty riled up about it." Rob's chair squeaked as he leaned back from his desk. "So tell me, why are you here?"

"I have a story for you."

"The Grand Army reunion is old news. It's over, done with. Besides,

I'm already writing a piece about General Stannard and that Indian scout."

"Put it aside," Garrett said. "This is a story that will take you and your desk around the corner, right alongside the rest of the regular reporters in this paper."

Sullivan made a face as if he'd swallowed something distasteful. "Come on, you and all the other reporters on this rag are keyhole peepers. So how can you pass this up?"

Garrett edged closer. "One way or other this story will get told. So choose. Be in at the beginning, or stay out of it and spend the rest of your career crammed in a hallway."

Rob's nod was minimal, but sufficient. He was hooked.

"I want the story in the next edition," Garrett said. "Not page one. Not yet. Put the item in one of the special columns…I think it's called—"

"'Around and About—A Column Containing Varied Items of Interest to *Inter Ocean* Readers'… I've read it a few times," Sullivan interrupted.

"Can't promise anything. Mr. Hosty decides, he's the editor." Rob still didn't look convinced. "What's the story?"

Over the next ten minutes Garrett told him. Then they left Powers hunched over his notebook, scribbling furiously.

Outside, the mist was replaced by a cold, steady wind. Garrett saw a row of hacks at the curb. "Can you make some special deliveries of the next edition?" he asked a newsboy, who was feeding a carrot to one of the horses.

The boy shrugged. "If it's worth my while."

"The names and places are on this card. Just see that these people get the paper, stuff them under the doors in their hotels and on the desks in their offices, whatever it takes."

Garrett tossed him a coin. The lad caught it midair, looked at the coin, decided it was a considerable amount and easily enough earned. "Can't beat that," he answered with a grin.

"What's next?" Louis asked.

"We just made the noise, now we wait for the echo. Best go about your business."

"I shall. This is the Lotus Club's poker night." For a moment Sullivan looked perplexed. "Oh, I almost forgot. The general sent this to my office. It's for you." He handed Garrett an envelope, then bowed slightly, an elegant gesture which came quite naturally to him. He took a step backwards and disappeared into the crowd.

Clouds were moving out towards the lake. Garrett smelled more rain coming. He continued walking, past office workers and clerks hurrying homeward, coats buttoned tight against the cold. Although he had seen no one following, he found himself instinctively looking over his shoulder. After a few blocks he slowed his pace, signaled an empty hack, and climbed aboard.

Garrett opened the rear door at 45 Eldridge Court and walked through the scullery into the kitchen. An enticing aroma emanated from the cast-iron stove, even though its oven doors were closed and the lids were down. Bernard and Eulah sat at the table drinking coffee. She showed Garrett into the front parlor and pulled the drapes shut, but left him to turn up the gas lamps and find a seat.

It was late afternoon and the embers from the fire glowed in the grate. Garrett added kindling, then sat in an armchair and listened to the steady patter of another day's rain against the windows. He took the general's envelope from his pocket. It contained a telegram from Washington. Garrett was reading it a second time when Charlotte came in carrying a tray with a pot of coffee. She placed it on the side table and poured out two cups. Watching her movements Garrett was reminded of how lucky he was that she was a part of his life. But he knew that luck was a fleeting thing. It had to be earned, then guarded. Garrett promised himself that, after he found Sam's killer, he would make a point of letting Charlotte know his true feelings.

"Evidently Pinkerton hasn't caught up with you yet. I trust you weren't followed." Before handing Garrett a cup, Charlotte placed a linen napkin on his lap. He smiled very slightly, just a twitch of the lips. She returned his smile, then sat in the armchair across from him.

Gesturing towards the envelope in his hand, she asked, "Good news?"

Garrett nodded. He told her about McGlynn's discovery of the hasp from an army belt buckle near Oates's body and how the general had asked a friend in the War Department to trace the serial number. "The owner of that belt killed Oates, or was there...left his calling card. And now I know who he is."

Charlotte looked worried. "You're determined to prove Caultrain's involved in this, aren't you?"

He started to speak, then glanced at the album still sitting on the side table where he'd left it the night before. Charlotte merely raised an eyebrow. Apparently Eulah had told her about their conversation regarding Iris. She seemed comfortable with this knowledge. He'd decided he wouldn't bring it up, if she didn't, so he continued.

"Caultrain has always harbored a grudge against me and General Stannard. He used the Powder River episode to make himself a hero and ended my army career."

"Caultrain is one problem, Sam's death the other. You know who killed him?"

"I'm pretty sure."

"You've been *pretty* sure before." She let him digest the remark. "At least we agree—it wasn't Caultrain. He wasn't even in St. Louis. Besides, would he really get involved in a phony bond scheme?"

"He's done worse. Gotten away with it, too." He leaned back and stretched his legs, balancing the cup on his lap. "I've heard the rumors. Caultrain is up for a big promotion—what he's always wanted."

"I lunched at the Union League Club yesterday, part of the army reunion festivities. My cousin, Iris Reynolds, joined me. I believe you've met?" Charlotte took a sip of coffee. "All in all, a very rewarding afternoon. Met old friends and made some new ones."

Garrett didn't know where Charlotte was going with this. Her tone sounded edgy. So he added, to let her know he was up on things, "Reynolds's Liberty Development buys, then sells, land. The market dropped this past year—the man has property but little ready cash. I figure Reynolds met with Brock in St. Louis. The plan was for Brock to print the phony bonds, then he and Reynolds would handle the distribution. I'm not sure how Caultrain fits into all of this…if he was just part of the property deal, or if he had a hand in the bond scheme, too, getting his share to cover his gambling debts. He always owed money, at least when he was at Fetterman."

Charlotte smiled.

Garrett continued. "The colonel is General Sheridan's newest protégé. His career is on the rise. If anyone or anything sullies his reputation, Sheridan will cut him loose. No doubt that's why he came to Chicago early. He has to get rid of any evidence linking him to Reynolds. But… would he be that careless, signing any kind of agreement?"

"Ah, he did. I'll soon have it." Charlotte briefly described her cousin's involvement with the colonel and his callous treatment. *Of course, Iris probably deserved it*, she thought. "For insurance, Iris found their contract and, unbeknownst to Augustus, hid it."

"It's always good to have insurance. Caultrain will destroy any papers or any person that can implicate him. Which makes him a dangerous man indeed."

Garrett stood up. "I need some whiskey with this." He poured a shot into his cup, then one into hers. "This all started with Oates," he tried to explain. "Reynolds and his group held regular high-stakes poker games—evidently part of their business strategy. Someone suckered Oates into one of these games. Naturally, he lost his shirt at first, but was able to pay up with his own cash. Later, I think he discovered that some of the cash he'd won was counterfeit. So he swapped it out with good bills from the general's safe. He probably always intended to replace the phony bills, before the general discovered them. Then, when he got even deeper in debt, someone got him to trade Lake View Vault shares for government bonds."

He sat down and glanced over at Charlotte. He couldn't read her expression, so he continued. "Somehow Oates discovered the bonds were phony, panicked and came to the Lotus Club. Reynolds's whole setup was crooked from the start. He spread his net pretty far and included the buildings surrounding the Eastwood site. Oates was not the only fish in the pond, just maybe the last to be reeled in."

Charlotte relaxed slightly, as if they'd passed some dangerous point in their conversation and now she felt she was on safer ground. "Oates wasn't a gambler. Why would he keep on playing?"

"Some have suggested that he was persuaded…by a woman." Garrett watched her reaction, which was stoic. Still, he wondered if she was involved. Had her relationship with Iris drawn her in? In any case, he still felt the need to talk, to tell her how he was piecing all of this together.

"One reason is money. Reynolds couldn't fund that many land purchases on his own. It's the bonds, that's the key. Bill Pinkerton thinks I have more of those phony government bonds. He won't stop 'til he gets them *and* me." He sat stiffly, holding himself tight, gripping his cup until Charlotte was afraid it would shatter.

She didn't comment but simply sat in the chair across from him, drinking her coffee and waiting for him to continue.

"Sam found one of those forged bonds in St. Louis and sent it here, to me, for safekeeping. I know Pinkerton's going to pin Brock's death on me. He's probably already decided Sam was involved in this. Figures that's why I wouldn't go looking for Brock's partner. 'Cause maybe it *was* Sam. Now it's up to me. I figure whoever killed Sam, killed Brock. It would have taken time and a lot of cash for Reynolds to amass that parcel of land. But he didn't have that much time, he needed money quickly and the bonds were the answer, so he partnered with Brock."

Charlotte relaxed slightly and asked, "Well, then, where are the rest of the bonds?"

"Wish I knew. Pinkerton's sent flyers to all the banks." Garrett managed to keep his voice steady. "Still, the right person could pass a good portion of them without getting caught."

Charlotte stood up. "I'll be at the Lotus Club most of the evening. That's a nasty rain out there. Why don't you spend the night? We can talk in the morning." She reached the door and turned. "The past week, when I've looked in your eyes, I see a future…us…together."

"What do you mean?"

"I mean, don't run off and do something foolish. Think of what you have here, now, and what you stand to lose."

The parlor was quiet and dark except for the flickering glow from the fireplace. Garrett remained in the armchair. He knew he'd been speaking to Charlotte without thinking. Only now did all the dangers and responsibilities close in on him. It was too late. He couldn't take his words back. Part of him wished he could continue sitting in this room. Charlotte's presence would be close to him, along with the sense of peace and contentment that he always felt in her company. However long or short, the time of peace would come to an end and then what?

Sam Wilkerson had been his partner. Whatever happened, he would find Sam's killer and bring him to justice. He owed the man. There are loyalties deeper than life or death, loyalties deep as hell itself.

# THIRTY-FOUR

*1882 was a record year for building in the city, with over 2,500 permits issued. From a construction standpoint Chicago had always had "luck." The city was home to both potential owners with vision, money, and courage, and architectural geniuses who developed new designs that made tall buildings possible. It also produced a new breed of contractor who revolutionized building practices. These men all had a firm grasp of building. They showed Chicagoans that—by careful buying of materials, painstaking guidance of the work, and organization of their sub-contractors—taller and taller buildings could be erected quickly and economically.*

The morning sky was bright but having second thoughts. Garrett could see clouds moving in from the west. More rain coming—not for a few hours—but it was on its way. He walked through the lobby of the Union Trust Bank and up to the reception desk. No one was there. He looked around, trying to decide on his next move, when he heard a familiar voice.

"Mr. Lyons. This is a surprise. But it is good to see you."

"Well, Forsyth, I'm here to see Major Shoup. Personal business."

"Personal is it? Well now, let's not keep you waiting." He signaled to a young clerk sitting behind a teller's cage. "Mr. Lyons to see the major."

"This way, sir." The young man stepped forward and led the way through the bank lobby, then up the stairs toward the mezzanine. Garrett followed.

Shoup's office was actually a large alcove overlooking the main lobby. A desk and two chairs stood atop an island of pristine carpet, which was positioned in front of the only window. Garrett sat in the nearest chair without being asked. When Shoup arrived he could see the whiskey in the man's eyes before he smelled it on his breath.

"I understand you wish to speak to me?" Shoup's words were more of a challenge than a question. "I suggest we would be better served meeting in a private office."

"This will do. Time we cleared the air."

As Shoup retreated behind his desk Garrett easily read the expression on his face. Here was a man who had never quite achieved what he felt was his due. A man who had toiled faithfully in the army, then was wounded but received neither glory nor medals. In the end he was ushered out and this job was arranged for him by General Sheridan, like a bone tossed to a favorite dog. So now he watched other officers reap the rewards and gain the positions that should have been his.

"I received a message this morning from General Stannard indicating that you'd ordered the Eastwood building site closed, claiming it was because of the explosion. There's more to it than that, isn't there?" Garrett spoke quietly, but with conviction.

"Figured right away you were working with Reynolds," he continued. "He would need someone on the inside who would know which properties were in jeopardy, so he could take them over cheap. You never did have any intention of letting that building get built." He lifted the lid of the cigar box on Shoup's desk and helped himself to a cigar. He sniffed it appreciatively, while looking steadily into the major's eyes.

"I wonder, how much do you owe McDonald? I'm guessing about four figures. Otherwise you wouldn't be stopping by Chapin & Gore's on a Sunday morning to chat with Reynolds, or running over to McDonald's office this early in the day."

The silence that followed lasted less than a minute, but was absolute.

"You're the one who lured Oates into those private poker games on Mike McDonald's orders. Augustus Reynolds took it from there. I'd bet even money he and McDonald are working together. What did

Reynolds promise you? A chairmanship at Central Casualty? You've always hated General Stannard. I think it goes way back. He was the soldier you never could be. So, for payback, you decided to take over his company. Maybe you were hoping McDonald would tear up your IOUs too?"

Garrett saw Shoup's back stiffen. The man didn't quite meet his eye, but Garrett could swear he wasn't looking away either. So he continued.

"Best you listen. I don't have your fancy West Point education, so it took me a while to figure things out. Of course Oates lost. But he paid up, even though it used up his cash reserves. That's when your buddy, Reynolds, offered him a deal. Oates could trade Lake View Vault shares for government bonds. Am I right? Oates probably felt it was a way out. I'm guessing it all went smooth as silk until he accidently discovered those bonds were phony. It set Oates thinking. Is that when he figured out the poker games were a setup? Unload some worthless bonds and at the same time ruin Central Casualty? In any case, he panicked."

Garrett tapped his cigar and let the ash fall onto the carpet. He spoke softly, confident he was on the right track. "Oates came to the Lotus Club that Monday evening, not to play cards, but to contact me. You see, General Stannard is a man who likes to reminisce. Over the years, probably on more than one occasion, he spoke to Oates about our relationship and my work with Pinkerton. We were all to meet at his office the next day. It never happened."

Garrett sat back and watched while Shoup absorbed this last information. He waited as the man began to consider a response. Garrett was used to it. The people he'd faced over cards for the past eight years had a pocketful of responses. He learned to watch their expressions as they sifted through them. Surprise...anger...fear...curiosity? He studied Shoup's face as the man considered, then discarded, the various possibilities, apparently deciding on the last one.

"What does this have to do with me?" he snapped. "Mr. Reynolds arranged those poker games. If Shelby Oates lost, it was bad luck. A gambler knows when to stop."

"Is that why you dash into King Mike's emporium twice a day?

I recognized your type, right off. You're a player who, having lost, clings to the frail hope your luck will turn. So you play every number. Then find out the number that comes up is the one you've just abandoned."

Shoup looked uncomfortable, as if he wanted Garrett to leave, but didn't know how to arrange it. He kept staring fixedly at the ceiling, carefully avoiding Garrett's eyes. His fingers drummed on the desk. When he finally answered he kept his voice controlled. "I don't know anything about phony government bonds."

"You just followed orders. From who? Reynolds?" Garrett waited for Shoup to react, then continued. "The bonds were Reynolds's easy money scheme. Of course you went along. Your job was just to cash a few of them here at Union Trust. Only you hatched a plan to get your hands on the whole lot, maybe cut Reynolds out. Are you the one who broke into Oates's safe?"

They sat another half-minute in silence. Garrett watched Shoup, thinking that maybe the man finally understood what he was up against—a no-win situation.

Finally Shoup said, "Look, I don't want trouble, neither do you."

"No one does, but sometimes we walk right into it. McDonald and Reynolds don't give a rat's ass about you. They do care about losing money. Someone is going to take a fall. Who do you think it'll be?" Garrett stood. "Will they kill you or have you killed? Do not underestimate them." That said, he left the mezzanine.

As he walked through the lobby he spied a copy of the *Inter Ocean* on the reception desk and picked it up. "Deliver this to Major Shoup immediately," he instructed the clerk. With that he left Union Trust and walked out onto LaSalle Street.

The porcelain clock on the dressing table was chiming ten when Charlotte finally woke. Garrett's side of the bed still bore his imprint. She rolled into it, letting bits and pieces of their conversation from the previous evening scroll through her mind.

She'd arrived home from the Lotus Club poker night and found Garrett stretched out on the bed. Although he looked rested, Charlotte sensed that sleep had not brought him peace of mind. She'd opened a bottle of whiskey, poured two glasses, and sat next to him. Garrett was a man who had to talk things out. And she was a willing listener. Over the next four hours he talked—about the general, Oates, phony bonds, and crooked card games. When he started, nothing he said made any sense. Then she began seeing things...dimly at first...memories, forgotten, now returned.

The air between them became heavy with unspoken fears and half-formed suspicions, until both were silent. It was one of those silences that can steal upon two people unawares. Finally, the whiskey gone, they lay side by side, simulating sleep while their open eyes stared uncertainly into the dark. And when she woke, he was gone.

Charlotte couldn't remember if it was memory or a sudden brainstorm. Whatever it was, it pushed its way up from her unconscious mind and screamed at her to get up, do something. The bedroom door opened. Charlotte looked toward it smiling, hoping to see Garrett. It was Eulah, carrying a breakfast tray.

"Bernard is downstairs drinking his third cup of coffee." Eulah's eyes made their second trip around the room, finally seeing what she was looking for. "Came in earlier and got your suit. It's pressed and on the chair by the window." Eulah handed her a cup. "Do I make a fresh pot or tell him to get the carriage?"

"Tell him to get the carriage. We have a lot of errands this morning."

Charlotte had never concerned herself with Augustus Reynolds's business dealings, legitimate or not, until now. According to Iris, he was in serious financial trouble. The night before, at the Lotus Club, Sullivan mentioned that Reynolds had decided to cancel construction of their new home. Although Adler tried to discourage him, Louis was not confident his partner had succeeded.

*Just how involved is Iris in Augustus's affairs?* Charlotte wondered. *Iris has always been headstrong and selfish...self-centered. Someone lured Oates into those card games and kept him there. But the bonds? Iris mentioned that she'd traveled to St. Louis with Augustus...*

Charlotte poured herself another cup of coffee. She needed time to think, to see if there was a pattern. Suddenly she shivered—not with cold, because the air in her bedroom was warm—the chill came from inside.

♠

Garrett had left the bank feeling somewhat satisfied. When you finally draw a winning hand it's worth the wait to play it out. Now he had some free time on his hands, so he decided to visit the Eastwood site. Why? Curiosity and a hunch. He was not really surprised that Shoup had halted construction. After that explosion, what else could be done? One last look around might yield more answers. It was worth a try.

Garrett stood at the entrance and stared at the remains of the Eastwood. The whole structure looked old, tired, desolate. He saw a skeleton crew halfheartedly clearing and stacking building materials. Froelich was nowhere in sight but Garrett saw Bailey sniffing around. He knew the man would not vacate his building that easily. He began a slow walk around the perimeter of the site. The damage to the foundation seemed to be concentrated in one area and looked extensive. Garrett didn't know what he was looking for, but figured he would know it when he saw it. He spied a shiny object in the rubble. He started to pick it up, then paused, sensing a nearby presence.

In one fluid movement Caultrain slid next to him. He stood so close Garrett could see every neatly trimmed hair on his upper lip. Caultrain's chest heaved rhythmically, but the revolver in his hand did not waver. Garrett backed away.

Caultrain smiled indulgently, as if humoring a child. "Don't know what you're doing here, don't care. I do know this is my lucky day."

"Time we finally settled things." Garrett spoke softly.

"Let's discuss this privately." Caultrain gestured towards a stairway, then nudged Garrett up the steps with the tip of his revolver. "Sometimes a person has to do things, for the greater good, to advance his career, reach his goal. Now I'm almost there!"

"Don't be too sure. You partnered with Reynolds on the scheme to buy up all that property. But you're Sheridan's protégé, so you had to clear your gambling debts or he'd toss you. Were you in on the bonds, too?"

"I have no idea what you're talking about. In any case, it's your word against mine. Who'll believe you?"

"Whoever reads the *Inter Ocean*, that's who." Garrett waited a moment then continued. "Remember the agreement you signed with Reynolds? I gave it to a reporter friend."

"Then I guess this is not *your* lucky day."

They had reached the fourth floor. Suddenly Garrett felt the butt of Caultrain's revolver smack the back of his head. Warm blood began dripping behind his ear and onto his shoulder. *Damn!* he thought. There is nothing like the panicked feeling a man gets when he discovers he's in desperate need of a gun and doesn't have one. He realized that he'd left his behind at Charlotte's.

He stumbled forward. Before he fell, he twisted around and grabbed Caultrain's ankle, flipping him over. The revolver dropped to the floor. Caultrain gripped Garrett by the neck and banged his head against the floor, again and again. Garrett sputtered for air, blinded by his own blood. With a desperate heave he managed to push Caultrain away. They rolled over and over, until half of Garrett's body hung over the edge of the fourth floor. He dug his heels into the steel framing and tried twisting away.

"You're taking the fall…for everything. I'll see to it," Caultrain shouted. "Even if you do have the contract, that proves nothing."

"If I go, you go with me!"

Garrett used his last bit of strength to pull Caultrain on top of him. He heard the man shriek before his fingers let go of his neck. And then they were sailing through the cold morning air.

Whump! They landed on the scaffolding. It shattered beneath them. Garrett's arm caught on the edge. His hand managed to grip a metal frame. He fell no farther.

Caultrain hung suspended in a dangling rope just below him.

"Help me," he yelled with a strangled cry.

Garrett's first reaction was to let him go. He looked into Caultrain's anguished face and remembered the general's words. "You are so wrapped up in your past you don't see what you have become." He reached a bloodied hand towards Caultrain.

"Letting you die would be too easy."

Just as Garrett grabbed Caultrain with his free arm he felt his other hand begin to loosen its grip.

*Well*, he thought, *maybe it'll be quick*.

He heard a dog barking. Then, just as he felt his fingers give way, his arm was grasped firmly from above and Froelich's face appeared over the edge of the scaffolding.

♠

Augustus Reynolds had been secreted behind a copy of the *Inter Ocean* for the past twenty minutes. The newspaper had arrived unexpectedly, along with his morning mail. He held it up at different distances from his eyes, turning it until he got the pages in focus. After reading Rob Powers's article, his face looked grave, his mouth pinched at the corners. He exhaled a cloud of smoke from his cigar. "You know what this means, don't you?" he asked, as he held the paper out to Iris.

She bit her lower lip thoughtfully, while tilting her head slightly to read the print. When she saw the expression on her husband's face, she tightened her lips and remained silent.

Up until now Augustus Reynolds's dealings with the rougher aspects of his business investments had always been peripheral. In other words, he preferred to reap the benefits of his endeavors while, at the same time, not having to see or know how certain things had evolved. Unfortunately, over the past six months the stock market had taken a downward plunge, along with his other investments. At first he was confident. After all, he'd weathered financial storms before. With Colonel Caultrain as his partner, the property deal should have gone smoothly. Then Caultrain was promoted to be General Sheridan's aide and threatened to back out of the deal. But finding and partnering with Brock had proven to be an unexpected windfall. Luckily, they were able to print and remove a good portion of the bonds before the explosion and fire. Brock was just in the wrong place at the wrong time—he'd been cleaning up loose ends. Augustus had not been worried, even when Brock was injured. That is, until he read the article in the *Inter Ocean.*

Evidently, someone *had* talked to that reporter. Even though the article did not name General Stannard specifically, he concluded that if the old man wasn't the source, it was probably Lyons. Stannard never had any real interest in Oates or Central Casualty. He simply carried on with the firm out of loyalty to his late wife's family. The article stated that Brock had decided to clear his conscience before he passed. He'd proclaimed his innocence and named his confederates with his dying breath. Reynolds figured William Pinkerton would be arriving at his door, sooner or later. For the past year that detective had been snooping into his affairs. Before long he'd make the connection between Reynolds, Brock, and the bonds.

Iris finally broke the silence. "What can I do?"

"Nothing." Reynolds finished his coffee. His hand shook as he set down the cup. He waited as Iris dutifully poured him another, adding a double shot of whiskey to it.

"And what exactly does 'nothing' mean?" she asked.

"Just that, nothing," he snapped. "If you want something to do, pack our bags. Call downstairs, have the porter order us a coach. I want it here within the hour."

"Where are we going?"

"Oak Ridge. We should leave the city, spend some time in the country. Do us both good, won't be more than a month or two. I can rest. Regain my strength."

"What about the bonds?"

Augustus put the paper down and spoke slowly, as if talking to a child. "Much too dangerous, my dear…and foolish. If Pinkerton comes around, and I'm certain he will, he won't find a thing. The bonds are not here. As a matter of fact I have closed the door on that deal. Washed my hands of it."

"We still have time to distribute the bonds. It's ready money. Haven't you always preached that the market sets the price? And you always told me to never give anything away. That's what you're doing.

You're throwing it all away. We've…I mean you've already set up the distribution."

"I've made up my mind. We leave for Oak Ridge, immediately." His voice became a whisper. "The bonds were just quick cash. Sticking to that plan will only put us in harm's way. The market will come back. There'll be money again."

He looked at her. Iris was wearing her hair gathered at the back of her neck. A sapphire glittered at her throat. It occurred to Augustus that she always wore something that matched her eyes. The whiskey and her smile were like magic to him, as always. He felt the blood surge up his face and hated himself for being so vulnerable. Suddenly he clutched his chest and grimaced. He felt a pain, sharp and intense. He looked at Iris and whispered, "…my medicine. In the valise…on the desk."

She stared at him.

"Hurry…hurry!" he gasped.

Iris picked up his valise and rummaged inside. After a few agonizing moments she held up a glass vial. "You mean this?"

"Yes, yes, I need it!" Reynolds was struggling to control himself.

"Where are the bonds, Augustus? Tell me now."

Iris leaned forward and listened as Augustus whispered. She saw the lines of strain etched deep into his face, the expression of anxiety in his eyes. Lately she'd observed too many moments when her husband had difficulty swallowing or took extra time to steady his hand. He would miss something she said to him, as if his mind were elsewhere, and ask to have it repeated. Iris looked at him. He seemed so very old.

Augustus reached out to her.

Iris held up the vial of medicine in front of him, then let it drop. An enigmatic smile lingered at the corner of her mouth as the glass shattered against the marble fireplace. She watched the expression on Augustus's face change from hope to panic.

At that moment she felt exuberant. All the trappings of widowhood—the money, the freedom—would be hers, without the tearful inconvenience of grief. She picked up her cloak and walked out the door.

# THIRTY-FIVE

*The firm of Burnham & Root announced the completion of the Montauk Block in the fall of 1882. The building was innovative in many ways. It was ten stories high and served by elevators, which made the top floors—with views of the surrounding city—prime office space. The plumbing and heating systems ran outside of the walls and were touted as being especially healthful. However, its real significance lay below the surface, as its spread foundation solved one of the most persistent problems in Chicago construction—how to erect tall buildings on soft sand and clay. John Root liked to describe it as a raft...a building floating, braced on a raft of iron and steel. The stone and brick façade was nothing more than a skin.*

Although the crowd in the lobby of the Grand Pacific Hotel was sparse for midday, the first floor saloon was packed. Businessmen and travelers crowded the tables or stood shoulder to shoulder at the bar. Garrett's right arm and shoulder still ached from his earlier confrontation with Caultrain. However, he found that, with practice, he could drink with his left hand. He had been practicing for a half hour before he spied the man he'd come to see. He walked over and tapped him on the back.

Shoup's initial look of surprise was immediately followed by a thin-lipped, sardonic smile. He motioned to the bar man. "I don't believe we have anything further to discuss, Lyons."

"Oh, I think we do. Recognized that U.S. Army belt you're wearing first time we met at the Eastwood site. Not usual issue, the kind us regular officers had. West Pointers, like yourself, wear one with custom, hand-stitched leather, am I right? Took a closer look during our recent discussion over at Union Trust."

Garrett paused for a reaction, got none, then moved on. "What happened to the buckle? Somehow, that particular belt doesn't look right with a plain, ordinary civilian buckle."

Shoup carefully avoided Garrett's eyes. "It's none of your business. Let's just say it's been missing for a while," he replied in clipped tones.

"I was just asking. Figure you lost it, the buckle I mean, near that warehouse by the river. 'Cause it was found next to the body of one Shelby Oates."

Shoup finished his whiskey in one gulp then turned to leave.

Garrett grabbed his arm and leaned close to his ear. His voice was soft, but held an unmistakable warning. "What happened?" His grip on Shoup's arm tightened.

"It was an accident," Shoup hissed. "We scuffled. The gun discharged. My word against yours."

"Why dump Oates's body in that burned-out warehouse?"

"Why not? I read about your warehouse exploits in the newspaper." A sardonic smile remained on Shoup's lips, but was gone from his eyes and replaced by his professional soldier's thousand-yard stare.

Garrett signaled the barman for another round. "Look, Oates is dead. How he died, or why, doesn't interest me. Only, Bill Pinkerton is determined to recover those bonds and he's not a man to come up empty handed. He won't let you out of Chicago with them. 'Course, once he has you and the bonds he'll probably tack on a murder charge."

"What are you saying, Lyons?"

"You probably have a good idea who killed Sam. And that should scare you. Does me."

The muscles in Shoup's jaw tightened, like an arrow hitting home.

"What I'm saying is...I'm giving you a chance. I came to Chicago to bury my partner and find his killer. Sam is tucked away at Rosehill

Cemetery. And what you've got stashed up in a room here at the Grand Pacific will help me nail his killer. I know it couldn't have been you. Why? You would never have been able to get the drop on Sam. So, you walk away *now* and leave it. And this doesn't go any further."

Shoup's nod was minimal, but sufficient.

"Good. But first we finish our whiskey."

♠

Charlotte stood outside the door of Reynolds's suite at the Palmer House. She raised her hand to knock, then hesitated. On her way there she'd still held a tenuous belief that her thoughts about Iris were a mistake, a misunderstanding. Only, now Charlotte realized she could no longer avoid facing the truth. She wanted a serious talk with Iris in order to settle things.

A porter came down the hall and rapped on the door. When there was no answer he said to her, "Here to tell Mr. Reynolds the coach he ordered is ready. Want to know if the boys can begin loading his bags."

When no one came to the door Charlotte jiggled the knob and found it unlocked, so she pushed it open. The sitting room was quiet. The porter followed behind her and turned up the lamp. As the room lightened she saw Augustus sprawled across the sofa. She rushed over and touched his hand. It was clammy and cold, his face pale, lips turning blue.

"Get a doctor. *Now!*" she ordered. Startled, the porter rushed out.

Augustus opened his eyes and stared vacantly at her. After a moment, he seemed to recognize Charlotte and tried to speak. His words were nothing but mumbled sounds. Frustrated, he pointed toward the fireplace.

Charlotte looked at the shattered medicine vial. "Do you have another?"

He nodded feebly.

"Where? Your valise?"

Not waiting for an answer, she went over and upended the case, scattering its contents across the desktop. She found another bottle of medicine and held it up in front of him.

He smiled gratefully.

Charlotte poured some of the liquid into his mouth and waited.

After a few moments his face seemed to gain more color and he stopped gasping for breath.

"What happened? Where's Iris?" she asked.

He glanced again at the shattered medicine vial. "Gone. Left...me."

Charlotte gave his hand a reassuring squeeze. She was on the verge of saying something else and then realized it would not help. She felt a deep sense of dread.

*Iris, what have you done?* She shivered as if her own words frightened her.

Garrett let himself into the suite at the Grand Pacific, using the key Shoup had reluctantly handed over. It didn't take him long to find the phony bonds hidden in the bedroom. He carried the satchel containing them out to the sitting room and placed it next to a small table in the shadows of one corner. He lit the gas lamp, then turned it down, so that whoever walked in could not see him, then sat and waited. The room felt warm. He unbuttoned his jacket and stared out the window.

Less than ten minutes passed before he heard the knob rattle and the door open. Shoup's partner entered the room, paused, then walked over and turned up the lamp.

"Whoever you're expecting, I assume it's not me," Garrett said.

If Iris Reynolds was surprised to see him, she didn't show it. She dropped her purse on the table. It landed with a thump. "Lyons! Why are you here?"

"Same thing you came for." He pointed to the satchel on the floor next to him. "If my presence here disturbs you, I'm glad. In any case, sit down."

Iris was profiled against the window. Her blonde hair, gathered at the back of her neck, glowed in the lamplight. She turned slowly and faced him. "Since we both want the same thing, I'm sure we can reach an amicable agreement."

Garrett shook his head. "I don't think so. Right now Bill Pinkerton is convinced I killed Brock. He's determined to bring me in and put a noose around my neck. I didn't kill him. You did. You were at the hospital Sunday morning and gave Brock the poison."

Her vivid blue eyes stared at him. "Are you sure? Did he talk?"

"He didn't have to."

"Well, then you have no proof. Besides, Brock was a forger, a crook, and a liar."

There was something in her manner—half-joking, half-threatening—that made Garrett wary. "You made quite an impression on Brother Andrew. He remembered every word of his conversation with you. And I just had a long talk with your husband's partner, Shoup."

"And who'll believe him. . .or Brother Andrew for that matter?"

"Bill Pinkerton. Of course, you just might be able to talk Pinkerton out of a hanging. Maybe you'll just get a long prison sentence instead."

Iris took a step back and looked him over. Then she smiled. The hem of her silk dress rustled softly as she walked across the carpet and moved closer to him. "It doesn't have to end like this. We should join forces. This is our chance. We can travel to New York or Washington, cash in those bonds. I can make you forget about Charlotte, about everything." Her voice became an intimate whisper, as warm and soft as the purring of a beautiful cat. She leaned closer and whispered, "Listen to me, Garrett. Imagine living out every dark dream of what you've ever wanted to do with a woman. I'll make it all real."

Garrett caught a whiff of lavender, faint and a little sweet, as Iris's hand touched his cheek. He felt her breath near his lips.

"For how long? I'd spend the next year looking over my shoulder, waiting for you to plunge a knife in my back. What about Sam?" he said.

"Who?"

"Sam Wilkerson. He was my partner. I set quite a store on Sam. He was more than a partner, he was a friend. I don't have too many of them. When a man's partner is killed, he does something about it. Besides, we were both Pinkerton agents. We watched each other's back. Mark my words, Bill Pinkerton won't let Sam's murder go unpunished. It's bad for business if one of your own gets killed and you don't do anything about it. It's like asking a dog to catch a rabbit, then to let it go. It can be done, but it's not a natural thing."

Garrett took a moment to gain his composure, then continued. "For a time I thought Brock killed Sam. But he was a forger, not a killer, wasn't in his nature. So then I asked myself, who murdered Sam? My partner was shot point blank, up close. Hard to believe, 'cause Sam Wilkerson was a crack shot. No one ever could get the drop on him. But that last time he never drew his gun. Took me some time, but I figured it all out. While Brock and your husband were in St. Louis to set up their plan for printing and distributing the bonds, you arranged to meet Sam."

He watched her face, saw his words, and their meaning, reach her eyes. After a moment she understood and her expression stiffened. When he resumed speaking his voice was calm, expressionless.

"At first nothing made sense. Why would Sam walk down *any* alley, alone, at night? It just wasn't in his nature. Then I remembered Sam had one weakness—pretty, young, blonde ladies. I figured Sam Wilkerson would walk down any alley to meet you."

Iris's lips parted, then pressed together, etching harsh lines from her mouth to her nostrils. She was about to speak. Then, sensing a presence, she turned. Charlotte was standing in the doorway. Iris stared at her cousin with bright, frightened eyes, pleading to be understood, hoping that loyalty was too precious not to be extended both ways. "Don't listen to him. He doesn't know what he's saying. He must be drunk. You believe in me, don't you?"

"I'm sure Charlotte would like to." Garrett felt the blood running slowly through his veins, heartbeat by heartbeat, and when he spoke his voice sounded like someone else's. "But you're the one who killed Sam Wilkerson and I'll see you take the rap for it. I promised Sam's mother and I keep a promise."

Charlotte's cheeks were flushed and there were tiny beads of sweat on her upper lip. Garrett looked into her eyes with sadness. He could think of no other words to say.

"I am sure Iris can provide us with a reasonable explanation." Charlotte's words were blunt.

Iris stepped back and leaned against the table. No one moved. After a while the silence became uneasy.

"Not like you to be at a loss for words, my dear. Maybe you should start by explaining what you did to your husband." Charlotte told Garrett about finding Reynolds, the broken medicine vial, and sending the porter for the doctor. Then she turned to her cousin. "Your husband will recover, which I'm sure you are pleased to hear." There was something so calm about Charlotte's voice that Garrett became uneasy.

"You have no proof, Charlotte. I am tired of your constant lectures on good manners…on being a good wife…on having a place in society." She looked at Garrett. "And I'm tired of your silly accusations. Did anyone see me? No! Besides, it was an accident!"

"I may not have proof, but I am certain you killed both Sam *and* Brock."

Inner turmoil showed clearly in Charlotte's eyes.

Suddenly Iris spun around. She had been fumbling in her purse as they spoke and now she flung it to the floor. Garrett was startled to see that she was pointing a revolver directly at his chest. She gestured to him to move away from the corner. "I'm through talking. This is my chance. I'm taking it. Those bonds will buy me freedom and a new life." With her free hand she grabbed the satchel.

Charlotte looked surprised, then stunned and, finally, hurt. "All these years, I guess I never saw who you truly were."

"Well, you see me now."

"Iris think…just think. Where you're going, there's no turning back. Maybe I can help."

Charlotte stepped toward Iris, her arms outstretched, pleading. Suddenly, there was a loud bang. Garrett watched in horror as Charlotte crumpled to the floor. He rushed over and knelt by her side.

"It just grazed my shoulder. I'm fine."

"You sure?"

"Yes…but she's taken the bonds. Go after her. Quickly."

Garrett rushed out the door and down the stairway. Charlotte retrieved her handkerchief and pressed it against the wound. Then she stumbled after him, clutching at her shoulder. She felt weak and had to stop several times to regain her composure. When she finally reached the hotel lobby she saw a crowd gathered at the Jackson Street entrance.

Voices were shouting, "Terrible it was...that carriage...came out of nowhere...poor woman...ran right out she did...someone get a doctor!"

Charlotte pushed through the crowd, but was stopped by Garrett before she could reach the street. He held her gently by the arms and looked her in the eye.

"I was too late. I couldn't stop her."

Charlotte struggled to look over his shoulder and saw a woman's crumpled body on the ground. It was Iris, the satchel next to her.

Garrett drew in his breath to speak, then saw in Charlotte's eyes the futility of it. He realized that whatever he said he would regret and saved himself the indignity. He released her and she knelt down to cradle Iris's lifeless body in her arms. She looked at Garrett as he picked up the satchel. Their eyes met and, though nothing was said, everything was understood.

# THIRTY-SIX

*As 1882 drew to a close Chicagoans had many reasons to be optimistic. The city now stretched over twelve miles along its lakefront and ten miles into the vastness of its suburbs. A new era of expansion and development was underway, resulting in not only Chicago's first skyscraper but the promise of more tall buildings to come. This new architecture was significant because it not only solved the technical problems of architects but also answered the needs of a booming commercial city.*

It was the tail end of a long day after an even longer week. Garrett was sitting in the general's office, staring out the window at a steel gray sky that mirrored his present mood. This past hour a hundred thoughts had raced through his head and he was unable to seize a single one. What he did know was that life is never what one expects it to be. Just as a person comes to the fringe of happiness…somehow it gets jerked away.

General Stannard sat across from him, a copy of the *Tribune* in his hand and a smile on his face. "By now, Phil Sheridan and his cronies have discovered that I still have some bite left in my bark." He twirled his cigar between two fingers, took several puffs, then blew smoke toward the ceiling. Genuinely pleased with himself, he added, "Seems Pinkerton recovered some phony government bonds, along with a notorious counterfeiter. William Pinkerton is the hero of the hour. He'll be busy basking in the U.S. government's glory, so you'll have no more problems with him."

When Garrett did not respond the general continued talking, more to himself than anyone else. "Sure, now, Shelby Oates got us in a mess. But the Eastwood Building was nothing more than a flanking maneuver, never the objective. It was expendable. I always considered that. Toss the howling dogs a bone, I say. Let Shoup, and his cronies at Union Trust, gnaw on it. That's all they're going to get."

"I did tell Shoup that if he turned over the bonds I'd let him walk. But I still have that buckle. I'm going to hold that in reserve, if he causes us trouble again."

"Same goes for Caultrain," the general contributed. "Iris had that contract, but we never did find it, so we have nothing concrete on him. Still, we're not done with him yet. Let him stew in his own juices for a while. We'll think of how to deal with him soon enough. In any case, I hear he's not quite Sheridan's favorite anymore. Hear he may soon be transferred to the arsenal in Baltimore. A dead end job shuffling papers. What I don't understand is why Reynolds doesn't have to answer for his part in all of this."

"Charlotte tells me that Iris's death was too much for him to bear. He's a shell of his former self. She doesn't expect he'll last longer than another month or two. Pinkerton probably figures he'll just let him fade away. That whole land grab of his fell apart in the end."

The general picked up a small framed print of his late wife. For a moment his eyes were gentle, faraway, remembering some past happiness. Then he added it to the box on his desk that contained other mementos that had adorned his office.

"The objective all along was using the Eastwood to bring down Central Casualty Insurance and to get ahold of that building site. Mary's father, Quentin, founded this company. Central Casualty was his life and therefore it was important to her. Mary had too many disappointments. Maybe I was one. So I could not lose it, you realize that? Now I think it's in good hands. I told you, didn't I? Had some inquiries from the Home Insurance Company. They want to move here and offered a good price. I may take it. Of course I'll be available. But I need you here to keep an eye on things…help me in the transition. What do you say?"

Garrett picked up his glass. He didn't drink from it, merely swirled the whiskey around, then put it down again. What he wanted was to see Charlotte, talk to her, try to make everything right again. Garrett wanted this so profoundly that it required a deep effort to keep listening to the general, let alone be civil to him. So, when he did speak, his voice held the dead calm of truth.

"Frankly, sir, I don't know what to do anymore."

The general smiled sympathetically. It seemed to him that you could find in the memory of every man the bittersweet shadow of a woman. There was a prolonged silence. When he spoke, it was quietly and with firm conviction. "It would just be a couple of months, 'til spring."

"Just a few weeks of my time, you said before." Garrett smiled.

The general nodded. "You know, I do *not* abandon my troops. I'll just be directing the campaign from the field tent, so to speak. Then I intend to sit by the fire this winter. Put out Mary's things the way she would have wanted them." There was something in the general's voice, a wistfulness, a memory of something he once had, but was now gone.

"Consider the fact that during this time you'll have money in your pocket and a place to bunk. We must think about today and always look forward to tomorrow. One never knows what will happen."

"Well, then, how can I refuse?" Garrett touched the drink to his lips, then drained it.

♠

Arranging Iris's funeral had been a long, tedious affair. Augustus was too ill to cope, thus it all became Charlotte's responsibility. Now she was sitting in her front parlor. The drapes were drawn. The embers of a fire bathed the room in a faint glow. The memory of the church, with the smell of incense and candle smoke, came back to her. The initial shock had passed and the reality of Iris's death settled upon her.

She glanced at the condolence cards scattered on the side table. Then she opened the album in her lap and began leafing through the pages, staring at familiar images—Iris, her father, her late husband. Old memories returned, things forgotten years ago that had been pushed into the oblivion at the edges of her mind. Her eyes glazed over and she absentmindedly unpinned Garrett's brooch from her blouse. She stared at the oval-shaped cameo edged in pearls. Amid the jumble of thoughts her late husband's words forced their way into clarity, *You would have made a good soldier. You don't know the meaning of fear.*

A person isn't afraid until they realize they have something to lose. When you love someone, you're terrified—there's so much at stake. Suddenly she rose and stood before the mirror, watching the teardrops run slowly down her face. She didn't like the expression of the woman who stared back at her. She refastened the brooch, then turned abruptly, gathered the condolence cards, shoved them into the album, and closed it.

At that moment Eulah entered. "Bernard's here, about the Lotus Club this Monday."

"He can make the usual arrangements." Charlotte pointed to the album. "And pack that up with the mourning hat and veil. I'll wear my lavender dress. Half mourning, as befits a cousin."

Eulah picked up the items. She started to speak, then thought better of it. Charlotte watched her leave. When the door closed she poured herself a whiskey and sat again before the fire.

There's only one way to restart a life and that is by facing the truth.

# AUTHOR'S NOTE

*Honor Above All* began as a short story published in a Western fiction magazine, which I then decided to expand into a novel. Garrett's story continues against the backdrop of Chicago's rebuilding after the Great Fire. I chose to set it in the year 1882, the beginning of the city's Golden Age of Architecture. Greater advances in construction were made in that period than in any other time.

Although the main characters in this book are fictional, readers may recognize more well known historical figures in Chicago's architectural and political arenas who are part of its story.

Those interested in exploring Chicago's history and architecture further may find this partial bibliography of interest. It is by no means a complete list of the sources I consulted while writing this novel.

♠

Andreas, Alfred T. *History of Chicago*, v. III (1871–1885). A. T. Andreas, 1884. [available online: https://archive.org/details/historyofchicago03andruoft]

Berger, Miles L. T*hey Built Chicago: Entrepreneurs Who Shaped a Great City's Architecture*. Bonus Books, 1992.

Dedmon, Emmett. *Fabulous Chicago*. Random House, 1953.

Duis, Perry. *Challenging Chicago: Coping with Everyday Life, 1837–1920.* University of Illinois Press, 1998.

Hines, Thomas S. *Burnham of Chicago: Architect and Planner.* University of Chicago Press, 1979.

Knight, Oliver. *Life and Manners in the Frontier Army.* University of Oklahoma Press, 1978.

Lindberg, Richard. *The Gambler King of Clark Street.* Southern Illinois University Press, 2009.

Longstreet, Stephen. *Chicago, 1860–1919.* McKay, 1973.

McPhaul, John J. *Deadlines & Monkeyshines: The Fabled World of Chicago Journalism.* Prentice-Hall, 1962.

Meeker, Arthur. *Prairie Avenue.* Knopf, 1949.

Miller, Donald L. *City of the Century: The Epic of Chicago and the Making of America.* Simon & Schuster, 1996.

Morn, Frank. *The Eye That Never Sleeps: A History of the Pinkerton National Detective Agency.* Indiana University Press, 1982.

Randall, Frank A. *History of the Development of Building Construction in Chicago.* University of Illinois Press, 1949.

Shultz, Earl, and Walter Simmons. *Offices in the Sky.* Bobbs-Merrill, 1959.

Starrett, Paul. *Changing the Skyline: An Autobiography.* McGraw-Hill, 1938.

Twombly, Robert. *Louis Sullivan: His Life and Work.* University of Chicago Press, 1986.

# ACKNOWLEDGMENTS

I will admit, writing can be solitary, but I have never found it to be lonely. Along the way I've had my own personal mentors to counsel me, guide me, lift my spirits, to keep me going as I took one step at a time.

My thanks to Percy Spurlark Parker, who critiqued my first short story and told me I had a "way with words"; Phyllis Choyke and Mary Sass, who started the journey with me; my early readers, Joanne Strecker and Mary Harris; and Grace Morgan, who set me on the right course when I floundered. And to Harriette Robinet, Helen Kossler, Rich Lindberg, and Eric Arnal, our present critique group…who listen intently and graciously suggest.

Finally, to Emily Victorson and Allium Press, who share my passion for Chicago present and past. Her keen eye and sharp pencil put the final polish on my story.

Again, I am grateful to all of you for your encouragement and help.

# ABOUT THE AUTHOR

Joan Bard-Collins was born in Chicago and grew up in northwest Indiana where the local library became her second home. Stories have always been a major part of her life—first listening, then reading, and now writing. From an early age she discovered that American history was one epic adventure after another.

She is a partner in her husband's architecture/engineering company. They share a passion for Chicago's architectural history. Over the years they have collected remnants from numerous, now demolished, Chicago buildings. She invites you to visit her at www.jbardcollins.com.

# ALSO PUBLISHED BY ALLIUM PRESS OF CHICAGO

Visit our website for more information:
www.alliumpress.com

## *Beautiful Dreamer*
## Joan Naper

Chicago in 1900 is bursting with opportunity, and Kitty Coakley is determined to make the most of it. The youngest of seven children born to Irish immigrants, she has little interest in becoming simply a housewife. Inspired by her entrepreneurial Aunt Mabel, who runs a millinery boutique at Marshall Field's, Kitty aspires to become an independent, modern woman. After her music teacher dashes her hopes of becoming a professional singer, she refuses to give up her dreams of a career. But when she is courted by not one, but two young men, her resolve is tested. Irish-Catholic Brian is familiar and has the approval of her traditional, working-class family. But wealthy, Protestant Henry, who is a young architect in Daniel Burnham's office, provides an entrée for Kitty into another, more exciting world. Will she sacrifice her ambitions and choose a life with one of these men?

◆

## *Company Orders*
## David J. Walker

Even a good man may feel driven to sign on with the devil. Paul Clark is a Catholic priest who's been on the fast track to becoming a bishop. But he suddenly faces a heart-wrenching problem, when choices he made as a young man come roaring back into his life. A mysterious woman, who claims to be with "an agency of the federal government," offers to solve his problem. But there's a price to pay—Father Clark must undertake some very un-priestly actions. An attack in a Chicago alley…a daring escape from a Mexican jail… and a fight to the death in a Guyanese jungle…all these, and more, must be survived in order to protect someone he loves. This priest is about to learn how much easier it is to preach love than to live it.

## *Set the Night on Fire*
## Libby Fischer Hellmann

Someone is trying to kill Lila Hilliard. During the Christmas holidays she returns from running errands to find her family home in flames, her father and brother trapped inside. Later, she is attacked by a mysterious man on a motorcycle. . . and the threats don't end there. As Lila desperately tries to piece together who is after her and why, she uncovers information about her father's past in Chicago during the volatile days of the late 1960s . . . information he never shared with her, but now threatens to destroy her. Part thriller, part historical novel, and part love story, *Set the Night on Fire* paints an unforgettable portrait of Chicago during a turbulent time: the riots at the Democratic Convention . . . the struggle for power between the Black Panthers and SDS . . . and a group of young idealists who tried to change the world.

◆

## *A Bitter Veil*
## Libby Fischer Hellmann

It all began with a line of Persian poetry . . . Anna and Nouri, both studying in Chicago, fall in love despite their very different backgrounds. Anna, who has never been close to her parents, is more than happy to return with Nouri to his native Iran, to be embraced by his wealthy family. Beginning their married life together in 1978, their world is abruptly turned upside down by the overthrow of the Shah and the rise of the Islamic Republic. Under the Ayatollah Khomeini and the Republican Guard, life becomes increasingly restricted and Anna must learn to exist in a transformed world, where none of the familiar Western rules apply. Random arrests and torture become the norm, women are required to wear hijab, and Anna discovers that she is no longer free to leave the country. As events reach a fevered pitch, Anna realizes that nothing is as she thought, and no one can be trusted. . .not even her husband.

*Her Mother's Secret*
Barbara Garland Polikoff

Fifteen-year-old Sarah, the daughter of Jewish immigrants, wants nothing more than to become an artist. But as she spreads her wings she must come to terms with the secrets that her family is only beginning to share with her. Replete with historical details that vividly evoke the Chicago of the 1890s, this moving coming-of-age story is set against the backdrop of a vibrant, turbulent city. Sarah moves between two very different worlds—the colorful immigrant neighborhood surrounding Hull House and the sophisticated, elegant World's Columbian Exposition. This novel eloquently captures the struggles of a young girl as she experiences the timeless emotions of friendship, family turmoil, loss…and first love.

A companion guide to *Her Mother's Secret* is available at www.alliumpress.com. In the guide you will find photographs of places mentioned in the novel, along with discussion questions, a list of read-alikes, and resources for further exploration of Sarah's time and place.

## THE EMILY CABOT MYSTERIES
Frances McNamara

### *Death at the Fair*

The 1893 World's Columbian Exposition provides a vibrant backdrop for the first book in the series. Emily Cabot, one of the first women graduate students at the University of Chicago, is eager to prove herself in the emerging field of sociology. While she is busy exploring the Exposition with her family and friends, her colleague, Dr. Stephen Chapman, is accused of murder. Emily sets out to search for the truth behind the crime, but is thwarted by the gamblers, thieves, and corrupt politicians who are ever-present in Chicago. A lynching that occurred in the dead man's past leads Emily to seek the assistance of the black activist Ida B. Wells.

◆

### *Death at Hull House*

After Emily Cabot is expelled from the University of Chicago, she finds work at Hull House, the famous settlement established by Jane Addams. There she quickly becomes involved in the political and social problems of the immigrant community. But when a man who works for a sweatshop owner is murdered in the Hull House parlor, Emily must determine whether one of her colleagues is responsible, or whether the real reason for the murder is revenge for a past tragedy in her own family. As a smallpox epidemic spreads through the impoverished west side of Chicago, the very existence of the settlement is threatened and Emily finds herself in jeopardy from both the deadly disease and a killer.

◆

### *Death at Pullman*

A model town at war with itself . . . George Pullman created an ideal community for his railroad car workers, complete with every amenity they could want or need. But when hard economic times hit in 1894, lay-offs follow and the workers can no longer pay their rent or buy food at the company store. Starving and desperate, they turn against their once benevolent employer. Emily Cabot and her friend Dr. Stephen Chapman bring much needed food and medical supplies to the town, hoping they can meet the immediate needs of the workers and keep them from resorting to violence. But when one young worker—suspected of being a spy—is murdered, and a bomb plot comes to light, Emily must race to discover the truth behind a tangled web of family and company alliances.

◆

*Death at Woods Hole*

Exhausted after the tumult of the Pullman Strike of 1894, Emily Cabot is looking forward to a restful summer visit to Cape Cod. She has plans to collect "beasties" for the Marine Biological Laboratory, alongside other visiting scientists from the University of Chicago. She also hopes to enjoy romantic clambakes with Dr. Stephen Chapman, although they must keep an important secret from their friends. But her summer takes a dramatic turn when she finds a dead man floating in a fish tank. In order to solve his murder she must first deal with dueling scientists, a testy local sheriff, the theft of a fortune, and uncooperative weather.

◆

*Death at Chinatown*

In the summer of 1896, amateur sleuth Emily Cabot meets two young Chinese women who have recently received medical degrees. She is inspired to make an important decision about her own life when she learns about the difficult choices they have made in order to pursue their careers. When one of the women is accused of poisoning a Chinese herbalist, Emily once again finds herself in the midst of a murder investigation. But, before the case can be solved, she must first settle a serious quarrel with her husband, help quell a political uprising, and overcome threats against her family. Timeless issues, such as restrictions on immigration, the conflict between Western and Eastern medicine, and women's struggle to balance family and work, are woven seamlessly throughout this riveting historical mystery.

*Bright and Yellow, Hard and Cold*
Tim Chapman

The search for elusive goals consumes three men...

McKinney, a forensic scientist, struggles with his deep, personal need to find the truth behind the evidence he investigates, even while the system shuts him out. Can he get justice for a wrongfully accused man while juggling life with a new girlfriend and a precocious teenage daughter?

Delroy gives up the hard-scrabble life on his family's Kentucky farm and ventures to the rough-and-tumble world of 1930s Chicago. Unable to find work, he reluctantly throws his hat in with the bank-robbing gangsters Alvin Karpis and Freddie Barker. Can he provide for his fiery young wife without risking his own life?

Gilbert is obsessed with the search for a cache of gold, hidden for nearly eighty years. As his hunt escalates he finds himself willing to use ever more extreme measures to attain his goal...including kidnapping, torture, and murder. Can he find the one person still left who will lead him to the glittering treasure? And will the trail of corpses he leaves behind include McKinney?

Part contemporary thriller, part historical novel, and part love story, *Bright and Yellow, Hard and Cold* masterfully weaves a tale of conflicted scientific ethics, economic hardship, and criminal frenzy, tempered with the redemption of family love.

*Shall We Not Revenge*
D. M. Pirrone

In the harsh early winter months of 1872, while Chicago is still smoldering from the Great Fire, Irish Catholic detective Frank Hanley is assigned the case of a murdered Orthodox Jewish rabbi. His investigation proves difficult when the neighborhood's Yiddish-speaking residents, wary of outsiders, are reluctant to talk.

But when the rabbi's headstrong daughter, Rivka, unexpectedly offers to help Hanley find her father's killer, the detective receives much more than the break he was looking for. Their pursuit of the truth draws Rivka and Hanley closer together and leads them to a relief organization run by the city's wealthy movers and shakers. Along the way, they uncover a web of political corruption, crooked cops, and well-buried ties to two notorious Irish thugs from Hanley's checkered past.

Even after he is kicked off the case, stripped of his badge, and thrown in jail, Hanley refuses to quit. With a personal vendetta to settle for an innocent life lost, he is determined to expose a complicated criminal scheme, not only for his own sake, but for Rivka's as well.

CPSIA information can be obtained
at www.ICGtesting.com
Printed in the USA
FFHW020842131118
49375696-53697FF

9 780989 053570